Lay Your Body Down

LITTLE DEATHS
BOOK TWO

TYLOR PAIGE

Content Notes

Lay Your Body Down is a dark(ish) vampire, mafia romance. Before reading, please be aware that some things in this book aren't for everyone, (and that's okay!) and to please be mindful of your mental health when going in. These topics are but are not limited to, dub con, cults, blood play, biting, violence, unintentional drug use, gambling, stalking, suicidal ideations, knife play, SA, kidnapping, torture, and overall violence.

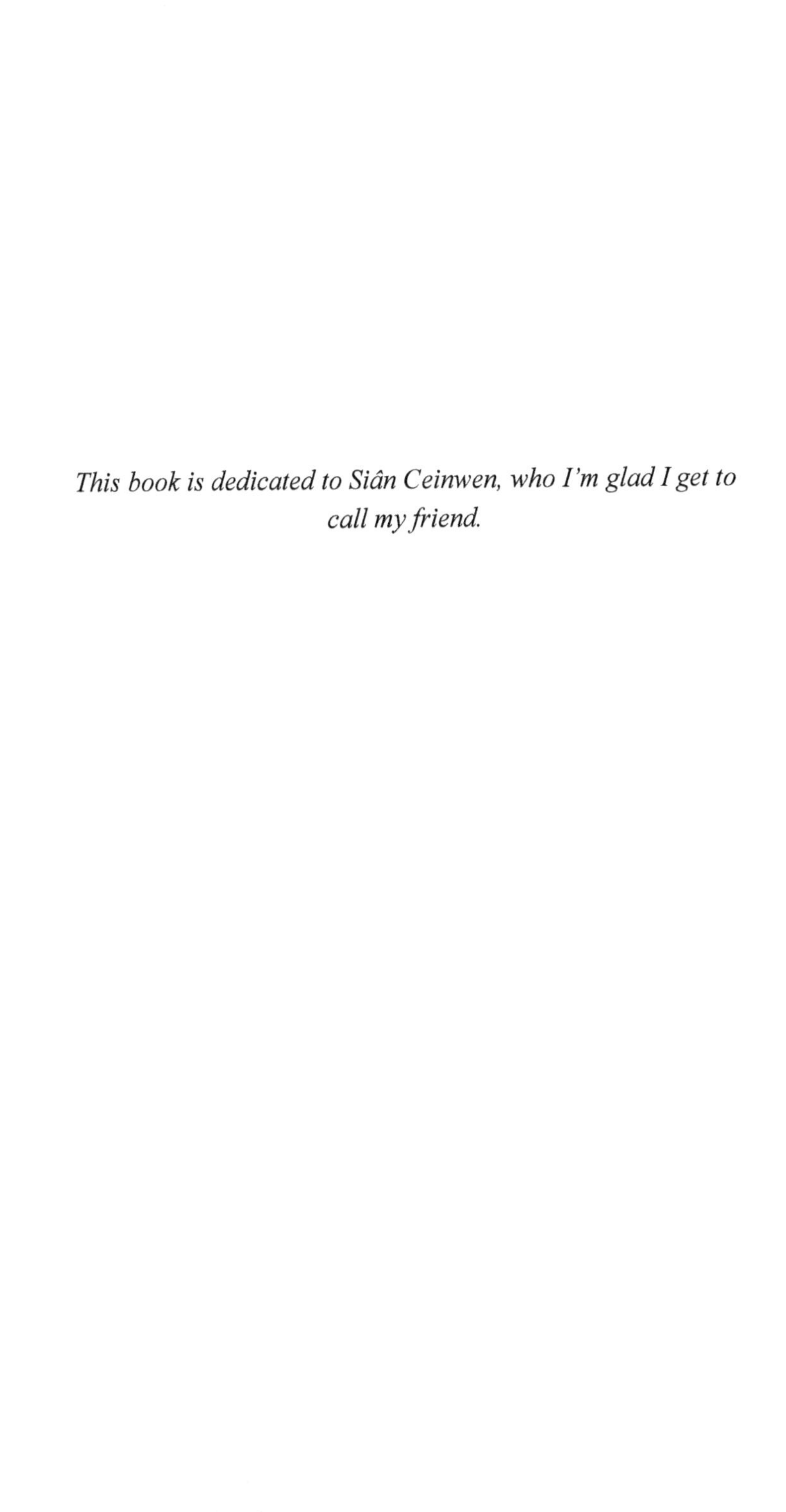

This book is dedicated to Siân Ceinwen, who I'm glad I get to call my friend.

CHAPTER 1

"Pick a card, any card."

A large sigh came from behind me. I turned to see Desi pinching the space between his eyes and shaking his head.

"Scout, no, it's not like—you don't just—okay, let me show you how it's done." He stepped forward, and I admired again how sleek he looked in all black, with the sleeves of his dress shirt rolled up to his elbows. He took his cards back from my nervous hands and stormed over to the guy we had taken from the wedding reception. The mark.

Desi turned back to me. His eyes, one blue and one green, were wild with a mix of excitement and irritation. I blanched.

"You're not a magician." He turned back to the mark. He was fighting against his restraints, but he'd been tied pretty tightly. The human's struggle was pointless. He was dying tonight regardless of how it happened. "You're not Harry fucking Houdini."

"Harry Houdini wasn't a magician. He was an escape artist." I corrected him, causing him to roll his eyes and let out a small growl from his throat.

"Scout. Focus. I don't want to spend all night on this."

"You got some other place to be?" The guy in the chair spat.

Desi slipped a hand into his dress pants and pulled out a pocket knife. He flicked it open with the expertise of someone who'd been killing people like this for the last three decades.

"As a matter of fact, I brought my girl to a wedding intending to dance with her. You're taking far too much time."

"Oh, well, I'm sorry for the inconvenience. Fuck you." The rather plain man attempted to kick Desi, but his ankles were bound by zip ties to the chair legs. "Why am I even here?"

"You're here because—" I started but was interrupted by Desi again. He clicked his tongue and shook his head at me. I furrowed my brow. I had agreed to do this with him, but his nitpicking drove me nuts.

"Don't tell him. Let him figure it out. Why do you think you're here?" Desi asked the man. Kevin, the man in the boring suit with the male-patterned baldness, glared at the immortal man standing before him.

"Fuck if I know. I was just attending my friend's wedding. I was doing nothing wrong."

"If you were doing nothing wrong, no one would have paid me good money to kill you."

"Kill me?" The man visibly paled, and it was as if he'd punched me in the gut. As someone who couldn't die unless you cut my head clean off, the concept of death was confusing to me. I wasn't afraid of it like he was. I didn't have to be.

"Scout, you there?" Desi snapped his fingers, causing me

to blink and swallow the lump in my throat. I shifted in my dress and stepped back up to his side.

"Yeah, sorry. It's just—I don't know."

"You don't know? How long have you been a vampire? You've done this a million times." He stared at me, his face full of confusion. I shook my head.

"Thousands," I clarified. "But not like this. I did it because I had to."

"Have to." He pointed out. He straightened his spine and stepped away as if he had all the time in the world. He looked around the room. It was a large office that Desi had taken time to cover with plastic to avoid a bloody mess. The father of the bride had welcomed everyone to his grand home for the reception and then hired Desi to do what he did best. "Just because you broke your curse doesn't mean you don't need blood to survive."

"I could use the blood banks." I crossed my arms defensively. I hated when he tried to tell me what to do. "I don't *need to do* anything."

"Yeah, but that's no fun." Desi grinned, his fangs flashing as he smiled. He turned back to the man in the chair. "Care to draw a card? If you make me do it, then I'll make sure you feel everything."

The man had beads of sweat slipping from his forehead to his chin, dripping onto his jacket. "Fine. Let's do this." His voice was shaky, as was the rest of him.

Desi nodded and pulled his tarot cards back out of his pants pockets. He closed his knife quickly, shuffled the deck, and then brought them to the man's bound hands. I watched with my stomach tightened as the man closed his eyes and fumbled with the cards, finally pulling out a card. Desi took it from him and lifted it to his eyes.

A smile slid onto his face so slow it sent chills up my spine. He turned to show me the card.

Six of Cups

I stared at the card, taking it all in. Desi had spent the last few months teaching me how to read the cards he treasured with his life.

The art on the card was a child, a boy, giving a gift to a younger girl. A flower in a large vase. What was the meaning of it again? I squinted as I recalled the words I had memorized.

I opened my mouth to recite them, and Desi shook his head slightly.

"Remember," he said softly. "You tailor the reading. Tarot isn't just memorization." He urged me to dig deep for the meaning of the card. I nodded and did as he asked.

"You slept with a girl when you were younger. You gave her your flower." My eyes darted from Desi to the man in the chair. Desi nodded approvingly and stepped back. He walked over to the large oak desk and leaned against it. He crossed his arms and waved a lazy hand at me, encouraging me to continue.

"Was it the bride?" I asked. The man who we had kidnapped from the reception snickered.

"This is stupid. You think you're some psychic or something?"

I widened my eyes excitedly. "I knew it! Okay, so you slept with the bride when you guys were younger."

I glanced at Desi, who was staring hard at me. He frowned and then kicked off the desk. "You want to do a three-card spread with him?"

"Three cards? Oh, come on. You're just giving people more time to find me." The man smirked.

Desi laughed dryly. "No one's coming for you, don't worry. Let's draw another. That was his past, now for his current."

Desi went to him and demanded he take another card. The man was more forceful when he snatched one from the deck this time.

Temperance

The angel with the cup.

I frowned. "Balance? Peace?" I tilted my head in confusion to Desi. He smirked and shook his head.

"It was reversed. Do you remember?" He coaxed. His voice was tender and almost calming. I took a deep breath and thought back.

"Temperance reversed means indulgence. You've been overdoing it." I gasped. "Are you still sleeping with her?" I accused the man. He laughed.

"This is all just a sham. You can literally figure things out with any card I draw. He told you about our affair. Her dad. He's never liked me. This is why he wants me dead? Because I'm fucking his prized pig? You can't possibly be okay with killing me over this."

"No. We're not killing you because of an affair. We're killing you because it wasn't consensual." Desi snapped at him. The man's mouth fell open and shut silently. His eyes went large, and his face suddenly regained its color, which was very red. Desi thrust the deck at me, and I fumbled to take them.

"Desi, I don't know if I can do this."

"Why not? You wanted to be involved." He reminded me.

"Yeah, but this is—"

Not what I expected.

"I saw your little black book. You've killed tons of people

like him. Humans, vamps, they're all the same. Evil. He's nothing." He thrust his arm out, pointing at the man. I flicked my nervous gaze at him.

"Yeah, but I had to break my curse. This isn't something I—"

"Scout, baby, nerd," Desi reached his hand out to touch my chin. He pinched it lightly, and somehow it helped me steady myself. I looked deep into his beautiful mismatched eyes and took a long breath. "You wanted this. You want to go to art school, don't you?"

I nodded.

"You want to get all the fancy pencils and paints?"

I nodded again. His face softened even more, and he curved his lips upwards. "Then you're going to do this. I'm going to hand you my knife, and you'll slash him from ear to ear, okay?"

His voice was so gentle in comparison to the words he was saying.

"Is this a joke?" Kevin interrupted our conversation. We both turned to him in mild surprise, almost as if we had forgotten about him completely.

"Why would this be a joke?" Desi let go of me and stared directly at him. "Do you think I'd waste my time dragging you all the way through this house, tie you up, draw my cards, just for a fucking joke?"

Desi brought his hand up as if he was going to slap him but then stopped himself. The man was cowering under Desi's frame. My vampire boyfriend sighed and dropped his hand. He looked at me, his eyes suddenly tired.

"I love you, but I really need this wrapped up. I was serious about taking you dancing."

My heart melted as he reached for my hand and squeezed.

"Finish this." Desi pulled his knife back out and offered it to me. I reached for it with slightly shaky hands. He locked eyes with me. They were hard and demanding. We stared at each other for a long moment before he blinked and quickly left the room. The man in the chair screamed as the door opened and shut, but it was useless. Between the music and the distance from the hall to this office, he wouldn't be heard.

"Why did he leave? Is he going to get more people? Who told you about me? You can't just kill me!" He screamed in my face.

"Was he telling the truth? Are you abusing her? The bride?" My mind went back to the ceremony. The human couple was so young and looked so happy. She didn't look like a victim. Tears began to well in my eyes, and my chin quivered. How could he do something so vile to someone like that?

"Is that blood? You guys cry blood? Jesus Christ, that's fucking horrible."

I gritted my teeth and wiped away the small line of blood that had managed to fall from my eyes. I glared at him. He flinched, and I saw his Adam's apple dip.

"Have you never met a vampire before?" I tilted my head curiously at him.

He snorted. "Why would I be stupid enough to inter-mingle with your kind?"

I blinked. "My kind?"

"Monsters." He spat.

Well, isn't that the pot calling the kettle black?

I ran my tongue across my fangs and extended my hand to him. I was done trying to argue with myself over right and wrong. "Draw the final card to determine your future."

There was a long moment where no one moved. I held

firm. Desi's hardened eyes and words of confidence flashed over and over in my mind.

I tapped my heel, and it made him jump. He grabbed a card and handed it to me. I took it, looked at it, and laughed.

"What? What does that mean?"

I flicked the card around with my fingers to show him.

The Fool

"It means you're gonna learn today."

With the speed that comes from being a vampire, an immortal with no fucks to give and the strength to do whatever I wanted, I flicked open the knife. I reached out, slicing his neck from shoulder to shoulder. His eyes went wide with shock as blood began spitting from his neck. He coughed, and I blanched as his blood flung across my face, hitting my icy cheeks.

I turned my head and stood up straight. He continued to struggle for a moment before going limp. A moment later, the door opened, and Desi returned. He brushed off his dress jacket and looked up at me. I blinked rapidly, and he raised his eyebrows and grinned.

"Is it weird that I find you incredibly attractive covered in blood?"

I looked back at the dead man slumped over in the chair. I kicked him, and he fell over with a thump. Desi started slowly and carefully toward me, stepping over the random blood spots. He was grinning at me, his fangs bared and his eyes wide.

Each step he took, I matched, moving backward. I bumped into the desk, and in a flash, he was pushing his body, hard and ready, against mine. He brought his hand up to tilt my chin toward him.

I leaned toward him, and before our lips met, I smiled and whispered to him.

"I think it'd be weird if you didn't."

"When we first met, you know, for the second time, I thought you were incredible. Now, you're fucking glorious." Desi pushed the skirt of my dress up. The layers of Chantilly lace bunched up at my hips as he urged me to spread my legs. He continued assaulting my bare skin, some of it covered in the human's blood, with kisses. He licked my collarbone and drug his tongue up my neck. I shivered and leaned into it.

I closed my eyes and reveled in the teasing he was so good at. He used his hands, mouth, and words to show me exactly what he wanted.

"When? Way back when, or at the movie theater?" I asked, and he let out a low chuckle. His lips found mine, and I could feel the rumble in his throat when he laughed.

"The second time. It's odd to think about, knowing you," he traced his fingers up my bare shoulders. "And loving you," he brought his hand down to cup my breast over my dress. His thumb rubbed over my nipple, and I bit down on my lip. "So long ago. It's like we were two different people."

Slowly, he pushed my dress down to expose my body to the cold air. I arched my back as he shifted to take a nipple into his mouth. I gasped, and my hands went to his dark, inky hair. I tugged his roots as he flicked his tongue over my peak.

He grabbed my ass and lifted me up, setting me on the desk. I spread my legs and let him between them. I threw my head back as his lips returned to my neck.

"Are you sure we should still be here? Desi," I called him by name when he didn't answer. He let out a low growl as his fingers traced the line of my underwear.

"It doesn't really matter. The mark is dead. We can do whatever."

"People won't miss him at the wedding?"

"Scout," he whined. His cock throbbed against my thigh. He was hard and ready. He sighed and brought his eyes to meet mine. He looked like he could murder me. "Are you bothered by him in here with us?"

I scrunched up my nose. He knew me too well. I nodded, and he rolled his eyes. He took a step back and offered his hand to pull me off the desk. I hopped off and readjusted my dress.

"I'm not saying we can't. I still want to, just not with an audience," I explained.

Desi glared at me. "He's dead."

"Stop. Don't make me feel bad about this."

He gave me another look but then put his hands up. "Fine. I won't fuck you in front of this dead guy, but I will not be leaving this wedding without having been inside you."

He stormed toward the large oak doors and opened them more calmly than I had expected. I blinked and started forward. My head turned slightly toward the dead body, the monster.

"And you just leave them there?"

Desi rolled his eyes again and sighed. "I get paid to kill them, not to deal with the rest."

"You'd think it'd be some sort of package deal." I started to crack a smile, but his growl made me stop, straighten, and leave the room with him.

"You're such a nerd. Get in, get out. Don't linger." He reminded me again. He reached for my hand as we started down the hallway. In the distance, we could hear the band playing in the grand hall for all of the partygoers.

"You were just lingering." I pointed out. He huffed but said nothing else. The music grew louder as we walked toward it. I suddenly stopped in my tracks. He paused and cocked an eyebrow at me. "I can't go back in there like this." I looked down at my dress. It was black, as per usual, but my bare skin, of which was plenty, had streaks of blood in various places.

"You want to leave?" He offered. I pouted and looked back up at him.

"You promised me dancing."

He laughed. "That I did. Let's see what I can do." Desi swiveled his head back and forth and then squeezed my hand. "Come with me." We turned and went back the other way.

I wondered for a moment if he had been here before with how well he navigated the place. We turned to the left, the right, and then through some doors. He took me up a staircase and then down another hallway. Then, finally, we stopped at the door. He opened it, let me in, and then pointed to the room's far end. There were two large windows.

He placed his hand lightly on the small of my back and urged me toward it. I stepped closer and saw that he had found a balcony. Those were doors, not windows.

Desi and I stepped outside with the moon shining bright

in the dark sky. The cool air hit my skin, and I shivered. Despite being cold by nature, goosebumps still appeared on my arms.

"Hm," Desi closed the doors, and I went to the edge of the balcony, peering over the edge. He joined me, putting his arm over my shoulder. "I really thought we'd be able to hear the music."

I smiled softly and turned to him. He was frowning and looking down at the ground. "That's okay. I still had fun tonight. I did my first official kill. Like paid kill." I boasted. He chuckled.

"That you did. I'm proud of you, Nerd. I figured I'd give you an easy one. A real asshole. It's the ones who you don't know why they're in your chair that are hard." His eyes took on a far-off look as if replaying some memory.

I reached for his hand on the railing and tilted my head to rest on his arm.

"Do you like it? Your job?"

"I like the perks. With the freedom to travel, I choose what jobs I take. The money's damn good."

He paused, and the silence between us stretched.

"You're asking if I like killing people," he looked down at me, his eyes suddenly tired. I flinched but nodded. He shook his head. "Please don't ask me stuff like that."

I pressed my lips together tightly and took a deep breath. His face suddenly relaxed, and he smiled. "You said you wanted to dance?"

I grinned and stepped back from the railing. "I did, but I need music."

"Say no more." Desi grinned as he pulled out his cell phone. We had both gotten new ones after the mess with Corrine.

Pride.

She had wanted me dead, so we had to go on the run for a bit. When she had calmed down enough to let me stay living my little undead life, we had to go get all new stuff for me that she had destroyed. A phone, my car, and most of my apartment.

"I'm not much of a romantic. What's a good sappy song?" Desi smirked up at me as he perused through his music. When I didn't answer immediately, he cocked an eyebrow in warning. "You've got about five seconds before we're slow dancing to *Fear of The Dark*."

I scrunched up my nose. While I enjoyed Iron Maiden just as much as he did, it didn't exactly scream romantic.

"Oh! Okay, I think I've got one. I'm going old school. Cover your ears," Desi ordered, and I giggled as I did as told. I turned around and closed my eyes.

A moment later, I felt Desi's hands cover my hands. Gently, he squeezed them and brought them down from my ears. I turned slowly and tried to guess the song. It wasn't rock, which surprised me.

"What is this?" I asked. The song was itching something in my brain. Almost as if the memory of it was on the tip of my tongue. It wasn't until I saw Desi's lips moving, whispering the lyrics directly to me, that it clicked.

Lights, by Journey.

"I remember this," I said softly as we moved. The memory was coming slowly, as if I was stepping into a warm bath. "You and I. A million years ago."

"I'd say thirty, but a million is close." He chuckled.

"Yes. It was Valentines, and I'd been so mad at you. We hadn't seen each other since Christmas. And I'd told you if you didn't show up, we were done." My vision blurred as I started to remember. "And then when I left work that day, there you were."

That was one of my favorite memories from that year I'd had with Desi before we turned. He had gotten all of his friends to stand on top of their cars in the snow at 2. A.M. and put on a concert for me.

"You know how much it cost me to get them there?" He laughed.

"It would have cost you more if I had broken up with you." I reminded him.

"Very true. It was worth every penny. Everything I've ever done for you has been worth it."

"Even selling your soul?"

"I'd do it again if I had to." He pulled me back up, and our lips met for a long, tender kiss.

No sooner did that song end did another smooth love song take its place. He pulled me tighter, and I pressed my head against his chest, inhaling his cologne.

"I love the way you smell." I sighed.

"I can get you a bottle of my cologne to spray on your stuff. It's a blue bottle."

I shook my head just a smidge, keeping my body close to his. "Not the same. I'd need to shove fireballs in all of my pockets to get it right."

He laughed. "Sorry."

"I like it. It's you. It's my Desi." I sighed deeply and closed my eyes. A sexier song came on, and almost as if rising from a deep slumber, I felt the tell-tale throb against my thigh.

I pulled away and raised an arm to spin. "When are we leaving?" I asked.

"Whenever you want to. I have no plans after this besides bed with you."

"Oh, so now you want a bed? A desk was just fine an hour ago."

"I was talking about sleeping." He grinned, flashing me his fangs. "I told you I'm not leaving this party without having been inside you."

"You're still on that?" I teased and did another spin and then dropped to my knees. I tilted my head up to see him staring down at me with a grin on his face and eyebrows high with surprise.

"I reached for his belt, unbuckled it quickly then straightened my posture and shimmied his pants down to his thighs. His dress shirt hung over what I was trying to get to. I pushed the black silk away, and my hands went to work, massaging his cock.

"Don't tease me," he murmured as I stroked him. I started to bring my other hand up, but he reached out and batted it away. He put his hands in my always-messy hair and pushed me gently forward. He was impatient and bucked his hips to tell me as such.

I smiled and leaned forward, flicking my tongue out to circle the tip. I loved how he responded to me when I used my mouth. I tried to tease him again with another fast lick, but he wasn't interested in playing anymore. He clenched a fistful of my hair and pushed me forward, and I eagerly took him into my mouth.

Always aware of my sharp fangs, I let them gently graze the length of his cock as I swirled my tongue around him and sucked. He swore, and I felt his weight shift as he relaxed his head back to enjoy what I was doing to him.

I continued using my hand to assist me as took his cock in and out of my mouth. I loved doing this to him. Not only giving him pleasure but knowing what he could do to me with this part of him turned me on immensely. I sucked and swirled and gently nipped at him. His breathing started to become more ragged.

"If you don't move, I'm going to come in your mouth," he warned. I looked up at him and saw him staring down at me. Without looking away, I took him as far as I could into the back of my throat and sucked as hard as possible. That sent him over the edge. He exploded, and I swallowed every ounce of his orgasm. I continued until he took a step back and pulled on his pants. He left his belt unbuckled as he scooped me up with one quick motion and set me down on top of the thin banister.

"Your turn," he growled.

"Desi, we can't! This railing—"

"Do you trust me?"

"What? Desi, my ass is not big enough—"

He pushed forward, spreading my legs. He put one hand on each of my thighs and tightened his grip. I looked at him, my eyes wide with terror over falling the three stories to the ground. His beautiful mismatched ones stared intensely at me as he ran his tongue across his fangs. "Do you trust me?" He repeated.

"Desi—"

"No, Desi," he gritted his teeth. His upper lip flinched as he stared me down. "Do you trust that I won't let you go?"

I swallowed the lump in my throat and fought past the pit in my stomach. I forced a nod even though I wasn't as sure as he was. His grin spread slowly over his face, sending a shiver of fear mixed with excitement through me.

Gripping me tightly, Desi dipped down and pushed my dress up past my knees. Instinctively, my hands flew to his, and I squeezed. I was shaking, and I had to shut my eyes tight.

"Scout, baby, Nerd," his voice was low and soothing. "Relax. Let me take care of you."

I forced myself to steady my breathing. My nerves

weren't any less shot, but I could pretend I wasn't scared shitless.

Desi feathered kisses on my thighs. They were so light it was almost a tickle. My body responded as it only did when he was involved. He reached my middle and planted his lips solid on my underwear. "I thought I told you to stop wearing this stuff," he muttered. He started to take his hand off my thigh, but I caught him and held him tightly. "Scout," he warned. "Either you help me, or I'll need the use of my hands."

I shook as I removed my hand from his wrist and grasped the railing tightly. He chuckled low and put his hand between my legs. He pealed my panties away from my bare lips and began slowly exploring my wetness. "Beautiful," he murmured before replacing his hand with his mouth.

My breath caught in my throat as he licked and lapped at my slit like it was his full-time job. My legs relaxed even further, and he used that chance to move closer, using his hands to spread my pussy open. He eased a finger inside me as his tongue ran up and over my clit. One finger turned into two, and suddenly the pleasure became overwhelming.

I gasped and let go of the railing. I swayed a bit, and Desi's free hand clamped down on me. "Nuh-uh," he murmured in-between tasting me. "You don't get to leave until you've come." He moved his fingers faster, digging deep into the most sensitive spot inside me. I gasped and pushed against him, eager to get to mine. Desi stopped lapping and spelling words and went straight to sucking, and I screamed. My hands dropped the railing completely in favor of his hair. I dug my fingers into his dark locks and pushed him deeper between my thighs as I rode my orgasm.

When I finally came down, Desi stood up and reached for

my waist. He was grinning ear to ear, and I wanted to punch him. He was too adorable for his own good. He helped me off the railing, and I straightened my dress. He did the same for his own wedding attire, and then he smiled again.

"You ready to go? I'd love to do that again at home."

"I don't understand why you're coming to me about this."

I had my hands shoved in my pockets, one hand playing with my cards, the other slowly unwrapping a fireball. I pulled the candy out of my pocket and popped it into my mouth, trying to keep casual. Arsenio raised an eyebrow expectantly. I sucked on the hard candy and replied. "Because I don't know who else to talk to about it."

"Sit, friend. Have a drink." He motioned to the expensive chair in his den that we were currently standing in. "Blood, whiskey?"

Suddenly a person appeared in the doorway. I turned to see a bloodshed woman smiling kindly at me. Arsenio nodded to her. "This is Fanny. She's my housekeeper. She has one of the more interesting deaths of a Bloodshed I've heard so far. Sucked dry by leeches."

"Full-time staff?" I ignored his explanation of her in favor of the more interesting bit. I was mildly surprised. Because of the business he conducted in his basement, Arsenio didn't like people in his home regularly.

"It was time. Plus, now I can enjoy my guest's company while Fanny prepares drinks. Two warmed, please." He nodded to his housekeeper, and she disappeared quickly. After she left, we sat down across from each other. Arsenio picked up a remote and pushed some buttons, turning on soft piano music. He grinned at me then. "So, what all do you need from me?"

I hated that I was here in the first place for this, but I had no other leads to the answers I sought. Arsenio, one of my closest friends, my fellow Seven Sin member, was also Scout's ex. I swallowed my bitterness and repeated my original question.

"I want to ask Scout to marry me."

"Again, this doesn't involve me in the slightest. You've already asked and received my blessing. Not that you needed it," he laughed. "If I had known that the reason we couldn't seem to make a connection was that she'd already had a taste of your blood, it would have saved me two solid years."

"Of your immortal life?" I smirked. He rolled his eyes and tossed me the middle finger.

"You keep pushing it, and I'll tell you all the dirty details, friend."

I gritted my teeth. Instant jealousy flared in me. Neither of our pasts were squeaky clean, but I didn't need to hear about Scout's intimate moments with another man. Especially if that man in question was Arsenio, the buff, Italian Adonis.

I leaned forward and rested my elbows on my knees. I clasped my hands together and sighed. "Do you think she'll say yes?"

He shrugged his shoulders. "Probably. I don't really talk to her too much these days." He paused and leaned forward himself, making direct eye contact with me. He opened his mouth, but just then, Fanny returned with a tray. It had a tea kettle and two mugs. Silently she poured us our drinks and handed them to us. We waited until she left to continue talking. Arsenio spoke first. "I feel like there is something else that is bothering you. What is it?"

I struggled to communicate my thoughts, but after a moment, Arsenio began to guess. "Is it because of your previous engagement to Aleida?"

I nodded and looked down, guilt swimming in my stomach. "There's a lot to deal with…" I paused. "With all that."

"How so?" He leaned back in his chair and raised a curious eyebrow.

"Well, for one, when I got my memory back, so did Aleida, Scout, and our parents."

His blood-red eyes went huge. "Oh. And now they're angry." He responded, not asked. He knew all too well how traditional Bloodborn families were.

"They are. I have gotten calls, emails, and even some certified mail, from pretty much everyone." I pressed my lips together and shook my head.

"Do they still expect you to marry her? Surely they can understand. It's been thirty years!" He exclaimed.

"I know. You'd think they'd relax some."

The phone call I had with my brother just last night rang through my mind.

"Good genes are good genes."

"So why did you lead with whether or not Scout would accept your proposal? It seems as if you're getting a little ahead of yourself."

"I am." I agreed. I finished my cup of blood and then asked for some of the cinnamon whiskey he kept here just for me. He stood up and went to the bar to pour me a drink. He poured himself one too and then returned to the conversation.

I took a sip and continued. "I just needed a reason to come here and talk."

He laughed. "Desiderio, my dearest friend. You never need a reason to visit. If you need help, I'm here. You want me to go with you to talk to your parents? Or what about Aleida herself? Have you spoken to her?"

I snorted. "I'm really trying to avoid her if I can. Which is probably what's causing the problem. Who knows what she's been telling her parents, who are then going to mine."

"She still wants to marry you?" His eyes went wide with skepticism. I made a sour face.

"I think if I offered, she would. Not out of love, but of duty."

"Desiderio," he paused and shook his head at me. "I think you need to have a sit down with everyone. If you truly want to marry Scout and have your parent's approval, then you need to explain to them what you two did."

I cringed. That was the last thing I wanted to do. My mom especially would lose her shit when I told her that not only did I let someone who wasn't approved by them drink my blood on her turning day, but later I turned it around and drank her blood as well.

"I don't think they'll like me." Scout sighed as she stared out the car window. I continued the drive to my parent's house.

"And why's that?" I tried to give her a reassuring smile, but it appeared awkward and forced. She saw right through it.

"Because I'm not your *betrothed*." She stuck her tongue out at the word and made a gagging motion with her finger.

"Well, I'm going to make them like you. They might not

right now, but they'll have no choice once they get to know you."

"Why is it so important to meet them? I've never met my parents."

"Yeah, but mine are—" I stopped myself. I felt like a jackass. She raised an eyebrow and glanced at me.

"What are yours exactly? Special? Are they like that guy with the Sunshine?" Her hand went to her side, where she'd been stabbed with a poison-dipped knife. I grimaced.

"Yes, and no. Pretentious as hell, yes. But not as violent."

"If they aren't going to kill us, why even bother? I don't need approval from anyone." I glanced at her and saw she was playing nervously with the frill on her dress.

"You're right. You don't. But I want to stop being harassed about not marrying Aleida. I have to show them why the marriage is off."

"This is all so dumb," she muttered and turned back to the window.

The rest of the ride was spent arguing in a similar fashion, and I found myself relieved to see my family home up ahead.

The Amato home was grand. My family had been living on the property for almost two hundred years. Over time they'd expanded and redid this part or that, but overall, it looked much like the home I'd been raised in.

"Jesus Christ, Desi, you grew up here?" Scout whistled when I stopped the car and helped her out on her side.

I laughed. "Yep. Born and raised."

"So it's literally just me that's poor. I'm the only poor vampire in existence." She laughed.

Not for long, if I had it my way. When we get married, my money will be your money.

"Come on, Nerd." I ignored her and motioned to the house.

"You first, Loser." She took my hand and leaned up on her tiptoes to give me a quick peck on the cheek. It put a small smile on my face. We then started up the long walkway to the door.

The door swung open before I could ring the bell.

"Peter? No shit, you're still here?" I exclaimed upon seeing the butler, the same fucking guy who'd been doing this my entire childhood.

"The benefits are worth it, Mr. Amato. It's good to see you too," the man snickered. While he looked just like every other vampire, eternally twenty-seven, his personality was of a man who was born five hundred years ago. "Your family has been anticipating your arrival."

I forced a smile and urged Scout to go into the house ahead of me. "Your jacket, Miss…?" Peter seemed confused that it wasn't Aleida that I had brought. While I hadn't told them I'd be bringing my girlfriend, I had told them all a dozen times that I was not with Aleida anymore.

"Scout." The brunette goddess with every part of me wrapped around her lightly tanned finger answered him confidently.

"Scout." Peter nodded, although his eyes appeared weary. "Scout…?"

"I don't have a last name."

I blinked, suddenly realizing that I had never thought to ask. The first time we knew each other or now. How did I not know that?

"Oh. Well, why don't I take you to the den where the Amato family is waiting."

Oh great. Everyone was here.

Peter took us down the familiar hallways and to my dad's office. Scout's eyes were wide with curiosity as we walked through the house. I guess it was more impressive if it wasn't your own history.

Peter walked into the room first, and all light chatter that had been going on ceased. "Your son, Desiderio, has arrived. He's brought a guest. Scout." He said her name as if he had a sour taste in his mouth. I remembered why I could never stand him as a child. He was an asshole.

I stepped into the room, and everyone's gaze turned to me. I glanced back to see that I was alone. I grinned nervously at my family and backed up. Scout stood next to the door, her feet bolted to the floor.

"Come on, it's okay," I said quietly. She shook her head. Her red eyes were large and almost as terrified as she had been the night I tongue fucked her on that balcony. I reached for her hand and pulled her forward and into the room.

Everyone stood then as if we had interrupted an important meeting. They stared at the two of us as if we were ghosts. I swallowed my nerves and introduced Scout to my family.

"Hey guys," I started awkwardly. My voice was beginning to shrink, much like my balls. "I brought my girlfriend."

"Girlfriend?" My older brother, Gianni, snapped.

"Shush!" My mom snapped right back. She was blinking rapidly and pressing her lips together tightly. "Desiderio, I'm confused."

"Well, let me do introductions, and then we can talk about other things. Scout, this is my mom, Gisella." I pointed to the dark-haired woman who had given birth to me. She smiled nervously at Scout.

"That's my dad, Eugenio. That's Gianni," I made a face at my brother. "And that's my older sister Caterina. Family, this is Scout."

"Scout who?" Caterina demanded. She went to stand next

to our mom. The two looked so similar. If they weren't vampires, you'd think they were sisters.

"I don't have a last name," Scout told them.

"She doesn't have a last name," I added right after her, feeling stupid.

"That doesn't make sense. She's Bloodborn, isn't she?" Caterina came forward and began to circle Scout as if apprising a dog. "Her eyes are red. What family do you come from?"

"I don't know. I was an orphan. What is this?" Scout turned to glare at me. "Did you not tell them about me?"

I gulped. "No, well, not exactly."

"Not exactly, my ass. He didn't say shit about bringing some—" Gianni started, but I stepped forward, and he shut his mouth quickly.

"I suggest you choose your next words wisely, brother." I glared at him. "I brought my girlfriend because I needed to get it through your guys' heads that I will not be following through with my engagement to Aleida Linotti."

"And why not?" My dad spoke suddenly. He straightened his suit jacket, and his face hardened. "That was a good match, Desiderio."

"To you, maybe." I stayed firm with my decision. "But not for me. There was nothing more to that relationship than a duty to our families."

"So? I did it, so did Cat. You think you get to just do whatever you want because you messed up your turning?" Gianni was furious, but I held my ground. I squeezed Scout's hand and took a deep breath.

"Yeah, and here's the reason behind it." I tilted my head at the short woman beside me. They all shifted their attention to Scout and glared. She shrunk beside me. "She's who I took the curse for."

"Her?" Caterina crossed her arms. "You don't even know her."

"Yes, I do," I scoffed. I was actually offended. "She's my soulmate."

"Soulmate?" My mom shook her head and came forward. She reached out for me and put her hands on my cheeks. "Oh sweetie, that's a silly notion. You don't just declare someone your soulmate. You have to—"

"Drink each other's blood?" Scout piped up from beside me. Her voice was tiny, but her words were heard loud and clear. Silence filled the room as they took in what she had said.

My mom pulled her hands from my face as if I were poison. She took a step back, and her mouth fell open in horror. "Desiderio, what did you do?" She asked, shaking her head. I grinned then, knowing that I had won this argument.

"I gave her my blood when she turned and drank from her shortly before I broke my curse. Sorry about your fucking luck."

CHAPTER 4

Desi

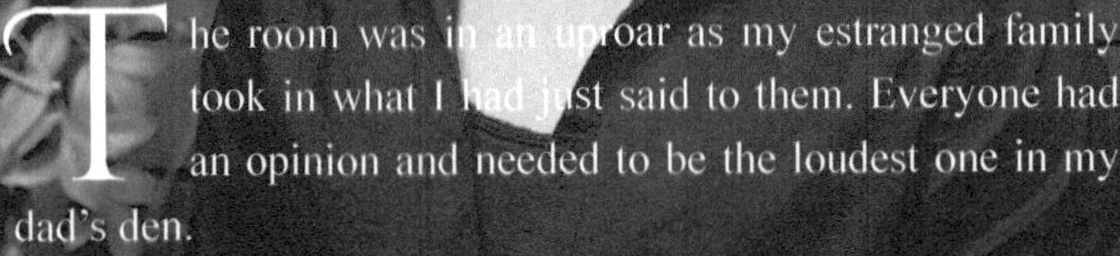

The room was in an uproar as my estranged family took in what I had just said to them. Everyone had an opinion and needed to be the loudest one in my dad's den.

Finally, my mom put her arms up and shouted at everyone. "Enough! Gianni, Caterina," she took a large breath, closed her eyes and turned toward Scout and me. "And Scout." Her voice was calmer in addressing the woman whose hand I was squeezing. "Please leave the den. Scout, I'll have Peter show you Desiderio's rooms. I'll have him bring up a tray of blood for you. We need to talk to our son alone."

I opened my mouth in protest, but the vampire woman who gave me life put her hand up. While she appeared twenty-seven, like everyone else in the room, her mind was of a woman who had lived a long time. She wasn't putting up with my shit. "Absolutely not. Go. All of you!" She waved to my older siblings. They pouted but stormed out, muttering about me.

Reluctantly, I let go of Scout and turned to her. Her red

eyes were large, and she was unsure what to do. I forced a smile, which, unfortunately, I knew was really rough. She saw right through it but didn't say anything. I cleared my throat. "I should probably talk to them in private. Go ahead with Peter. You can explore my bedroom and see what I was like as a teen." I wiggled my eyebrows in an attempt to get her excited.

She nodded and started toward the door. Peter was there to greet her and escort her out. I rolled my eyes. Gianni probably sprinted to get the butler. He was so fucking petty.

Peter closed the door behind us, and then a large slap on my dad's desk caused me to jump and turn.

"How could you do such a thing, Desiderio!" He bellowed. I gulped. I stared, open-mouthed, at the man who looked similar to me, but his style made us total opposites. I was wearing a worn Pantera shirt, while he had on a grey three-piece suit. "Does her family know?"

"Scout's?" I cocked my head in confusion.

"Aleida!" The vein in his forehead bulged, matching his blood-red eyes. "Does the Linotti family know what you did with that girl?" He spat.

"I don't know. Dad, it's been thirty years. We've gone this long without each other. I think you guys trying to push this is absurd."

"We had no memory of the deal. Nor did they. To us, it's as if you are still engaged to be married." My mother spoke in a much softer tone. Both me and my dad spun our heads to look at her. She sighed deeply. "Desiderio, why did you do this? To get back at us?"

I looked around the room and scoffed. I had grown up knowing that all of the Amato wealth would one day be mine, provided I followed their rules. If that was the case, I didn't want it. "You turned your back on me when I turned. I've been the black sheep of the family just because I don't look like you, and you expect me to give you what you want?"

"This is the vampire you took that curse for?" My dad smirked. "You gave up everything for a Bloodborn with no family line? It's incredulous. How could you?"

"Eugenio, yelling isn't getting us anywhere." My mom went to him behind his desk and urged him down into his chair. She pointed to one of the leather chairs Gianni had been sitting in. I sat too, and for a long moment, the room was quiet. Finally, my mother continued the discussion. "We haven't seen you in person since you broke your curse. Now that you remember things tell us how this happened."

"You mean the sex or the curse?"

My dad slammed his fist on his desk so hard it shook. "God damn it!"

My mom reached for his shoulders and shoved him back down. She shot daggers at me with her glare that caused me to shrink into my seat. "This isn't a joke, Desiderio."

I licked my lips and blinked, trying to figure out where to begin.

"Okay. I met Scout in nineteen-ninety-three and fell in love for the first time."

I waited for my parents to let my bold statement set in.

They had introduced me to Aleida Linotti in nineteen-eighty-nine.

My mom blinked and then raised an eyebrow. "Why didn't you tell us about this other Bloodborn woman? Perhaps we could have figured things out."

"I didn't know she was a vampire. We were both unturned. I thought she was human."

"So you knew you shouldn't have pursued her then." My Dad reprimanded me.

I agreed with him. "I'm fully aware. I'd spent weeks

trying to figure out how to end things before I turned. Our birthdays are one night apart. I decided to wait until she turned twenty-seven and then call it."

But I hadn't.

I had chosen to break up with Aleida instead, but in an attempt to be honest, I told Scout about what I had done to both of them. That I was cheating, and she was the other woman. That had caused the fight on the bridge.

"But she did turn." my mom shook her head in confusion.

"Yeah. But neither of us was prepared for it. We were out in public when she dropped to the ground. I thought she was really dying. Then, I panicked when she woke back up and needed blood. We were alone. I couldn't just let her die." I threw my hands up. They knew that. When your human heart dies, and you return as a vampire, you need blood immediately, or you die for good. I had minutes to save her.

"You chose to give her your blood? Permanently sealing your fates." My mother mourned the loss of a perfectly good match between the Amato and Linotti families. "You tied yourself to her without thinking about everything, Desiderio," she scolded lightly.

I shook my head. "I was thinking very clearly that night. I knew what I was doing."

"How did the curse happen?" My dad was growing impatient. His dark hair, the same inky black as mine, normally styled back, was frazzled from the stress of my grand entrance.

"Well," I rested my hands in my lap like a child. "I let her drink my blood, and then she slipped into sleep again. I took her home and went back to my apartment. I didn't know what to do. It was my birthday, I was turning come nightfall, and it would be a big thing."

I swallowed the pit in my stomach, remembering how fucking shitty I felt going to the diner and finding that Scout not only was working that night, but she was our waitress. She looked at me, sulking in my seat next to Aleida in her vampire form, and was done with me. It had shattered me so completely that I realized maybe it was best I do what my family had wanted and marry the blonde woman with family ties and the personality of a sponge.

"I hadn't turned when the restaurant we were all at got robbed. Guys with guns were everywhere, demanding we put our hands up. I was still human, so I had no choice but to listen to them. But they shot anyway. Everyone collapsed, including me, and I panicked. I started praying for help."

"And someone answered." My dad stood and started to pace the den. It was his favorite room in the house. He kept it dark and the fireplace going at all times. It always reminded me of those commercials where Santa reads stories next to a fire. Except with the smell of cigars permanently seeped into the walls and floor. "If you call a demon, they will answer." He didn't look at me as he put his hands behind his back.

"I begged to go back. For them to not let me die as a human. I needed to turn, so I could save my soulmate. He agreed, but well, you know the rest."

"Desiderio," my mother groaned again. "What a disaster." She pinched the space between her eyes. "What are we going to do?"

"You're going to give me your approval to marry Scout." I stood and stared at her with hard eyes.

"You're joking. We can't approve that." My dad laughed. "She doesn't even have a last name. Our family will be shamed."

"More than it already has? You tossed me away when I

came home with two different colored eyes, Dad. Don't pretend like things have suddenly changed."

"But they have. Desiderio, you have a chance to fix things. The Linotti family is still interested."

"But I'm not." I pressed. "And I doubt Aleida is either. We're different people, living in different times. It's not going to happen."

We continued back and forth for the rest of the night until we were all exhausted. Finally, I turned and left the room. I couldn't keep talking in circles with them. It was getting early. "I'll deal with this tomorrow night." I tossed over my shoulder before I left.

I went to my room and found Scout waiting for me in bed. I quickly stripped down and climbed in next to her.

"How'd it go?" she asked.

"Not great. They still don't get it. Their brains are so rooted in tradition it's hard for them to understand how I could break them with no fucks given." I rolled onto my side and pulled her into my embrace. Her skin was soft and exactly what I needed right now. I relaxed against her and closed my eyes. "I'm sorry you had to spend hours in here alone."

She laughed lightly, which ignited the flame in my heart. I needed her in my life, and I refused to give that laugh up.

"It wasn't terrible. I explored some. Teenage human Desi was a lot like adult vampire Desi."

"Yeah?"

"When did you last live here?" she asked.

I squinted, trying to remember. "I moved out with my buddies when I graduated high school. So, nineteen-eighty-five?"

"I found all your Iron Maiden tapes. They were in a

shoebox underneath the Van Halen poster on your desk. You have quite the collection."

I laughed. "I went to as many of their concerts as I could when I was in school. Even when my parents refused to give me permission. I'd find someone to drive me five hours just to see them and buy a shirt."

"I found pictures. Of you and your friends. They look like a fun group."

"Yeah? You don't remember them?" I sat up on my elbows, and she turned slightly to look at me. "You met most of them that night you met me."

She furrowed her brow. "I don't. Not specifically, anyway. I remember a group of long-haired grunge-heads taking up one of my tables all night, and then when I clocked out, they catcalled me from their car. And then you, I remember you." She reached up and put her soft hand on my rough cheek. She smiled. "You were leaning against the wall, trying to act like you were different from all of those guys."

"I was." I defended. "I had the balls to talk to you."

"Yeah, but you shouldn't have." She removed her hand, and the shadow of Aleida and what I had done returned, engulfing Scout and mine's relationship again. I sighed and fell back onto my pillow.

"I was stupid back then. I thought I could have you all to myself and still make my parents happy by pretending I was with Aleida."

"Are all of those people in the picture vampires?" She changed the subject after my confession sat heavily between us. I smiled, remembering the crew.

"Nah. They're all old men now. Mid-to-late fifties. Kids, careers, wives. All that picket fence stuff."

All the stuff I wouldn't mind having.

I closed my eyes and moved to rest my head against her. I

loved sleeping next to her. It was easier to relax and actually dream. Her slow, steady breathing told me that she felt the same.

That next night I was determined to get my parents to see that Scout was who I was meant to be with, whether they liked it or not. I found my family all at the dining room table sipping warm cups of blood and chatting, presumably about me.

"Good evening," I said to them.

Gianni snickered. "Where's your girlfriend?"

"Where's your wife? Fucking some random vampire across town?" I shot back. I reached for the teapot and poured myself a cup.

My brother glared at me and said nothing. I was probably right. He had chosen to marry for name and money. My sister as well, and now they were both in unhappy marriages.

"She is pretty, but besides that I presume is good sex, she can't provide much else." My sister shrugged. I felt my cheeks flush.

"Caterina, stop being vulgar," our mother scolded.

"What? I mean, how else could someone with no last name, Bloodborn or not, have pulled an Amato?" My sister brushed back her long, dark hair and smirked. I rolled my eyes. I always found it uncomfortable how proud they were of our last name. It was just a word.

"She is rather pretty. Is she from another country?" My mother asked kindly. I noticed that my father had been stewing silently on the other side of the table. He refused to look at me.

"No, although she thinks her family may have come from Mexico. If you guys gave her a chance, you'd like her."

"Why? We've given you many chances, and we still don't like you." Gianni shot at me. He looked so much like our father that it was almost comical. My brother was far too stupid to take control of all our dad did. It was probably why our dad had yet to retire.

"So you intend on marrying this woman? When?" my dad asked finally. I blinked.

"Yes. I don't know. I haven't really thought about dates yet. There's no real rush."

We're immortal.

"I made the painful call to the Linotti's last night. It was embarrassing." My mother faked a sniffle. She was stiff and regal, as always.

"I'm sorry. I wish I had told you thirty years ago," I told her. She sniffled again but said nothing.

"We have no choice but to accept your future with the orphan," my dad said flatly.

My mood lifted slightly. "Does that mean I can have the ring?" I asked.

"That ring had been for the marriage we had arranged," he replied sharply.

"No. It had been for the marriage I went through with. There were no stipulations. Grandma said I could have it. Where is she now? I'll go visit her."

There was a slight pause as my four family members exchanged silent looks.

"What?"

"When you got your curse, Grandma gave me the ring to save for when we thought you were ready." Gianni grinned at me. My mouth fell open as I took in his words. I shut it quickly, realizing how stupid I looked.

"Okay, well, give it back. It's mine."

"Not a fucking chance, baby brother."

CHAPTER 5

"You are such a loser!" I shouted at him as I leaped out of his car, slamming the door behind me. I hadn't even waited for him to stop. He finished parking and hurried to catch me.

"Oh, come on, it wasn't that bad!" He exclaimed.

I stopped and turned quickly. I was fuming. "Wasn't that bad? I spent the last three days getting glares from your entire family as you argued with them over how to break our blood bond. I was mortified! Desi, why did you take me there?"

He blinked as if suddenly realizing what he had put me through. "That's not what we were arguing about. They know we can't break it, nor do I want to." He gave me a pointed look. I rolled my eyes and threw my hands up.

"That's not the point. It was embarrassing."

"I had to show them you. That you're why I can't be with Aleida."

"*Can't?* Desi, you can be with whoever the fuck you want. I don't give a shit." I bared my fangs for a moment and then whipped back around. I started back toward our apartment.

"Don't say shit like that." He protested and reached for my arm. He grabbed it, but I pulled it out of his grasp. He managed to get hold of it again, and I turned. I glared at him with blazing eyes.

"If you don't think I'll rip my arm out of my fucking socket to get away from you, you're mistaken. Let go of me. You. Fucking. Loser." I said those last words slowly and with as much menace as I could muster. He flinched as if each word stung. He dropped my arm and slumped.

"I'm sorry. You know I don't care what they think."

"Then why did you insist I go with you?" I continued walking to the building. I pulled my keys out and unlocked the door. He followed me in and up the stairs to the apartment we now shared. He had insisted I move in with him after his fellow Seven Sin member attempted to have me killed. I tried to slam the door in his face, but he caught it, stepped inside, and slammed it for me.

"Because I want them to like you!" He threw his hands up. Silence suddenly filled the room as I turned and stared at him. He looked down and shoved his hands in his pockets.

"What?" I asked my voice hardly a level above a whisper.

"I mean, it doesn't change things between us if they don't, but eventually, when we get married and stuff, I want them to accept you as part of the family."

Marriage? And stuff? What did that even mean?

I opened my mouth to say something but was interrupted by a sudden knock on the door. He sighed and looked like he was going to ignore it, but it came again. He went to the door quickly and ripped it open.

"What?" He snapped at my neighbor across the hall, Amy. She had once been human, but when she turned twenty-seven, she took the plunge, literally. She threw herself down the stairs, breaking her neck. The next time we saw her, she had turned into a Bloodshed.

"A package came for you guys. The guy asked me to keep it until you got back. Here." She shoved it at him, and he closed the door quickly. He turned, examining the small box.

I took his momentary distraction to turn and go to our bedroom.

I couldn't handle talking about *marriage and stuff.*

Needing to get the memories of our trip off of me, I changed quickly. It was nearly morning, and I was exhausted. I removed my jeans and hoodie and slipped on a tank top and short pajama shorts. I sighed with relief as I removed my bra. I glanced at the bed. It was so inviting. I needed a good day's sleep.

Desi came into the room, shoving something in his pocket. I was going to ask, but he saw me, and his face morphed from stress to lust in an instant. I rolled my eyes as he scrambled to get out of his travel clothes. I noticed he was very hard in his boxers.

"Are you coming to bed?" I asked, despite already knowing the answer. I changed my tone and asked, "What was in the box?"

"Nothing. Just something I ordered online for the apartment," he lied. I knew that face all too well. He set the box down and hurried to join me in bed. I raised the covers to let him in.

"I won't take you there ever again if you don't want. I'm sorry I put you through that," he said.

"You're not getting any brownie points now. What's done is done. I hope you accomplished what you wanted with the trip," I said, my words clipped.

He tried to pull me into his arms, but I elbowed him away.

"I'm not in the mood." Those words still continued to echo in my brain.

Marriage and stuff.

"Oh, come on. I just want to hold you. Nothing devious." He tried to protest. I turned my back to him and forced myself to try to sleep. With a large sigh, I heard him click the lights off and lay down himself.

"You know, I don't care about your lineage. I love you," he said from behind me.

"I love you too." I smiled softly.

"We can still do all that stuff with or without their approval."

I stiffened.

"What stuff?" I could hear the squeak in my voice. I turned to look at him in the dark. He raised his eyes but was looking at the mattress, not me.

"You know, all that stuff couples do when they commit to each other."

Marriage and stuff.

"Is that what you really want? Or is that what society has trained you to want?" I asked.

He didn't reply.

"Desi, we just found each other again. I'm happy just dating you. We live together now, which is huge for me. I've never done that with someone I cared for. Can we just enjoy life as it is?" I pleaded for him to understand.

He hesitated but eventually nodded. "Sure, I just thought that was stuff you wanted."

I laughed. Was he trying to save face, or was he being honest? I don't know what was worse. "We're still getting to know each other. I like this stage."

"I know you." He tried to defend, but I shook my head.

"No, you don't. What style of art do I do?"

He opened and shut his mouth.

"What's my favorite color?" I tossed at him.

He didn't know that one either.

"Here's one for you. I lied to your family. I have a last name. What is it?

His eyes grew wide, and he scrunched up his mouth.

Point made.

I gave him a tight smile and turned back around. "Goodnight, Desiderio." I forced myself to fall asleep and let him stew in that.

No sooner had our alarm gone off was he in my face interrogating me.

"Okay, you got me. What's your last name?"

I gave him a funny look as I stretched. What was he talking about? He asked again, and I remembered our mini argument before bed. I smirked. "Your guess is as good as mine."

His eyebrows shot up, and suddenly I felt bad.

"I told you. I was a ward of the state. I was dropped off at the fire station when I was a kid."

"Yeah, but you never had any leads to your lineage? I mean, you're what— Hispanic?" He eyed me.

I glanced down at my body. It was obvious that I had come from some sort of Latin descent. My skin was lightly tanned, and my hair naturally dark. I'd always been told to check 'Hispanic' for all the boxes on formal papers.

"You've got an accent."

"Barely." I laughed. He scowled, and I relented. "There's been some leads. I spent a lot of time in Mexico when I first turned, trying to find my family. I didn't really get anywhere."

"Was Scout the name you were born with?"

I shook my head and frowned. "No, the fire station gave

me that name. I don't know much else past that." I got out of bed, went to the bathroom, and started the shower. "Can we call this whole thing even?"

I pulled off my pajamas and threw him my shirt. In a flash, he was joining me in the shower.

Worked every time.

We spent the night relaxing and watching movies. We were doing a horror marathon as we caught up on laundry. In between movies, I scooped up clothes for another load and reached for the pants Desi had worn the night before. I started going through his pockets when I found a folded piece of paper. I opened it and saw that it was a handwritten letter.

"D,

Long time no talk. I heard you talked to Tully. Why didn't you call me? I might have known where Elvie was. I see how I rank.

Anyway, word has spread about you exploding Corrine's brain. Typical of the baby of the family to get what he wants. We still all have to follow the rules.

If you haven't heard, I've hunkered down with Tully. We run a little thing over here that I think you'd get a kick out of. You should come. Bring your little lady. What did you tell Corrine she was? Your soulmate? How romantic. Bring the girl and have a good time with us. If you're going to break the rules, we want to meet the reason for it.

See you soon,

Dante

After I read the letter, I glanced back at Desi, sorting socks on the bed. I cocked my head and asked. "Who's Dante?"

His head shot up so fast, and he saw the letter in my hand. He tried to lean forward and snatch it, but I stepped back.

Dante must be someone important.

"Is he one of the Sins? Tully, you've said that name before. No, I think you've said Dante too. It is!" I bounced excitedly as my brain started working out the puzzle. Desi's eyes grew wide with horror as he watched me figure it out.

He stood up and went to me, taking the letter back. I didn't fight it, but I didn't need to. I had read it already.

"They know about me. Desi, they are inviting us to go visit!"

He rolled his eyes, but I could see his resolve softening. His lip twitched with irritation, but he said nothing. When I continued to plead with my large eyes, he responded.

"We're not going. Dante and Tully are not two people I want you to meet."

"You always say that. Which ones are they?" I brought my hands up to try to count. "Pride, Greed, Sloth, Wrath, I've met those," I paused to look directly at him on the last one. He had hidden from me that he was Wrath for months. It still was a surprise sometimes. He sighed deeply and crossed his arms as I continued. "So that leaves Lust, Envy, and Gluttony."

"That is correct," he replied dryly.

"Well, I won't be able to guess unless we meet them."

He shook his head again, but I continued to plead with him.

"Desi, come on. Please! For me. I had such a crappy weekend. You owe me!"

He blinked and let out a laugh. "I *owe* you? I thought we were even?"

"Yes, but now I want to do this. Can we please?"

He stared up at the ceiling as if weighing his options. He'd be irritated the entire time if he took me, and we'd probably fight. If he didn't take me, I'd be irritated, and we'd probably fight.

"I have absolutely no good reason to take you to meet them. They're bad news."

I scoffed. "You say that about all of you guys. I call bullshit."

"Really? You don't think we're bad?" He stepped up to me, urging my legs apart with his foot. My heart skipped as my body pulsed with the thought of his touch. "One of us has an illegal fight club in his basement, another runs a large drug ring across the country, and I murder people for a living. I think you've gravely misunderstood things." He bore his gaze down on me, but I didn't flinch. I steeled myself and grinned up at him.

"I don't think so." I put my hands up and placed them on his bare chest. My fingers traced the blood-red bat tattoo that told me who he was and what he did. It marked him as a Seven Sin. A large shiver went through him with my touch. "And even if I am wrong, I don't care. I love you anyway."

Instinctively, his arms went around me, enveloping me in a hug. I inhaled the smell of him and sighed.

"I'm sorry for freaking you out about the future," he muttered into my hair as he kissed it tenderly.

"Then make it up to me by letting me meet your friends." I giggled. He took a step away, letting me go. He stared at me for a long time.

"You're way too cute for an undead girl." He sighed deeply. "I'll think about it."

"I'm not going to forget," I said, and he gave me a look before returning to the socks on the bed. Licking my lips, I rattled off a large string of numbers. He turned and cocked an eyebrow.

"What is that?"

I smiled at him smugly. "Dante's phone number. I'm calling him." I hurried for my phone and began putting in the number. He leaped off the bed and attempted to bring me back to the mattress by wrapping his hands around my waist.

"How did you—"

"It was on the back of the letter. Ssh, it's ringing!" I wiggled under him. "Hello? Is this Dante? Desi's friend? I saw your letter. I'm Scout."

He snatched the phone from me and playfully pushed me away. He brought it to his ear and glared at me.

"Hello? Who is Scout? Is that D's girlfriend?" The voice was loud, and I could hear it clearly through the speaker.

"Dante," Desi replied curtly.

"D! I knew you'd call. Your lady has a nice voice. Did you like the cards I sent you?"

"Cut it," Desi snapped.

"So? What say you?" The man on the other side asked. I could almost hear the grin in his voice. Desi glanced at me, sitting beside him on the bed. I leaned forward, letting my breasts spill out of my tank top. His eyes flicked to them with a look of yearning before back to my face, at which he glared. The voice repeated the offer of invitation, and Desi finally replied.

"Give us a week, and we'll be there."

"Are you ready?" I asked while I skipped to Desi's car to start toward New Jersey.

"I am, but I really don't think you are." He snickered as he jingled his keys and followed behind me at a much slower pace. He was less than enthused about taking me to meet his two Seven Sin brothers, Tully and Dante, and had been vocal about it all week. "Do you have everything you need?"

"I think so. You said one week, so that's what I packed for." I eyed him carefully, trying to see if he was hiding something. He'd been off since he had agreed to visit the pair. He wouldn't tell me why, only that it wasn't a good idea.

I went to my side of the car and reached for the handle. I tugged it only to find it still locked. I turned my head to protest and saw Desi still standing with me instead of on the driver's side. I grinned, but he didn't smile back. In fact, he looked uncomfortable.

He shifted nervously on his feet, his hands stuffed inside his pockets.

"What's up? Unlock the car, Loser." I laughed lightly, and I watched his Adam's apple bob before he pressed his lips tightly together.

"I want to give you something before we go."

I raised my eyebrows. "You got me something? Desi, we packed enough fireballs to last me a lifetime. You a week." I teased him, and finally, he relaxed slightly. A tiny smile spread over his face, and he shook his head. He then pulled his hand out of his pocket and shoved it toward me.

I looked down at his closed fist and cocked my head to the side. He stepped forward, closing the small gap between us then. As soon as he was within reach of me, he opened his hand and revealed a small, white, folded square of tissue paper. I plucked it tenderly out of his hand and eyed the clear tape on it.

"What's this?"

"Open it." He urged me, nodding his head. I took it in both hands and carefully tore into the wrapping paper. A thin gold chain fell into my palm, and my heart stopped. Completely fucking stopped.

He took the paper from me as I lifted the chain to see exactly what the gift was.

"Oh, Desi," I sighed, staring at the necklace in shock. "I love it." My fingers went to the pendent. In gothic lettering, it spelled out DESI. "And there's a bat underneath it!" I ran my fingers over the name and design fused to it.

"It matches mine."

My head shot up as he moved the collar of his shirt, revealing a gold necklace that said SCOUT, with a small bat attached. Suddenly, I felt like complete putty. I started to falter, and he caught me.

"You okay?" He chuckled. I nodded and stood straighter, taking a deep breath.

"Yeah. Desi, I love this. I love you." I turned to let him put it on me. His name rested at the base of my neck. When I turned back to him, I leaned up and planted a kiss on his lips.

"I thought you would." He looked down as if I had embarrassed him with how I reacted to his gift. He shoved his hands in his pockets and rocked on his shoes. "You ready?"

I nodded, and he pushed the button to unlock the car. I hugged him once more before I hopped into the car. He moved much slower, climbing in and buckling himself silently. He glanced at me, grinning like an idiot and holding the necklace. He smiled, but then his face turned serious.

"Ohio to New Jersey is almost seven hours. I don't want to stop."

"I already went to the bathroom, and I packed blood." I raised the backpack in my lap, and the recyclable metal bottles filled with blood clanked together inside. "Come on, let's have a good trip. I'll let you have control of the radio." I promised.

He grinned and put out his hand. I dug into my bag and pulled out a cinnamon ball, handing it to him. He popped it into his mouth, flashed a smile, and reached for the phone in his pocket. He connected it to his car, and a moment later, we were pulling out of the parking lot while *Too Hot For Teacher* blared in our ears.

I loved his music.

I pulled out my sketchpad and doodled as I bobbed my head and sang to the playlist filled with Guns N' Roses, Van Halen, and plenty of Iron Maiden.

Desi drove in mostly silence, not relaxing even an iota the entire time we drove. It was a little unnerving. Despite trying to get him to loosen up and get as excited as I was about our vacation, he was still tense.

"It's not like you're missing anything." I tried to offer him, but he responded by tightening his grip on the wheel.

"That's not the point. I just don't think this is a good idea."

"How so? I've got you here with me, and Corrine already promised she wouldn't try to kill me anymore. There's no reason to be scared."

His jaw tensed. "I'm not scared. I'm…" he paused, and I looked up from my cartoon doodle. His tongue flicked over his lips, and he continued. "I'm worried about myself. It's a guy thing. I change when I'm around them. I turn into an asshole."

I blinked and raised my eyebrows. "More than you are already?"

He scowled. "Yes. And I don't want you to feel like I'm neglecting you or that I've changed. I'm going to try to be conscious of it, but it's just the environment. Tully and Dante like to party, and they party hard."

"And you think I can't hang?" I crossed my arms over my chest. "I can party just as hard as the next guy."

"Really? Is that why you've spent the last few years as an assistant manager for a movie theater?" He side-eyed me, and I could almost hear the rest of that unspoken sentence. *Nerd.*

"I'm responsible. But I'm still fun. Do you think you'd have more fun if I weren't there?"

He didn't respond, which in itself was a response.

"Wow. Okay," I sat up straighter in my seat. "I'll show you that I can hang just as much as the rest of your little gang." I put up air quotes at the end, which I knew would annoy him. It did.

"Don't call us—" he huffed, and then I saw his eyes roll while still focusing on the road. "Fine. You want to play and party with us, by all means. But I've told you before that you shouldn't trust any of us."

I waved my hands at him. "Yes, I know. The Seven Sins are bad. Yes, even you. I'm a big girl. I can hold my own. By the end of the week, you'll be groveling at my feet, begging me to go back to the nerdy girl you came with."

He shook his head and laughed. His shoulders finally relaxed, and he smiled for the first time in what felt like days. "I admire the enthusiasm. It's sure to be an eventful week."

I grinned. "Yes. And then we can return back home and continue on with our regularly scheduled programming."

"Which is?"

"Me finding a new job, applying for art schools. Then once I get in somewhere, I need to start looking for a place to stay. Not every school lets vampires stay on campus."

"Whoa, hold up," Desi took his hand off the wheel and put it up in the air. "What do you mean, look for a place to stay? You've got a place. You live with me."

"Yeah, but there's no real good schools around here. Especially blood-friendly." I cocked an eyebrow at the panicked man beside me. What was his problem? "This has always been the plan." I reminded him.

"School, yeah, but not you moving. I thought you liked living together."

"I do. This isn't some slight on you. If you're that upset about it, come with me. Worst case scenario, you can find a place close by if I end up staying on campus."

"Why would you stay on campus if I had an apartment near the school?" he demanded.

I blinked. "Well, now it's because you're acting like some — I don't even know. I don't like this." I waved my arms around wildly. "Whatever this is."

He gritted his teeth and gripped the wheel tight again. "It

just makes me more comfortable to have you close to me. To know you're safe."

I laughed. "Do you think I can't handle myself? I've spent the last thirty years on my own as a vampire. I don't need saving. I live with you because I like you, not because I need you. Get that shit out of your head now."

"Why are we even fighting about this?" He threw up his hands. "You haven't even gotten into a school. This is dumb."

"Because it will happen, eventually."

"Will it?" He shot back, and his shitty remark had me speechless. I opened and closed my mouth. Then, I turned my head to look out into the dark.

Fuck you.

"Scout, I'm sorry. That was a shitty thing for me to say. I'm just—"

"Nah, you don't get to take that back. I don't know what's going on with you, but you better figure it out before we get back home. Otherwise, I'll move out before I even start applying to places." I didn't bother to look at him as I said it.

I closed my eyes and pressed my forehead against the cold window. I was naturally cold, but it still felt good on my skin.

"I don't want to fight. I love you," Desi whispered when there was a slight delay between songs. His words stung, and I felt them in my stomach. I took a deep breath and sat up. I grabbed my bag and pulled out the bottles. We were about halfway to New Jersey.

I unscrewed one and offered it to him. He took it with a soft murmur of thanks. I drank from my own bottle and reached for his phone. He was right. I loved him too, and I hated fighting with him. I went through his music and switched to my music.

I turned the volume up and sang along with all the female-led bands that filled the playlist. Maria Maria was the first to play, and I saw Desi roll his eyes when Cleo De La Rosa's voice came through. He was not a fan of punk-pop. Eventually, the tension in the car disappeared, and we were back to joking and singing along to The Cranberries on our way to visit two of the Seven Sins.

Boredom eventually began to set in, and I pulled out my tarot cards. Desi had gifted me my set after my side had fully healed from the Sunshine. He had surprised me with the cards and offered to teach me how to read and understand them.

I opened the deck and set them down on my sketchpad. Desi glanced at my lap.

"Doing a spread?" He grinned. He loved it when I took an interest in the cards. Besides cinnamon candy and horror movies, Tarot was one of his favorite things.

I shrugged and let out a small yawn. "Yeah, I guess. I haven't played with them in a while. I didn't bring any of my books, though." I frowned. Desi chuckled and tapped his temple.

"I'm your reference book. Do your spread, and I'll fill in any gaps."

"Do you want me to tell you the question?" I looked up at him. He shot me a look that I wasn't sure how to interpret.

"Only if you want me to know." Again, I could hear the rest of his words, unspoken.

Why wouldn't you want me to know?

Something in my stomach made me hold back from telling him. I swallowed and closed my eyes, letting myself think about the question. As I thought, one hand drifted to the dip in my neck, where his name sat. It suddenly felt warm against my otherwise chilly skin, but it was a comforting warmth.

What will lead me to true happiness?

That had always been the goal. For so long, my curse made me run toward a finish line I'd never cross. I begged for real answers and thought that breaking my curse would reveal everything, but it hadn't. I still had questions, and I still felt sad. Why?

I squeezed the necklace, then dropped it quickly to draw a three-card spread. It was my go-to, as I hadn't memorized any other ones yet. Past, present, future.

Queen of Cups, Three of Pentacles, The Moon.

I scrunched my nose and squinted my eyes, staring at the cards. While Desi had spent hours teaching me, and we'd gone through books on it, I still wasn't as skilled as he was at finding the answers instantly.

"What did you draw?" he asked finally.

I rattled off the small list. I saw one side of his smile turn up. He recognized instantly that I had done the only spread I could remember.

"Queen of cups. Okay. So, let's talk about it," he started. "Was your question a negative or positive one?"

"You told me I didn't have to tell you," I responded quickly. Guilt swirled in my stomach, and Desi blinked as if he'd been slapped.

"Were any of your cards upside down?" he asked.

"The Moon."

He didn't say anything for a moment but finally sighed and looked over at me. "I think this one's on you. My advice can only take you so far. If you want to ask them a personal question, you have to read them and decide for yourself what they say."

I stared at them as I felt like the shittiest person in the car. He was only trying to help, and I copped an attitude. Actually, we'd been going from one fight to another this entire car ride. What was going on? We never fought this much.

I stared back at the cards on my lap and tried to interpret them from memory.

The Queen of Cups was drawn in reference to my past, which wasn't really all that great. I was fixated on my happiness, which was Desi. *Is Desi.* I glanced at him again, but he was hyper-focused on the road.

The present card was the Three of Pentacles. I knew that one! It's the start of a journey. Which is my new life, curse-free.

The Moon reversed was for my future. I took the card in my hands and examined it closer. Everything about this card screamed negative vibes to me. Cheating, lying, danger. How could that future lead to happiness?

"I don't think I did it right," I said flatly.

"No?" Desi cocked his head and reached for my hand, squeezing it gently. "It takes a while to figure it all out. Maybe when we get to the hotel, I can help you with a different spread. Or we can work on rewording questions to better help the cards respond."

I nodded and put the cards back in their box. Desi's cards were so old he lost their case ages ago. He kept them in his pocket, sometimes secured with a rubber band, sometimes loose. I wasn't sure I'd ever have that strong connection with my own deck.

"We're getting a hotel?" I asked, relaxing into my seat. I stretched my legs some and yawned again. I glanced at my phone. "We're getting close."

"Yep. Based on our arrival time, we won't have long to get inside and socialize with Dante and Tully. I figured we would want to get a good day's sleep and refresh before visiting. We'll be staying with them the rest of the week."

"Really?" I blinked in surprise. He smirked, but his eyes darkened. I watched as he turned off the highway when he saw a sign for a blood-friendly hotel. His lips curled up, and his fangs showed as he growled slightly at our plans for the upcoming week.

"They insisted."

CHAPTER 7

Desi

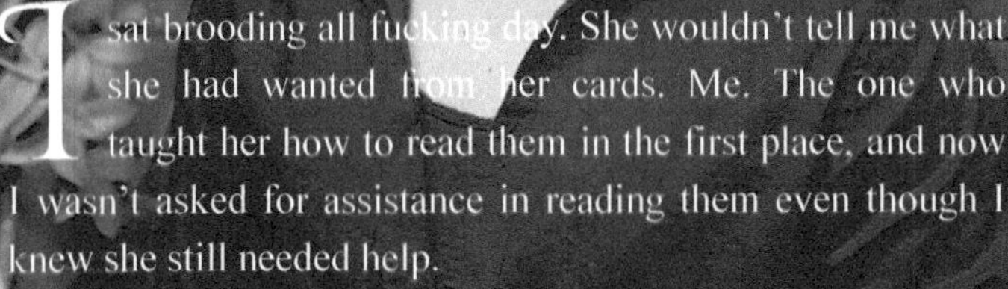

I sat brooding all fucking day. She wouldn't tell me what she had wanted from her cards. Me. The one who taught her how to read them in the first place, and now I wasn't asked for assistance in reading them even though I knew she still needed help.

And why? Because she was asking them about me. *About us.* Which only made the cards she pulled even fucking worse.

Queen of Cups, Three of Pentacles, The Moon reversed.

If she did the past, present, and future spread, which I was almost sure she did, that meant that we basically looked past each other's flaws just so we could fuck. Now she realizes this and second-guessing our relationship. Finally, to top it all fucking off, The Moon reversed is saying that one of us is going to cheat.

I never deep-dived why my cards always told the truth about everything, but I wondered how on-the-mark hers could be. Until tonight she never seemed to take much of an interest in them past politeness toward me. Maybe you had to really believe in their power for them to guide you.

God, I hoped so.

I tossed and turned all day. It was bad enough that we were visiting my two least favorite Sins, but to top it all off, I had to worry about Scout's cards predicting that she'd cheat on me with one of them.

However, those worries were relaxed as soon as I woke and called Tully to let him know we were in town.

"Toulouse, we made it." I yawned into the phone. I sat up in bed and watched as Scout did the same, stretching and grinding sleep out of her eyes. *God, even fresh out of slumber, she was gorgeous.*

"It's about damn time." He laughed. "Me and Dante have been waiting all week. When are you coming over?"

"We have to shower and check out. Give us a few hours. We're staying with you, right?" I wanted to clarify our original agreement. They often forgot things.

"Yeah, yeah. You sure you want your little lady staying under the same roof as us?" He goaded.

"Tully," I growled, glancing back at Scout. She had gotten out of bed and was quickly undressing to head to the shower. My cock pulsed as I stared at her beautiful body. "Don't start."

"Whoa, I could say the same for you, buddy. I forgot what a temper you have." He clicked his tongue, which only unnerved me more. Toulouse always had a way of getting under my skin. "Yes, I have rooms for you two to stay in and have your privacy. I even made sure it was away from the tables. Although I do insist you guys come check out the setup at least once."

"Sure. Whatever, I'm gonna go. Text me the address, and we'll see you soon." I hung up quickly to join Scout in the shower. I needed to touch her and show her that I wasn't going anywhere regardless of what she may have read in her cards. And neither was she.

———

Only minutes after coming deep inside her, we were dressed and checking out of the hotel.

"Can we do that again later?" I laughed, putting my arms around her and holding her close to my chest.

She giggled, and it was like singing directly to my soul. "I'd be down for that. Hopefully, Tully has a big enough shower."

"Or maybe a bath. That could be interesting."

Her eyes and smile grew wide with the idea, making me ready to go again.

We got into my car, and I typed the address into my GPS. Just as I was putting my phone up to put the car into reverse, I received a text from Corrine.

> Corrine: Dante tells me you're visiting New Jersey. Check your email. I have a few jobs for you.

I sighed deeply. I hadn't planned on making this a working trip. I ignored the text and backed out of the parking spot to start the trek to Tully and Dante's.

I didn't have to do the jobs if I didn't want to. For the most part, I could take or leave whatever I was offered. Unless I made a special deal with someone, but that was rare. I'd have to see what Corinne offered before I took the gig.

"You look irritated again," Scout said, interrupting my brooding. I relaxed my brow and forced a smile.

"Sorry. I told you, being around those two makes me anxious. It's mob mentality with them."

"Oh really?" She smirked. "What, you turn into a burping, farting, frat boy?"

I laughed. She had no idea how wrong and right she was.

"Something like that. Remember—" I started, but she interrupted me with her tongue hanging out and blood-red eyes looking at the roof of the car.

"I know, I know. The Sins are not to be trusted. Even you."

I patted her thigh and gave her the same sarcastic smile she was giving me. "Good girl."

"Oh, don't start that." She warned with a look so sharp it caused a moment of silence before we both erupted in laughter.

"So, is there any real last-minute advice you can give me about them?" she asked. I pressed my lips together and thought. It had been years since I'd seen them both in person. But time didn't alter some things.

"I wouldn't tell Tully anything specific about yourself. Like if he asks about something personal, keep it vague. He holds on to that shit," I muttered. Flashes of harsh memories flew through my mind. I swallowed and continued. "As far as Dante goes, don't…" I paused, knowing that anything I told her in warning would reveal what Sin he was. "Don't talk to Dante."

She started to laugh, but when she saw me not smiling with her, she frowned. "Seriously? How am I supposed to not talk to the reason we're here? You don't think that'll look weird?"

"Oh, it will, but he'll know why and as long as you stay with me, he won't test it."

"Gluttony, Envy, and Lust. Those are the ones left, right?"

My jaw tightened. "Yes."

"Interesting."

The address we had been given turned us into a parking lot of what looked like—

"Is this a sex store? Oh my god! Is one of them Lust?" The squeal that came from my girlfriend's mouth as she realized this made the pit in my stomach drop so hard I struggled to breathe. She was practically bouncing in her seat as I parked and stopped the car.

"Finally! One that makes fucking sense! Oh, please don't tell me he's doing something absolutely disgusting." She frowned. I tilted my head in confusion. Her eyes darkened. "You know, with minors and stuff." She kept her voice low.

"Oh God, no. At least, I doubt it. We're deplorable vampires, sure, but I don't think any of us are interested in that. I wouldn't take you somewhere like that." I assured her, and she let out a large exhale and then resumed her excitement.

"Good. Okay, let's go. I want to meet Lust."

"Can you please stop saying that?" I swallowed my jealousy as I got out of the car and joined her in walking toward the door. The shop was a large square building with giant neon signs all over. The biggest one was on the roof. It said **Night Work**. The name of the shop itself didn't scream sex-toy shop, but the blowup in the front and all the signs that listed what they were selling told us exactly what we were going to expect upon going inside.

I walked in, shaking my head at how painfully obnoxious this was, even for Toulouse. Scout grabbed my hand and pulled me in, as I was slightly reluctant. House music was playing at an oddly comfortable level, and I blinked at how harsh the lighting was in here.

A bloodshed vampire woman greeted us from behind the large counter. She smiled kindly. "Hello. Welcome to Night Work. Is there anything specific you're looking for today?"

I saw Scout open her mouth and I quickly clamped my hand over it. She nipped me, her fangs piercing the palm of my hand just enough for me to jerk away. "No. Just looking around, thanks."

"Okay, well, if you need any help, my name is Sharon, and I'll be happy to help you. Clothes and the dressing room are over there." She pointed to the left. We turned and saw she was correct. "Anal play and vibrators are in that room, along with all the lubes, lotions, oils, bondage, and all leather gear are in the second. Movies and magazines are on the wall over here." She quickly rattled off everything, and I realized I was starting to get a little embarrassed. Scout giggling like she was a teenager beside me wasn't helping.

"What do you want to look at first?" My immortal girlfriend asked me. I scowled.

"Nothing. We're not here for that."

"Oh, come on. Some of this can be fun." She thrust out her lower lip and pulled me toward the room that was clearly labeled TOYS.

"I don't know," I said, feeling kind of stupid. It wasn't like either of us was innocent or celibate during our thirty years apart. We'd discussed our past.

"You know, sex gets way better when you realize that toys are your teammates, not your enemy."

We both turned quickly to see a tall vampire leaning against a rack of robes and smirking at us.

Toulouse.

Despite myself, I grinned and hurried to greet him. He

hadn't changed even a little. He uncrossed his arms and pulled me in for a bear hug. "It's been too long, baby brother. You look good!" he exclaimed, patting me on the back.

I laughed, and when we parted stepped back, I looked at him. It was like stepping through time. He wore a baseball cap backward, his blonde hair peeking out the front hole. He had a faded green plaid button shirt over his white t-shirt, and his jeans were acid-washed. He was even wearing the same yellow converse.

"Holy shit. It's like seeing a ghost." I blinked.

He snickered. "I don't need the fancy duds like Arsenio and Elvie. You uh, done shopping?" He glanced behind me at Scout. Instantly I straightened. I had forgotten about her for a moment. "Because I can bring you guys on back and over to my place."

"You live next door?" I reached for Scout's hand and started off with Tully.

"Yeah. It's connected to the shop. Actually, you guys might want to go get your stuff. Then I'll take you down." He stopped short and turned. Scout bumped into my shoulder, and it caused him to look at her. He grinned and extended his hand.

"I'm Tully."

"Scout. You're Lust?" She blurted. I wanted to stomp on her shoe. Tully blinked and shot a look at me. I sighed and shook my head in annoyance.

"Uh, yeah. Nice to meet you, Scout. We've all been anxious to see the vampire that's changed the rules for us."

"Oh?" Scout cocked her head, and it made me squeeze her hand tighter. Didn't I warn her enough?

"Go, get your bags, and I'll take you down." He flicked his attention back to me. I nodded and started out, pulling

Scout behind me. She tugged against me, causing me to pause. I turned and eyed her with caution.

"Aren't you coming with me?"

"Do you need her help?" Tully answered for her. I could have punched him. I gritted my teeth and took a long, deep breath.

"Remember what I told you." I looked down at our hands as I let go and rushed out of the sex store to get our bags.

"Lemme guess—" I could hear Tully being a smart-ass from behind me, but there was little I could do about it. I moved fast, collecting our shit and hurrying back inside. I cringed, hearing Scout's giggles as Tully entertained her.

They both stopped laughing and turned when I came back. Instant irritation rose up in my throat.

"Ready?" Tully asked. I nodded. Scout smiled and returned to my side. She took her suitcase from my hand, and three of us went into the back room together. It was a large storage room, with another door in the far back that had several locks on it. Tully took out a set of keys and started unlocking them. He finally got it open and urged us in.

There were immediate steps, and Scout stumbled for a second before Tully flicked on the lights. We were in a fully finished hallway. The walls were dimly lit, and a soft red carpet was on the floor. The walls were lined with off-white wallpaper and random pictures of still life.

I kept looking at them as we passed, and Tully commented on them.

"I had a chick once who was really into painting."

"I like painting," Scout told him. I glanced as Tully grinned and leaned toward her, way too interested in that little factoid.

"Yeah? I'd love to see some of your work."

He was in front of us, and I reached out and kicked the

back of his knee. He faulted for only a second before continuing on.

"Dante and I were actually setting up a game for tonight if you want to join us."

"Game?" Scout asked as we reached the end of the long tunnel. We were at a large door and could hear voices and music from the other side. Tully turned to us and smiled wide.

"You didn't think I made my fortunes selling fake cocks and ball gags, did you?"

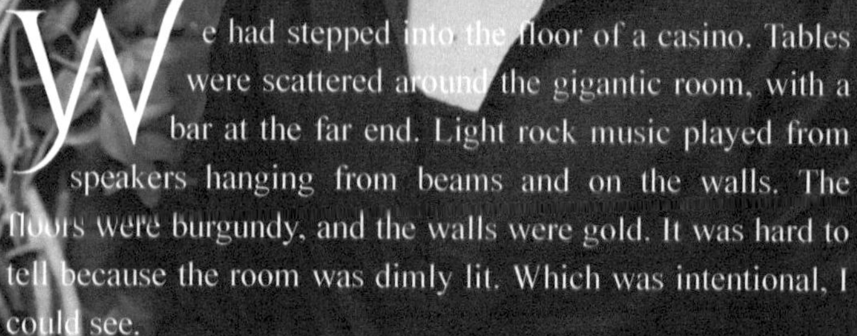

CHAPTER 8

Desi

We had stepped into the floor of a casino. Tables were scattered around the gigantic room, with a bar at the far end. Light rock music played from speakers hanging from beams and on the walls. The floors were burgundy, and the walls were gold. It was hard to tell because the room was dimly lit. Which was intentional, I could see.

"Where are we?" Scout gasped as Tully led us further into the room, closing the door behind us. People in white dress shirts and black pants were walking around fixing chairs, preparing tables, and shuffling cards. Some women in red cocktail dresses carried trays and other small things toward the bar.

"My house. My basement. You like it?" Tully turned to me and wiggled his eyebrows, waiting for praise.

I didn't.

"It's like Vegas," she laughed. "No slots?"

Tully's face darkened for only a second before the slimy smile returned. "It's just a card club."

"And the sex shop is the front. Because you earn all of your money here," Scout pushed, and I bit my lip. I hated her curiosity sometimes. It seemed to get us in more trouble than it ever helped.

Tully clicked his tongue and pretended to cock a gun at her. "You got it, babe. You want to play?"

"No!" I interrupted their conversation, dropping our bags and putting my hand up. I then brought it around her and pulled her to me. "She's not playing with you."

"Ugh, is this who you are now that you've wifed up?" Tully gave me an exaggerated grimace.

"We're not married." Scout stiffened and stepped away from me. "We're just dating. I could hang. What card games do you play?"

"Poker, mostly. Different versions at different tables. You play?" Tully flicked his tongue over his fangs as he shot a shit-eating grin at me before returning his attention to Scout.

This was bad. This was really bad.

Scout, shut the fuck up.

I gritted my teeth and tried to shout it telepathically but to no avail. She opened her mouth and played right into Tully's hands.

"No. I can learn, though. Although it'd be just for fun. I didn't bring money to blow."

"Oh, I wouldn't worry about that. We take all sorts of payments here. Money, blood, whatever is agreed upon. Let me show you around." Tully extended his arm, and suddenly it was behind her back, urging her forward. They started away from me, leaving me standing there, dumbfounded by the door.

"Leave your things. I'll have someone take them to your room," Tully said, not looking at me.

"Is Dante here?" Scout's head turned to and fro, looking for Tully's partner-in-crime.

"Yeah, you want to meet him?" Tully turned his head back to me. His eyes were blazing with excitement. It was like watching Satan himself work his magic on Eve. He grinned, his fangs shining in the light.

I swallowed. I had to tread carefully. The more I tried to get her to leave, the more she wanted to stay. I followed them, keeping a pace or two behind. Just close enough to protect her but far enough to let her think she had control of the situation.

She didn't.

"Dante has his own table he likes to hold court at." Tully glanced at the watch on his wrist. "He should be coming down any time now."

"Do you play or just keep everything running?" Scout asked him. Tully's hand remained firm on her lower back. Every time his hand twitched, so did my eye.

"A little of both. If I find the game interesting enough, I'll sit down." A cocktail waitress passed by carrying a tray with a big bowl on it. Tully plucked something from it and grinned. "Sometimes it's fun just to watch. Would you like to try some candy?" I was just about to protest when Tully popped it into his own mouth and winked at me.

"Is this who I think it is?" A loud, familiar voice shouted from the far right of the room. All three of us turned to see a dark-haired vamp striding toward us with his arms wide open.

Dante.

"Speak of the devil." Tully chuckled and bent low to whisper in Scout's ear. "Meet Envy."

I took a step forward, and instantly Tully stepped away and gave me a tight, knowing smile.

My momentary attention lapse allowed Dante to rush toward Scout and lift her up into a hug as if they were old friends. "You're gorgeous! No wonder D blew his load over you!"

I groaned at the disgusting choice of words. He put Scout down and turned his attention to me. He grabbed me and lifted me just as he had her. "How's it been, man? Good, by the looks of you!"

He dropped me hard, and I stumbled back. Regaining my feet, I straightened and looked at my old friend and fellow Sin.

Dante was just like Tully. They hadn't changed. He was wearing a hockey jersey and ripped jeans. His dark hair was styled just the same as it had been the last time I had seen him. And he still kept the goatee. Facial hair on a vampire, especially a Bloodborn, was rare. He and Arsenio were the only ones I had ever met with it. Which I think Dante liked. It was kind of unsettling. Like he purposely wanted to stick out in the blood community but blend in with the humans. You couldn't hide the red eyes, though.

Dante's casual stance and genuine smile relaxed me enough to put my hand out and shake his, a real smile of my own spreading on my face.

"Good. I'm doing really good. You guys, too, apparently."

He laughed. "Oh yeah. This, paired with my own stuff, has set us up real nice."

I raised my eyebrows. "Your own stuff?"

His expression darkened for only a moment before returning to its friendly smile. "I'll show you in a bit. It's nothing you'd be interested in. You're still playing with your cards?" His eyes flicked down to my pocket, which in fact, held my tarot deck. I nodded.

"Good. Keeps the work entertaining, I'm sure."

Just then, my phone vibrated in my pocket. I glanced around the small circle we had formed and pulled it out. Corinne was calling. I knew if I didn't take the call, she'd just harass me until I did. I put a finger up and excused myself for a second.

"Yeah?" I snapped when I answered. I looked toward the trio. They were more than happy to entertain Scout while I was busy.

"I have a job. It's urgent." Corinne ignored my attitude.

"Apparently. What part of not working during my vacation didn't you get?"

"I know. This isn't for me. Ginata called it in."

I frowned. "Gina? That's not—" I paused. "Is she alright?"

"She seems okay. It was a short email request. Just that she had someone that needed taking care of as soon as possible."

"Where is she even? I'm not flying out somewhere, even if it is for her. She'll have to wait."

"It's in New York City."

I sighed.

God damn it.

"Is it going to be a whole deal, or can I get in and out?"

"He's easy to find."

"Then why doesn't she do it?" I hissed through clenched teeth. Tully had just brushed a strand of hair behind Scout's ear. She was talking animatedly, and he was nodding as if he gave a fuck. I knew better.

"She wants to keep it quiet. She wouldn't have asked if she didn't have to. You know that." Corinne reminded me.

"Fine. Send me the name and details. I'll do it tonight.

That's it. I'm shutting my phone off if you call again for this."

"I'll give Ginata your regards." She hung up before I could, and a moment later, the details about the guy I needed to kill were coming through via text.

I shoved my phone into my pocket and returned back to the group. "We've got to go. I need to go do something for Ginata." I looked at the three and reached out for Scout's hand. She frowned but started to reach for me, only to have her wrist snatched by Tully.

"Hold on, just because you have to work doesn't mean she has to go too. We can keep her company while you go do your thing."

I blinked, trying to comprehend what the fuck just happened. Tully removed his hand from Scout's body, and her arm fell to her side. She looked at me, her beautiful face begging me to let her stay.

"Ginata? That's a name you don't hear often enough. Speaking of," Dante exchanged a look with Tully, and they both grinned at me. "You know what she's got going on in her territory, right? I wouldn't be opposed to a little of that action right here." His gaze flicked to the unknowing Scout.

My eyes nearly came out of my head. Ginata kept multiple men in her bed. Did he just ask about the three of us sharing Scout?

Oh, hell no.

I thought my brain would explode when suddenly Tully put his hands up and stepped between Dante and me. "Hey, it was just a joke. A bad joke." He glared at his partner, who had a tight, awkward smile. "You go. We'll take care of your little girlfriend. She can play some games with us at my table, and when you come back, you can join us. I promise no one will touch her."

"Unless she wants it," Tully said over his shoulder.

I snapped. I let out a snarl and threw myself at the large body in the middle. Dante tried to catch and shove me back, but I was faster while he was stockier. I saw red as I ran through him and rushed toward Tully, who was backing away quickly. "Hey! Don't fucking kill me just because of my mouth! Jesus Christ, Desiderio have you not gotten control of your anger yet?"

"There's a reason he's Wrath, Tully," Dante reminded him as he stood up again. He left me alone as I stalked forward and caught Tully against a wall. I thrust my hand against his throat and tightened. I lifted him up as he tried to swat me away, eventually giving up.

"You touch my girlfriend, and they'll be Six Sins." I let go of his throat, and he crumpled to the floor.

"Alright, alright. Point made. I was just having a little fun. Touchy touchy." He groaned as he got back up and dusted off his clothes.

I stalked back to Scout and tried to steady my heaving chest. I wasn't so sure smoke wasn't about to come out of my nose. She stared up at me with eyes so bold they dared me to tell her what to do, which oddly calmed me down. I knew if I forced her to come with me, she would fight me just to stay. I pressed my lips together tightly and then reached for her hand. She let me take it, but I only squeezed it once before releasing her.

"Please, be smart. I love you."

"I love you too," she said softly and then stood on her tiptoes to give me a quick peck on the lips. "Be safe, and come back quick."

"I always do."

I turned to Dante. "Show me out."

He gave me a tight smile and patted me on the back as he

led me away from Scout and to a door, which took us to the main house.

"Look, Tully just likes fucking with you. You're our little brother. The more pissed off you get, the more he will poke at you."

"Scout is not something to joke about with me," I said sharply. He brought me through their large house and then followed me to my car, which wasn't far. The sex store was right next door.

"I'll keep that in mind and make sure Tully does too. You go kill whoever, and you can take her upstairs and do whatever you want with her when you get back. Okay?"

I climbed into my car and rolled the window down. "Thanks. I'll be back soon."

I sped to New York City, which was only about a half hour away. Corinne had promised that it'd be easy, but the guy had been tipped off, and I spent a good hour trying to hunt his ass down. Finally, I cornered him in his own car, trying to make a getaway.

"Hi, George!" I greeted him, slipping into the passenger's side. He jumped nearly a foot in the air and tried to unbuckle himself, but I quickly locked the door and snatched the keys from his hand. I then grabbed his wrist tight. "You get out, and I'll make your death slow."

"Why? Isn't me leaving town enough for her?" He cried out. I tilted my head, and for a moment, I grew curious. This Bloodshed vampire was conventionally attractive. Built like he was a gym junkie, and his face wasn't bad. He did fit her type.

"What did you do that warranted Ginata to ask me to come for you?" I twisted in my seat to pull out my knife roll while still holding tight to George.

"I turned! That's all. I swear. I was one of her familiars

for almost three years, and we talked about my turning when my birthday came. Then she decided I wasn't allowed to anymore, and I chose to do it anyway. Please, don't kill me because of that. Just let me leave."

"How did you do it?"

"Do what?"

"Turn." I sighed. I wasn't sure why I always asked. Morbid curiosity?

"I turned the heat on in my bedroom and laid under a rug."

"What?" *That made no sense.* "Like, you smothered yourself? That worked?" I tried to envision it, but it just sounded absurd. He nodded, his eyes still scared shitless.

"I got it soaking wet with bleach. It didn't take long."

"Why are you guys always trying to outdo the next one? What happened to a good, old-fashioned noose over a strong beam?"

"Please, let me go," he pleaded again.

"I can't do that. Surely you've spent enough time around Ginata to know that once I've been sent for, there are no take-backs."

He started to cry then. Streams of blood exploded from his eyes, and suddenly I felt a little bad for him. I struggled to believe that Ginata would want someone killed for something so dumb, so he must be lying. "Look, I'll just make this quick for you." I let go of his wrist and set my knife roll on my lap. I unbuckled it and grabbed the largest knife in the pack out. "This should take your head off in only a few quick whacks."

And it did. He didn't fight me much, and within half an hour, I was exiting his car to climb back into my own. My clothes were saturated with his blood, and the ride back to New Jersey wasn't exactly pleasant.

The entire drive back, my stomach churned with nervousness. Was Scout okay? Was she safe with Dante watching over her? It made me go even faster, and soon I was sprinting back into their house and down to the basement.

The room was now full and loud. People, vampires and humans, were all sitting at tables or at the bar, chatting and laughing. I scanned the dark room, looking for Scout, and finally, I found her slumped in a seat at a busy table.

I stormed over, looking for Dante as I moved through the crowd. He was nowhere to be seen. However, when I reached Scout's table, my stomach dropped. Blood nearly came up through my throat as I saw a very satisfied-looking Tully sitting across from Scout. She looked up at me, and fear flooded my system as I looked down at her face. Thin red lines dripped down her cheeks as she cried.

I cupped her face and kissed her quickly, trying to soothe her. "Shh, what's wrong? What happened? Where's Dante? I demanded, glaring at Tully.

Tully grinned. "He had to take a call. It's fine. I kept her company." His eyes widened, and slowly it all started to take shape—why Scout was upset. I looked at the table in front of her, where her cards lay. It was a shit hand.

She didn't know how to play.

"What were you playing?" I demanded, focusing back on Scout. My question only caused her to begin shaking as she cried. Her head dropped down, and she refused to answer.

"It was just a simple game of poker. I think she just got in a little over her head. It's fine," he tried to calm me down, but seeing that it wasn't working turned to Scout. "They'll be more games, sweetie."

I rested my hands on her shoulders and squeezed. "What did you bet?"

Although I was looking at her, the question had been directed at Toulouse. He knew it and took great pleasure in answering me.

"She bet an orgasm."

"What the fuck does that mean?" Desi snarled, squeezing my kneecaps so tightly I thought he might accidentally bust them. I was shaking with my ridiculous sobbing. I couldn't answer him. I didn't know the answer myself. Desi repeated the question to Tully, who was sitting across the table, grinning like a cat who caught the mouse.

"She already told you. We were playing cards, and she lost. Now she has to pay the house."

"You really think I'm going to let my girlfriend fuck you?" Desi let go of me and stood. I looked up, trying to steady my breathing. I brushed the salty blood from my cheeks and stared at Tully. If he was scared of Desi, he didn't show it. Lust versus Wrath.

Who would win?

"No. Of course not. She doesn't have to give me my orgasm. But she can give me hers." He turned his gaze on me, and I shivered. My stomach rolled so hard that I almost threw up.

I fucked up bad.

"Toulouse—" Desi started toward him. His steps were slow and calculated. Flashbacks to when he nearly tore off Arsenio's arm flew through my mind. Was he going to kill his fellow Seven Sin? Because of my idiocy?

"D!" Dante's booming voice came from behind us. We all turned to see him storming over, his eyes wide with confusion and almost a panic. He had his hands up and rushed to put himself between Lust and Wrath. "What happened?"

"This stupid fuck thinks he can play games," Desi snarled, turning back to Tully.

"I don't think anything. We played. She lost. I am *owed*." Tully flicked his tongue over his fangs in such a way I found absolutely repulsive.

Dante sighed. "Fuck. I was only gone a minute." He glanced at me but only spoke to his brothers. "What did she bet?"

"An orgasm," Tully said with a bored expression. As if he was talking about who won a local election.

Dante blinked his red eyes rapidly for a moment, trying to comprehend what he had just said. He turned his head slowly to Tully. "You bet Desiderio Amato's girlfriend that if she lost a round of cards, she'd have to give you an orgasm? How did you see that playing out? Are you fucking stupid?" He reached out and slapped him across the face. "Have you been eating the candy again?"

Tully's head snapped back, but he only laughed. "Maybe. I don't get the opportunity to fuck with our baby brother enough. Maybe if he came around more often, I'd be more inclined to be sensitive to his situation." He glanced at me and winked. I gagged.

"Tully, you can't possibly think—" Dante started, but Tully stood up suddenly and pushed his chest into Dante's.

"Oh, I do think. Now, why don't we take this somewhere

else to discuss how I'll be paid?" While the rest of the room was alive and loud, our table had gone icy silent.

Finally, I grew brave and stood. "Fine. Let's go."

The three Sins all turned to me with varying emotions. Dante looked shocked, Tully looked excited, and Desi looked…outraged.

Tully moved first. He came around and tried to put his arm around me, but I shrugged away. My hand went to the charm around my neck. Desi's name. My fingers clung to it as if it were a rosary. I said a silent prayer to the powers that be, begging for a way out of this mess.

"This way." Tully told us without missing a beat. My feet were frozen to the spot. I looked desperately at Desi, but he didn't look at me. He strode right past me, following Tully through a black door near the bar. Dante stayed behind and rested his hand on my lower back. I jumped and looked up at him. His smile was kind, but his eyes were wary.

"Did you eat any of the candy?"

I frowned. Had I? I couldn't remember. Tully had offered, but I wasn't sure if I had accepted any.

He shook his head and sighed. "Come on. Let's see what we can do."

I nodded and let him push me toward the door. Which led to a long hallway. There were a few dark doors, but we went past them all, and toward the end of the hall, we could hear Desi and Tully yelling from inside a room.

"Care to guess which door they went through?" Dante chuckled, attempting to relax me. It didn't. We reached the room, and he opened the door quickly.

The room was a mid-sized conference room. There was a large oval table in the center of the room with a dozen chairs around it. A TV was on the wall and a mini fridge in the corner. Desi and Tully were standing across the table, glaring and screaming at each other.

"You're lucky I don't rip your fucking face off right now," Desi threatened.

Tully laughed. "I dare you to try. You may have anger issues, brother, but don't forget your place."

There was silence as Dante and I entered the room. Dante shut the door behind us. "Why don't we all sit down?" He pulled out a chair for me, and I sat quickly. Desi, still refusing to look at me, sat across from Tully, and Dante sat next to me.

"Look, I'm reasonable. She was the one who agreed to the bet when I suggested it, but I kept the phrasing loose. She doesn't have to touch me if she doesn't want." Tully spoke to my boyfriend as if I weren't here. I swallowed and opened my mouth to speak, but Desi did the same. It was as if I were an object and not a person.

"What are you suggesting?" Desi put his hands on the table and clenched them as hard as his teeth were.

"I asked for an orgasm. So she can give me hers." Tully shrugged. Again, he seemed downright bored. I was half-expecting a yawn.

"If you don't get on with it, I'll use my cards when I kill you," Desi growled.

"As form of payment, I want to watch her masturbate to completion."

My eyes flew open, and I blinked rapidly. My heart sped up, attempting to leap right out of my chest. My stomach lurched again, and blood began to rise in my throat. I swallowed it down and tried my hardest not to cry.

"Uh, no?" Desi laughed.

"Now hold on. This could work," Dante interrupted, raising his arms again. My mouth fell open.

I thought he was on my side!

He glanced at me, offered me a sad smile, and looked at Desi. "I think this might be the lesser of evils. Tully still gets paid, and Scout is untouched."

"In a way, I still get to watch," Tully snickered. Desi stood up suddenly, and the room was alive with tension. The other two rose quickly, and I felt as if I were witnessing a stand-off. Tully watched Desi with an expression that I could only describe as—*smug*. "You can take my offer to watch her come by herself, or I can take her and make you watch. You want to see my cock sliding in and out of her? We can make that happen, Desiderio."

It was almost a full minute of silence before. Finally, Desi glanced at me. Suddenly he looked exhausted and defeated. He gritted his teeth and sighed. "Fine."

Tully clapped and grinned at me then. I felt faint. How did this even happen?

One minute there was a group of us all playing a friendly game of Poker. Dante had been showing me the ropes, but he was called away for business. That was when the bets and the game suddenly got harder. Tully had trapped me in a false sense of security. Others around the table were betting outlandish things and winning, so I thought I could too.

"What would you like to bet?"

My mind was blank. I shrugged. "I have no money with me."

Tully looked around the table and picked up another piece of candy from the bowl in front of him. He sat back and then chuckled. "What about an orgasm?"

The table began to laugh with him, and my cheeks flushed. I began to laugh too. He couldn't be serious.

"Sure," I smirked. "I've got good cards."

But I didn't. I had a shit hand, as it turned out. I lost within a minute of betting.

"So, how is this going to work? You can't ask her to do it here," Dante said, interrupting my thoughts. Horror filled my face as I shook my head.

Oh God, please, no. Not with Desi right here. He can't see this.

"Nah, we'll take her to one of my other rooms. I've got one with a two-way mirror. Get her some candy."

"Candy?" I asked, my voice squeaking out.

"Don't worry about it. Just eat it, and you'll be fine." Tully said sharply. His Jersey accent was thicker, and his eyes were cold and almost dead-like.

I closed my eyes tightly. Wishing this wasn't real.

"Fine." Desi snapped. My eyes popped open, and tears suddenly started with little warning. They slid down my cheeks as I stared at Desi, so angry, so—*disappointed.*

Dante went to the door and opened it. Tully followed him. Desi then came and snatched my hand from my face. He held onto my wrist and tugged me out of the room. I stumbled and tried to stop the crying.

"Go with them. I'll be back."

"Where are you going?" I cried out in panic.

"Don't worry about it." He snapped and disappeared into another room.

In the hallway, a waitress appeared out of nowhere with a tray of the candy everyone ate. Dante took a fistful and then offered them to me. I was hesitant, but he looked down at me, pleading for me to eat them. I took them gingerly and put them in my mouth. They dissolved almost instantly, and I found my brain to be—*fuzzy.*

Desi had warned me not to trust them, and I hadn't listened.

Tully took the lead, taking us back down the hall. We entered another door, and I thought I was going to faint. If I was thinking normally, I would have.

Tully was a deviant.

He did indeed have a room with a two-way mirror. Which, given their gambling business, I could understand. I've seen movies. What had me struggling to breathe was the chairs—as in multiple, all in a row.

For an audience.

How many people were going to watch—*me*?

"You can go right through here, Scout," Tully said in a much kinder tone. He tried to be friendly, but I couldn't look at him with anything but disgust. Dante let go of my arm.

"Go with him, Scout." Desi's voice caused me to snap to attention. I looked past Dante to see that he had returned from wherever he had gone.

"But—" I started to protest, but Desi stared at the mirror. All emotion was gone from his face.

"Go." His voice was so harsh I moved quickly, stumbling over the chairs. I blinked, trying to get control of my mind again, but I couldn't.

Tully took me to the other room. There were chairs, a couch, and a table. I chose the couch, plopping down on it like a child.

"Just make yourself comfortable. I guess it's good you're wearing a skirt. Do you have any requests?"

"Requests?" I looked up at him in confusion. My eyes went large and a goofy smile spread on my face, despite my stomach being filled with fear.

He chuckled. "I own a sex store. What do you need to get you there?"

When I didn't answer immediately, he started rattling off items we had seen when we first arrived.

"Lube? Magazine? Something to sit on, or maybe stick to the wall? I've got tons of vibrators, stuff to suck your clit, balls to stuff inside you. Or we can go old school with a good old-fashioned cock? I can get you a dildo bigger than what Desiderio's packing if you want." He wiggled his eyebrows and beamed. My mouth fell open, but no words came out. His offer didn't sound too bad, I supposed.

He sighed and crossed his arms. "I think you had too much candy. You're taking the piss out of all of this. I'll take your boyfriend upstairs; he can pick some stuff out. Hold tight, princess." He shut the door behind him, and it was then that I saw there was no doorknob on my side. I was trapped.

I clutched the cushion and kept my legs tightly against each other. Could I do this? I asked myself, and oddly enough, I replied back.

Yes.

After some time, Tully returned, carrying a red plastic bag. He emptied it on the table. My stomach fluttered and my core pulsed.

"Sorry about the delay. Feel free to take and use whatever gets you there. Since this is my payment, you'll need to be in view of the mirror. At least you can't see the other side."

I stared at him, blinking, but nothing more. "Consider this a gift. You guys can take it home afterward. I can't sell it anyway." He laughed. Tully and I stared at each other for a long moment. I knew I should be upset, but once again, a silly smile spread onto my face. He shook his head and sighed.

"Alright, I'll leave you to it." He left quickly, locking me in the room with a chair, a table, and a selection of sex toys.

Shakily, I stood and went to the table. I swallowed the spit in my mouth, but it didn't help. All I could think about was who was on the other side of the mirror and what they were doing. What they were thinking. God, were they going to help themselves while I did the same? The thought made my stomach flutter and I tightened my core.

That was kind of hot.

On the table, there were vibrators, some large, some could fit in the palm of my hand. There were a handful of magazines with naked men and a pillow with a dildo standing straight up on it.

I could do it completely alone, with no assistance from Tully's store. I clenched my core and ruled that option out. There was no way I could get aroused enough right now.

Or could I?

The idea of them all sitting out there, waiting for me, wanting me…

Tentatively, I grabbed one of the smaller vibrators. My face flooded with shame as I turned and went to the chair in the middle of the room, directly in front of the mirror. I stared at it before sitting down. When I did, I was stiff as a board.

Maybe I should have had more candy.

I closed my eyes and tried to steady my breathing, but it proved unattainable. I shoved the small vibrator between my tense thighs and pushed the button. It hummed to life, and I gasped. No, I had just the right amount of candy to relax me, I decided.

Suddenly, I heard a click, and then Tully's voice came through the ceiling. "Spread your legs, sweetie. You're not going to come like that."

His words came out in almost a tender way. As if he was genuinely concerned and wanted me to get this done just as quickly as I did. It was bullshit, but somehow it did relax me.

My thighs drifted apart, and I moved the vibrator. It was touching my skin, but not the parts that mattered. I heard the click again.

"Are you wearing panties? Maybe you should take them off."

As if in a trance, I stood and did as the Seven Sin named Lust directed. I reached behind me and raised my skirt. I grabbed my black boy shorts and slowly brought them down my legs. They reached my ankles, and I kicked them off. Suddenly, I could breathe. Long, deep, and slow.

"Good girl. Now sit down and show me what you were hiding."

The way he said those words.

Good girl.

My mind erased Tully, and replaced his voice with Desi's. I would do anything for Desi.

I licked my lips and sat back down. I did as told, raising my skirt and spreading my thighs apart. I was completely bare to whoever was on the other side, and my stomach tingled with the thought. I swallowed my nerves and slowly brought my fingers down. I was surprised to find myself wet.

I made a lazy circle over my clit and found myself getting more aroused.

"There are other things you can use." Lust offered. "Did you see the rabbit?"

I stood and returned to the table, looking for what he wanted. I reached for the vibrator with the anatomically correct cock and the small rabbit ears attached to it. I've seen these before but never used them myself. I was intrigued.

"Good girl, Scout. Now come back to the chair and try it out."

Once again, I did as told without an argument. I took the vibrator and returned to my spotlight. I played with my wetness for a moment before taking the vibrator down between my legs. My heart sped up slightly as I spread my thighs and started to take the rubber cock into my soaking pussy.

I gasped and blinked, trying to fully grasp what I was doing. I knew I was doing it, yet, I couldn't care enough to stop it. I pushed it until I couldn't take anymore and then removed it some, pushing it back in. Soon, I was thrusting along with it. I closed my eyes and bit my lip.

"Why don't you press the button on it?"

I brought my head back up and looked down. I found the button and then nearly screamed as the ears hummed to life, attacking my clit with pleasure.

"Keep up the rhythm."

I did as requested. The fake cock inside me, pressing hard on my g-spot, had me panting, and the ears thrumming on my clit had me screaming. I closed my eyes and rode the vibrator as if it were a real man under me. Suddenly, I couldn't hold it back, and my body exploded into orgasmic spasms. I shoved the cock as far as I could, coming all over it.

I kept my eyes closed as I came down from my orgasm. Clarity hit me finally, and I blinked. I removed the vibrator from my body and stood up quickly. I bent down to snatch my underwear up. I quickly slipped them back on and went to the door. I brushed my hair behind my ear with shaky hands as I knocked on the door.

It opened then. I walked out and stopped short. My eyes went wide, and my jaw went slack as I took in the bloody scene in front of me. Desi stood over Tully and Dante. His face was splashed with blood, and his hands looked like he'd dipped them in a bucket of red paint. His chest was heaving. And he turned to look at me, murder in his eyes.

"You fucking happy?"

CHAPTER 10

Scout

Desi dragged me through Tully's massive home by the wrist.

Tully.

Lust.

What had I done?

I was too stunned to pay attention to the decor or the people watching my boyfriend pull me through the poker room and up the stairs. I could only focus on how tight he was gripping me and the blood. The blood. So much blood.

I didn't find my voice until Desi opened a pair of giant doors and threw me into the dark room. I hit the floor with a yelp. It was only then that my brain comprehended that he had taken me up at least three flights of stairs and down a long hall.

"Are you proud of that?" He snarled. I scrambled to my feet and smoothed my skirt down. He stomped into the room without shutting the door. He stalked over to me, and I started walking backward. I swallowed the lump in my throat.

"What? I had to—" I protested. His eyes looked murderous. His chest was heaving, and he looked as if his sanity was hanging on by a thread. His eyes widened, and I could almost see his brain exploding.

"You had to? I told you not to play games with him. Scout, I fucking told you not to get involved with us." I bumped against a wall, and Desi closed in on me. He grabbed my chin, pinching it tightly between his fingers. I clenched my jaw and steeled my nerves. He tilted my head up to force me to lock eyes with his. His words came out so cold they chilled me to the bone. "You play with the Seven Sins, and you will lose every time."

Then, just like that, he let me go and stalked out of the room. I debated following him, explaining that I hadn't wanted to, the candy had confused my mind, but my body refused to let me move. He turned back to me at the doors.

"You can sleep here today. I don't want to be anywhere near you."

The doors slammed closed, and I blinked. I slid down to the floor and blinked. I couldn't cry anymore. This entire night seemed almost too insane to be real.

Eventually, I got up and locked the door. I turned back to the room in which Desi had tossed me. It was a suite. There was a bathroom off to the side and another small room that was almost a living room. I didn't plan on using the latter, though. I just needed a shower and a bed.

I realized then that I didn't have any of my clothes. So I stripped down, took a shower, and climbed into the giant bed bare. Exhaustion took me quickly, with my last thought of the night being that I shouldn't have enjoyed that as much as I did.

The next night, I had no choice but to put on the same clothes I had worn before. They smelled of smoke and had crusted spots of blood in the spots in which Desi had touched me.

There had been so much blood.

I sat there with a dry mouth and a sunk stomach, afraid to leave the room. He hadn't told me I couldn't leave, but he had been so angry that I didn't want to test him.

I'd seen him angry before. He was Wrath, the literal Sin itself. But never at me. Surely, if I could explain to him what that candy did to my brain, he'd understand.

A knock on the door took my attention from my thoughts. I went to it, quickly unlocking the door and letting in Desi, much to my surprise. He stepped in cautiously, hands stuffed in his pockets and eyes to the floor.

"I have your clothes." He motioned to the hall. I peered out and saw our suitcase. I grabbed it and brought it inside.

"Thanks."

"I don't want you participating in any of their games. Toulouse or Dante's. I think we can both agree that last night was an introduction to what kind of currency they use here."

I nodded. "Are they alright?" I asked, recalling them unconscious on the floor of that room. Desi's eyebrows furrowed.

"They'll be fine. They took advantage of the situation, and I didn't like that."

"What situation?"

"You, being alone. I wouldn't have let that happen."

I crossed my arms. I didn't like this whole possessive thing he was doing. "You think that? Because if you had spent all night acting like this, I probably would have still played with him just because you said not to."

He licked his lips and glared at me. "Oh? So what, you want to fuck him then?"

"No, but I do enjoy pissing you off."

"Well, I bet you're fucking ecstatic then." He started back

out, stalking away from me. I followed behind him but stopped at my door.

"What am I supposed to do?" I called after him. He didn't pause or turn back. Instead, he just shouted over his shoulder.

"I don't fucking care. Change those clothes, for one. You smell like a turtle tank."

I frowned, then lifted my shirt to my nose and sniffed. It didn't smell that bad. He reached the edge of the carpeted stairs and looked at me.

"I'm going downstairs with Tully and Dante. You can come but can't play until you learn poker. You gotta be able to stand a chance with them."

"Or what?" I smirked. He shook his head, and a small, almost evil grin slid onto his face.

"Or they'll end up killing you."

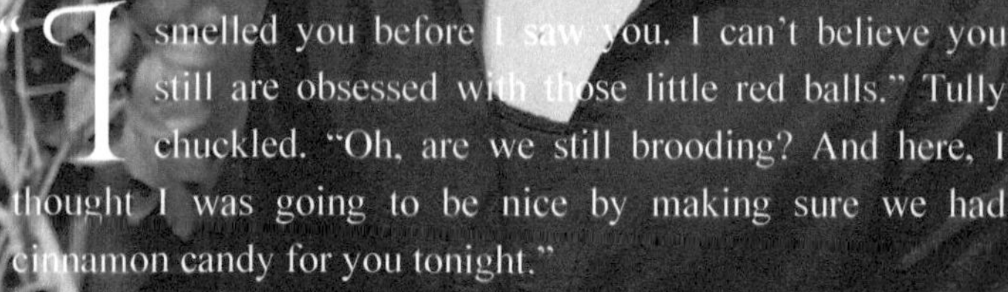

"**I** smelled you before I saw you. I can't believe you still are obsessed with those little red balls." Tully chuckled. "Oh, are we still brooding? And here, I thought I was going to be nice by making sure we had cinnamon candy for you tonight."

I glared at him from across the room as he picked up a bag and nodded to me.

"Candy won't sway me," I said, sarcastically. He sauntered over and offered me the bag. I stared at it. My mouth beginning to water. Despite myself, I did want them. I inhaled deeply.

I eyed Tully warily. He grinned, his fangs glinting in the light. "It just might."

The fireballs were almost a comfort item at this point in my immortal life. While I didn't need them to survive, like blood, I did revel in the burn on my tongue when I had them.

"I see you dressed appropriately tonight," he said.

"Like you were dressed nice yesterday?" I shot back. I shifted uncomfortably. Considering how everyone else was dressed the night before, I had opted for something nicer tonight. Dress pants, a short sleeved white button up, and black suspenders. It wasn't a tuxedo or anything, but still not the band shirts and boots I preferred.

Scout's footsteps were heard up above us and I stilled. Tully and I shared a look. I watched his Adam's apple bob with nervousness.

Good.

I snatched the bag of candy from him. I gave him a tight smile and returned to the stairs to make sure I escorted her around. As I waited for her to come down, I opened the bag to see that the candy was smaller than the normal fireballs I ate, but they appeared the same in every other way. I grabbed two and popped them in my mouth just as Scout came down the stairs.

She had changed into a clean dress. When she saw me at the bottom, she glowered. I ignored it. I was still too damn pissed about everything. However, the candy was easing my mind some. I could suck on these all night and keep my mouth shut.

I smiled, and found that it didn't come as hard as it had moments before. It must have been a bad one, because Scout cringed away from me. I cocked my head and she jumped, causing me to chuckle.

"You want to go downstairs with everyone?" I asked. She eyed me suspiciously.

"I just need some blood. I don't have to go down there," she said, her voice soft.

"Bullshit. Live a little. You wanted to meet my family. Let's do it." I found the words tumbling out of my mouth surprising. Was I really okay with this?

I offered her my hand, and she was still hesitant. I tight-ened my brows. I reached for her and she flinched back. I blinked. I flicked my tongue over the rapidly dissolving candy and scowled at her. "Come on."

"I ain't your bitch."

I blinked. My mouth opened and closed for a moment before responding. "You sure fucked yourself like you were one in heat. No, you're not my bitch, but I can treat you like it if you really fucking want." I spat.

"I'm leaving. We're done here." She turned, but I grabbed her.

"Stop! Scout—" My mind was all over the place. One moment I was angry, the next I was relaxed, and then confused when I switched back.

She ripped herself from my grip and spun back to look at me. "Choose your next words carefully."

I swallowed and nodded. "Fine. Let's go get some blood, and we'll play some cards. No bullshit."

"Fine."

I didn't try to take her hand this time. Instead, I led her downstairs to the poker room with one hand on the small of her back, and the other in my pocket, popping more candy in my mouth. They dissolved fast.

The room was full of people already betting their life's savings, blood, bodies, and God knows what else. It was crowded, and I tightened my hold on Scout's waist. She found my hand and squeezed it as I took her through the party to a red, unlabeled door guarded by a bouncer.

He looked down at me and then nodded, letting us in. The door was shut behind us, and I squinted to see through the thick cigar smoke circling the room.

It was a private poker game, Dante, a group of unfamiliar vampires, and a pair of humans sat around a green velvet lined table. The air was warm, and the smell of fresh blood lingered.

What were they playing for?

"Hey! I didn't think you guys would be back after last night." Tully's voice came from behind us. I turned to see him come in and walk to the empty seat next to Dante. He sat down and motioned for us to join the table. When we didn't move right away, he shared a look with Dante. They grinned. "Oh come on, bygones and all that. Look, our bruises are all healed and everything. Come sit and play with us."

"She's not playing," I snarled.

Dante snapped his fingers and sighed. He looked almost bored. Suddenly two Bloodsheds stood up from the table and, leaving their cards and chips behind, left the room, and Dante motioned for us to sit. I was still hesitant, but finally, I did and Scout joined me.

She reached for the cards left on the table, but I snatched them up before she could. I gave her a pointed look. It wasn't meant to be malicious, but it was firm.

You don't get to play.

Her eyes went to the floor.

Trust me, Nerd.

I sighed, and slipped another piece of candy in my mouth. My stomach was going crazy with nerves, and the familiar taste helped relax me.

I tossed both sets of cards at the dealer, who quickly scooped everything up and began shuffling them again.

I reached for Scout's hand under the table, and she took it. I looked down at her and she gave me a small smile. Her eyes were weary, and I could almost hear her thoughts.

I didn't want to fight anymore, either. This isn't us.

A woman came in with a tray of tall glasses and small bowls of candy.

I took two glasses and she set a bowl in front of me. I offered Scout a drink, and she took it eagerly. I slid the bowl towards her and she grimaced, pushing it away. I cocked an eyebrow, but said nothing. I opted for one in my pocket, and popped it into my mouth.

"No candy tonight?" Tully asked Scout. She jerked at his voice and shook her head.

What was that?

I glared at Tully. His eyes flicked to me, and he rolled his eyes.

I watched him as the cards were dealt to everyone but Scout. He was staring hard at my girlfriend, and she was squirming uncomfortably. Did I miss something last night?

The stress of watching those two stare at each other made me reach into my pocket for more candy. It was helping me keep my mouth shut.

Scout finished one glass of blood and requested another. She didn't speak once, and let us play, while she drank and sat beside me quietly.

Each game I got more confident and my shoulders relaxed. I began to laugh and joke with my Seven Sins brothers. Last night's fiasco was beginning to seem ridiculous and just a blip in our immortal timeline.

Who cared?

A few jokes were made at her expense, but I laughed right along with them. I knew I was being a jackass, but it really didn't seem like a big deal. She seemed to be just fine now.

"Desi?" Scout's voice called to me through the fog. I blinked, and looked over at her.

"What's up, Nerd?" I smirked.

"Are you okay? Are you eating their—"

"Why don't you let her play, just one game?" Tully interrupted her. My brain was too sluggish to really focus on multiple people. So I turned to my Seven Sin brother.

Lust.

I had been declining his offer for her to play all night, and I did again, but Scout finally decided to open her mouth and speak over me.

"Deal me in."

The table went silent. Everyone looked at me, and then my girlfriend beside me. I turned to her, and was surprised to hear her speak up against my wishes. "You don't own me."

My jaw tightened again, and I continued to glare at her, but I didn't say anything.

"What are you betting?" Tully interrupted us. I was still struggling to hold focus, but I continued to try to push through the fog.

No. Please, Scout. No.

"Five dollars."

Everyone but me laughed. In fact, my stomach turned so suddenly I thought I was going to vomit all my candy up. And that would hurt like a bitch.

Tully leaned forward. "The minimum bet is a grand, sweetie. You want to play for blood or body?"

"What's that?" she asked.

Jesus Christ. My breathing became shallow and I couldn't speak.

"I don't want your blood. So if you want, you can play for your body. You lose. The winner takes you."

"Takes me?" Her voice came out so tiny. A hard rock dropped in my stomach.

"Kind of like yesterday, but with two players instead of one. How confident are you, little lady?" Tully's smile was snake-like. I gripped the table, but I couldn't get my body to move. I'd jump over the table and murder him now if I could.

"Look, we'll play an easy one. Who's up for Texas Hold 'em?" Dante suggested.

"She's not playing," I snarled. Finally, my body was

working with my brain. Tully stood, and I kicked my chair back, doing the same.

"You may have grown a pair, but you're in my territory, little brother. If she wants to play, she'll get to play. Sit down." Tully's silly smile and relaxed manner had disappeared completely as he stared me down. My chest rose with heavy breathing, but finally, I snatched my chair back up and did as told.

What choice did I have now?

The dealer dealt the cards, giving her two. Scout took them with shaky hands and clutched them to her chest after she looked at them.

She was going to lose.

She was horrible at this. I had seen her cards.

Two of clubs and seven of diamonds.

I tossed chips into the middle without looking at my hand. Everyone else took the time to look at their cards before sliding their bets forward. I watched her close her eyes tightly, knowing she was trying her hardest to remember how to play. She was hopeless. Her tell was so bad.

Nausea continued to stir in my stomach. I gulped down a full glass of blood and popped a piece of candy in my mouth.

I flicked my eyes to Scout and saw that she was visibly panicking. Her hands held those cards so tightly they were shaking against her tits.

The thought of someone else touching what was mine... no!

"I like your necklace," Tully said to her. Her hand went to my name around her neck and squeezed. "Why don't you toss that in there to symbolize your bet?"

"She doesn't need to. We all know what's going to happen if she loses," I snapped. Tully chuckled but didn't argue further. He had only said it to goad me.

Everyone put in their bets. I added more, but she didn't move when they looked her way. Her eyes were shut again and her lips were moving, as if reciting the rules to herself.

The dealer set three cards face up on the table, and everyone leaned in. Six of hearts, ace of spades, and queen of hearts. I recalled her cards and gritted my teeth.

She was completely fucked.

I was the first person up after the flop. I checked, and, to my relief, so did the human and vampire after Scout. Tully gave me a sly grin and put two more chips in. There was a moment of silence, all except a low growl, that was coming from my throat, as Dante matched the bet. I scowled at Tully as he slid his chips forward before everyone looked at Scout.

Don't.

She set her cards down with shaky hands and unclasped the necklace I had given her only days ago. It was as if she was letting me go completely, and my soul was completely fucking crushed. She set it on top of the pot, and I had to fight back the tears glistening in my eyes.

The dealer dealt the turn, and I caught sight of the ten of diamonds in her hand. It hadn't improved her hand. She and I checked again, as did the vampire, but again, Tully made a bet. Her chin quivered when it came to her turn. She didn't have anything to bet, and her cards were shit.

"No more jewelry?" Tully said, craning his neck to look at her. "Why not toss your panties onto the table?"

Her head shot up and she furiously shook her head. He laughed, and his eyes grew dark. "I suggest you do something — otherwise, I'll consider it a fold."

Pressing her lips together tightly, she stood, brought her hands under her dress, and tugged her underwear off. Mortification flooded her cheeks as she folded the black boy shorts and placed them beside my necklace. "All in."

"Good girl."

His purring was a jolt to my system. I stood up again and people began calling for me to relax. I blinked rapidly and sat down.

What was going on with me? This wasn't like me. I didn't just follow orders. Tully should be on the ground, not telling me what to do.

I said a silent prayer that he did not win as the dealer laid out the river, a two of spades. I couldn't believe my luck. *Her luck.* It wasn't a high pair, but she actually had something.

Tully bet again, though, and I dreaded seeing his hand, sure that he must be able to beat a pair of twos. Dante folded, and I matched Tully's bet. The vampire I didn't know folded as well, which only left Scout, Tully, and me to show our hands. Scout was visibly losing it, swiveling her head to look at us.

Tully was grinning at me. He took such delight in screwing with me. He knew how much Scout meant to me and what I did to get her back. How could he?

Because he was a Seven Sin. That's how. I reached forward and grabbed a handful of candy. I tossed them back, and I felt them almost instantly dissolve.

Tully threw his cards down first, revealing an ace and queen of clubs.

My stomach turned so hard when I saw his two-pair. Scout let out a small cry and dropped her cards face-up in front of her. Everyone stared at them in shock. She slumped in her seat as tears sprang from her eyes. Sharp cries escaped the table, with someone swearing and another laughing.

"Desiderio? Your hand."

I blinked and raised my head.

What did he say?

The candy was really strong. The flavor was weird. I felt weird. Tully repeated hisself.

I set my cards down slowly, and everyone leaned in. Relief washed over the table as they saw my six of spades and six of diamonds. Trip sixes beats a two-pair. She was saved.

I won.

I won.

She wouldn't be forced to sleep with a stranger. Scout slumped in her seat, relief washing over her.

Loud noises rang through the room, but I couldn't focus on anything other than how close we had come to disaster. And now, that was over. But then, Tully cocked his head and opened his mouth.

"Aren't you going to take your prize?" His eyes were dark and almost… hypnotic.

My mouth opened without my permission.

"Stand up." I barked at Scout. My mind suddenly went blank, and only Tully's words echoed in there.

"Take. Your. Prize."

CHAPTER 12

"Desi, please. You can't." I wiggled under his hold, trying to escape, but he shoved his hips against my ass.

He had stood up after Tully made a comment about taking his prize.

He couldn't have been serious.

But something in Desi's eyes flipped. Both blue and green, were as blank as the rest of his face as he kicked the chair out from under me and then snatched me up, shoving my face onto the table.

He was hard against me, his cock pulsed against my nakedness under the dress.

"This isn't you," I pleaded.

He laughed coldly. This wasn't Desi. A shiver of terror ran through my body as he shoved my dress halfway up my back, exposing me to the table.

Tully cleared his throat. "You're a Seven Sin, act like it."

Desi bent over, crushing his body against mine. "Baby, this has always been me. I warned you about who I was, remember?"

His tongue flicked across my ear and I tried to jerk away. Tears began to slide down my face, and my chin trembled as I fought back sobs. He stood back up and grabbed my wrists, squeezing them tight. My mouth fell open in a sharp cry as he kept squeezing. I thought he was going to snap them in half!

I tried to kick him, but he pressed further against my naked body, and shoved my legs apart. He yanked my hands to my back and adjusted his own hands so that only one was needed to hold them there. I continued to fight, but froze when I heard his belt unbuckle and a zipper go down.

"Desi, please. Not here, not in front of everyone," I pleaded, tears streaming down my face against my will. "If you really want this, let's go upstairs," I urged.

"Why? No one cares here? It's not like we haven't seen worse," Tully said. "Scout, be a good girl, and let him take his prize."

Desi shifted, grinding his hard length against me, and I tried to kick him again.

"Be a good girl for me," Desi mumbled as his free hand reached between my thighs and spread my lips. I tightened my body and tried to move, but he was stronger. His fingers attempted to play with my most private parts, but I was shutting down.

When he realized that, he pulled me up and grabbed the front of my dress. My back was arched at such an angle I gasped, trying to breathe. He let go of my hands and I began to try to cover myself with my dress, but he was stronger than me. While I was pushing my skirt down, his hand had went to my collar, clenching it tight. He pulled it hard. It stretched only a little before tearing like paper. I scrambled to hold the two halves of my dress together, but he kept pulling, exposing me completely to the disgusting onlookers.

His hands went to my back as I attempted to save my

dress. He ripped the clasp off with such force it stung and he pulled it down. Then, he pushed my arms away from my clothes, ensuring everyone got a look at my body.

I sobbed then. I couldn't contain it anymore.

"Brown. Dante and I wondered what color her nipples were, considering how light her tan was," Tully smirked.

My hands flew to my chest, and Desi let me cover myself.

Was this nightmare over?

Desi shoved me back down on the table, assuring me that it was not. His hard cock throbbed against my exposed backside and his fingers returned to my thighs. He poked and prodded but I remained dry, despite my legs beginning to wobble.

I closed my eyes but I couldn't stop crying. Blood ran down my face in droves.

I felt him reach forward and I opened an eye to see him grabbing a cup of blood. He paused, and reached for the pot in the middle of the table instead. It had all the chips, my underwear, and my necklace. Had the necklace caused a reaction in him? Was he going to stop this madness?

He abandoned the blood and grabbed the necklace. I threw my hands out when he let me go. I looked around, trying to make eye contact with someone, anyone, but I soon realized that there was no one here who was going to help me. It wasn't that they couldn't, but that they didn't want to. These people thrived on the pain of others.

I was moving so much against him that Desi struggled to put the necklace back on me, but finally, he clasped it around my neck. Then, he reached for the panties.

He was! He was going to help me. I knew this was all an act.

Relief washed over me for a split moment before

suddenly he snatched my hair and tugged hard! I let out a sharp cry of pain, mixed with surprise and heartbreak.

Tully stood then, and came over to stand beside my boyfriend. He bent beside me and locked his hard, evil, eyes on me.

"You know, I love how your hair looks like you've just been fucked. In the pictures, and even when we first met." He reached out and ran his thumb down my cheek, smearing my blood tears. He grinned as he cocked his head, his fangs flashing at me.

"Tell me, how wet did you get for me and my brother last night? It couldn't have just been the vibrator between your thighs?"

I gulped, trying to steady my breathing. I would not answer him.

"Desiderio, I thought you had a good girl, but she seems to be acting very, very bad." Tully stood back up and looked at his fellow Seven Sin. "I think we're all ready to see you take your prize."

My spine stiffened as Desi shifted again, his cock hard against me. His fist was still in my hair, and he throbbed, telling me that this really was happening.

I shook my head, and decided I wasn't just going to let it happen.

"I am not. Your. Bitch."

Tully shoved my panties into my mouth as far as he could and repeated the phrase, loudly, almost screaming it.

Desi's body reacted to him. He grabbed my wrists again and pulled them tight to my back with one hand, and with the other, he pulled his pants and boxers down.

Freeing himself, he leaned into my body. I watched in horror as he reached for the glass of blood again, and dipped two fingers in it.

I tried to scream, but Tully's hand shoved my head down against the table and held it down. I blinked at how hard the impact had been. It stunned me long enough for Desi to bring the fingers covered in blood down between my legs and slip them inside me.

I began to choke from the sobs, as I was completely helpless. Tully kept one hand on my head and moved another to press on my back, pinning me down, as Desi's hand moved in and out of me.

I was convulsing with sobs, but that only seemed to spur Tully and Desi on. Tully kept urging Desi to hurt me, and Desi didn't say anything. It was as if his mind had been completely turned off.

A shout from Tully made Desi quickly remove his fingers and replace them with his cock, thrusting into me as hard as he could, causing me to scream through my gag.

I closed my eyes as tightly as possible as Desi thrust into me like a wild animal, grunting and panting with no real emotion.

The whole time Tully kept his hands firmly on me and called me every vulgar thing in the book as he urged Desi to *take his prize.*

Finally, Desi let out a loud groan and shoved himself as deep as he could, exploding inside me. He pulled away from me a moment later, and I was set free. Both men let go of me and I collapsed onto the ground.

"I didn't think you'd actually have the balls, brother." Tully laughed. Desi didn't speak.

I struggled to get to my feet, ripping my underwear from my mouth. I glanced at Desi. His pants were still down at his thighs and his eyes closed.

"Fuck you," I said, and with shaky legs, I exited the room, naked, horrified, and done.

I turned back to a silent card game. Everyone was looking at me strangely.

"Are we playing?"

The cards were dealt again, and we played mostly silent for a few games. The tension in the air was almost palpable.

"I didn't think you'd have the balls, baby brother," Tully said after winning a particularly tense game. "I guess you've earned some of my respect."

I smirked. "I didn't come here for your respect. Do you have any more candy?" I reached into my pocket but found the bag empty.

"You might want to chill on those." Dante raised his eyebrows. "You'll end up betting your entire bank account."

"What do you mean?"

Tully and Dante shared a look, and then Dante replied.

"Those are from Elvie. She made those specifically for the house. That's how we make our money. They make you do things, think things you wouldn't normally do."

"Yeah? Like what?" I was skeptical. As a vampire, I'd

done some stupid stuff in my afterlife, but I was always fully aware of my inebriation. I felt fine.

"Like rape your girlfriend," the human snickered.

I blinked.

"What did you just say?" I leaned forward, and he flinched away, his eyes wide with terror.

"I— I— I've had the stuff. The blood and the candy. Both do different things. You're not yourself. Surely you wouldn't have done that sober?"

I blinked and tried to comprehend what he was saying. It didn't make sense. Do what?

"D, are you okay? Look, it was just a game. We thought it'd be funny to get you a little high. No big deal." Tully tried explaining things to me, but my brain just couldn't compute. I was high? I felt fine.

"I'm not high," I said, and everyone stared at me. Tully smirked.

"Not anymore. It's been an hour since your girl left. You ran out of the candy I gave you before that."

"I haven't been high all night," I insisted, but when I tried to remember anything from after I woke up, I couldn't. It was all a fog.

"No, you are. And if you're not then you and your little girlfriend are freakier than I thought." Tully laughed.

"What are you talking about?"

"Are you not— do you know what you just did?" Dante's brows furrowed.

"When?" I demanded, slapping my hands on the table.

"Jesus Christ, Tully," Dante whined. "He took too much. You shouldn't have given him an entire bag of his favorite flavor."

"Oh, come on, it was just fun. A little brotherly hazing. I haven't seen the fucker in a decade or so. He'll get over it." Tully snickered and tapped his cards on the table. "Let's keep playing. Finish this round and then you can go sort shit out upstairs. D- I'll even let you take what you and Scout want from the shop. She really seemed to like the vibrator. Maybe you can grab a few of those before you leave."

I continued to blink. I was struggling to hold it together. What had I done?

"Was she here? Scout?"

The room grew deadly silent again, and I stood. I squinted, and I realized I could remember bits and pieces. She had been here.

I remembered her crying, her taking off the necklace.

Then, it all hit at once.

My fingers, covered in blood, shoving into her unwilling body.

Her crying as Tully held her down. The room laughing as I…

When it was all finally clear, I was horrified. I leaned over and gagged, which turned into vomit in an instant.

"There it is. He remembers. Siân, can you get someone in here to clean this up?" Tully sighed and snapped his fingers at the dealer.

I closed my eyes as the smell of blood, cinnamon, and bile filled the room.

What had I done to her? Scout, my— my soulmate.

I wiped my mouth and ran from the room and through the gamblers. As I ran, I saw the candy bowls on all the tables. This was his scam the entire time. He had everyone giving away their lives just by offering them some fucking sugar.

I sprinted up the stairs to the house, where I had just tossed Scout aside. I had barely acknowledged her after I— I couldn't even say it. I was going to get sick again. I paused to get control of myself again before continuing through the house to her.

I reached the suite where she had slept last night and turned the handle. It was locked. I pounded on the door with my open palm.

"Scout! We need to talk! That wasn't what you think it was!" I pounded again but was met with icy silence. Her ignoring me was frustrating. If I could see her face to face, I could explain everything.

"Come on! Let's not fight about this! I'll do whatever you want. Just open the door, please, Scout, please!" I pleaded. Soon, my palm became my fists, and I beat on the door in a frantic.

I tried the door again, but it was still locked. With a cry of anguish, I pulled out my pocket knife and flicked it open. I bent down and began twisting the tip into the little hole. I felt the mechanics relax and unlock, and it turned when I tried the handle again. I stuffed the knife back in my pocket and confidently pushed the door. Only, it barely budged.

What the hell?

"Scout! Did you put something in front of the door? Come on!" I snarled. This was really starting to piss me off. "This is a fucking joke, right? Let me in!"

I continued to call to her from the other side of the door. I shoved against it time and time again. I was getting in to see her, to explain to her everything. If she knew that it wasn't all me that had done that to her, she'd understand.

I wasn't a monster.

I couldn't be.

I loved her.

The sound of splintering wood caused me to take a step away from the door triumphantly.

I looked at the large crack from the top of the door down

to the handle. I braced myself and continued attacking the door. A few more large breaks in the door, and whatever had been behind it fell. I shoved the door open and stormed inside.

"Scout, baby, Ner—" I started to say, but the cool breeze from an open window stopped me dead in my tracks. I ran to the window in horror. I put half my body out and scanned the ground below. We were two stories up. There wasn't a ladder of any sort hanging.

Did she jump?

"Scout!" I screamed to the sky but there was no answer. I squinted, trying to see the inside the thick woods behind the house. There was no doubt in my mind she had gone that way. She'd be hidden from the curious eyes and the eventual sun.

I looked up, and my heart splintered, just like the door I had spent hours throwing myself against, trying to get to her. It had all been in vain. In the time I had spent trying to fight for her, to get her back, breaking that *fucking* door down, she had taken the opportunity to escape. And I could do nothing about it because the sun was coming up.

CHAPTER 14

Desi

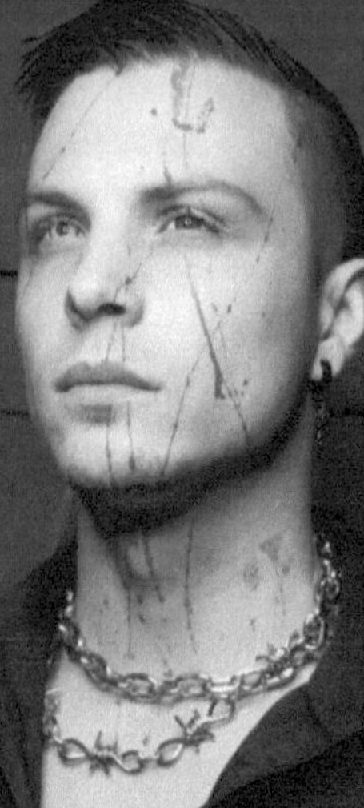

I went around her room, looking for clues as to what was going through her mind when she jumped out the second-story window.

I flicked the lights on and found the suitcase I had brought her last night. It was still on her bed, open. I started pulling her things out, looking for… I wasn't sure exactly. It didn't look like she took anything.

I went back to the window and stared out. I could make it to her. I could find her and get her somewhere safe if I left right now. Then, we'd talk. I'd explain and apologize, and we'd figure it out together.

We always did.

I tossed a leg out and was starting to bring the other out when I heard a rustling from behind me. I turned and nearly fell from being startled by Dante sprinting over to me. He ripped me from the window and tossed me on the carpet.

"What the hell?"

"You can't be serious." Dante stared down at me, shaking his head. "The sun is already rising."

"So? She left out that window, and if I don't get to her,

she'll die of exposure." I stood and stepped forward, but Dante's massive hand came out and shoved against my chest. He pushed me back until the back of my knees hit the bed. I fell onto the mattress.

"You can't go out there. Scout is smart. She's gonna be fine. You need to give her time to cool off."

"Fuck that! I'm leaving." I sat up, but suddenly I was tackled back to the bed by Dante the fucking bear.

"Tully! Get in here, you asshole!" He screamed as I fought against him.

"What?" Tully's sarcastic voice came into the room before his body did.

"He's trying to go outside."

"He can't. The sun is out."

"Exactly, numb nuts. Help me!"

I managed to get my knee in position to knee him right in the balls, but he caught me and rolled me over. He shoved my arms up over my head, and I was suddenly seized by Tully.

"Don't think I won't knock your scrawny little ass out if you keep fighting." He clutched my wrists tight. "Stop moving, or I'll tie your ass to a chair for the day."

Dante moved away from me, climbed off the bed, and left the room, only to return with a bundle of red rope. Tully shoved me down on the bed. I flew back up, but it was enough to catch me off guard and for Tully to grab me again, this time with a firmer hold around my chest. I stared at Dante as he unraveled the rope. My expression caused him to laugh.

"Tully's store has just about everything."

"You did not." I glared at them, but there was little I could do since Tully had me in a fucking bear hug of sorts. He stood us up and I tried to push out of his grasp, but he was strong, and spun me around, pushing me back onto the bed.

Before I could fight them off, Tully had me on my back, spread eagled as he sat on my chest. Dante was grabbing my wrists and quickly attached me to the bed. I kicked and snarled at Tully as Dante went under the bed and popped out the other side, handing him the rope.

He pulled it tight to my chest as I fought them, but they ignored me.

"You're good at this," I muttered, as they did another lap under the bed and around my chest. He hadn't done just normal knots. It was almost a braiding technique.

"I'm into Shibari," Dante responded.

"I could have gone my whole life without knowing how good you are at this."

Dante chuckled. "That fucking mouth of yours. Always getting you into trouble." Tightening the rope.

"My mouth had nothing to do with this," I snapped and tried to fight the restraints to no avail.

"Didn't it? Maybe if you hadn't been so overly protective over her, I wouldn't have wanted to push it." Tully stood once they had secured me from my hips up and climbed off the bed to let Dante continue tying up the rest of my body.

Tully crossed his arms over his chest and grinned at me from the sidelines.

"Why did you do this? Because I was happy?"

Tully's smug smile fell from his face, and an angry snarl took its place. "You don't get to be special, baby brother. I wasn't allowed to be happy. Why should you?"

Ludovica.

Guilt hit my stomach for only a moment before I steeled myself again. His heartache was no excuse for doing this to me. To us.

"Look, you wanna go after the chick after the sun goes down, by all means. But we can't let you die on our watch.

Corrine will have our ass." Dante stood, and Tully followed suit.

"Maybe take this time to think things through. Figure out where she could have gone, what you're going to do when you get to her, all that jazz." Tully yawned and turned toward the door.

"This is all because of you. I fucking hate you." I lifted my head and spat. Tully turned back to me and raised an eyebrow.

"Really? Because you two were fighting before you got here, am I wrong? And why was that, exactly, Desiderio?" He sauntered slowly to me, with his hands in his pockets. I flinched when he bent down over the bed, getting his face inches in front of mine. "Is it maybe because you got involved with a total stranger?"

A shiver went through me, but I refused to look away from him. He wanted that. I was not going to let him win.

"What are you talking about?" I lifted my head to see the room.

He smirked and stood back up, taking a few steps back. He paced the room while Dante chose to pull up another chair off to the side. Toulouse put his hands behind his back and walked back and forth pensively.

"I heard about your past. Before you turned. You were gonna be married off to a rich Bloodborn girl. A good breeding match, sources say."

"Who?" I demanded.

"Sources. Don't worry about it," he snapped.

"You dropped the rich bitch for a human you barely knew. Then, she turned, and you thought you'd get your family on board with it after the curse was broken. How'd that go, Amato?"

I clenched my jaw but said nothing. He laughed.

"I heard you couldn't even tell them her last name."

Gianni. He had spoken to my brother.

That bastard.

With all of my strength, I loudly cried as I fought against the ropes. It was hopeless. Dante was too good at the Shibari. Tully watched me with amusement and waited for me to stop struggling before he continued to taunt me.

"What else don't you know about your supposed soulmate?"

"Her last name doesn't fucking matter." I shook my head.

"Why, because you're gonna give her yours? So romantic." He rolled his eyes. "What about her passions? Surely working as a shift manager at a movie theater wasn't her dream job."

"She's an artist."

"What kind of art does she do?" The sarcasm in his voice was so thick it fell over me like a warm, wet blanket.

"She—" I stopped short. What did that even mean? "She draws."

"With what? Pencils, pens? What does she draw on? Canvas or paper? What style does she draw in Desiderio?"

My head fell back onto the pillows, suddenly feeling like absolute shit. I couldn't answer any of his rapid-fire questions.

"What about her past? What was she doing the entire time you were getting those ten-thousand souls for her?"

I didn't know that either. I hadn't thought to ask.

"We all have pasts we'd rather not speak about. It's not my place to ask." I responded lamely.

"It's not your place? You're her fucking soulmate, and you're telling me you can't even tell me what her favorite color is?"

I did know that one. But it didn't make me feel any better.

"Maybe it was a good thing you did what you did. I wonder how much of that was the candy and how much of that was the real Wrath coming out."

My fury returned with a vengeance, and I pulled at my restraints. "You're fucking dead! When I get out of this fucking rope I—"

"Aw, are you trying to threaten us? Threaten *me*? Who do you fucking think you are?" Tully's tone went from amused to psycho level pissed in an instant.

"I can take you out of those restraints and we can fucking go—" Tully started stalking around the room, patting his chest and spitting.

"Tully shut the fuck up." Dante stood. "Desiderio, no one in this room is threatened by you. Stop fighting your restraints. You're going to hurt yourself."

"I'm going to burn this place to the fucking ground," I said through clenched teeth.

"What was that?" Tully tilted his head and smiled at me. "Baby brother throwing a fit? Nice try. Come on," he snapped and Dante. "lay there and stew you stupid fuck."

Dante and him left quickly. Dante, before shutting the door, cleared his throat. "We'll be back when the sun goes down. Try to sleep and get Tully out of your head. It does no good to stew."

He acted as if he didn't know me. Wrath did not back down.

"You'd think Lust would be more sympathetic to the man in love," I muttered. He snickered.

"Don't be stupid. Love and Lust don't make sense togeth-er." He shut the door and left me tied to the bed, lights on, with the room trashed from my previous ransacking, trying to figure Scout out.

As I sat there, Toulouse's words echoed in my head. I didn't really know Scout. I knew her adorable smile, soft body, and snarky voice. But that was all surface stuff. I only knew what she had shown me, which wasn't much. Scout was protective of her past, and I never thought to push it. As her partner, I should have.

I should want to know about her time in Mexico. Or what art style she preferred. I didn't know shit about her comics. Sure, I'd watch her draw, but I never once thought to ask about those things. I should have.

Things started to go sour, I realized, after the visit with my parents. They had asked the same things Tully had today, and I hadn't been able to tell them anything more than her first name. She saw that, yet I still never bothered to try to get to know her.

I gave up after a while, and switched gears. I fell asleep, with the promise on my lips to Tully, that I would burn his place to the ground.

Dante and Tully woke me up hours later when they came to untie me. Tully grew impatient in Dante's work, and eventually pulled out a knife, cutting me free.

I sat up and stretched, and then smiled at them. They shared a confused look but offered to take me downstairs and see me out.

As we went down, I told them what I had come to realize while bound to that bed about Scout and I. Dante looked at me with skepticism in his eyes.

"I agree with most of that, but she definitely ran because of what you did at the poker table, not because you don't know if she likes Dali or Van Gogh."

I flinched. I didn't want to think about that. That wasn't me. Her Desi. That was Wrath.

"Do you need anything before you take off?" We had reached the ground level and were standing in front of the door that led to the underground poker tables.

"You guys heading down already?" I ignored the original question.

"Yeah, I mean, we have nothing going on. Why? You want to play a bit before you go?" The look on Tully's face was confusion, and surprise.

I shrugged. "I've had some time to calm down. A few rounds of blood and I'll be good to go. She sent me a text a few hours ago." I shoved my hand in my pocket and pulled out my phone. "She just needed a few hours to calm down. I'm meeting her at a hotel around midnight," I lied. Both Envy and Lust relaxed and then smiled.

"Hell yeah, good. Let's play some before you head out then." Tully patted me on the back and together, we went downstairs.

I had to force a few glasses of blood down, and play two full games of poker before I excused myself.

"I'm gonna go grab my bags and be off." I went around the table and gave a quick side hug to both Dante and Tully. "It's been real," I muttered.

"I left a raincoat for you by the door. Grab it on the way out," Dante said.

"Good luck. It was nice seeing you," Tully said.

"Was it?" I asked and quickly fled the room before another argument could start.

I sped to the door that Tully had led Scout and I down two nights ago. While only being in there once, I remembered it well. I hurried along the hallway, past the doors, until I found the boiler room.

When I accidentally found this room before, I hadn't given it much thought. But now, it was perfect for what I needed. I went to the water heater, and smiled when I saw it was gas.

Stupid fucks.

I looked around the room. This was too easy. I grabbed the box of spray paint and dropped them right next to the water heater. Then, I went for the T&P valve.

There was some water on the floor under the drip pipe. Looking at the heater, it was old. The room itself probably hadn't been touched in years. It was full of random tools and boxes of cardboard and other DIY shit. Probably Dante's doing, by the looks of it.

I started digging through the boxes until I found a wrench. Moving faster, I got the valve off and tossed it on the ground.

There we go.

I fled the room, wrench still in hand. I sped up the stairs, thought the gamblers, and slammed the door behind me. I then sped to the kitchen and turned on every burner on the oversized stove. Then, as one final fuck you. I went to the den, where I had watched Tully puff on a cigar.

The fire was rolling, and I grabbed a throw blanket from a chair and stuck it halfway in the fireplace. Then, I went behind the small bar and swung my wrench across all the glass bottles.

There. That should do some damage.

I left through the front, grabbing the raincoat Dante had mentioned as I went.

As soon as I had the coat on, I began to sprint around the house. That boiler did not have long at this point. I had to start looking for her at the spot in which she dropped from her room. It was raining pretty hard, but I still looked for something. A scrap of clothing, something from her bag, her blood. Nothing.

I turned then and stormed into the thick forest, in which I was sure she had gone after her leap. There was nowhere else to go. And then— there was the boom.

The house behind the woods exploded. I turned around to look and all I saw was orange and red flames. I was mildly impressed, as I was unsure a house this big would go up so easily, but sure enough, it did.

I swung back around, and continued to scream for her. Over the fire, I called for her. Over and over again.

"Scout! Nerd! Are you okay?" I shouted and screamed, pleading for her to respond. The dirt was soggy from the rain, and my shoes sank into the ground with every step. The trees were thick, and while they stopped much of the rain from reaching the ground, it only amplified the noise. Between the heavy rain and the house burning down, If Scout was in here, she wouldn't be able to hear me. But yet, I continued to shout my pleas for her to return to me.

I spent the night wandering the dark forest, and finally, I came out on the other side just as the rain had cleared. I had reached a highway. I wasn't sure how far I had walked, but my gut sank as I realized what she had most likely done. I turned and walked back into the woods. The sun was rising, but the trees were so thick and dense that I was confident I'd be able to hide in the trees.

Eventually, I fell against a tree. I was tired. I needed sleep. I tried to get up and keep moving, but my body resisted. I gave up, finding a spot on the ground that was dark and not too wet. Sleep overtook me, and I couldn't have woken up if I wanted to.

Sometime later, when it was night again, I woke up. I groaned, stiff and colder than usual. I sat up, and something fell from my chest. I blinked as my eyes adjusted to my surroundings and looked down to see what it was. I froze, staring down at it.

It was a tarot card.

My hands shook from the cold and the fear as I reached for the card and flipped it over.

The Fool.

I looked up and saw a dark shadow a few feet away from me.

"Scout?" I whispered. The figure was still for a moment before their foot was brought up and shoved hard into my face before I could react.

I sprinted away in the dark, my steps covered by the rain and the leaves littering the forest floor. Desi was lying unconscious under a tree, and I didn't know how long that would last. I needed to get as far as possible from him and whatever that large boom had been a few hours ago.

I wasn't even sure why I went to him while he was sleeping. It was stupid, and I hated myself for that small moment of weakness.

I flew through the woods, dodging trees and jumping over branches. My vampire speed and stamina were in full use tonight, but it wasn't a perfect science. Eventually, I tripped over a large tree root.

My face collided with the mud, and I scrambled up. My chest was heaving, and my heart was trying to escape my body. I gulped and got back up. Confident I was far enough away from him, I walked.

I shifted the backpack on my shoulders. The nearly empty aluminum cans of blood clanged inside, reminding me that I needed to get somewhere by morning. But where?

That was why I stayed under the protection of the trees this far. Where could I go where I wouldn't be found?

I gave up my apartment to move into Desi's. Going home was not an option.

Just thinking about Desi and the memories we had made at his place caused my heart to race and my hands to shake. Everything was tainted now. I had finally seen the real him, and that wasn't my Desi.

He really was Wrath.

I tripped again, falling on my bare knees. I could feel them scraping, and I let out a small grunt as I struggled to get back up. I was tired. I had planned on sleeping for a bit, but then I heard him calling for me. I wouldn't be able to sleep if he was in here. It was too dangerous.

I wiped the dirt off my legs and saw the tiny cuts quickly sealing back up. Small injuries like this were painless, but the sight of my blood struck a small shred of fear in me.

He'd smell it.

I bent down to stretch my shirt enough to wipe the blood off my knees. It didn't look like much, but it was definitely enough for a vampire trained on the scent of my blood to find me. I needed to get away from here.

I closed my eyes tightly, took a deep breath, and steadied myself. I was letting his presence shake me. I was making stupid mistakes, which would get me in trouble. I opened my eyes and started forward, eyes on the ground in front of me.

My body hurt all over. The skin that was exposed to the elements was cold and damp. Bruises were constantly coming and going, the direct result of my vampirism, but the places I had covered were damaged in ways my genes couldn't fix.

Desi.

What had happened? I sniffled and forced back tears. I had spent the last day since he forced himself on me, crying.

I couldn't get it out of my head. All of it. The smell of cigar smoke and blood, the rock music playing in the background, and the feel of green felt on my face as Tully held me down and urged Desi to take my body against my will. Despite my vampire blood doing its magic to heal the bruises and the damage he did between my legs, I could still feel the phantom pain of his attack. His blood-covered fingers shoved inside me, forcing my body to respond, despite the tearing pain. The burn of my bare breasts as he thrust into me, causing them to rub against the felt, and my cheeks were itchy and raw feeling from all the tears.

And then, when he finally stopped. When he let go of me and let me fall to the floor. The shame, shock, and heartbreak flooded my system all at once. There was nothing the vampire blood running through my veins could heal. I had been broken beyond repair.

Once he was done with me, I fled the room with only one thought in my mind.

Run.

I ran up to my room as fast as I could, holding on to what was left of my dress. I threw on some clothes and snatched my backpack off the floor. I wasn't sure how much time I had, but I wasn't going to waste a precious second of it. I only hesitated once before jumping out the window.

Worst case scenario, I hobble until whatever bone breaks can heal. Hours at most.

So I leaped. Some part of my foot did snap, and there was a sharp pain as I walked, but I was correct in that my body healed within a few hours. As long as my head was still attached to my body, I'd survive.

I always did.

That was the most bitter part about it all. Once again, I

was alone, left to figure things out. But I could do it. I always had. I didn't need Desi. I never did.

The woods were great at shielding any light, but my blood supply was running low. As I reached the edge of the woods, I sat down and stared at the highway.

I would have to flag someone down and hope they'd take me to a blood bank.

Not only did they make sure vampires were fed, but they also had resources to help me get somewhere safe.

I pulled my backpack off my shoulders and dropped it between my legs, opening it. Inside were empty canisters, my wallet and I.D., and the dress he had torn from my body. I wasn't able to leave it in that house. I pushed the dress aside to get the only other item in the bag— my tarot cards, minus **The Fool**.

I reached for the last canister with blood and my cards. I drank and shuffled my cards as I sat, trying to find serenity in the sound of moving cars and nothing else.

I looked at the cards in my hands and felt sick. These were full of negative vibes. I couldn't bring these with me wherever I was going.

I finished my last bottle and tossed it back in my bag. I took a deep breath and shuffled my cards one last time. I drew three cards, placing them on the moist, cold, ground.

Past, present, future.

I flipped them over to reveal the Five of Cups, Ten of Swords, and the Three of Swords.

I racked my brain, trying to remember what I'd been taught.

Five of cups, my past. Fives were always bad.

Regret.

My heart cried as I thought of Desi. Happy Desi, with his weird smile and mismatched eyes.

I licked my lips and focused on the next card.

Ten of Swords. Tens were always an end. The Ten of Swords card was a rough one. The person lay on the ground with ten long blades in his back. Pain. So what did that mean for me? The text came back to me from my lesson book.

Betrayal, painful endings, loss.

All of that paired with the card before it. Desi and I were over. There was no coming back from what happened in that room. What he did to me.

Finally, I stared at the last card I had drawn. The Three of Swords. I remember the first time I had ever drawn that card. Desi and I were hiding in an abandoned building in the middle of nowhere. I could still see his face darken and hear his words clear as day in my head as he told me what that card was.

"It's the card for broken hearts."

I stared at it for a long time. My mind ran through the relationship that was restarted without us knowing at the movie theater. That first time seeing him. My heart knew what my mind didn't. It remembered him, even if I wasn't allowed to.

I stiffened when I heard the faintest voice, his voice, calling my name. He was awake. I stood quickly, grabbing the cards and slinging the bag over my shoulder.

Desi and I were meant for each other, but not like this. I refused to be his punching bag.

A small gust of wind came through, sending a cold chill through my already cold body. I turned away from the highway to stare back at the trees. He called for me again, but the voice was louder. It was closer.

The wind came again, and I took a deep breath. Tears welled up in my eyes, but I refused to let them fall. I looked down at the deck in my hand and grabbed the three cards I had drawn, still sitting on top. I raised the rest of the deck and let the wind take them.

The three cards I had in my hand, I looked around for a place to leave them. This would be my last message to Desiderio Amato.

My mind was racing. Panic over how close he could be versus the distance to the road was causing my mind to become blurry. Quickly, I pulled the bag off again and unzipped it, grabbing out the dress. I had brought it to remind me of what he had done to me. It was apt, I realized. I went to the nearest tree and crumpled the torn garment into a ball. I then took the cards and placed them in a row. Past, Present, Future.

My scent was all over it. If he came close enough, he'd find it.

I stood then and hiked my bag over my shoulder. I braced myself and started the run up the hill and to the highway.

The hill was steeper than I thought, but I finally reached the iron railings. I flipped over them, scraping my thighs as I went, but finally, I felt safe. I stuck my thumb out. I glanced at the woods only once as I started walking backward beside the busy road, and spat on the ground.

Fucking Wrath, man.

CHAPTER 16

Scout

Afew people slowed down for me, but when they saw my vampire-red eyes, wet clothes, and my entire body in a ragged state, they sped back up. I made sure to flip them off before they disappeared.

When the sun rose, I had to abandon the hope that I'd be picked up and fled to the trees. Thankfully, I think I was far enough away from Tully and Dante's estate, that I could take breaks as needed. If it was still even there. I had heard the loud boom and the saw the flames. The fire had to be from their mansion.

I couldn't help the suspicious feeling creeping in my belly, telling me Desi had something to do with that large boom. I tried not to rest too long, just in case. I kept pushing through my burning throat and aching legs. Just a few more feet, then a few more, and I'd be safe.

I went back to the road at nightfall and took an exit into the city. The signs told me I had made it about twenty miles. It was better than nothing.

Thankfully, there were lots of signs telling me where to

find the blood-friendly businesses, and a bank was not far off the exit.

When I entered the bright, overly clean building, I was greeted by a Bloodshed in all white. I waved half-heartedly and then collapsed.

I woke up in a hospital bed. I was still in my own clothes, but I was hooked up to an IV.

Gross. I drink my blood, not inject it.

I peeled the tape off my hand and removed the device. I wasn't sure how long they had been feeding me, but I felt much stronger than I had when I walked in.

Me rousing must have set off some alarm because as I swung my filthy legs over the bed, another Bloodshed in a stark white uniform came in, holding a clipboard and smiling way too wide. I grimaced.

"Look, thanks for the blood. I need to get going. I can pay for what you gave me and what I'll need for a few days."

"Whoa, hold on." He put his hands up and cocked his head. "We'd like to talk to you a bit first."

"Why?" I demanded. I eyed him up and down. I could tear his throat out in seconds if I wanted. I'd taken down bigger vamps.

"Well, your state when you walked into the bank was rather concerning. You were in desperate need of blood and rest, so we had our security put you in a room." He waved his arms around the simple room. "But one of our men noticed some things that have us worried."

I snickered. "Worried *for* me? Dude, you should be worried *about* me." I stood to go, and he thrust his hand out, pushing me back down. I blinked.

"Who attacked you?" he asked quickly. I raised my eyebrows in shock.

"What? No one," I lied. Flashes of Desi's blank eyes as he threw me against that table, and Tully holding me down went through my brain. I shoved them away quickly, but the vampire in front of me saw me flinch.

"The security guard informed us that blood was coming from between your legs. We had one of our female doctors come in and give you a brief check. While your body healed, naturally, your underwear and inner thighs were still crusted with blood. I'm going to ask again." He paused and waited for me to look at him. "Who hurt you?"

I steeled myself, straightening my spine and gritting my teeth. "No one of importance. I'm fine now, as you said." I swallowed deeply and refrained from saying what was on the tip of my tongue. It sickened me just to think about.

The blood isn't even mine.

"Are you safe? Is someone coming for you?"

Yes.

I licked my lips and shook my head. "No."

"How old are you?"

I rolled my eyes and tried to think.

"Fifty-five. Does that matter?"

He scribbled on his clipboard. "Not really. Sometimes the older the vampire, the braver they are. Humans know of our existence, so it's a dangerous world for the blood community. Vampire hunting is almost a hobby now. There's no shame in seeking help if someone is trying to hurt you. We're not just a blood resource, you know." He looked at me with a small smile.

I sighed. He really seemed to mean well, but I didn't care. I needed to get out of here before Desi found me. "Thanks. I know. I've seen the pamphlets. I just need some blood to fill my backpack, and I'll be good."

He stared at me for a long time before he relented. "Okay. We can't legally keep you here. We just want every vampire to be happy, healthy, and safe. Let's get you what you need and see you on your way. Miss—"

I pressed my lips together, racking my brain. I didn't want to give him my real name. "Felicia," I said. He knew I was lying but nodded and led me to the lobby to get my blood.

Filling my backpack with enough blood to last me at least four days, I thanked them and started off into the night. I had been unconscious all day, apparently. I had lost a lot of time, which was concerning. Desi could have found a way to move with the sun up. I wouldn't rule anything out.

In my current state, there was no way I would get a ride from anyone. I looked like a drowned vampire bat, and that was before they stopped to talk to me. As Desi would say, I smelled like a turtle tank.

I had to choose my moves wisely. Thankfully, the blood bank didn't make me pay for anything, but now I had to decide what to do come morning. I needed a place to stay, but all I had in my wallet were debit and credit cards. The moment I used one, Desi would find me.

I found a blood shelter and asked to stay a day. They had a bed, but the room was cramped. I slept in a room with a dozen other vampires down on their luck. The shelter had no shower or soap in the bathroom, so I could only splash water on myself, which was useless. I held my backpack tight to my chest just in case one of them got brave enough to rob me.

When nightfall came, I knew I was running out of resources. I had to use my cards to pull out my money. I didn't know what to do other than keep moving, and I couldn't do that in these clothes with no shower.

"Where's the nearest ATM?" I asked the attendant at the shelter. He was a Bloodshed with boredom in his eyes.

"Down the street at the liquor store. Are you staying another night?"

I shook my head and started out the door. "No. Thanks for the help."

I ran out into the night and looked over my shoulder constantly as I ran my card through the machine. I winced, looking at the total I had there. With a deep inhale, I clicked the buttons to remove it all.

Seeing it come out in twenty-dollar bills, it looked like enough to tide me for months. However, counting it as I removed them from the slot, I had only a few weeks if I was lucky.

I asked the clerk at the liquor store to call me a cab, and surprisingly, he did. It was an agonizing wait, but finally, I was picked up.

"Where to?"

Good question.

Did I go back to Ohio? Where I had been living the last few years? Did I go back to mine and Desi's place? No. That was his now. I didn't want it.

"Bus station, please." I decided. That only bought me more time to think about it.

Every step of the way, my stomach physically ached as I used my money. The cab ride, the bus fare. All of it, slowly, my stack of twenties were dwindling. I stepped up to the ticket booth and braced myself, deciding to head somewhere safe.

"One ticket to Los Angeles, please."

The man eyed me with suspicion. "Vampire?"

I sighed and stuffed my hands in my pockets. I rocked on my heels. "Yes, sir."

"You'll need to wait for a blood bus."

I snickered. "They have us on separate busses now?"

"It's a three-day bus ride. It's required. These busses have special windows to keep the sun out and supply you with blood during your trip."

"Let me guess, it costs more than a human bus?"

"You are correct." He nodded. "Do you still want to ride?"

I gulped, considering my options. They were minimal and getting smaller by the minute. Finally, I snatched my backpack off my shoulder and got my wallet out. "Yeah, I'll take the ticket."

"Phone number?"

"What?" I blinked. "I don't have one," I said quickly. I swallowed the knot in my throat. I had left it in my room on purpose.

The man in the booth gave me a confused look but sighed and typed something into his computer. "You'll need a printed ticket then."

I paid and turned to find somewhere to sit while I waited. Ticket in hand, I shrugged my bag back on my shoulders and went to the comfiest looking seat. Which was basically the seat with the least amount of cracks in the fake red leather.

I glanced at the clock on the wall, then the ticket in my hand. Four hours.

I blew air out of my mouth and turned my attention to the TV attached to the wall. It played a sitcom from twenty years ago at a very low volume with the subtitles on. I was never a big TV person.

I preferred movies.

Thoughts of Desi and I at work flashed in my mind, and I quickly shoved them away in favor of the couple on the screen arguing over who got them into the easily fixable mess.

I wasn't entirely sure how long I sat there, staring at the television. I only looked away when someone came to sit next to me. I turned to see a strikingly beautiful Bloodborn woman smiling at me. I stared stupidly at her in confusion as she kept grinning.

"Scout. What an interesting name. That was what I said when I first heard about you."

"Yeah? When was that?" I crossed my arms under my chest but didn't relax.

"Word travels fast throughout my family. You've basically had an amber alert on you for days now. I'm glad I found you first."

It struck me then. She was a Sin. She was the only one I hadn't met yet.

Gluttony.

Gluttony was gorgeous, which kind of threw me for a loop. While I had never seen an unattractive vampire, I still expected her to be. Dante and Arsenio both had facial hair, a rare sight in the blood world. And Desi, while he did have an anger issue, was the sweetest vampire I knew. An ugly vampire could happen too. But no, she was extremely pretty, even for our standards.

My mouth fell open and I struggled to find words. She laughed lightly and reached a thin, gloved hand to brush a large lock of shiny auburn hair behind her pale ear. Her red lips turned upward as her fangs flashed.

Everything about her looked perfectly made. She was dressed in a slick pencil skirt and a white blouse that went up to her chin. Her red eyes were almost hidden underneath her thick eyelashes and perfectly executed makeup.

"Where are you going?" She spoke, causing me to blink and look away, almost bashfully.

I licked my lips and pressed them tightly together. Desi's warnings about never trusting any of his fellow Seven Sins members came to mind.

I'm not telling you shit.

She sighed. "I know what they did to you. I want to help."

I smirked. "How do you plan on doing that?"

"Toss the ticket and come with me."

I cocked an eyebrow. "What makes you think I'm stupid enough to do that?"

Her big warm eyes suddenly turned into icy slits. "I can keep you safe. I'm the only Sin that Desi won't come near."

The expression on her face made me falter in my original decision. *Could I trust her?*

"Why won't he?"

She laughed and moved in closer. I shivered as her lips brushed against my ear. "Because he's afraid of me," she whispered.

I blinked as she pulled back to stare at me, expectedly.

"What about the others? Someone had to have called you."

She shook her head. "In my territory you'll never have to worry about men like Desi, Tully, or Dante, for that matter. Come with me. You'll be safe, and we can make you happy."

"We?"

"Yes. I consider each and every person in my territory important. We all strive to work together to make everyone happy. You'll see."

"Where is this place?"

"I wouldn't be too worried about that. Plus, I don't need to shout out my location here." She glanced around and nodded to the cameras in the room's corners. "When he gets here he'll look at those."

"And you're not worried about him seeing you?"

She shook her head and crinkled her nose. "Nah. I'm sure he'll be shocked and confused, but we'll be long gone by then."

"But he'll still try to come find me," I pushed.

"He can try all he wants but once you're a part of my clan, we won't let him take you. Come, Scout." She reached out her hand and I stared at it for a long time before taking it. She helped me stand and then pulled me in for a tight embrace. "You're going to be so much happier with us."

CHAPTER 17

Desi

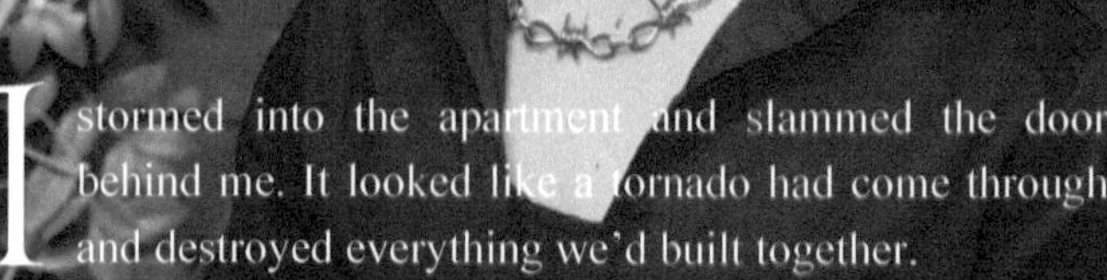

I stormed into the apartment and slammed the door behind me. It looked like a tornado had come through and destroyed everything we'd built together.

I'd gone through every shoebox, read every scrap of paper, pulled out all of her pockets in her dresses, and still, I found nothing that could point to where she'd gone.

It'd been weeks, almost a full month now, since that night at Tully's and not even a hint that she was coming back to me. I was miserable.

I kicked my way through the torn pillows and broken art projects tossed on the floor, all the way to the bathroom. I couldn't remember the last time I showered, which made me realize I needed one.

I started taking my clothes off and saw myself in the mirror. I did a double take.

I looked horrible. I went to the sink and stared at my reflection. My eyes were bloodshot, my face gaunt, and I had bags under my eyes so large they looked almost like large purple bruises.

This is what she does to me. She drives me insane.

I showered as if preparing for my funeral. When I stepped out, cold air washed over me and I stumbled out of the room and to my bed—our bed. I passed out before I could take my towel off.

———

I woke up sometime in the middle of the night, naked, confused, and thirsty. I put on a pair of lounge pants and grabbed a drink from the fridge. I glanced at the empty plastic container on top of it. It used to be filled with fireballs, but then I threw them all over the living room, hoping she had hidden something in the jar. She hadn't; and I hadn't bothered to pick them back up.

In fact, I haven't had cinnamon since she that horrible night.

I took another long swig of the cold blood and fell against the fridge. Another night with no leads and no clue what to do. I hated living without her. None of this felt right. My entire existence was reliant on her being by my side.

It was odd to think about, considering I had spent thirty plus years without her. I had no clue I needed her until I had my memories back. I had known back then, in 1994, that I had wanted to spend my eternity with her, and I didn't get to take that back. I didn't want to.

I tossed the bottle in the trash once I drained it, and returned to the bedroom. This room looked like the ones before it. Everything was shredded and tossed about.

Once I had her back, I'd get it cleaned up, of course. None of this was done out of anger, but more like… mania. I was out of my fucking mind without her.

I looked around the room, as if I hadn't already searched

everything, but then decided to go to the closet again. Who knows, maybe sixteen times a charm?

I started going through the hangers. They were now empty. All the clothes had been removed, checked, then tossed on the floor. I reached for the boxes of random trinkets she had and went through those again to no avail, and then finally, I dropped down to start going through the mountains of rumpled clothes.

I spent an hour picking up things, shaking them good, checking pockets, then tossing them aside. Nothing. Again. I knew this routine, but there was comfort in trying, so I kept at it. I was ready to be done with this for the night when I tossed a dress bag behind me and heard a clink as it hit the wood floor.

I spun around to snatch it back up. I shook it again and frowned. I swore I heard something in that bag. I opened it then and started digging in it. I found the tags, a small bag of extra buttons, and a key.

I ripped my arm out in shock and stared at the tiny bronze item as if it held the cure to my sanity. What was this key for, and how did it relate to Scout?

I kicked through the clothes to leave the closet and plopped down on my bed. I turned the key over and found a small number engraved on it. I brought it within inches of my face and stared hard at it until I concluded that it was a phone number.

Despite the time of night, I called. Almost everywhere had a night shift these days. It was smart business. Sure enough, there was a click and then I heard, "Lopez Storage."

"Storage? As in units?" I asked the man who answered.

His reply came with a loud yawn of boredom. "That's the one. How can I help you?"

"I—" I blinked, trying to come up with something fast. "I

found my key. It has the phone number on it but not the unit information. It's been so long, I can't remember."

"Name on the unit?"

"Scout."

"Is that the last name?" I could hear clicking of a keyboard in the background.

"First."

I continued to hear the clicking but then finally his voice returned. "I'm sorry, but no one is renting a unit by that name, first or last. Maybe it's an old key?"

"You don't keep records of old renters?" I accused.

"Not after ten years. Sorry."

"All good. Thanks," I hung up. Tossing my phone on the bed. I stared at the key. Something about this didn't sit right. Why would she keep the key if she no longer used the storage? I turned it over again and blinked a few times, as if I wasn't seeing this right. There was a unit number on it. How did I miss that before?

I picked up my phone and searched the phone number with the name, Lopez storage. Sure enough, a location came up. Los Angeles.

I started clicking on links, trying to find exactly where this place was. It was in the middle of a neighborhood called, Echo Park.

I began reading pages on the community, the shops, and the history, I was fascinated by it all. Had this been where Scout had grown up? Finally, after an hour, I moved to figuring out how to get there. Fast was key.

I started checking flights. As I began to book one, a notification popped up, asking me if I was a vampire. I clicked yes, and was told I couldn't board that specific flight. I would have to get a blood specific flight.

How dumb.

So, I searched and finally found one in five days for L.A. I bought the ticket and then looked around. Maybe a little cleaning would do me some good.

I went to work getting the apartment back in shape. My mind was relaxed some, now that I had a clue about Scout's potential whereabouts. Was this once her home? Maybe she went back.

It took me until morning, but finally, the apartment was ready for her to come home.

I slept somewhat peacefully that day. Not entirely, but the bags under my eyes were a little lighter in the evening.

With days between me and the plane ride, I had nothing to do besides pack. I was laying in bed, holding The Fool card in my hands, flicking it between my fingers, wondering why she left it for me, when my phone rang.

I looked at it, and cocked an eyebrow when my brother's name appeared on the screen. I debated refusing the call, but finally clicked the green button.

"Yes?"

"You really like this woman?"

I sat up. "I do." My heart began racing and my stomach churned with nerves. Gianni never called me unless it was important.

"But you don't know her."

"I do. Just not in the traditional sense," I defended. "What is a last name anyway?"

"Everything," he said firmly. I gulped.

"I want to come visit you two. Her, mostly. I'm curious. Perhaps she has a lineage that is far more impressive than ours."

My mouth fell open. "No! I mean, why?"

"Do you really want to argue this with me? If I approve you'll get the ring you want."

I licked my lips, remembering what he had over me. I did want that ring.

"She's not here right now. I'm actually going to go get her later this week."

"Oh? Where did she go?"

Fuck if I know.

"Los Angeles," I lied. "I'll be back on Monday."

"I could take a trip. I do enjoy the sights. When do you leave? I'll go with you."

I wasn't entirely sure how to protest, but offered the excuse, "We have to take a special flight. It might be filled already."

"Oh yeah, the blood flights. They are segregating more and more these days. I prefer it, myself. They don't usually fill all the seats. Where did you book your flight? I'll buy a ticket."

I told him, despite not wanting to. The image of that ring I desperately wanted from him flashed in my mind. That would be the perfect way to bring her home to me. I would find her, we would talk, and then when she opened the door to our apartment I could get on one knee.

If I wanted that to happen, I'd have to suffer through a weekend with Gianni.

"Good! I'm booked. I'll see you at the airport."

The phone clicked off, and I stared down at it for a moment before tossing it aside and grabbing for my laptop. I started planning my trip more thoroughly. I booked a hotel and a rental car.

Sometime later, I got up to stretch my legs. I glanced at the mirror again as I passed by and paused. She couldn't see me like this. I was a mess. It wasn't enough for me to clean up our home, I had to clean up myself too.

I started with laundry, then started stretching and going

for runs when I woke up. The days leading up to my flight I made sure I was drinking enough blood and getting out to breathe fresh air. By the time I was heading for the airport, I felt almost normal, minus the hole in my heart.

Gianni was waiting for me in a three piece suit. I looked like trash standing next to him in my band tee and leather jacket. He stood when he saw me and eyed me up and down with a look of amusement on his face.

He snapped his fingers a few times then laughed. "That's where I've seen that look. You look like you came out of the eighties."

"I did," I said sharply. "I wanted to make sure people could tell us apart." I smirked. He and I both hated how much we looked alike. His face fell and then he pointed to his eyes.

"Oh I think they'll know who's who." His red eyes lit as he stared into my cursed ones.

I flipped him off and we sat down across from each other, waiting for our flight. He had brought his tablet, and chose to read something rather than converse, which was fine with me. I put my ear buds in and put on my music.

The plane ride was much the same. We chatted some. He wanted to know more about Scout, but when I continued to not know the answers to things he turned away from me and back to his tablet.

The car rental wasn't far from the airport, so we were able to pick it up right away. From there I put the GPS on started off.

"Where are we going exactly?"

"I'm going to take you to your hotel first, and then I'll go get Scout," I lied.

"Why? I'd love to meet her again. I want to give her an honest chance to win over my approval. I'll be nice this time. Let's just go straight there."

"I don't know if she'd be into that," I said, making another excuse. Gianni was silent for a moment before responding.

"What did you do?"

"What?" I glanced at him but looked away quickly.

"Don't play stupid. There's a reason you've been avoiding her and I meeting again. Why? Is she even here? Did I fly out with you for no reason?" His voice became agitated.

I gulped. "I don't know."

"Don't know what? What you did or where she is?"

I know what I did.

"I don't know where she is."

"So why are we here?" He snarled through clenched teeth.

"I'm trying to find her. I have a lead."

"And what's that?"

"A storage unit key. I think she may have something here."

"Like what?"

"Honestly, Gianni," I sighed and reached for my phone to change courses. I spoke into the phone, telling it to take us to the storage units. "I have no fucking clue."

We drove in silence after that. Well, silence for me. My older brother spent the drive lecturing me.

"See, this is why Mom, Dad, and all of us, can't take you seriously. All you had to do was marry Aleida and everything would have been fine!"

After a solid hour of listening to him, I snapped.

"Really? That's all? Don't give me that bullshit. Marriage is just the beginning of a life I never wanted anyway. Fuck all of that."

"You enjoy being the embarrassment of the family?" His red eyes went wide with fury.

"I'd rather everyone avoid me than have a wife I don't like, kids I don't want, and a giant mansion that's more prison than home."

He scoffed at my statement, but he finally shut up. I knew I had hit home with that last statement. He had all of those things.

We pulled into the business and drove through the chain link gates.

"I'm looking for row sixteen, unit P," I said as we began drifting slowly through the lot.

"There, turn right up at the next row." Gianni pointed and I did so. I hunched over as I moved even slower through the aisle, looking up at the letters on the units.

I was at L when I saw a figure leaning against a unit ahead of us. I stopped the car short and turned my brights on. It was a woman. She turned and stared at us, and my stomach turned.

I turned my brights off and started toward her, where she was leaning against the unit I was looking for. I stopped, turned the car off, and stepped out.

"Hello," I said. She flicked a flashlight on and turned it toward me. I flinched at the harsh light.

"Who are you?" She demanded. Her voice carried a thick Latin accent.

"Can you take that off my eyes? I'll talk to you just fine without it."

She did so, poising it at the ground. I blinked, letting my eyes adjust, and then looked at her. She was a lightly tanned woman of about mid-forties. Her long dark hair had a few grays and tiny wrinkles around her eyes.

"My name is Desiderio Amato." I put my hands up to

show her I wouldn't hurt her. "I'm… Scout left this key at our apartment."

"Where is she now?" The woman demanded.

"I don't know." I admitted. "I'm trying to find her. I thought this key might have some answers. Who are you?"

"I'm her foster sister. The storage unit called me when you came through. They know no one comes for that unit." She paused, then pulled a key from her pocket that matched mine. "You can't get in here without both keys."

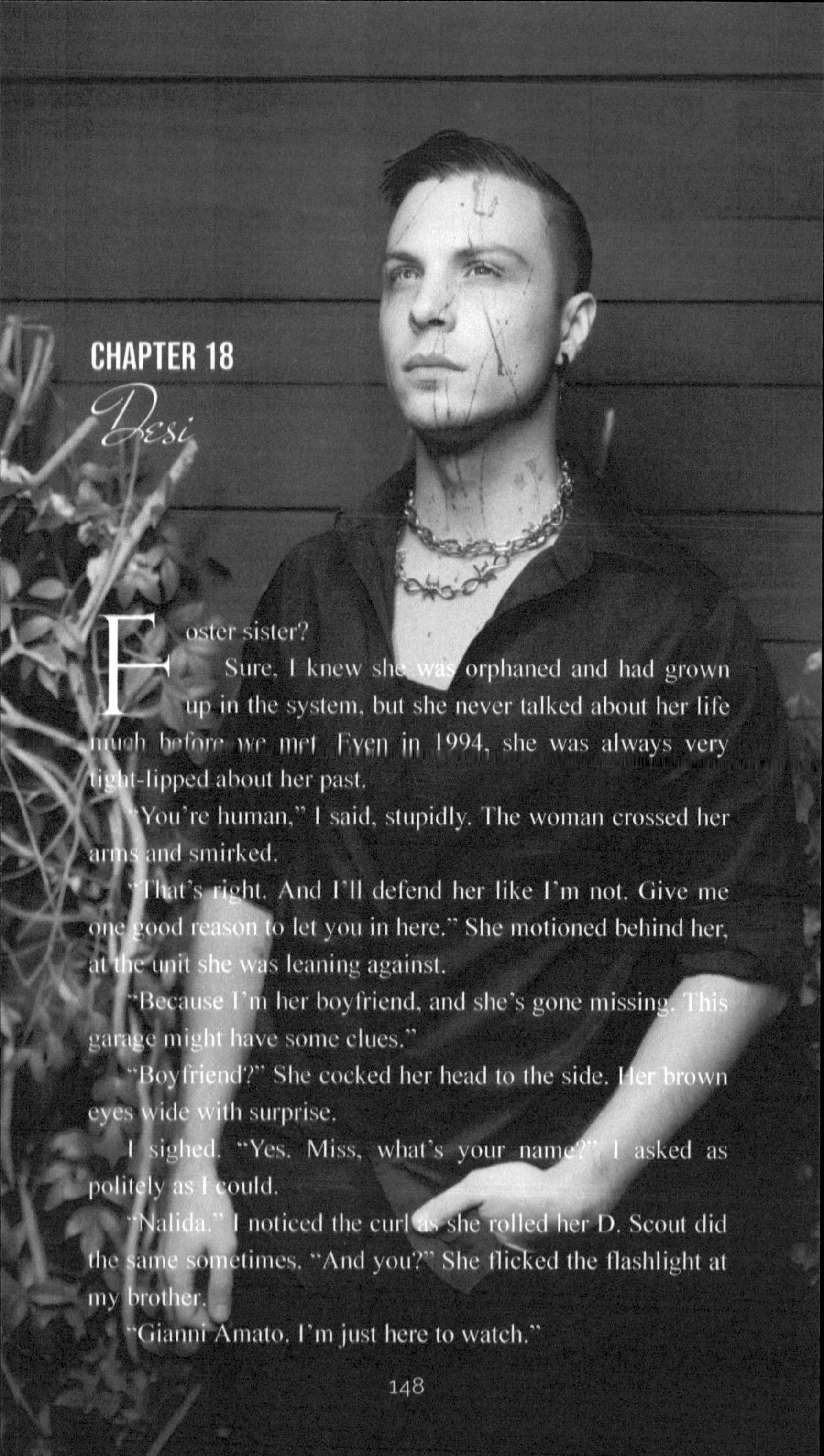

CHAPTER 18

Desi

Foster sister?

Sure, I knew she was orphaned and had grown up in the system, but she never talked about her life much before we met. Even in 1994, she was always very tight-lipped about her past.

"You're human," I said, stupidly. The woman crossed her arms and smirked.

"That's right. And I'll defend her like I'm not. Give me one good reason to let you in here." She motioned behind her, at the unit she was leaning against.

"Because I'm her boyfriend, and she's gone missing. This garage might have some clues."

"Boyfriend?" She cocked her head to the side. Her brown eyes wide with surprise.

I sighed. "Yes. Miss, what's your name?" I asked as politely as I could.

"Nalida." I noticed the curl as she rolled her D. Scout did the same sometimes. "And you?" She flicked the flashlight at my brother.

"Gianni Amato. I'm just here to watch."

Nalida nodded, and then directed her attention back at me. "Tell me something about her. To show me you're not lying about who you are."

I gulped. "When was the last time you saw her?" I asked, carefully.

"Ten years ago."

"Okay, so she was cursed, and now she's not. I was cursed too, and we were part of each other's. We broke them together, and discovered that we knew each other before we turned, in 1994."

She didn't seem fazed. I took a deep breath and thought harder. "She has a tattoo of a broken heart between her tits, and a fat devil on her ankle. I took her to go get that for her twenty-seventh birthday."

"What's her last name?" Nalida demanded and I froze.

"This again? I don't know." I threw up my hands. "I have no fucking clue. She never told me. Even after I asked. If she has one it's a fucking secret."

The woman stared at me for a long time before turning away and pulling her key out again. "Come here, we need both keys."

Relief washed over me as I hurried to unlock the storage shed with her. "What is her last name?" I asked as she bent down and started pulling the door up.

"She doesn't have one. You can go through this, but only with me present."

"Deal. Thank you so much."

I took a step back to allow Nalida to enter the unit and find the light. I blinked as the harshness of it filled my eyes, but then I looked around to see dozens of rather unassuming, brown cardboard boxes, a few card tables, and a bird cage in the back.

"Come on in, but be careful with everything."

"What exactly is this all?" I asked as the three of us stepped inside. "Did she move and forget to come back for stuff?"

"No, not really. These are her memories."

I turned away from a box I was just about to open to stare at the middle-aged woman. She looked tired, deflated, and just, sad.

"Scout never wants to talk about her past," I said lamely. Nalida perked up and nodded.

"Maybe some of these boxes will provide some insight. Here, this one I think has photos."

She marched toward a box and opened it, pulling out albums. She handed one to me and one to Gianni. He took it with a confused look, but then opened it anyway and began looking through it.

"Lemme see that whole box. I said and plopped down on the concrete. She had a dozen or so large photo albums all completely full.

"I didn't know she liked taking pictures."

"Oh yes. When we were traveling through Mexico," she put her hand on one of the pages I was looking at. The photos were of Scout and a much younger Nalida, dressed in hiking gear and grinning at the camera. "She took so many photos. She had bags full of film that she'd have to mail to my boyfriend back home." She laughed. "She wanted to remember every moment. Every little thing we did, there's a picture for."

It warmed my barely-beating heart, looking at Scout happy. She was grinning ear to ear in all of these albums. When I met her for the second time, she barely smiled. What had happened?

"Looks like you ladies had a lot of fun in your younger years," Gianni said.

"So much fun. I know it was kind of crazy to run off with a vampire to Mexico for a few years, but Scout always kept me safe. I felt comfortable with her."

I found a photo of Scout holding a massive black and red bird. "Is that who the cage was for?" I nodded to the metal cage in the corner.

Nalida looked at the photo and smiled. "Alfie. Yes, that was her pet bird. She found him in Mexico and brought him back with us. She loved him so much."

"What happened?"

Her face fell and she gave me a tight smile. "He was an old bird when she bought him. One day he went to bed and never woke up. She left shortly after he passed away."

"Was that the last time you saw her?"

She nodded. "Scout acts hard and tough, but Alfie's passing really hit her hard. And when things get hard, she runs."

A chill went through me. Nalida didn't know how true that was.

"What else is in here?" I asked brightly, setting the last album back in the box and standing.

"Well, there's souvenirs from Mexico, some of her art, some diaries from her childhood, and from Mexico."

"What exactly were you doing there?" Gianni asked suddenly. For the most part, he'd been pretty quiet. Only speaking when directly spoken to.

"Looking for her family. When we were growing up Scout never seemed to care much about them. Or if she did she didn't tell anyone. We were all without families." She shrugged. "But then one day she knocked on my door, a vampire, and asked me to go find them with her."

"And you did." I smiled.

Nalida grew silent for a long moment, debating whether

to tell us about something. "Have you ever heard of Magdalena Solís?"

"No," I said.

"Yes," Gianni said, kicking off the wall he'd been leaning against and stepping forward with interest. "Is she related to her?"

"I don't know."

"Who is this Magdalena?"

"The High Priestess of Blood," she said and then crossed herself.

I blinked. Nalida stared at me as if I should know that. Gianni sighed.

"She's a very well-known vampire. A queen, some say, of the dark world. I've never met her myself, but I hear good things."

Nalida grimaced. "I guess to a person who does what she does, sure."

"What does she do?" I asked.

"Large blood orgies, mostly." Gianni grinned, flashing his fangs at Nalida and I. "Ritualistic sacrifices, eating still-beating hearts. Brutal stuff."

Nalida's eyes went wide and I reached for her arm. "It's fine. He won't do anything. Tell me about this high priestess."

"I didn't look into it too much," she sighed and looked around the room. "But basically, she is a vampire like you." She pointed to my brother. "A Bloodborn. Before Magdalena even turned she was drinking blood, and became popular. She had a cult of men in the sixties.

Humans started coming up missing or dead, eventually catching up to her. She was sentenced to prison for fifty years."

"And she survived?" I asked, incredulous. "How?"

Nalida scrunched up her nose. "According to the internet, the rumors are that she stayed only until she truly turned. When she rose up into her vampire form she killed everyone in that prison who tried to stop her escape. Now she lives a free queen, doing whatever she pleases."

"So the legends go," Gianni added and she nodded.

"What does this have to do with Scout?" I asked.

She blinked and furrowed her brow.

"Scout wanted to find her and see if she could help her locate any other Bloodborn families."

"And did you? Find her?" I asked. Nalida shook her head.

"No. The High Priestess keeps her den a secret. We traveled for years looking for a clue and got nowhere."

"So you came back," I said, not really a question.

"I convinced her to. I wanted to settle down with my boyfriend. Now my husband. I was aging, and she was not." She shrugged.

"And you didn't want to turn?" I tilted my head, curious.

"I'm Catholic. Suicide is a mortal sin. Even if we don't truly die. I could never."

A cold silence fell over the storage unit. I quickly moved on to another box, this one was full of sketch pads.

"She has tons of these at our apartment." I grinned at Gianni, as if to say, *"See, I do know stuff about her."*

"She wanted to do comics." Nalida laughed. "She had this one guy she drew just about everywhere in Mexico. It was like, her tag or something."

"Gum Man?" I asked, flashing her a sketch of a little cartoon guy with the name emblazoned underneath his pegged legs.

"Yes! Gum Man!" She laughed. "She had a whole collection for him. Let's see if it's in here." She started digging through the notebooks with me and then found what she was looking for. She took the one out of my hands and traded me. "You'll love these. Here."

I opened the book and grinned. There he was, Gum Man.

"What style is that?" Gianni asked over my shoulder. We both looked up at him.

"I never knew much about her art," Nalida admitted. "Other than that she loved getting a laugh from everyone with this guy." She pointed at the drawing I had paused on. The green cartoon character was sitting down, covered in pink goo. Underneath was the title, written in her handwriting.

Gum Man had the hiccups.

It was adorable, and I found myself wanting to bring this out of the unit and back home. I perused the pages as Nalida and Gianni spoke about Mexico, and Scout's journey to finding her real family.

Gum Man went to the dentist.

"Did you guys meet any Bloodborns?" I asked, pausing at a particularly cute drawing of Scout's.

"Some. But many were weary to talk to us. A vampire traveling with a human that she wasn't feeding on? That was odd back then."

Gum Man took his dog for a walk.

"You guys grew up in foster care, you said?"

"Yes, we met in high school. We were in a home together for about a year before we were separated. Both of us aged out of the system."

Gum Man has gas.

"And she had no biological siblings?"

"Not that she knew of."

"What about you?" I interrupted them, suddenly curious about the woman we sat with now.

"Me? I do have a sister. We were separated in the eighties."

"Were you orphaned too?"

"No. My mother wasn't a very good caretaker and my father left when we were in elementary school. I turned out okay, though," she added, defensively.

"My apologies," Gianni put his hands on my shoulders and gripped tightly. I flinched. "My brother has an inability to understand manners sometimes. Actually, quite often."

"It's fine. Scout does too. You guys seem like a good match." She laughed.

"I have to ask, but how did she go through the foster care system without a last name?"

Nalida bit her lip. "Well, not exactly. She had one, has, I guess. Not entirely sure how things work when you're a vampire and you live forever. They gave her one to use for legal documents, but she dropped it as soon as she could."

"What was it?"

"Smith."

Scout Smith. *How original.*

"Well, if we went by that, I'm sure she has lots of family." Gianni snickered. Nalida gave him a nod. "There were lots of kids named Smith in homes I passed through. She wasn't anything special to them."

She is to me.

"I wonder," Gianni started, taking his hands off of me. "If we could be of help to her. To find her family. Her blood relatives."

"You really think you could find The High Priestess?" Nalida raised an eyebrow, skeptical. I was too. Sure, the Amato name had connections, but I doubted we were that high on the chain of things.

"Perhaps. I'll ask around. Are you sure there is absolutely

nothing else you can share with us Nalida? Someone she talked to of interest? Maybe we can read those diaries of hers. Or what about any past lovers? Were they human or vampires?"

She glanced at me and blushed. I tightened my jaw, but said nothing.

"I can't remember every man she dated. Not that there were a lot! It's just been so long."

"Why did she entrust you with this?" I motioned around the room. "No offense."

"Scout never really had many people she could trust. Even the men in her life only knew very little. She knew that giving me the extra key that her memories would be safe."

"I'm sorry if I made you uncomfortable." I offered her a small, awkward smile.

She waved it off. "You're fine."

"Who is this?" Gianni held up a piece of paper with some writing on it. The paper was a faded yellow now, once white.

Nalida took it from him and read it. Her eyes lit up suddenly and she handed it to me. "Oh! I forgot about this. This might actually be a lead. This man came looking for her. When I told him I hadn't heard from her in a few years, he gave me his information and asked me to pass it on. I tried to call her, but she had changed her number. That was about six years ago. When I couldn't reach her I came out here and put the paper in a box so it wouldn't get lost."

"Was he human or vampire?" I asked.

Nalida's eyes took on a far off look as she tried to recall. "Vampire."

"Bloodborn or Bloodshed?" Gianni asked.

"He had the red eyes."

"And did he say why he was looking for her?" He pushed.

She shook her head. "No. He was very… secretive. He wouldn't tell me anything."

I stared down at the paper. "Okay, if he's alive, we'll find him. Nalida," I looked up at her, desperation firmly on my face. "What could I give you to take all of this home with me?"

"**W**hat do you think about a promotion?" I continued toward Yorick, my boss. He watched me with his icy-blue vampire eyes as I carried a tray of half-finished expensive drinks back from a high table.

"Promotion? To what?" I glanced at him as I set my tray down on the bar. The glasses made a slight clinking sound as they teetered.

I straightened in my heels and crossed my arms over the rhinestone-covered bra that he called a uniform.

"Bartender. I think you'd be good at it." He crossed his arms over his, which was covered in an expensive suit, and smiled. "It comes with a raise and better tips."

"Did you get your head knocked in again?" I joked, referring to how he decided to end his human life.

"No," he laughed with me. "One tree falling on me was enough. Seriously, I want you to do this. I said larger tips!"

"What did you just say?" My eyes went wide. He rolled his eyes.

"Tips. Puh!" He exaggerated the last consonant and now I

was the one to be embarrassed. A voice from my past echoed the word I thought Yorick had said in my ears and I shuddered.

"What's going to happen with Landon?" I motioned to the current bartender.

The blue-eyed, shaggy haired blonde turned and grinned. "What's up?" he asked, coming over to us.

"I want Scout to learn under you. Show her how to bartend." Yorick turned to me, his decision made. "You'll start tomorrow night."

I nodded and the manager of Gilmore's disappeared back into his office. I reached for my tray and started back toward the kitchen. I placed the glasses in the sink and returned to the floor.

It was a slow night, and for which I was grateful. I had been working here for about a month now, and these times were few and far between. While the tips were good and I was happy to have gotten a job so quickly, I was worn out.

When Ginata had brought me here straight from New Jersey, she had told me that Gilmore's was the nicest bar in all of New York for vampires. The rich came here to conduct business.

"As long as you be a good girl, you'll be very happy here."

I had shuddered at how she said it, but I was still determined to move on and do what she said. Be happy.

And for the most part, I was. I hadn't seen Ginata since that first night. She got me a job and my apartment and then promised she'd see me soon. I'd be bothered about her absence if I had time to entertain company but I wasn't. This job kept me... busy.

I couldn't even say exhausted, because my vampire body didn't really let me feel aches or tired-ness for long. But my brain weeped for some kind of relief that I had yet to give it since I had left that house.

I was zoned out for the millionth time, but shoved back into reality by air being blown into my face. I blinked and focused my eyes on Landon, elbows leaning on the bar, smiling at me. "Penny for your thoughts?"

I gave him a half-hearted smile and shrugged. "Just enjoying the slow night. It's a nice change of pace."

Together, we shared a look around the large, dim room. Everything was either silver, black, or royal blue. Sleek. There were booths with tall walls for privacy lined all across the wall, and high tables for those just wanting a quick drink with an old friend. Jazz music played in the background as vampire women dressed just like me, in skimpy uniforms and hi-ponytails, walked around servicing the customers. Normally, the room was full. Today was an exception.

He laughed and slapped the counter, straightening his back. "Savor it. They never last. You want a shot?" He was already reaching for a tiny glass, already knowing my answer. I looked around the dark room. No one needed my attention so I scooted onto a black leather stool and relaxed my back. I watched the handsome vampire as he stared at his wall of bottles.

"Can I surprise you?"

"You always do. Just—" I put a finger up and he waved me away.

"No cinnamon. I know." He reached for the top shelf vodka and a dark brown bottle. He poured a little of each into my small glass, and then added a spritz of lemon pop. He slid it over to me and stuck his tongue out playfully. I smiled, despite myself.

"It's called, The Mind Eraser."

"Oh? I don't recall asking for that." I reached for it and

quickly tossed it into my mouth. The brown bottle had been some kind of coffee liqueur. It burned my throat, but I knew it'd make me feel better soon. "Not bad," I told him, giving him the glass back.

"I figured you could use it. I'll teach you how to make it tomorrow."

"Yeah, what is with that?" I tilted my head toward Yorick's office door. "Why am I being put on bartending instead of any of the other waitresses? I just started."

"Probably because of your mouth." He smirked. "You don't exactly have a customer service voice."

"What's that mean?" I slid off the chair and put my hand on my hip. "I do fine with tips."

"Yeah, to the guys who like sass. Everyone else shoots you dirty looks when you leave their tables." He pointed out.

"If I'm so terrible, why do I still have a job?"

"Ginata's recommendation supersedes everything. Yorick likes to keep her happy."

Oh.

"That's why I'm getting a raise?" I grimaced and glanced back at the room. Prue, one of my fellow waitresses, smiled kindly at me. She deserved the higher wage more than I did.

"I may have had an opinion when asked about who I wanted to work with." A coy smile slid onto his already gorgeous face and my stomach fluttered.

"Is that right? I feel so honored." I placed my hand over my chest, right over my broken heart tattoo.

"You should! It's a coveted position."

"I bet it is." It was then that one of my tables was waving to me, so I hurried over to service them. The rest of the night suddenly picked up, and when I had a moment to breathe, it was closing time.

"I jinxed myself," I told Prue as we were sitting in the

back, changing out of our uniforms and into our street clothes. "We were having such a slow day."

I pulled off the rhinestone booty shorts and bra. Opting for my own less flashy underwear and shorts. I slipped on a loose black shirt and pulled the tie out of my hair, letting the messy locks fall over my shoulders. My black heels were replaced with sneakers, and I was ready to head back to my modest apartment.

My new friend laughed as she changed into a pink velvet track suit. She pushed her blonde hair back and stared down at me. I was the shortest person, so everyone had to look down at me. "If you relax too loudly the customers sense it and come running. Ugh, but enough server talk." We grabbed our bags and started out the front.

We walked through the upscale bar, now empty, arm in arm. "Word is Landon asked for you specifically to be his bartender partner."

"I did hear that from somewhere." Landon's voice came from behind us. Prue and I paused, turning slightly as he caught up with us.

"Why is she so special?" Prue pouted. We kept moving, weaving through tables.

"Are you jealous?" Landon laughed, and when we reached the front doors, he opened them for us.

"A little bit." She admitted. "I've openly voiced my interest in working with you a few times."

"Yeah, but in what way?" Landon shot back.

My gorgeous blue-eyed girl friend laughed. "Fair enough. I'd be lying if I said I wouldn't mind adding you to my bed sometime." Prue smirked, eyeing the handsome man up and down. The look she was giving him made me almost blush.

Landon shook his head and blew her off with an arm

wave as we started toward our separate rides. "I think your bed's pretty full, thanks."

Prue and I climbed into her convertible and she started out of the parking lot and toward my place.

"He likes you. Landon. And he's a cute one." She smirked.

"I hadn't noticed," I said, staring at the window. I was only half-lying.

"He's built like a football player. I'm seriously jealous."

"Of what? We're not—" I protested.

"But he wants to be."

"That doesn't mean anything. It takes two."

"Or three, or four." Prue laughed and then sighed with a smile. "I would love to make him my fourth."

"Don't Kyle, Joshua, and Alex, have a say?" I raised an eyebrow, genuinely curious. She shrugged.

"Only if I want them to. You should try it. I will never be monogamous again."

I laughed. "I don't know if that's my lifestyle. I'm actually quite content with me, myself, and I." I raised my hand and wiggled my fingers at her.

"You mean, you, yourself, and your vibrator."

We laughed together and she turned the music up, finishing our ride from work with no more talk about her current, and what she assumed was my future relationships.

"Thanks, but my last one ended pretty fucking shitty. Hard pass."

"We'll see." She smiled.

I walked into my apartment building and ran up the stairs when I saw my neighbor, Benji, coming out to say hi.

"Scout, is that you?" He called but I was already closing my door.

I leaned against it and let out a huff. I needed to bounce, like yesterday. At least to a better apartment.

I dropped my bag next to the door and kicked my shoes off.

I looked around my tiny studio apartment. It was bare, besides a pile of dirty clothes, a few sketch pads, and my very secondhand furniture. The only thing that was new in the entire apartment was my mattress I had finally earned the money for two weeks ago. I didn't even have a frame. It rested against the wall until I needed to sleep, in which I'd set it on the floor in front of the couch. I felt like I was back in the eighties, freshly kicked out on my own and one step above homelessness.

A hot shower warmed my cold vampire skin, my marshmallow scented body scrub refreshed me and got all the sticky alcohol and fingerprints from guests that were too friendly off of me.

I tossed on a clean shirt and panties and lowered my mattress to the floor. My comforter and pillow sat folded on the couch. Crawling onto the bed, I reached for them and made myself as comfortable as possible.

I realized as I was relaxing my body, that I hadn't even bothered to turn on any lights. For some reason it really bothered me. Was this my life now?

I had spent the last month, wallowing.

Wallowing.

Even as an immortal being, I couldn't keep living like this. This was fucking pathetic.

That next day, I went into Gilmore's with a smile on my face and my stomach in knots.

"Do you want this?" Prue offered me a giant red pill in the changing room. I glanced at it and refused.

"I'm good. Again. Thanks," I muttered. Everyone here

took the pills, and no one knew what was in them. I had a sneaking suspicion that Ginata was getting them from Ludovica, and if they were anything like the candy Tully and Dante had at their underground casino, I wanted no part in it.

Prue shrugged and popped it into her mouth, chasing it with a gulp of blood from her reusable bottle. She swallowed and stared at me. "It just makes you feel happier, is all. I don't get why you wouldn't want that."

"Being happy all the time is overrated. I enjoy the rage boiling inside me at all times." I replied without missing a beat.

We changed into our uniforms and walked out onto the floor when Landon called me.

"Scout, come on! Time is money, and we're losing time!"

I cocked my head, considering his words. What was time for us immortals? He rolled his eyes and motioned again for me to join him.

"Did you forget you weren't slinging trays tonight?" he asked as I pushed through the half door to go behind the bar with him.

"No, I guess I just— still didn't believe it?" I cringed.

"Well, believe it. I want you back here with me from now on." Landon's chiseled face was stern when he looked at me, and it sent butterflies to my stomach, causing the knots to loosen, then tighten quickly again. I pressed my ruby lips together and nodded.

"Okay, make me a sex on the beach." He crossed his arms and stared at me blankly. I did the same.

"What's in it?"

He sighed. "That's your job. I'm the customer. I don't know what's in it. I just know all my girlfriends are drinking them and I want one too."

"Okay, well I don't have a way to look them up."

"You still don't have a phone?"

I shook my head. I'd been avoiding it. I looked down at the floor. Flashes of the reason for my hesitance to put down roots went through my mind. They were interrupted my Landon reaching out and touching my chin. I jerked away and stared at him with wide, shocked eyes.

"You know, you're safe here."

"What?" I snapped.

"I don't know what brought you here, to Ginata's territory, but you're safe now."

I stared at him for a long moment. I would never, ever, tell anyone what Desi had done to me. I reached for the necklace I still wore around my neck with his name. I couldn't help it. I had tried to take it off, but I couldn't bring myself to.

I wanted to bury him and his memory, but I couldn't if I continued to hide from him.

"Scout?"

I blinked away the red liquid pooling in my eyes and looked up into the handsome vampires blue ones.

"Tonight, after work, we're going to get you a phone. And my number is the first one you're gonna put in there."

I nodded, although I still felt unsure about it. "And you'll teach me how to make a sex on the beach?" My voice came out soft, and almost desperate. He grinned.

"I'd like to teach you a whole lot more, if you let me."

My stomach went fucking crazy. The butterflies used their tiny butterfly hands to unravel all the knots I'd spent a month tying and were rising up into my chest.

Just like Prue had last night as we left work, I eyed Landon up and down. Ideas of what he could show me started playing through my mind. Would that be so bad?

Yes. I wasn't ready to forget Desi.

"What do you say?" He offered me his hand to shake, and I stared at it like an idiot.

"To what?"

"Will you give me a chance?" My gaze returned to his face, and I saw promise and an honesty in his expression that I had never seen in Desi's. Not now, not in 1994, not ever. I gulped, and when I responded, it came out so quiet I was sure he couldn't hear it, but I wasn't going to take it back. I was sure of what I wanted. But I knew that eventually, I had to move forward.

"Yes."

CHAPTER 20

"Ginata is coming in tonight. She'll be taking her usual booth and wants her usual served all night. Prudence, I want you on her table."

I stood behind the counter with Landon as we listened to Yorick go through his evening meeting before the shift. Landon knocked his elbow into mine and made a quick silly face, causing me to let out a small giggle. Yorick shot us a look and I straightened up.

"She's bringing her men tonight." His eyes darkened for only a moment before moving on to remind the waitresses that just because a familiar offers themselves, we're still on the clock and needed to act appropriately. He looked pointedly to Sol, a pretty, dark haired vampire who came here after her home country made the vampire laws unbearable. Last night she had spent a little too much time indulging in a young man with a red ribbon around his neck.

"Thankfully, we were able to cover your tables, but let's not put that burden on others, okay everyone?" Yorick said to everyone.

"I don't need any more flashbacks. Okay?" Prue smirked.

I watched as Bette, a blonde vampire who's legs were taller than my body, put her arm around Sol and giggled with our newest co-worker about Prue's comment. Prue had been trampled to death during a fight she self-inserted herself in, at naturally, a bar. Yorick clapped his hands and everyone separated. The doors were opened to the public and vampires started trickling in. It only took about five minutes before Landon and I were hard at work making extravagant cocktails for the elite.

"Two Blood Cosmos and a Bloody Mary plain." Sol came up and handed me her paper with the order on it.

I grinned. "On it." And began to prepare her drinks.

"Wow, it only took a week and you're faster than I am." Landon teased from across the bar where he was filling martini glasses with chilled blood and olives.

"It helps when you don't stop and flirt every time someone comes up here." I laughed. He shook his head.

"No, see, it helps quite a bit."

Just then, he slid the drinks across the counter to a pair of buxom brunettes and in return I watched them both slide fifty dollar bills to him. My mouth fell open and I glared at him.

Touché.

As the night went on, I found myself continuously checking the door. It was almost midnight and still, no Ginata. I glanced at the booth directly in the center in the back. It sat empty with a small place card that read, *"reserved"*.

Then, as if I had thought a little too hard about her, the energy in the building shifted. Voices seemed to lower, heads all turned, and then there she was, striding in like the queen she was.

Dressed in a plum-colored cocktail dress, her bright hair shone as it rested all around her. Her smile was stunning as she walked into the room, accompanied by three giant vampire men, all in different colored suits, but looking just as regal as her.

"Those were the men Yorick was talking about?" I whispered to Landon, who had appeared by my side.

"*Her* men. Leo, Elias, and Cap."

"Cap?" The entire room paused to watch the foursome walk to their table and take a seat. Ginata sat in the middle, with two blondes on her left side, and a raven haired man on her right.

"Capricorn. He's the blonde farthest from her. He used to work with me here. He's her latest. He replaced George."

"Latest?" I stared at the group, taking them all in, piece by piece. Prue hurried over and began to take their orders. Ginata seemed bored, and the men all rushed to make sure the attention returned to her as the room erupted back into play. Conversations restarted, the music grew louder, and movement continued.

"Yeah, her last boyfriend, George, he was her familiar. He left out of the blue. She likes to keep three men at all times. So she brought Cap in."

I blinked. Ginata stretched her neck, letting the other blonde bend down and kiss her bare skin. The dark haired man on the other side rubbed her shoulders and it hit me then. They were all—together.

"Wow, so is that why Prue does it too? Polyamorous relationships?" I asked aloud. Landon laughed. I frowned. "What? This is all new to me."

"Apparently. Prue isn't special. They aren't the minority. Most relationships in Ginata's territory are polyamory."

"Since when?" I shot back, skeptical.

"Since always. Haven't you noticed?"

"Well, no. I guess not. I haven't had much time to socialize." I tilted my head then and stared at him. "Are you part of a…"

He grinned, flashing his fangs and sticking his tongue out. "I have been. But I'm currently running solo."

"Multiple women or men?"

I was genuinely curious, but our conversation was interrupted by Yorick coming to the counter.

"Ginata wants to see you at her table. Go take a break."

I pointed to my chest and he nodded. "Go. He'll be fine."

I took a deep breath and steeled myself. Landon patted me on the back. "You'll be fine. Just don't let her smell your fear." He laughed.

I rolled my eyes but did find his words comforting. I left the bar and strolled as confidently as possible to her table.

"Scout. Beautiful, come sit," she purred as I reached the group. I looked at the vampire man with the dark hair and sharp cheekbones. He scooted closer to her and I slid in beside him. "These are my men, Cap, Leo," she pointed to the men on her left. "And this is Elias." She patted the dark-haired vampire's lap, then turned to them. "This is the one I was telling you about."

"What about me?" I asked, a little nastier than I had intended. I flinched slightly and she shrugged.

"Who you once belonged to, is all. Nothing of importance." She leaned forward, her breasts spilled over her dress. I couldn't help but glance down. When my eyes returned to her face, her red eyes were bright with amusement. "How have you been? Safe?" Her smile slid off her face and her expression turned into one of genuine concern. I nodded.

"Yes. Very. Thank you. I haven't heard from him since I got here." I put my hands in my lap and looked down. I didn't want to talk about that.

She sat back triumphantly. "See, I told you. He doesn't

have the balls to come into my world. As long as you remain with us you'll never have to worry about Wrath ever again."

"Thank you," I whispered. Suddenly her hand reached out and found my chin. She lifted my face and smiled kindly at me.

"None of this sadness. We don't do that here. Here," she offered me a bowl with the pills. I shook my head, but her eyes lowered into slits. "Take one." Her voice was firmer, and I found myself reaching for one. I put it in my mouth and Leo slid his glass to me. I took it shakily, and when Ginata repeated herself, I finally took the pill.

"Good. Now, we can relax and have a good time. How are you liking the selection in my territory?"

"Selection?" I asked. Prue came to our table and asked me what I wanted to drink. I shook my head. "I'm only taking a break."

"Oh no, darling. She'll take a Blood Martini. She'll be with us all night."

"I can't," I protested. "Landon needs me up there."

Ginata waved my concerns away and picked up her own red drink. "He'll be fine. I want to talk to you, and that's all that matters. Tell me about all the men you've sampled. Or women, we don't discriminate here. We only *encourage*." She laughed and the men around her joined in too.

"I haven't. I'm not really looking for anything like that."

"Why? Because of *him*?" She spat the last word, as if she had been the one hurt by my ex, and not me. "He's gone. Forget about him."

"You know what they say," Leo said. I looked at him with surprise. It was quite easy to forget the men were even here.

"The best way to get over someone is to get on top of someone else." Cap finished his sentence. The table agreed with him.

"Exactly." Ginata nodded and leaned forward again. "So what say you? Why not have a little fun? You don't have to be in love. If that's even a thing these days." She snickered.

"You don't believe in love?" I asked.

"I don't believe it's necessary to have a good fuck." She licked her fangs and sat back with a thump. "And I know a thing or two about a good fuck." Her arms reached out and both men beside her jumped slightly as her hands roamed under the table.

"Scout, have you ever had a ménage?"

I blinked.

Oh no.

"Ginata, I'm not really interested in you like that."

She laughed. "Not me, silly. We're exclusive. It's not an invite. I was just asking to be friendly. You, my new friend, need to loosen up."

Prue brought me my drink and Ginata insisted I start drinking. I was not a fan of blood mixed with alcohol, but I drank it anyway. She repeated her question and I shook my head.

"No. Just one on one."

"Please don't tell me it's only been Desiderio." She grimaced, her nose scrunching and her tongue flapping out as if she had tasted poison. "That you've been saving yourself for thirty years."

"No, there's been others. Just not in groups." I glanced at her partners and felt suddenly like a giant asshole. "No offense. I'm not judging, it's just never been my thing."

"Well it should be," she said firmly, reaching for the newest drink Prue had brought her. She had been here maybe an hour and had already consumed four cocktails. She was drunk. "And it will be soon, I'm sure. You can not tell me there's not one vampire here that hasn't caught your eye?"

My eyes flicked to the bar before I could stop myself and she saw it. Her face lit up as if I had just handed her a puppy. "A coworker? There's been lots of flirting, I bet." She winked at me. Normally, it would have made my stomach sour, but I smiled and laughed along with her.

"Some. Okay, a lot," I blurted. I realized that this must be the effect of the happy pills everyone took here. Honestly, it wasn't a terrible feeling. "He is really cute."

"What's his name?" she asked, putting her elbows on the table and resting her face in her palms.

"Landon. He's got pretty eyes," I revealed.

"I really do like Bloodsheds more than Bloodborns, if I'm being honest," she confessed. "They're more grateful to be here. And you'll find that they are also very hungry to please." Her gaze flicked to her partners, but if they heard her they didn't acknowledge it. They were speaking low amongst themselves.

"You should sleep with him." Ginata's eyes lit up. "He's huge, I bet his cock is just as impressive!"

"Don't!" I gasped, reaching out to put my hand over her mouth. I pulled back as I realized how bold I was being with the highest ranking person in this area.

With the Seven Sin of Gluttony.

She only laughed at my reaction, causing me to laugh as well. "He'll hear you!" I hissed.

She shrugged. "Good. Maybe it'll cause one of you to make a move. I'm sure he's just been dying to give you a go. Just go for it, no one cares here." She waved her hand dismissively at my worries.

As the night went on, I was fed more happy pills and drinks, as was she. I felt beyond elated, and I was disappointed when Prue came over to tell us that the sun would be up in two hours.

When we climbed out of the booth, I saw that all the other patrons were gone.

Ginata hugged me tightly before she left with her crew. "Please, for me, try him out. In fact, try the entire lifestyle out. Don't be afraid to sample more than one person if you get invited. I think you'll be pleasantly surprised."

"I really don't know if it's for me." I protested one more time, but now, I wasn't entirely confident in my answer. She had spent the entire night selling me on multiple men. Would it be that bad to try it?

Ginata kissed me on the lips quickly before leaving and I stood there, dumbstruck for a long moment. Had that entire night seriously happened?

"I hate you." Prue came over, looping her arm through mine and dragging me to the changing rooms. "You got to spend a whole night with Ginata and her gorgeous men. Tell me everything."

I tried my best to regale her with stories from my night, but most of them were centered around Ginata trying to get me to sleep with Landon. I didn't need that getting back to him. We still had to work together.

"Are you going to fuck Landon now?" Prue asked suddenly as we walking out the door. I stopped short and turned.

"What?"

"That's why she came, wasn't it? To get you to stop being such a prude. That's what everyone was saying all night."

I sighed and kept walking. "No, not necessarily," I lied. "We talked about other stuff."

Prue sighed and then stopped in the parking lot. She pulled out her cell phone. "I can't give you a ride home. My guys need me home right after work."

"What? Why didn't you say something before?" My

mouth fell open and looked around the lot. "How am I supposed to get home?"

"I can give you a ride." Landon's voice came from the doors of the club. He was stepping out just as she had abandoned me. My stomach knotted, and I glanced at Prue. She was grinning at me.

"I'll stomp you," I growled with annoyance. She laughed.

"Can't be worse than when I was trampled flat." She smacked her hands together, laughing at the way she was accidentally turned into a vampire. "Go have fun. Real fun." She ordered and turned quickly, leaving me with Landon.

He reached me and glanced at the convertible screeching out of the parking lot. "You walking?"

"No, I'll ride you. I mean, with you." I blinked and blood rushed to my face.

He burst into laughter. "I mean, both sound good, but I can take you home with your purity in tact if you'd prefer." He winked and my stomach fluttered again.

We went to his car and he opened the door for me. I started to duck inside but he reached for my hand, causing me to pause. I looked up at him then, and watched him bend down. I closed my eyes and let our lips connect in such a soft, gentle way that I temporarily forgot about the man whose name I still wore around my neck.

Nightmares. The fucking nightmares.

Not entirely sure where they came from, but god damn they were horrible.

It was about a week or so after Gianni and I had come back from California. Nalida, Scout's old human friend, had let me take some stuff home with me, and I had been going through it all, trying to figure out exactly who the woman I was in love with was.

I fell asleep with the lights on, still in my jeans, with sketches of Gum Man surrounding me when the first dream came.

Scout was laughing, and smiling. She looked beautiful. It was the most vivid image I had seen of her since she had ran away from me two months ago. I could almost reach out and touch her. I started to but then I ripped my arm back when I saw who she was smiling at. It wasn't me.

The face was blurry, but the bright blonde hair was not.

She was with someone else.

Her voice called out to him, but it was muffled, I couldn't

hear clear words. Just the inflection of them. She was happy. And then, she was gasping.

I watched, unable to leave the situation, as he picked her up and sat her on a couch. He bent down and shuffled himself between her legs.

Dream me tried to get her attention. I screamed. I called out her name from the corner, but she closed her eyes, as if trying to drown me out. I watched in horror as he slipped her panties off and his head dipped underneath her skirt. I had to watch as she gripped his hair and let her head fall back in ecstasy.

I woke up covered in sweat and blood from my eyes smeared against my cheeks and pillowcase.

I leapt up and ripped my clothes off. I stormed into the shower. Despite watching her come with someone else, I was still hard for her. I hated myself for it. I sat in the freezing water until I could calm down and process what I had seen.

I spent that entire night trying to piece it together. It had been too vivid to be made up by my brain alone. But she wouldn't. Not my girl. Not my Nerd. Scout would never let someone near her.

Not if she still loved me.

Once again, I fell asleep out of sheer exhaustion, and another nightmare came.

It was her and the blonde again. They weren't in the bare room from before. This appeared to be an apartment. It was his, I realized. I was able to walk around it, as if I were there. But I wasn't. I tried to ignore the sounds from Scout as he kissed her topless body.

Those were my tits to enjoy. Not his.

I clenched my teeth and worked on memorizing as much as I could before I woke up. I saw a photo and bent down to pick up the frame. My hand went through it, as if I were a ghost. What the hell was this all?

Every day for weeks, while I slept, I dreamt of the couple fucking. He took her in every which way he could think of. His place, what I assumed was hers, a car— which was all kinds of hell considering I was stuck up front listening to it, only inches from them.

I knew they couldn't see me, but I still felt the need to act like it didn't bother me. I would look away, sometimes yawn, and occasionally I'd even comment on his prowess.

"I've made her come so much harder. This is— tepid." I smirked one time after he took her against a wall. I forced myself in my dreams to pretend as if it didn't bother me in the slightest. Every night when I woke up I was either screaming or sobbing miserably for hours. It was killing me.

I started keeping a notebook beside my bed. I wrote down as much as I could recall. These were my clues to finding her.

A knock on my door one night caused me to jump from surprise. I hadn't had an interaction with another being since the nightmares started. I had started ordering my blood to be delivered and left outside. There was no need to knock. Who could it be?

The deep sound came again and I hurried to see what it was. It was my brother, Gianni.

I opened it quickly. "What are you doing here?"

He was standing there, almost bored. He was holding something large covered in a deep red cloth. "I have something for you."

I eyed the cloth warily. "What is it?"

"If you let me inside, I'll show you."

I stepped aside to let him in. "Why didn't you call?" I asked as he came into my apartment.

"I thought a surprise would be fun. I need something flat to put this."

I motioned to the coffee table with some of Scout's notebooks. I moved them to let him set the thing down. He did so and quickly ripped off the ruby-colored fabric.

A tiny black thing made a small squeak in a metal cage.

"What the fuck is that?" My mouth fell open as I stared into the cage.

"A gift. From Magdalena Solís herself."

"Who?" I crouched to see the creature that was continuing to make tiny little chirping sounds.

"The High Priestess of Blood. I found her for you. You're welcome, by the way. She was rather interested in your girlfriend's situation, and wants to help."

I tilted my head. "And her solution is a bird?"

"A Dracula parrot. Just like the one Scout had once upon a time."

I blinked with surprise.

"Oh wow. I see no red." I stood back up and dusted off my knees.

"He's a baby. Barely a hatchling. It'll develop in time. The High Priestess has tons of them in her territory."

"So she just gave you one?"

"To give to you. When you find your girlfriend, offer her the bird."

"You think that'll work?"

"Better than nothing." Gianni shrugged. "And you don't turn down a gift from the High Priestess."

I rolled my eyes. "Is she really that special?"

"Yes. Baby brother, I'm once again disappointed yet not surprised that you don't know who is who. I was very lucky to have been granted a meeting with her."

"Meeting? Or more?" I snickered. His red eyes grew cold

and small, which only confirmed. Gianni may act like he's all business, but I grew up with the fucker. He thought with his dick just like any other man.

He sneered at me. "I think you'll find the High Priestess very interesting."

I raised my eyebrows, suspicious. "You think?" I cocked my head to the bird. "What do I feed it?"

"Figs."

"What the fuck is a fig?" I threw my hands up. I didn't eat food.

Gianni sighed and reached for a second bag I hadn't noticed before. He opened it and removed a purple onion. He handed it to me.

"This. You can get it at any human grocery store. That's all they eat."

I stared down at it in disgust. The thought of even storing human food in my apartment made me sick.

"I've got to go. I was just dropping him off before I went back home. I have to report everything to Dad." He turned to leave but I put my hand out.

"Wait! It's a he? What's his name?"

My brother paused and raised an eyebrow at me. "I didn't name it. Why would I?" He went to the door and grabbed the handle. "When you have your girlfriend back, call me. I still want to talk to her. Especially now."

"Why? Is she related to the High Priestess?"

"I have gotten some new leads that she may be interested in." He ignored my question. "Who knows, little brother," he paused to look at me and grinned. "You may just get the ring and approval from the Amato family yet."

The door opened and shut quickly, leaving me alone with a fig and the bird.

There was an awkward silence as I took in my new situation. I went to the couch and sat down to get a good look at the animal.

"Why, hello," I said, sticking my fingers through the cage. The inky black blob scuttled forward. I smiled and was just about to click my tongue at him when I felt a sharp sting as he nipped me!

"Ouch!" I yelped as I pulled my hand away. "What was that for?" A tiny drop of blood spilled before my skin could heal.

I frowned and stood up, fig in hand. "Maybe you're hungry. I'll feed you and then we'll figure out your name."

I went to the kitchen and grabbed myself a bottle of blood. I cut his food up and then brought my drink along with me to feed him.

Carefully, I unlocked the cage and stuck the fruit in quickly. I scrunched my nose up as the smell of bird shit and moldy fruit wafted over to me. This was why I didn't do animals.

"Let's think." I took a sip of my drink. "What would Scout name you? She likes movies. Horror, mostly. You are a Dracula bird, which lends itself to many a joke."

I stared at the tiny little bird pecking at his dinner. He didn't respond. I sighed and leaned on my knees. "I wish she were here to see you. She'd have something to call you in an instant."

I stood then and looked around. I saw the bag Gianni had left me. There were only a few figs in there. I grabbed my keys and left then. Maybe the bird would be good for me, I thought. I was finally getting out of the apartment.

As I walked through the overly lit aisles of the human store, I thought about Scout and the bird. She really would love it. I could see her now, face lit up with excitement when she sees him for the first time. I wanted to give her lots of those moments.

I wanted her to come home to an all-new world. Everything she ever wanted, I would give to her. I got the bird, but now what?

Art school.

Before we went to Tully's, she had her heart set on getting a formal education. Comics. I was going to make sure she got to school, if I had to carry her to and from class each and every night. She would get to do it.

I found the figs and put all of them in my basket. I wasn't sure how many I needed, but the less times I came here, the better. I was getting weird looks from the late-night humans shopping.

Fuck 'em all, my parrot needed these figs.

I couldn't figure out how to self scan produce, so I had to see a cashier. It was a whole big thing and when I was done I decided I would have someone else do my shopping for the bird from now on.

I reached my car and got in, tossing the bags on my passenger side. Just as I reached for the wheel, something bright flashed in my vision and I froze.

How was this happening? I wasn't asleep!

Suddenly, I was taken from my car and transported to… a locker room? Green lockers ran along the walls. There were benches and a few sinks off to the side. I was in a gym, maybe.

The familiar sound of Scout in the throes made me jerk to find her. I groaned and my stomach knotted as I found her with her legs wrapped around the blonde guy once again. His pants were pulled down just enough to get his cock out and plunge it inside her.

Scout's eyes were closed as she hung onto him. She was gasping, and panting, and he was whispering things to her that I couldn't hear. Which was fine, because usually it was cheesy bullshit that he probably said to any woman he was fucking.

But then, I heard something that made me freeze completely.

"I think we should add another to our relationship. Paulo. I'd love to watch him fuck you."

Who the fuck was Paulo? I stormed over to them, and despite knowing his face would be blurry to me, I got as close as I could to try to look him dead in his eyes.

"We are still getting to know each other, and you want to add in someone else?" Scout said, not opening her eyes. "Why so fast? I don't think I can handle two men."

The one inside her thrust harder into her, causing her head to hit the metal lockers with a large thud. The thin metal doors rattled and her eyes popped open.

"I know you can. We'll start with just you two, and then when you're comfortable, I'll join in."

"What makes you think I'll ever be comfortable with that? I'm barely comfortable with you. If you want to see him fuck someone so bad, why doesn't he fuck you?" She spat.

"Because I don't want to fuck him. I want you to be so thoroughly fucked, you'll never think about him ever again." He grabbed the necklace around her throat and tugged on it. She reached up and pushed his hand away.

"You think I think about him?"

"I know you do. Every time you close your eyes, whose name do you call for?" His mouth went to her neck and he grazed the skin with his teeth. She gasped, closing her eyes, and then he thrust again, making her call out.

"We shouldn't be doing this. I still don't know if I'm ready." Scout ignored his question.

"What? Fooling around in Gilmore's? Being together while you're still in love with someone?"

His hand went to her tit and began fondling it harshly. I was always surprised at how rough he got with her and her response to it. While it was never as enthusiastic as orgasms with me, she was still enjoying it.

"Say my name," he demanded and she ignored him again. He repeated it through clenched teeth as he coaxed her to climax, and then finally she screamed.

"Desi!"

My heart stopped.

He stopped.

She stopped.

Time stopped.

He ripped himself away from her, letting her fall to the ground in a crumple.

"It's Landon. Actually."

He stormed out of the locker room and in an instant, I was back in my car. Time resumed and I quickly turned my car on and drove home. I didn't know what to think.

She called my name. That's all I needed. I was going to go find my girl.

CHAPTER 22

Desi

"Have you heard of a place called Gilmore's?"

"Oh, it's nice to hear from you, little brother. I'm doing fine since you burned my house down. Thanks for that," Tully snapped from the other side of the phone call.

"That's a shame. I thought I had you all trapped," I muttered.

"Ha, nice try. No, you just killed the fifty or so vamps and their familiars. Dante and I were the only survivors."

"How unfortunate," I said with no feeling behind it. It was just a number to me, nothing more.

"Is that Desiderio?" I heard Dante's voice in the background. "Tell him he's a fucking dick!" he shouted.

"You're a fuck—" Tully started.

"I heard him." I rolled my eyes. "Did you hear my first question? I need to find a place called Gilmore's."

I laid down in my bed and closed my eyes. I pinched the bridge of my nose and sighed. A loud squawk rang out from the other room and I lifted my head to snatch a pillow and toss it at the door to close it.

"What the hell is that?" Tully asked.

"It's a fucking bird, what do you think?" I snapped.

"You got an animal? Why?"

"I called you with questions, not the other way around," I reminded him.

"Right. Gilmore's? That's in New York. Hold on, Dante get over here." I could hear him asking our fellow Sin brother about the place in question.

"He thinks it's part of Ginata's territory."

"It's nice. But good luck getting to see her," Dante said from behind Tully. "She's too busy to entertain these days."

"Yeah, we had to call Corrine to host us until we could find a new place to settle down in. The humans weren't as amused as you were about the fire." Tully complained.

"You know how much gear I've had to move in the last two months?" Dante shouted. "A fucking lot!"

"Why would you keep your arms business right next to Tully's shit? That's on you," I argued.

"I told him the same thing," Tully smirked.

"What is Ginata even doing?" I tried to focus on the phone call, rather than the bird who never shut the fuck up. It was proving difficult.

"You know, that's a good question. I can't even get her on the phone," Tully whined.

"Anyway," Dante's voice was suddenly louder. He must have stolen the phone from Tully. "It's in New York. Nice place. I'm sure you can get a table, but you wouldn't be seeing Gina. Why?"

I didn't know how to answer that. How did I even begin to explain that I was seeing Scout in my dreams? I wasn't sure if it was her past or present, but it was real, and she was there.

"You want a friend to go with you?

"Nah, I've got this. Just business."

"Be careful. You know how she gets when she thinks you're stepping on her toes."

"Oh I remember."

Ginata was almost more spoiled than Ludovica. Take what she thought was hers, and there would be hell to pay.

Good thing Scout isn't hers.

"God damn, does it always sound like that?" Tully asked. I sighed. The bird, that I decided was now named Tippi, was still fussing.

"He does. I can't get him to stop unless he's sleeping."

"Put a blanket over him."

"Oh, thanks for the tip. I didn't think of that one!" I faked enthusiasm and hung up.

New York, why was I surprised? Ginata was born and bred in the city. I shouldn't be shocked she took some of it over.

I got up and went to the bird. "What the hell is your problem?" I moaned. "It's almost morning. Go to sleep!" His curtain had fallen, so I bent down to pick it up. I covered him and finally, there was some semblance of quiet.

I passed out on the couch, and thankfully, I didn't dream of Scout and Landon. Between my nightmares when I was asleep and Tippi when I was awake, I was going crazy.

It took me a few days, but not only did I track down the club, but I secured a reservation at the end of the week. I called Corinne and got Ginata's updated phone number. I called it, but only got her voicemail.

"Gina, it's Desiderio. I'm coming to visit. I think you may have something of mine. Call me back, we need to catch up while I'm there."

I received a text back, instead of a call.

She must just not have wanted to see Tully and Dante, which to be fair, I understood. I told her where I'd be and she promised she'd be there.

I just needed to find a fucking sitter.

I went across the hall to Amy.

"This is Tippi. Can you watch him?" I asked, showing her the bird.

She was more than happy to do something for me. Even after Scout moved in, she had continued to flirt with me, but I never reciprocated. Still, I thanked her and started packing to head across the country again.

I was surprised at how irritating I found traveling now. Before, having an apartment was unthinkable.Now, I craved the normalcy. The almost-human lifestyle. Was I getting soft?

Frantic knocks on my door threw me out of my thoughts and back to reality. I hurried to it, and opened it to find a terrified Amy being held by the neck by a tall, darker skinned Bloodborn with rage in his eyes.

"This is Jaime. He's looking for you."

"Are you Desiderio Amato? The one with the cursed eyes." The vampire's Spanish accent was thick, I struggled to understand at first. I rolled my eyes, and pointed to my face. I nodded.

"I am. Who are you?" I asked slowly, confused.

"Why does she have the High Priestess' gift?"

"The bird?" I grimaced. "She's watching it while I leave town for a bit. Why?"

"See?" Amy let out a small cry of panic. "I told you. Can you let me go now?"

Jaime dropped the back of her neck and she scurried back across the hall.

"Have you found her?" he demanded. I crossed my arms defensively.

"Who?"

"The vampire you call Scout."

"No, I'm on my way now, actually."

"I will go with," he said.

I laughed. "Uh, no?"

I gave him a solid once over. This guy was built like Arsenio. Tall, and twice my size in muscle. He had a long dark pony-tail and was wearing jeans and a plain red shirt. When my eyes returned to his face, I saw determination.

"Who sent you?"

"The High Priestess of Blood."

"Why don't you come inside and we can talk privately," I suggested against my better judgement. I opened the door wider to let him in and he stomped inside.

"You need any blood?" I offered.

"No."

"Okay, well you can sit there." I pointed to the couch. He walked over and plopped down. I chose to stand. I crossed my arms again and tried to figure out how to approach this conversation. "Why do you want Scout?"

"The High Priestess wants to see her."

"And who are you to her?"

"Who?"

"Scout." I gritted my teeth.

"She is my sister."

I blinked. It was as if the world around me dropped. She had a brother? "You sound so sure."

"I am. She looks just like the our mother, and the high priestess as well."

"Your mother, is she alive?"

He shook his head sadly. "Our parents died when Scout was very young."

"How did she get here, if you're from—" I hesitated.

"Mexico," he snickered. "We are different ages. I was a teenager when she was born. My father brought her to America."

"And your mother?" I demanded.

"Humans killed her. If you sit, I will tell you our story."

I did as told, grabbing a chair from the dining room table. He definitely had my interest now.

"The High Priestess was taken by humans and imprisoned in nineteen sixty-three. She was sixteen."

"For what?"

I vaguely remember Gianni talking about her, but I couldn't think of any details. Jaime rolled his eyes and shook his head. "They had found our vampire coven. They did not know what we really were, only that humans had been killed. She took the blame, as she was still human, and others were not. But she knew eventually when she turned, they would discover the truth and they'd come for all of us."

He paused, and I nodded. He continued.

"Plans were eventually put in place. It was decided that my mother would take the High Priestess' place in the prison."

"But she was a vampire too." I cocked my head, confused. Jaime's eyes began to shine and then hardened.

"Sacrifices had to be made for the greater good. My mother would take her place so the High Priestess could move us and protect the coven."

I scrunched my eyes, trying to do the math.

If she was sixteen in sixty-three, then she'd turn into a full vampire in seventy-four. Scout and I are only a day apart in age, so that would have made us… seven?

"Scout told me that she was found as a toddler." I eyed the vampire with suspicion. Things weren't adding up. He nodded.

"The child being born wasn't part of the plan. When she was born, my mother did not want to trade places anymore. The High Priestess felt betrayed by her sister. She demanded the baby be killed."

"She wanted Scout murdered?"

He nodded. "Our Priestess knows best. If my mother did not trade her, we would all have been killed."

"So they ran?"

"My father did. He left with the baby, and returned without her."

"Is he still alive?"

He shook his head, his eyes suddenly steely. "No."

A shiver ran through me. Something told me it wasn't humans who had killed him.

"What do you want with Scout?"

"The High Priestess wants her forgiveness, and for her to join her court."

"Court?"

He nodded. "She is important to us."

"Must not be that important if you were going to kill her," I tossed at him. He gave me a tight smile and nod.

"Yes. We want to give apologies. It was not because she did not love her niece. She had to choose between her entire coven or one. She did what was best. She saved us."

Silence fell over the room for a long moment while I took in his words. Did I dare trust him?

"What else can you tell me about her lineage?"

He blinked and his brows furrowed.

"Was she born Scout? Does she have a last name?"

"Her name is Julieta."

Julieta.

I slapped my thighs and stood up. I gave him an apologetic smile and shrugged. "Well, I'm sorry, but I don't know where she's at. I've been looking for her for a few months now. Everything so far has been dead leads. This one probably will be too."

He stood too. "I will join you."

"No!" I threw out a hand and then froze. It was then that it all hit me. I had researched Magdalena after we had returned from California. There was a reason she was called the High Priestess of Blood. She was fucking brutal. Live human sacrifices, and horrible torture methods flashed through my brain. I could very well be giving Scout to these people just for them to perform something monstrous on her.

"How did you find me?" I asked, trying to stall to give me time to think.

"The bird. It called for me."

That's why it never shut the fuck up.

It felt like pieces to a large puzzle were all falling into place, but they were the random middle pieces. Nothing was clear yet, but there were clusters of answers to questions I had been asking myself for weeks.

Gianni.

I had found it odd for him to come to me. Especially with a gift. I should have known it couldn't be trusted.

"Does the High Priestess have powers beyond those of a normal Bloodborn?" I asked. He grinned.

"You can only imagine."

"Does Scout?"

"That has yet to be seen."

Ah, so that's why they want her. They want to see if she's got some magic that the High Priestess also has.

"I've been lying to you." I slumped my shoulders and looked toward the ground. I brushed my hair back and sighed. "I can't find her because she doesn't want me to find her."

"Your brother told us you were soulmates. There is a bond beyond this world, no?"

I flinched. "I thought we were."

"That bond can not be broken. If you know how to listen, your bonds will tell you how to find her." Jaime spoke softer, more gentle. There was almost a sympathy in his red eyes.

I blinked. Was that why I had been having the night-mares? Our bond? Was she reaching out to me? Or I to her? Why was it only when she was with someone… intimately?

"How do you know?" I demanded.

He grinned. "Because I too, have offered someone my blood as they turned. It's common practice where I come from. A soulmate's bond can not be broken. Do you see her when she is not here?"

Slowly, I nodded. I was weary to answer him, but I had no one else to talk to about this. I was desperate.

"Have either of you drank from each other after creating that first bond?"

I gulped, suddenly embarrassed. I nodded again. He grinned.

"It was pleasure beyond your wildest belief, wasn't it?"

I chuckled. "It was."

"The more you do it, the stronger your bond becomes." He reached for his pocket and pulled out his wallet. He then handed me a card. "Listen to what your heart is telling your mind. It will lead you to her. Then," he flicked the card in my hands. "You will call me." He turned toward the door and started away.

"How do I know you won't hurt her?" I called to him as I stood, frozen to the spot. He turned.

"I think you underestimate a woman's power. It's not her that should be afraid, but me." And with that, he left, quieter than he had come.

I stared down at the card in my hands. It was simple, just a name and number.

I had a choice now. After I found Scout, I could tell her about Jaime and risk them hurting her. Or, I could throw this in the trash and forget he ever existed. The question was— what could she forgive?

"**A**re you alright? God, your face!" Prue came into the changing room and let out a gasp. I looked up, wiping the blood tears from my cheeks.

"I'm fine," I sniffled. "Just— Landon stuff."

"Did you guys have a fight? I thought things were going really good." She came to sit on the bench besides me. She put her arm around me and pulled me into her embrace.

"Not really a fight, just—" I wasn't even sure how to put it into words. How could I tell her I couldn't stop thinking about my ex long enough to focus on him and what he wanted? "I don't think it's gonna work out."

"What? Why?" she demanded. She pulled away from me and stood, going to grab paper towels. She went to the sink and got them damp. She handed them to me and I cleaned my face.

I shrugged. I really wasn't about to tell her what Landon wanted me, or rather us, to do. She would only take his side. I couldn't tell anyone here. Monogamy was a dirty word in Ginata's territory.

Prue offered me a hug. "Well, whatever's going on, I hope

you can figure it out. Worst case scenario, you try someone else. Or a few," she laughed.

I rolled my eyes. "That's the problem. I don't want a few. Or a lot."

"Nonsense. You just haven't found someone you click with yet. Has Landon mentioned anyone?"

She helped me stand and we walked to the sink to freshen up before we went onto the floor. I took a deep breath and steeled myself. I tightened my pony-tail and adjusted my bra.

"When was the last time you guys did it?"

I pressed my ruby lips together, my emotions getting the better of me again. "Did what?"

"Sex." She stared at me as if I were an idiot. I looked down.

"Oh, well we—"

She paused and blinked rapidly into the mirror. "Wow, so that's why you're fighting."

"Yes, I know," I replied curtly, and turned, leaving the changing room.

I put on a smile and went to the bar, where Landon forced a smile back at me. I joined him behind it.

"Hey baby, you okay?" he asked.

I nodded. "All good. Where are you at with orders?"

I glanced at the full bar.

"Everyone's taken care of right now. Thanks."

Uncomfortable silence fell between us for a moment. I looked away and thankfully, someone wanted my attention.

Work kept us too busy to dwell on the silent fight we were having behind closed doors. That was, until a handsome stranger came to sit directly in front of me.

"Hi," he said. His voice reminded me of warm chocolate. Smooth and rich. I looked up and found myself flirting a little.

"Hi. How can I help you?"

"Scout, this is my friend, Paulo." Landon came up behind me, putting his arms around me. He kissed my neck, causing me to let out an involuntary giggle. I was about to elbow him away when he whispered in my ear. "I want you two to fuck."

I froze. My eyes shot over to his friend. Chocolate colored hair, icy blue eyes, and a jawline for days. He winked, and I clenched my thighs together. I swallowed. "Landon, we talked about this."

"I know. But I don't care if we haven't yet. I want this. Please, Scout. For me."

"I don't know." I shook my head and pulled myself from his grasp. Paulo spoke then, causing me further embarrassment.

"I think we could have a lot of fun together."

"Oh yeah?" I asked, refusing to look at him any further. I went about making him a drink, even though he didn't ask. He looked like a whiskey on the rocks guy.

"Landon tells me you've never tried more than one man at a time."

I gritted my teeth. "That's right."

"You don't think you'd like having hands all over you, focusing on your pleasure and nothing else?" He leaned forward and grinned.

I slid his drink over to him and put my hands on my hips. I turned to Landon and glared. "What is this? A sales pitch at my job?"

He shrugged. "I thought maybe if you saw the product you'd be more interested in buying in."

"Well I'm not. Please, drop it."

The evening continued, with Paulo drinking at the bar while he and Landon spoke. Sometimes I heard them laughing, other times they were staring at me and speaking in low tones. All of it had my stomach in nervous flutters.

Eventually, I needed a break. I threw a towel down and fled the bar. I could feel the two men staring at my ass as I ran. Prue saw me leaving the floor and followed me.

"Please tell me you're gonna fuck them both tonight."

"Jesus Prue! Keep it down!" I said in a loud whisper. The door hadn't even fully closed. I smacked her arm lightly and she only laughed. "I haven't even fucked the one, what makes you think I'm going to start with both?"

"Oh come on, they are practically salivating at the bar every time you move. Landon picked a hot vamp."

"He wants to watch," I revealed, unsure of why. I wasn't going to actually do it. Her eyes lit up and she grinned excitedly.

"Ooh. You should get on all fours, and then have Landon in the front so you can blow him while his friend can fuck you. What's his name?"

I crossed my arms. The image of that scenario danced in my mind. "Paulo, and no. I'm not doing it."

"Why not?" Her face hardened, and suddenly she was defensive. "You're acting like a prude."

"I'm not a prude," I protested. "I just don't want to focus on multiple people."

"But that's the best part." She raised her hands and pinched her fingers together. "You don't have to. They are going to focus on you. Scout, have you ever came so hard you squirted?"

"Prue!" I let out a scream. She laughed.

"Let them take you home tonight and have fun. You won't regret it."

I sighed. When I first arrived at work, I was sure I would

not do what Landon wanted. Now, I wasn't as confident that I'd say no to a threesome with him and Paulo.

"New topic. It's already been decided." She waved the dark thoughts away dismissively. "I guess the bouncers had a problem earlier." She turned away from me, heading to the mirror to reapply her makeup.

"Really?" I joined her, interested in the gossip. We rarely had stories about the bouncers. She nodded.

"Yep. Some Bloodborn, no offense," she paused and looked at me with an awkward smile. "Some Bloodborn showed up with a reservation, but he was in jeans and a t-shirt." She scrunched up her nose. "Obviously they refused to let him in. I guess he tried to start a fight with Hawk."

I stiffened. Alarms were going off in my head.

Jeans and a t-shirt?

"What did he look like?"

Prue shrugged. "I don't know. I didn't bother asking. Go see Hawk. Why, were you expecting someone?" She raised an eyebrow and a slow smile slid onto her face. "Did you find someone on your own? I bet Paulo and Landon wouldn't mind sharing." She wiggled her eyebrows and I scowled.

"Fuck off." I spun around and went to go see the bouncers. I stormed through the building, my heart racing. My stomach was riddled with fear.

"Hawk?" When I found the giant Bloodshed vampire I was looking for, I tapped him on his shoulder. He looked down and smiled kindly.

"Scout. What are you up to?"

"I heard the drama." It took everything in me to play it casual. Inside I was dying. I crossed my arms and cocked my hip. "I'm nosy. What happened?"

He laughed. "It was nothing that serious. This stuff

happens more than you guys hear about. It was just a weird Bloodborn trying to get in without following the dress code."

"Weird how?" I asked.

"Sunglasses, Iron Maiden shirt. Boots." He stuck out his tongue in distaste.

"Did he have a reservation?"

Hawk nodded. "Yeah, but rules are rules. No suit, no entry. I told him to come back tomorrow night with nicer clothes."

"And he got angry?" I furrowed my brows in confusion.

"They always do. He tried to throw Ginata's name out there, which was the deciding factor to turn him away. He tried to say she was meeting him tonight." He gave me a pointed look. "And then tried to be all— you're making a mistake. Ginata isn't going to be happy. Blah blah blah. As if she had the time to fuck with someone weird like him."

"Weird?" It was then that all the hairs on my head stood on edge. Nerves tightened around my insides, and I knew what he would say before he did.

"Yeah, the sunglasses. We got into it, there was some shoving and his glasses fell off. Dude had one blue eye, one green."

The world around me became blurry. I blinked, trying to process things.

He found me.

"Scout?" Hawk called for me, but I was too lost in thought. How? Ginata promised me safety. Hawk waved his giant hand in front of my face, but I didn't respond.

"Darren, some assistance over here." Hawk's voice seemed far away, and I suddenly felt lightheaded. Suddenly, hard, cold hands were holding me up from my armpits, and I slumped in their grasp.

"I just need to sit down," I said, trying to process everything.

"Let's get her inside." I heard Hawk again, and the arms under my arms were carrying me in one quick motion. I looked up to see Darren, Hawk's blonde counterpart. His face was serious as he carried me to an empty booth.

"Get her some blood!" he barked and a moment later a glass was brought to my lips. I didn't want to drink but he pressed the glass against my mouth, urging me to. Finally, I obliged. I did feel better.

"Is this vampire an issue? We can put him on our black-list," Darren offered.

Here's my chance. Say yes. Tell them to never let him in here. That he's dangerous.

I shook my head. "No, I don't— this has nothing to do with that. I've just been on my feet a lot. I forgot to drink. I'll get some more blood in me and I'll be fine," I lied.

"Are you sure?" He was skeptical, but I nodded.

"Yeah, you know how it goes. You get so into work you forget about small stuff like that. I'll be fine. Thanks for saving me." I patted him on the shoulder playfully. He didn't seem to believe me, but sighed and stood to go.

"Why don't you get yourself some red pills? You've been looking a little off these days." His tone was kind, and I knew he meant well. I forced a smile.

"Yeah, I'll grab some from Landon. Thanks Darren."

He left me then, and I slumped down in the booth.

Desi found me.

Suddenly, my flight response kicked in. I needed to get out of here before he stormed through those doors. Before everyone knew exactly what he had done. I leapt up and let out a scream when hands clamped down on my shoulders.

"Hey! Calm down, it's me," Landon laughed and spun me

around. I relaxed, closing my eyes. I forced myself to steady my breathing. "You want to go home?"

"What time is it?" I asked, looking around. It was then that I realized that all the patrons were gone. Waitresses were cleaning up and the music had been turned off. "Oh. Yeah, I guess."

"Do I get to go home with you?" he asked. I looked up into his eyes. They were so kind, so soft, so… not *Desi's*.

I pressed my lips together. I needed Landon. I needed to do this to keep thoughts of Desi away. He didn't own me. I owned me.

"And what about Paulo? Is he coming too?"

I blinked, and Landon nodded to someone behind me. I turned and saw the very handsome Paulo waving and grinning at me. My core tightened.

Could I really sleep with two men at the same time? It was one thing to be making out with someone that wasn't Desi. It hurt every single time. My heart shattered each time Landon touched me. It was why I had only fantasized about sex, and nothing more. I couldn't, but maybe this was what needed to be done. Did I push it even further, taking not only him, but Paulo too, into my bed? Would having these men to focus on keep me from thinking about the vampire who hurt me? My soulmate?

No.

"Yes," I replied.

CHAPTER 24

Scout

I wonder what he's doing right now. Where could he have gone?

"Do you want a pill? It'll relax you," Paulo asked me, causing me to blink and force my mind to return to his upscale apartment.

"No, I'm good. I don't really like those." I glanced at the bowl of red pills on his coffee table. They were literally handed out like candy everywhere. He frowned, but took two for himself and popped them into his mouth.

"Ginata says they've got dried blood in them along with all the other stuff to make everything feel good. That's why it does what it does to us." Landon smiled, grabbing some too.

I was skeptical. "What does it do, other than make you high?"

They shared a look on the couch they were also sharing, then looked at me across from them. "It helps you loosen up. Look," Landon sighed and brushed his hair back. "Everyone is really uptight when they first come to Ginata's colony. The pills help you embrace the lifestyle. Come on," he slid the bowl across the table, but I simply stared down at it, my hands firmly in my lap. "It's fine. Ginata wants us to do this."

"Ginata wants us to have a threesome?" I blurted. I cringed at how blunt it was, but the pair I went home with just laughed.

"Yes. Actually, she encourages us all to live a poly-lifestyle. For so long women have been forced to service men and their pleasures, but Ginata wants us to be better," Paulo explained.

Landon stood and came over to me. He sat down and put his hand on my thigh. I stiffened. "We are here to make sure you always have the best time. Let us do our jobs." He smiled and I took a large breath.

Paulo joined me then, and I shuddered as his hand went to the other thigh. Together, as if minds in sync, they began to urge my legs apart.

My knees knocked together and they stopped. Landon pressed his body against me and began kissing my neck. "Relax, and let us give you the best orgasm you've ever had."

"Have you ever been bitten?"

"What?"

"Can I," he paused, running fingers so lightly across my thighs it tickled. *"Bite you?"*

I blinked rapidly.

"Are you going to bite me?" I asked, my voice soft and airy. Memories of the times Desi and I had bitten each other, and how good it felt, rushed through my mind.

Would two bites feel even better?

"What? God no. Vampire blood? That's poisonous." Paulo scooted away quickly, as if I had in fact bitten him. I shook my head.

"No it's not. I've done it."

"How? Scout, sweetie," Landon's voice came out shaky and confused. He reached for my chin, pinched it, and turned me to look at him. "You can not have possibly drank from another vampire's body and survived."

"You know that's how Bloodborn's turn, right?" I gave them a look and they furrowed their brows in confusion. Did they really not know? I shook my head. I was not giving a lecture on blood bonds tonight.

I straightened and slapped his hand away. "I have and did. Look." I pulled up my skirt and spread my thighs then. I pointed to the two small fang marks that was my permanent reminder of the first time Desi and had taken blood from me.

The two Bloodshed vampires leaned in and examined the scar. Paulo ran his finger against it and swore.

"What does that even mean?" he asked Landon, more than me. Landon shook his head.

"I have no idea." He looked to me then. "What happened to the other vampire? Did they die?"

"No. He's still alive and well, to my knowledge, and I have drank from him. We were fine. It's fine." I threw up my hands and closed my legs. "We don't have to. It's just really nice. It feels super good. I don't know who's been telling you otherwise."

"Was he like you? A Bloodborn?" Paulo asked. I swallowed.

"Yes. But that stuff really doesn't matter. We're all the same other than eye color."

"No, not really. There's lots of things we can't do that you can," he shot back harshly.

"Like what?" I smirked.

"Have kids," Paulo said, his voice dripping with sadness.

I blinked. "Really?"

"You didn't know?" Landon and Paulo shared a look.

I shook my head. "No. I guess I never thought about it. I mean, I know legacy families and their weird obsession with keeping things pure, but I didn't think—" I paused, trying to really consider their words. I guess I hadn't heard of any mixed vampires. Or Bloodsheds that had children. "Having children isn't really common anyway." I shrugged it off.

"You would say that. You have that choice. We don't." Paulo's eyes darkened.

"Uh, yeah, but you also had the choice to become a vampire. I didn't." I pointed to my chest. "Don't try to guilt trip me for something I can't control. This whole night is too much for me. I want to go home." I stood up and started to step over them but Landon reached for my hand.

"Please, don't go. Paulo is just—" he paused and I looked down at them. Paulo was scowling but Landon was giving him a look that relaxed him. "It's a sensitive subject. Actually, let's get off this couch and go to the bedroom." He stood then and started to tug my arm toward what I could only assume was Paulo's bed.

Paulo stood then and his arm went to my back, slowly drifting down, squeezing my ass. He bent down and I found myself tilting my head away from him, letting my hair fall to the side. His fangs lightly trailed against the exposed area, and my skin prickled with anticipation. But then he pulled away.

"I can't bite you, but let me show you all the other ways I can please you."

I sighed, and let them take me to the bedroom.

The room was nice, just as the rest of his apartment. His bed was ridiculously large, and was covered in royal blue silk bedding.

Paulo went forward and pulled out his cell phone. Music

began playing lightly throughout the room. I was unfamiliar with the song, but it did relax me.

I sat down on the bed and Landon bent down instantly. He reached for my leg and lifted it to unlace my boots.

I felt movement and suddenly I had large, warm arms on my shoulders. I closed my eyes and tilted my neck as Paulo urged the straps of my dress down my arms. He began to kiss my bare skin, and I swallowed the large lump in my throat.

"Oh, this is different. Usually, I pop in mid-thrust."

My eyes flew open and I looked around quickly. That voice. That stupid, sarcastic—

Desi.

My lips began to tremble and I was completely frozen. There he was, standing behind Landon, arms crossed and watching me.

"Oh wow, two cocks now? I knew that stupid fuck on the floor couldn't do the job." He kicked his foot out and it went through Landon, as if he were a ghost.

What the fuck was happening?

Desi's eyes went wide then and his head flew back up to mine. Panic in his face.

"You can see me this time?" he asked.

I nodded and closed my eyes as Landon finished my shoes and was kissing up my legs. "Yes."

"Well, this is interesting." I could hear the smirk in his voice. "Why now, I wonder? Is it a distance thing? Or is it something else?"

"I'm so confused," I said.

"It always is the first time. Just let us do the work," Landon said and pushed my thighs apart. He kissed me between them, moving closer to my core. I tightened my muscles, but he didn't notice. All the while, Paulo's hands were on my breasts, my dress pulled down. He rubbed me through my thin bra, my nipples perked up at the friction.

"I wonder if together they'll be able to manage giving you something worth bragging about."

I kept trying to forget the Desi ghost, but he kept reminding me of his presence with his snarky comments. Surely this was just my imagination going wild from the stress of what I was doing.

"This isn't real," I gasped as Paulo's hand slipped under my bra.

"Oh, it very much is," both Desi and Paulo said almost in unison.

Oh dear God. I glared at Desi and he only laughed.

He began to walk, hands in his pockets, around the bed.

"This has been happening for weeks. I've been sent to watch every time you let that stupid fuck on the floor inside you. If I wasn't so sure I broke my curse, I'd wonder if this was part of it."

What? I furrowed my brow, confused even more. Did he say he saw us? How could he see us having sex if we hadn't actually done it yet?

Paulo backed up and Landon stood to urge me back onto the bed. I fell onto the mattress and Landon climbed onto the bed with us. Both of them removed their shirts, then raised the comforter, to let me climb underneath.

"Scout, now that you can hear me, I have to ask. Is this really what you want?"

I closed my eyes, and decided then that I wouldn't open them until this was over. There was no way I'd be able to focus when I had Desi inches from the bed.

This wasn't real. This was just first-time nerves.

I nodded, knowing that I had to be careful how I

responded to the voice I wasn't sure was even real. Landon and Paulo could hear me regardless.

One of them reached for my hips and I lifted my body to let them grab my underwear and start tugging them off of me.

"Really? Why are you so tense then? They look like they are trying to fuck a mannequin."

I bit my tongue.

Hands were all over my body, and I couldn't tell who was who. Which I wasn't sure I liked. I popped one eye open just as someone shifted their body between my legs. Paulo's head popped up and he flicked his tongue over his lips.

"Ooh, have fun with that one. He looks like he thinks he's really good at eating pussy because no one's ever told him otherwise."

I gasped with surprise as a mouth went to my nipple. I shifted to see Landon nipping and sucking at my breast while his hand was on the other one, teasing it a little too hard. It took my attention off Desi and Paulo.

Paulo took that as the green light and he shifted lower and spread me even further.

"Can he even find your clit?" Desi asked.

I growled, which caused Paulo to laugh. I stiffened as finally his tongue made contact with my body, parting my lips.

"Ha! See, I told you. He thinks he's a God."

Despite wanting to ignore him, I opened both of my eyes and turned my head. To Landon and Paulo, I was staring at the wall. But I was actually inches away from Desi's shit-eating grin.

This was real.

Somehow, I knew, this was fucking real.

Desi bent down just so he could whisper in my ear.

"This is weird, isn't it?"

I nodded. I was trying really hard to focus on Paulo. His fingers were exploring. He slid one finger inside me and I let out a moan. It didn't necessarily feel good, but it was hard to think about pleasure when I had Desi laughing in my face.

"Fake moans. Bravo." He clapped. "I can't tell you how good it feels to hear those every single time. Have you actually had an orgasm since you started fucking this guy?"

"Yes!" I shouted. Fuck it. If he thought I'd been screwing Landon all this time, might as well let him keep thinking it.

Both men on the bed chuckled. Paulo then sat up. I perked my head up and watched as quickly both men began removing the rest of their clothes. Both Paulo and Landon were wearing whitey-tighties. I cringed as I watched them struggle with their long socks. They were eager and reminded me of teenagers. I watched in embarrassment as the moment they were both out of their undies, they high-fived.

"Where did you find these guys? Did they do a beer bong before this? Hm," Desi frowned. I looked to see what he was looking at. His gaze had flicked over to the naked men holding their cocks and tugging emphatically, while nodding eagerly to each other. "Nothing makes you feel better about yourself than seeing the new guy she's fucking is very unimpressive. Both of them."

I sighed. He wasn't wrong.

Just then, Paulo leaned forward, moving past me to his nightstand. He opened the drawer and pulled out two condoms. He tossed one to Landon, and quickly opened one for himself, sliding it on with ease.

"Was this your way of saying 'Fuck you'? The first few times it really stung, not gonna lie. Now, it's more hilarious than anything."

I had to bite my tongue from asking who he got his information from. Obviously someone had been telling him lies. But why?

"Why is that?" I asked aloud. Both men that I was for sure were real, gave me weird looks.

"Just because we can't produce children doesn't mean we shouldn't be safe," Paulo defended himself as he slid the condom on. I sat up fully then, covering my breasts. Everything about Paulo just rubbed me the wrong way.

"Scout, are you sure you don't want a pill?" Landon asked, reaching his hand out for me.

"What pill? Don't take it." Suddenly Desi's sarcasm was gone. His voice was full of panic. My gaze flashed to him. He had stood and was looking almost— scared.

"I told you I'm okay. No pills for me. Let's—" I took a deep breath. "Let's fucking do this."

"Alright." Paulo grinned and crawled back to me. "Where do you want me?"

"I swear if you let him take your ass before me my feelings are really gonna be hurt."

I glared at Desi, who was rolling his eyes and laughing.

I shook my head. "You said to let you guys do your thing, so I'll trust you to do so." I flinched almost, giving them permission.

"Okay, and if you want to stop we need to have a safe word." Landon looked at Paulo for confirmation. They nodded to each other.

"Please don't say pinapple," Desi mocked.

"Pineapple?" Paulo suggested.

"No!" I yelped as if I'd been pinched. I scanned the room quickly. "Uh—" I panicked, my mind coming up blank.

"Cinnamon," Landon said.

My eyes shot to Desi, who had been pacing. He stopped

dead in his tracks and his eyes went huge. "Don't you fucking dare."

I tightened my resolve and turned to my partners. "Cinnamon is a good one. I don't see myself ever saying that."

"Good. Now lay back, and let's see how many times we can make you come." Landon grinned, almost matter of factly. I didn't feel as sure as he did.

I slid back down and slammed my eyes closed. I let my legs fall wide open.

Paulo moved back between them. He picked my lower half up and pulled me to him. I forced moans as he thrust into me, attempting to coax an orgasm.

"He fucks just as good as he eats pussy. Lucky you." The sarcasm was thick with Desi.

Landon moved closer to my face. I turned away from Desi so Landon could urge his cock into my mouth.

"Not a fan of this. Two at the same time? You're surprising me every single night. This isn't you, and it really shows. It's gonna be embarrassing when some really shitty lays tell everyone that *you* were the bad one in bed."

I forced myself to buck my hips and groan loudly as Paulo treated my vagina like a rodeo horse and Landon seemed to be pretending to be a jackhammer against my mouth. This wasn't even remotely pleasurable for me.

I started counting then, which helped me drown out the grunts from the men on the bed, and the annoyed growls from the one pacing and watching.

Finally, Paulo let out a loud groan which caused Landon to pause and me to raise an eyebrow. He stiffened as he came and then Landon took his place, attempting to give me pleasure.

My body was raw and sore as he pushed inside me. I grimaced.

"Same," Desi smirked as he saw my reaction.

"You like it rough?" Landon smiled down at me. Paulo, having left the bed to dispose of his condom, had returned to kiss my body again.

"Jesus, this is so cringy," Desi laughed.

Something in me snapped then. I sat up and pulled Landon to me. I wrapped my legs around him and rolled us over, putting me on top. I moved my hips, pushing my body down as much as possible, attempting to get him deeper.

Paulo moved behind us, putting his hands on my breasts and kissing my neck as I rode his friend.

I began putting my all into gasping, panting, and calling out their names.

Some pleasure began to tease me, but I knew I wouldn't be coming tonight, so I soon faked one for all of our sakes. I shuddered, let out a small scream, and finally, I dropped against him and said. "I love you."

Landon chuckled lightly. "See, I told you this was a good idea. Just wait until we add another to this." He then started thrusting against me to get his orgasm, and not even a minute later, we were done.

I moved off of him. I felt— disgusting. And not because I'd been with two men at the same time.

Both men moved to clean up, leaving me alone for a moment. I looked for Desi, who was leaning his back against a corner of the room, arms crossed and scowling.

"How does it feel to have fucked all of us tonight?" he asked, before disappearing.

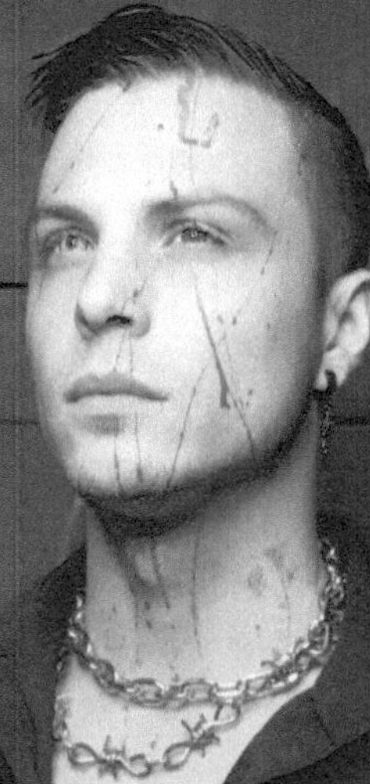

CHAPTER 25

She doesn't fucking love him.

She can't. She fucking cant. She loves me.

I love her.

We're soulmates.

I paced the hotel room I'd been returned to after those two depressing cocks removed themselves from Scout's body. Even if I wasn't there to distract her, I doubted she would have had a good time.

My fists opened and closed. I wanted to kill them both. I could. Both Bloodsheds were just plain embarrassing to the blood community. No one would miss them. If I saw them anytime soon, there was a chance I'd really fucking do it.

My phone rang as I stormed from wall to wall. I paused to rip it from my pocket. Ludovica's name flashed across the screen. I smashed the green button and answered.

"What?" I snapped.

Her child-like voice sighed. "Oh, baby brother. Did you find her?"

I didn't answer so she continued. "I heard that Ginata had

taken her, and that you had found her den. Is she going to give her back?"

"What do you think she is, a fucking dog?" I yelled into the phone. "She's my girlfriend. And no, I haven't even seen Ginata yet."

"Dante said she's been dodging him the last few years. You too? That's odd." I could hear the frown in her voice.

"It is. She refuses to answer my calls. Only texting, claiming she's busy. I am going to try again tonight."

"Be safe, little brother," she warned. I rolled my eyes.

"I've spent thirty years as the deadliest member of our family, and now you tell me to be safe? Do you think I've gone soft?" I asked.

"No, it's just— something's off in Ginata's territory. Don't take any of the pills there. Those come from me and are even worse than the stuff I send to the guys."

"Worse?" I gulped. Guilt pooled in my stomach again, as I recalled what I had done under their influence. I could only imagine what happened to all the other people who visited that house and ate them.

"Definitely. And she gets so many, it's just— weird. Desiderio, be careful. Where are you right now?"

I looked around my trashed hotel room. When I had returned to the room, I had a bit of a meltdown. I'd be paying to fix this. I sighed. "A hotel. Why?"

"I'll join you. Don't do anything rash."

Too late.

"Desiderio, please. Let me help you."

"Like you did last time?" I snapped. The last time I saw her in person, she had planned a kidnapping and murder attempt on Scout.

"That was different. Before she... she proved herself," her voice trembled.

"With what? She didn't have to prove shit to you Ludovica. You should have trusted me."

"I did. It was her I didn't trust. But I do now and want to help you get her back. We need her."

"Why?"

"Sunshine."

I blinked. Sunshine was the poison Charles Matheson had created. He was Corrine's ex, and a monster. He was the epitome of vampire elitism. I thought my family, the Amato's, were bad, this guy put them to shame. Matheson was cruel, just like the poison he had created.

Scout had been stabbed with a knife dipped in the golden liquid. As did Aleida, for that matter.

"What does that have to do with anything?"

"She healed quick from it. Your ex took a lot longer, and all the others we've tested aren't doing great either. She's special."

My blood ran cold. "You think I'm going to let you get your hands on Scout to test that shit on her?" I spat.

"No," Ludovica replied calmly. "I want some of her blood. I want to study her lineage. Why is she reacting to things differently than others?"

I grew silent. That was a good question. The vampire that had visited me at my apartment came to mind. He had come all the way from Mexico, claiming that Scout was the niece of a high priestess. Could she really have special blood?

"If you hurt her, I will end up killing you. That's not an empty threat amongst friends," I told her. There was a pause, and I could almost see little Ludovica considering my words.

"I understand. Learning how Sunshine works, and if there's a way to combat it is worth it. I won't touch her without her permission. Where exactly are you?"

I rattled off the address.

"K, don't be stupid. I'll be there soon."

I hung up with her, and looked around the room.

Shit.

I needed to clean this up. There was no way I'd be able to sleep here with the blankets torn to shreds. Hopefully room service could bring me some more.

Ludovica knocked my hotel room door that next night.

"How did you catch a plane so quick?" I asked.

She laughed. "Private flight. How are you? You look terrible." She pushed herself inside my room and sighed. "Why am I surprised?"

I cringed as I looked around at it as well. I had attempted to fix what I could, but other things, such as the coffee maker, a few lamps, and one of the nightstands, had been reduced to a broken pile on the floor.

I shut the door and watched as she stepped over everything to sit at the desk. She was dressed in a pink ruffled dress, and her innocent face held annoyance.

"Elvie," I started, moving slow, and sitting on the edge of the bed. "You said you think Scout is special. How so?"

She smiled, her fangs, much like everything else about her, were tiny and almost childlike.

"Well, at first I thought it was just pure luck that she had healed fast from the Sunshine. Corrine and I have been trying to recreate it, and we've come up with an almost exact copycat recipe. Nothing in it strikes out as the key to her not reacting like the others. But then, I heard about your guys'…" she gave me a knowing look and I blinked in confusion. "Kink? You drank her blood, and you didn't die."

"So? Arsenio was the one who told me about it. He said he's done it before," I defended. I didn't judge her on whatever she liked to do in bed. I was a little offended. She shook her head.

"No he hasn't. When have you ever heard Arsenio not brag about ridiculous stuff just for attention? I've done my research, little brother." She tapped her temple. "Did she ever drink from you?"

I licked my lips, and then nodded. "What happened both times?"

My eyes went to the ceiling. I couldn't believe I was having this conversation with the vampire I considered family. "When I drank from her, the bite made her sick, but that was because I drank too much. She tasted…" I couldn't look Ludovica in the eye as I spoke. "Really good. She had to go home and rest. And then her leg looked weird for a few weeks."

"How so?" She cocked her head.

"It was almost like a zombie bite, like in the movies? It was green and purple. You could see her veins and broken blood vessels. I was really worried for a while, but then it finally healed and she only had a small scar from my teeth."

"It scarred? Interesting." She leaned forward, her eyes alight with excitement. "What about you? When she drank from you?"

I shook my head. "That wasn't necessarily from pleasure. She had lost a lot of blood and I was the only resource available."

"Did it feel good then too?" She smiled, and I cringed.

"This is really weird. It feels like you're getting your rocks off by hearing about me doing it."

She rolled her eyes. "Please. I like hearing about it because I've never heard of any vampires drinking from each other and surviving. Past the first time to fully transition, of course."

I nodded. That was all part of the process. Your human

body died, and to complete the change from human to vampire you had to drink from another Bloodborn.

"Our blood is poisonous. That's why we like humans so much. To answer your original question, yes. I think Scout is special. But in what ways?" She pouted her lips and tapped her chin thoughtfully.

I struggled to come up with a way to bring it up, but finally decided to just bite the bullet. "Ludovica, have you heard of Magdalena, the High Priestess of Blood?"

Her eyes lit up and she straightened her spine. "Yes. She has a colony in Mexico. What about her?"

"Is she special?"

She rocked her head side to side. "Some people think so. I've heard some people say she was the reincarnation of an Aztec Goddess. She has quite a devoted following. I've only heard stories though, and they're all horrific. It keeps me from heading to see myself. Why?"

I hesitated. Did I start telling others before I told Scout? If she really is related to this once Aztec Goddess, maybe she was special. But, she could also be in danger.

"I'm going to tell you something, and in return, I want your help. Scout may need our protection. All of ours," I stressed. She nodded.

"Deal. What do you know?" She leaned in and I found myself doing so as well.

"I think she may be related to Magdalena. Someone came to my place, claiming he was her brother, which would make Scout the High Priestess' niece."

"Does the brother have special powers?" she asked quickly, her eyes lighting up. I shrugged.

"How would I know? He literally just showed up looking for her. I wasn't trying to get his whole life story. I'm not even sure it's true."

She scowled. "Does it sound plausible?"

I frowned. "Well, Scout has no family. She is Hispanic, and he claimed his parents fled to United States to save her from Magdalena. Maybe?"

"Hmm," She stood then, and continued tapping her chin. "I think you're right in trying to protect her. If he's looking for her, there's probably a reason for it. Maybe she's getting weak or something. When was this?"

"Right before I left to come here."

She blinked and then it hit me why she was staring at me like that.

"I don't know if he followed me."

"Okay, well we need to find Scout then. She may actually be in danger."

"I know where she's at." I glanced at the clock by the now-broken TV. "Or where she's going. She works at an upscale nightclub."

"Let's go." She started toward the door but I stopped.

"I can't. They kicked me out last night for not following the dress code." I scowled.

"Oh? What were you wearing?"

I looked down at my feet, slightly embarrassed. "Basically this." I motioned to myself, wearing a grey undershirt, a blue plaid flannel over it, and ripped jeans. Yesterday I had on a different shirt.

My little sister with the eye for fashion rolled her eyes.

"What are they, a suit and tie?"

"Something like that," I mumbled.

"What's the name of her work? I'll send someone to watch, and tomorrow night we'll go. You'll be presentable then." She walked to the door and turned, looking around the room again. "Desiderio," she sighed. "Get your shit together." She shook her head as she excited.

The next night she burst into my room with a dress bag. She tossed it on the bed, and demanded I go get dressed.

"Shower and do your hair too." She pinched her nose, and I shot her the middle finger before doing as told.

The suit she had brought me was all black, including the dress shirt. It was slimming and fit perfectly, which given her expertise, was not surprising. I did my hair as she directed with a comb and some gel, and slid the black dress shoes on. I forced a smile in the mirror, and Ludovica grimaced.

"Never do that smile in public, ever. Come on." She reached for my hand and started pulling me out of the room.

She had chosen a pink cocktail dress, which I was almost sure she'd brought. It was covered in pink feathers and looked just as ridiculous as all her other clothing.

She had a town car waiting for us. We slid into the back and it took us to the club.

Just like the other night, there were vampires lined up outside.

"I text Ginata earlier, and she put us on the list. She's not joining us, but we'll get in quick. Come on." She reached for my hand when the car stopped and pulled me out. Begrudgingly, I followed her out and to the front of the line.

The bouncer from before was the one to greet us. He recognized me immediately. "I see you've found someone to steal a suit from."

I bit my tongue as my rage began to flare. Everything about this place pissed me right the fuck off. Elvie cleared her throat.

"Ginata is our sister. We're here visiting and wanted a drink. She said there would be a table for us."

He scowled, but looked at his tablet. "Name?"

"Ludovica."

He found it quickly and nodded. He stepped aside and let us in. "Enjoy your night," he said rather curtly.

We were met by a cocktail waitress dressed in a silver rhinestone bra and shorts. She took us through the dark room and sat us at a table in the back, away from prying eyes.

All the while, I scanned the room for Scout. She was nowhere to be seen.

"So, how were Dante and Tully?" Ludovica asked, after a second waitress took our drink orders, and brought us a bowl of red pills. I slid the bowl away from me and shrugged. "I heard you burned their house down."

I nodded. "They haven't changed. Quite literally. Tully was still in his old hockey jerseys. Still annoying as hell."

That made her eyes sparkle and she laughed. "Oh, how I miss the good old days with all of us in one place."

"We should do it sometime. A weekend or something," I shrugged. Her face paled and she shook her head vehemently.

"Oh no. Tully and I— it's too hard," she swallowed and just then the waitress brought her a large glass of blood and me a glass of cinnamon whiskey. She waited until the server was gone to finish her thought. "We don't get the ending you and Scout get."

There was awkward silence for a moment as I considered her words. Tully had also mentioned something to that effect, and guilt welled up inside my gut. Was I the lucky one out of all of us?

Scout was still nowhere in sight, but I finally caught a glimpse of a familiar shape. It was his movements I caught first, as I had seen those so many times it was a joke at this point, but his face only confirmed it. That was Landon behind the bar. I clenched my fists under the table and could feel the heat rising out of my body as I fought the urge to use my cards on him. He would die a slow death.

"Elvie," I started, trying to calm myself. "Have you ever heard of soulmates that when one is far away and doing something, the other person gets transported like a ghost and is forced to watch but not interact with them?"

Her face told it all. Her mouth fell open and her eyes went wide. "No! Did you? When? Tell me everything. What was she doing when it happened?"

I nodded and raised my glass. I pointed to Landon before taking a large gulp.

"Having sex with that guy."

CHAPTER 26

Desi

"This is insane. I've—I've never heard of anything like this before. Do you know what that means?"

Elvie was gushing after I explained to her everything that had been happening to me over the last few weeks. I had blown her mind.

She sat back, stunned. Her eyes glazed over as she took in what I had just said.

"I really don't. Do you?" I finished my third drink, and caught our waitresses gaze. She was talking animatedly with a group of fellow waitresses, and appeared to be in distress. She turned back toward them and a moment later, a different vampire woman left the group and came toward us, smiling wide.

"Hi, so Prue, your original waitress has to leave. She has a family emergency. We're going to get you a new waitress for the night. Can I help you while we shift some things around?"

"Fireball, three fingers, no ice."

She grinned tightly and looked toward Ludovica.

"Just another glass of blood please. Warmed."

The stand-in rushed away, leaving us to our conversation. Elvie's face was still washed in shock.

"Desiderio, I think she really might be something special. That's why they want her. *They know*." The words came out of her mouth and slid down my body in an icy chill.

And then, there she was.

"Hi, I'm Scout and I'll be taking over for—" her voice caught in her throat as her eyes ran across the booth. "Desi."

She barely glanced at Ludovica. Her eyes were locked on mine. I had to look away. Shame filled my face. The last time we were truly in the same room together, I had hurt her.

She looked beautiful. Her long messy hair was in a high pony-tail, just like the other waitresses. Her uniform was tight and sexy, but the tattoos covering her body made her look fun. The red lips, her beautiful face, all of it, Scout. In the flesh.

"Why are you here?" she asked sharply.

The sudden change in her face and demeanor caused my stomach to turn so hard I almost threw up the alcohol. I swallowed it down and took a long, steady breath.

"To get you back," I said. I sat up straight. "Come on, we're leaving."

"Oh, is that how that works? Nice fucking try. You should leave."

"Scout, we need to talk to you about some things. You can't stay here." Elvie reached her hand out but Scout took a step back as if it were poison.

"And I should believe you?"

She turned around and stormed off toward the bar, where her boyfriend stood beside our drinks. They had a small conversation, glancing at our table, and then she scowled. A moment later she was sliding them onto a tray and bringing them over. She slapped them down so hard the liquid in both glasses spilled over the rims and onto the table.

"Did you tell him who you're serving tonight?" I asked, my voice low and mocking.

She glared. "If I did, you'd be kicked out."

"We're guests of Ginata's," Ludovica said calmly. I noticed she looked at Scout as if she were seeing the Aztec Goddess herself. "We won't hurt you."

"You're psycho."

"We're the ones keeping you safe," Ludovica argued.

Scout laughed and put her hand on her hip. "Keeping me safe? The only person I need to be protected from is *him*." She shot a look at me.

A moment later, Landon stepped up beside her. He put his hand on her hip and my jaw instantly clenched. I started to emit a low growl that I couldn't control.

"Is everything okay here?" he asked us with a tight smile.

"Yes. It's fine," Scout told him through clenched teeth.

"It didn't look fine from the bar." He furrowed his brow. "What's going on. Do you know each other?" He looked from me to Scout.

"It doesn't matter. It's fine." With Landon's hand assisting her, Scout turned around and took a step away from the table. As she started away, she turned her head and we made full eye contact for the first time. "He's just some stupid fucking loser."

A full week passed with me sitting at that club, watching Scout work. Ludovica decided to stay in the colony, but she needed time to dig up more information on Magdalena, so she didn't return to the club.

That first night stung. Scout didn't speak to me after Landon's pop in. The second night I requested her as my waitress again. To which, after a very generous tip to the owner, I was allowed. She didn't speak to me then either. The third night was much of the same, but I did get one request at the end of the night.

"Please, don't follow me home tonight."

"Why? Is Landon taking you home? I've noticed that I've gotten some sleep lately. That's a nice change of pace."

"What does that even mean?" she mumbled, leaning into the table.

"Every single time you've fucked, I've seen it," I told her.

She gave me a look I couldn't put my finger on, but said nothing.

"But, based on that threesome, him and his little buddy aren't much of a competition. Together or solo," I smirked.

She frowned, her lips trembling for a moment. But then she straightened her spine and shook her head. "It doesn't matter either way. He's not you and that alone is fantastic."

"Fantastic?" I laughed. "That's not the word I'd use to describe what I've seen."

"Oh yeah? And what word would you use?"

I thought for a moment, before smirking and answering her. "Tepid."

She stormed away then, and despite her request, I did follow her home. I didn't try to go in. I just made sure she got into her apartment safely. And I did again the next day, and the next.

Each day, she got bolder. She would say smart comments to me, and I'd respond just as snarky. She'd storm off, and a half hour later return to do it all over again. It became a routine that I didn't entirely mind.

At the end of the week, toward the end of her shift, she

came over and gave me a new drink.

"I wouldn't bother tomorrow. I won't be here all weekend."

"Why?" I demanded.

"Landon is taking me away for the weekend."

"Where? With that other frat guy?"

She refused to look at me, I noticed. In fact, she didn't look happy at all. "Him, and possibly a third. They want me to try it out."

"Try out what?" I spat.

Three men? No fucking way.

"It's normal here, Desi. Every woman has multiple men."

"Okay, that's all good and dandy, but is it what you want?"

"It doesn't really matter what I want."

"That's what consent is, isn't it?" I scoffed, and her head shot up. Her eyes turned from sad to pissed in an instant.

"You're the last one to ever lecture me on consent. Maybe I will take all three. Or maybe twelve. I don't care how many men I'm with, as long as none of them are you."

It was as if she had thrown water in my face. I sat back, stunned.

"Look," she relaxed and rolled her eyes. She leaned against my table and nodded to the bar, where Landon had been working all week. "I'm just letting you know I won't be here all weekend. I'll be on a boat with some of his friends for a few nights."

"A boat? Where are you going?" I demanded.

"Nowhere. We're just floating. He's got a friend coming in from Europe. It's whatever." She waved off my concerns. "Just don't bother coming in. I won't be here."

"What the fuck do you expect me to do?"

She scoffed. "Like I really give a fuck. Desi, give it up."

She turned away then, and I reached out to grab her wrist. She stopped short as my fingers wrapped around her small arm. "I'm going to suggest you take your hand off me before I rip it off your body and bash your head in with it," she said through clenched teeth, not looking at me. Her tone told me that she'd do it. I let go and instantly apologized.

She ignored me, and we didn't speak the rest of the night. I felt horrible for grabbing her like that. I ended up leaving early. I slid her tip under my glass and booked it for my vehicle. I wanted to wait to see her home, but I needed to rethink my plans.

If she was planning on taking three cocks just to spite me, I had to figure out how to stop it. I couldn't watch that. Two was enough. Fuck, one was enough, if I was honest with myself. Every time I had to see her smile as someone else felt the pleasure that came from sex with her, I died a little inside.

I returned to my hotel and paced until exhaustion made me sleep. I had to think of something to stop her from getting on that boat.

Out of sheer desperation, I called Ginata when I woke up. She didn't answer, which was to be expected. She instead text me right away.

Me: I need help. Scout is getting on a boat this weekend. Where can I find that?

Ginata: Why are you drawn to this vampire so hard? It's unusual for you, Desiderio.

Me: We're soulmates. It's hard to explain.

Ginata: I think the entire concept is outdated. Surely you can't think you are the only true love for her?

I clenched my phone tightly, staring at the message. I could hear the sarcasm in her voice. God, she hadn't changed either.

> Me: She is mine, and I am hers. Where is the boat?

She didn't reply, so I decided I'd get showered and find the thing myself. I was pulling on my coat when I finally got a reply back.

> Ginata: I think you highly underestimate the allure of our way of life. Good luck, Desiderio.

I shook my head and shoved the phone into my pocket. Fuck her. Ginata really thought that three stranger cocks were better for Scout than mine? I spent three decades pining after Scout. I killed ten-thousand people just to get her back. I wasn't going to lose her over three dicks who combined gave her maybe six inches.

I was just about to storm out of my room when a frantic knock came from the other side. I ripped the door open to find Ludovica smiling wide up at me.

"I'm leaving," I snarled.

She nodded. "Take this." She pulled out a flask and handed it to me. I raised it to my face to get a better look. It was a smooth, jet black with a faint cross on the front.

"What is it?" I shook it, hearing liquid sloshing around.

"I don't have a name for it yet, but if sunshine touches you, pour that on or in the affected area."

"You're a chemist now?" I smirked.

"I dabble."

I raised my eyebrows and shoved the flask into my pocket. "You think I'll need this?"

She frowned. "I have no idea. Something about this place gives me bad vibes. Be safe, Desiderio." She put her small hand on my forearm as an act of compassion. I stared at it for a moment before nodding and brushing past her.

"Thanks. I've got to go."

Getting in my rental car, I had no idea where to even begin looking for Scout and the boat she was probably already on.

So, instead, I drove to the bar. I was let in without hesitation, as I was Ginata's VIP guest. I went straight to the bar, where an unfamiliar vampire was taking drink orders. He came over with a polite smile and asked me what drink I wanted.

"Actually, I'm looking for Landon. I'm supposed to be meeting him and his girlfriend," I called out. The new bartender grinned wide.

"Ah, so you're their fourth? Good for you. I hear good things about the girl. She's Bloodborn."

I clenched my teeth together and forced a nod. He looked uneasy but pulled out his phone anyway.

"I'll text him. You know you don't have to hide here. You can take off the glasses." He pointed to my face.

I blinked. I had grown so used to wearing them in public over the last three decades I often times forgot about them completely. I chose to leave them on.

The bartender went to help other patrons but, within five minutes, returned to me with a dock address.

"The party is there. Have fun." He winked.

I fought the urge to rip out his throat and instead thanked him and quickly exited before I did something stupid.

The address was easy to find with my phone. Thankfully, I was there in thirty minutes, and the boat was still attached to the dock.

Lights were on all over, and music was blaring loudly from somewhere inside of it. As I stepped out of my car, I noticed someone large standing on the dock.

Security.

I strolled over to him, hands in my pockets and everything. I smiled at him, but he didn't smile back.

"I'm here to meet with Scout and Landon," I told him.

"The party is full. Go back the other way."

I opened my mouth and furrowed my brows. "I'm confused. They invited me here. For the—" I paused, swallowing the lump in my throat. "Fun."

The man laughed, causing my blood to start boiling. "Fun? I've heard stories about the people already up there. Fun is not what they are gonna do tonight."

I crossed my arms. "Yeah? And what are they planning?"

"Let's put it this way, when that group is done with that pretty little Bloodborn, no one else will want her."

"What the hell are you talking about?"

Red. My vision was turning red.

The man eyed me with suspicion and shook his head. He pointed to my car. "Leave. Before, I don't give you the option."

My tongue ran over my fangs, and I laughed out loud.

"I love your confidence. I suggest you move and let me on that boat before I make it the last thing you hear."

He scoffed. "You? I'm twice your size, easily. What are you gonna do?"

I raised my fists up and cracked my knuckles. It'd been a long time since I dealt with an asshole like this. I grinned as I slid my glasses off. He looked at me with surprise, and I stepped forward. "Oh, I'm so glad you asked."

CHAPTER 27

Scout

The bottle felt hot in my dress pocket. The liquid inside the tiny vial burned my side almost as hard as it had when I'd been stabbed months ago.

Sunshine.

Ginata had come to my apartment after my shift. She'd warned me that Desi would try to come for me, and I needed to be prepared.

"Prepared for what?" I asked as she tried to offer me the bottle of amber liquid. I stared at it without taking it.

She thrust it into my hand, and I flinched, almost dropping it. "Prepared to kill him if you need to. Desiderio is a monster that's been left unchecked for too long."

"Kill him? Aren't you supposed to be family?" I clutched the bottle only because I didn't want it to drop and break all over me. I recognized what it was immediately.

She crossed her arms and huffed. "That vampire has not been a brother to me in many years, if ever. He needs to be taken out."

"Then why don't you do it?" I replied sharply. I wasn't a

pawn to use in some Seven Sins game I wasn't aware of. She rolled her eyes.

"Because I can't. I'm not telling you to do anything to him. Just— if you start to feel afraid of him again, you've got something to stop him."

"He won't find me," I said, although even I didn't believe it. She gave me a knowing smile.

"We all know how smart Desiderio is. If he wants you, he'll have you. Take care, Scout. I need to go before the sun comes out." She left just as quickly as she had come, leaving me stressed all day about it.

But now, I was here on the boat, down below with Landon, Paulo, and some other Bloodshed vampire, they introduced me to named Kyle. I wasn't too enthused by the way he looked at me. In fact, I wanted to leave as soon as possible.

The music had been turned up loud and I'd been given a drink. I didn't want to get drunk, but the idea that in a few hours I'd be in bed down below with all of them with Desi possibly watching as some weird ghost thing was terrifying. So, I drank.

Landon came over to where I was sitting with my legs locked tightly and my drink shaking in my hands. He put his arm around me and grinned.

"Hey, are you okay?"

I forced a smile despite my shaking stomach. "Yeah, just a little nervous. How does this even work?"

He laughed. "We'll take the lead again. You just sit back like last time." He leaned forward and pressed a chaste kiss on my forehead. "We'll be taking off soon. We forgot some stuff and had to send someone to grab them."

"What stuff?" I tilted my head.

He laughed and took a long gulp of his beer. "Lube, stuff to stretch you, and more alcohol."

Stuff to what?

I blinked and licked my lips. I couldn't do this. I had to get out now. This was too much for me. I leapt up, spilling my drink. "I need to get some cold air."

"You want me to go with you?" Landon asked, standing with me. I shook my head.

"No, I'm good. I just need a minute. Go, have fun with your friends." I eyed Paulo and Kyle. They were laughing and looking at me with hungry eyes.

I sprinted up the stairs and onto the deck. I was on solid ground when I heard the lurching of the large boat taking off. I let out a small gasp and wavered as the boat began to rock slightly.

I went slowly to the edge and grabbed the metal railing tight. I stared out into the dark and felt a tear slide down the left side of my face. What was I doing? I was miserable. This wasn't the life I wanted.

I wanted Desi.

"You okay?"

The familiar voice caused me to spin around so quickly I almost fell over the railing. Anger filled me instantly, replacing the sadness in seconds.

"How did you get on board?" I hissed. Desi stood there, looking so fucking charming. He had that sarcastic smile I adored, and his hands stuffed in his pockets as if he were out for a casual stroll and we just happened to meet.

"Do you want me to leave?" He tilted his head and raised his eyebrows.

"Yes," I said firmly. "I told you we were over."

"Yeah, but why?" He took a step forward and I scooted to the left. He froze. We stared at each other and when he moved again, so did I. "Scout, this is stupid. I've learned my lesson. Come home." He extended his hand. I shook my head and gulped.

"No, Desi. I can't. I'm not—"

"My bitch?" His words were ice and his eyes suddenly turned from amused to rage.

I nodded and slowly, my hand went to my pocket where the the bottle sat at my hip. I reached into it, Desi watched me do so cautiously. He straightened and took a step back as I pulled out the small bottle with the sharp knife attached to the cork top.

"Yeah. Did you forget what you did to me?" I asked, my voice starting to shake as the horrible memories of that night began to flood my brain.

"I—" Desi opened and closed his mouth. He seemed to be struggling to find the words. *Good.*

Confidence soared in me. I looked toward the stairs where Landon and his friends were still partying loudly. They couldn't hear us. Ginata's suggestion came to my mind then. Maybe I should just end this once and for all. Could I truly be free then?

I walked backward, toward the back of the boat. I had a plan— kind of. I walked until I hit the railing with my back. Desi followed me slowly, his arms out, almost as if he was ready to pounce at any minute.

"Do you know what this is?" I pulled out the Sunshine from my pocket. A gust of cold air suddenly ran through us. It blew my hair all over and I shivered.

"Yes. How did you get it?" he asked. His words were just as cautious as his stance.

"Doesn't matter. If you come any closer, I'll uncap this and use it."

He blinked. His mismatched eyes processed what I said

and he straightened. Slowly, I uncapped it and pulled the short blade drenched in the vampire poison out. It dripped onto the wooden floor between my feet.

"You shouldn't make empty threats to someone like me. Either fucking do it or not." He stepped toward me and snatched the bottle from my hand. Without another thought I lurched forward with the tiny knife and sunk it into his right pectoral. He gasped and stumbled back, taking the blade with him. He dropped the glass bottle and it shattered, the liquid splashing all over. I leapt up and fell against the railing. I let out a small scream as I scrambled to hold onto it.

When I regained my balance I looked for Desi. He had fallen to his knees and stared in horror at the knife in his chest.

My heart was beating furiously as I watched him respond to me stabbing him. He gulped and his shocked expression turned into one of annoyance. Finally, his eyes found mine again as he wrapped a hand around the knife. Tensing his jaw, he yanked. It made a loud squelching sound, and blood poured from the wound as he tossed the blade into the water.

What had I done?

"Did that make you feel good?" he gasped as he struggled to stand back up. "Hurting me like I hurt you?"

Keeping his eyes locked on mine, he placed one hand over the hole and the other dove into his pocket. He then pulled out a flask. I watched with wide eyes as he used his teeth to flick the cap open. He then poured it's contents into his mouth and when it was all gone, he tossed that too into the water.

He closed his eyes and took a long, deep breath. Then, he removed the hand off his chest. The blood had stopped spilling out. A slow smile spread over his face, and he reopened his eyes. Smirking, he slid his jacket off and pulled the shirt off completely. My mouth fell open as I saw that the gash I had created from stabbing him was gone. The blood he'd lost was the only indicator he'd been hurt.

Desi stared at me, his entire body heaving. I stared at his chest, my eyes raked over his bare form. The flashes of all the times his arms embraced me shoved through my pain. I hated how I still wanted him.

I shook my head and turned quickly away from him. I couldn't do this. I couldn't be with Landon, Paulo, and Kyle all at once. They didn't love me. They were robots, living in Ginata's fucked up community. They were told to be with me and they blindly followed. That wasn't something I wanted. But, I couldn't go home either. Whether I wanted to or not.

I gripped the railing and steeled myself. I lifted my leg, put a boot on the first rail, and pulled myself up.

"Scout—"

My name on his lips spurred me onward. I scrambled up and threw my hands out to balance myself. I was teetering, and my nerves were freaking out. I closed my eyes tightly as the wind came back with vengeance. I could not let myself look at the water. The sound of it lapping the moving boat was already terrifying enough.

Suddenly, thick, familiar arms were wrapped around my hips, holding me firm. "Scout, stop."

"What do you think happens when a Bloodborn commits suicide?" I asked, keeping my eyes closed. My voice was shaky, as I began to make a decision. I didn't want to do this anymore. Any of it. I had spent too long hoping that once my curse was broken I'd find happiness, but that never happened. I was still—me.

I leaned forward and Desi held me tighter. "You end up like me."

What?

My eyes popped open and I looked down at him. He was staring up at me, with his beautiful cursed eyes. Was that true? Would I still live, but be forced to bare the mark of what I had done?

"You didn't kill yourself," I said. He smirked.

"Didn't I? At that diner, three men came in shooting and I stood up to shield you from a bullet. If I had just let them shoot you, I would have died that night and turned into the proper Bloodborn I was meant to be, and you would have healed just fine. I knew what I was doing."

I took in his words. He gave up his royal blood status —for me?

"And I'd do it again." His voice came out softer, almost comforting. I found my heart wanting to give in, but I couldn't. I turned back toward the water defiantly.

"I'm going to pull you down now," he said carefully, and began to hold my weight more.

"Why so you can rape me again?" I snapped and suddenly his arms dropped me so quick I let out a scream as I lurched forward and lost all footing.

"What?" I heard him say as I slipped and fell into the water.

It was ice hitting ice. I felt my always-cold body hit that water with such force I lost my breath. Water filled my lungs as I scrambled to kick and wave my arms above water.

Finally, my head popped up and I began spitting out the water. I kicked as hard as I could to keep afloat as I pushed for air. A splash beside me caused me to dip back under the water just as I had managed a full gulp of air.

Strong arms wrapped around me and together, we kicked and fought against the waves to reach the surface.

Our heads found themselves again touching cold air and this time, with Desi's hands holding me steady, we remained above the water. "Are you fucking insane?" I coughed.

"Are you?" he shouted. We both kicked and began moving toward the boat quickly moving away from us. We were too far from the dock to swim to it, we'd have to catch the boat. "You think I did that on purpose?"

"What? Rape me?" I said the words again and he hissed.

"Stop saying that. Will you fucking listen to me for a minute?"

"Why?" I demanded. "Give me," I paused, my head dipping under the water. "One good reason why I should listen to you."

"Because I was under the influence," he said.

"What are you talking about?" I paddled harder.

"They gave me candy. It came from Elvie, it had something in it that made me not myself."

The candy.

I blinked, and stopped swimming for a minute. I fell down under the water again and Desi reached for me, pulling me back up.

"Scout, come on. Please don't give up. Not like this," he pleaded.

"You had the candy?" I sputtered. I turned to face him in the water.

"A shit ton of it. I'm sorry. I didn't know. It made my mind— blank."

I knew exactly what he meant. When Tully took me to that room the night before my assault, I felt blank too.

In the water, Desi held onto me, both of us kicking to stay above water. He pulled me tighter to him and I broke.

"Desi," my chin quivered as the realization that we had to talk about this finally hit me. "I said no. I asked you to stop."

"Yeah but—" he stopped defending himself when he saw

the tears streaming down my wet face. "Scout, I— I'm sorry."

"I know." I sniffled. I let go of him and turned toward the boat. "Let's get back on the boat and we can talk about it later."

He tried to reach for me again, but I turned back and dove under the water to swim faster. I reached the boat in record time and started looking for the ladder Landon had told me about.

Desi found it first and called me over to it. Begrudgingly I did so, and together, we climbed back onto the boat.

Falling over the rails in heavy, wet heaps, we must have finally alerted the party downstairs that Desi was here. The music stopped and footsteps could be heard coming up the stairs. I panicked and looked toward a sopping wet and bare-chested Desi. He was blinking rapidly, trying to get his bearings.

"What the hell? Who are you?" Landon demanded. I sat up and opened my mouth. A coughing fit came as water left my chest. He hurried over to me and shoved his hands under my arms.

"Don't you dare touch her," Desi growled. We both turned as he stood and clenched his fists.

I pushed Landon away and scrambled up. My clothes were heavy with water and were pulling me down.

"Aren't you the creep that's been harassing her every night? Oh, I'm done. You're dead," Landon snarled.

Paulo and Kyle came forward, standing beside their friend.

Desi looked at them and laughed.

"Woah, what's with his eyes?" Kyle asked.

"That's—not right. Something's wrong with him," Paulo said, shaking his head and taking a step back.

"That's right. There is something wrong with me," Desi said, moving closer. His damp boots made a wet, squishing sound on the wood.

"He's psychotic," Landon smirked, but the uneasiness was clear on his face.

"And? Is that a problem?" Desi's eyes flicked to me as he asked. That was a good question. It had so many layers to it the three men I was supposed to take to bed tonight wouldn't understand.

There was a long pause as I tried to decide what I wanted to do. Did I dare follow my heart that needed Desi more than life, or listen to my brain that shouted that he was a walking red flag?

Taking a deep breath, I stepped toward Desi. He grinned, and then launched at Landon.

CHAPTER 28

Blood was splattered across my face before I could react. I stiffened and stared at the scene in front of me. Desi with his face shoved into Landon's dismembered throat. Pieces of skin and tissue flew into the air as Desi lifted his head and spit them out.

Screams rang out from Kyle and Paulo as they fled. Their frantic yelling caused me to snap out of it and hurry to tear Desi off Landon's limp body. I dropped down to my knees and looked at him. His ice-blue eyes were blank and he was convulsing, coughing up more blood. I reached for his cheek, and Desi snatched me by the wrist.

"You wouldn't be doing that if you knew what he had planned for you tonight."

I looked up at him and glared. "Get over yourself. If the biggest issue you have is who I'm fucking then you're one sad little man."

"He," Desi let go of me and stood up. He kicked the barely-alive vampire. "Was going to sacrifice you to a fertility demon."

"What?" I sat back as if Landon were poison. "Do those even exist?"

"Who even fucking knows. Seems pretty contradicting to me, but who knows with these brainless fucks. Ginata is doing weird shit here. We need to go." He extended his hand to me and I stared at it for a long moment before taking it.

"You can't just leave him like this." I glanced down. Landon was still choking, but the vampire blood was healing his wound already. "He'll be fine in five minutes. He'll come after us."

Desi raised an eyebrow. "Your teeth are just as sharp as mine are. Finish the job."

"You started it!" I protested, letting go of his hand and crossing my arms under my chest.

Desi put his hands up in protest. "Look, if you want him and his friends to run a train on you and then sacrifice you to Satan by all means, let him live. But I'm not touching that again." He grimaced and stuck out his tongue. "His blood tastes horrendous."

I sighed and looked from Desi to Landon. He had a point, but Landon? Goofy, sweet Landon couldn't possibly have planned something so… insane.

"Scout, Nerd, baby, I'm going to get one of the others. They'll show you. Hold him down just in case," he warned me as he left, following the path the others had taken when they ran.

I stared down at Landon. The rate of which the tendons, muscles, and skin were growing back was alarming. Was I setting myself up to be murdered in two minutes?

"Was he telling the truth?" I demanded, lifting my boot and stomping it onto his chest.

Landon's eyes moved. They blinked and then found me. His eyes went wide as I repeated my question. He tried to turn his head but his neck wasn't fully healed and he stopped short. I pushed my weight into my foot, crushing him further.

"Why?" I asked, my heart breaking a little. Not over Landon, but the trust he had let me build by being with him. "You were supposed to be safe. You were—" I frowned, replaying our entire relationship. Then, Desi reappeared, pulling Paulo along while holding a knife to his throat. "Boring," I finished. I stepped over Landon.

"Tell her the truth. Why you brought her here," Desi demanded.

"Fuck you," Paulo spat.

Desi pressed the knife further into his throat. "I've killed ten-thousand people just to know that woman's name. I have no problem killing you if you roll your eyes again. Speak."

"It's not fair! You disgusting… Bloodborns!" Paulo cried out. I cocked my head in confusion. His face contorted as if it pained him to explain himself. "You have no idea how privileged you are. We just want what you have."

"What do I have?" I pointed to myself. I was the poorest vampire I knew.

"The chance to have a legacy," he said, softer. Paulo began to cry then, blood tears streamed down his face. "To have a family."

I blinked. A family? That's what this was all about? Baby bats?

More vampires?

Jesus Christ.

"You were gonna murder me to try to have kids? With who? I'm the only fucking one with eggs!" I dropped my foot from Landon and stormed over to the crying Bloodshed. "What kind of logic is this?"

"It's easy to find another willing participant once we can reproduce. We just needed someone special." Landon's voice came out raspy from behind us. I spun around to see my now ex-boyfriend standing and rubbing his throat.

"Special? Bloodborns aren't special. What the hell is going on here?"

"Bloodborns, as a whole aren't, but you are," Paulo said and without hesitation Desi slit his throat. The vampire dropped to the ground and Desi went down with him, using the knife paired with his inhuman strength to bring the weapon deeper through his neck. Paulo fought but was no match for Desiderio Amato, the Seven Sin of Wrath.

"What does he mean? I'm special?" I asked.

"Ginata told us!" Landon exclaimed. He kept his distance, which was smart. "You've got some kind of power beyond normal Bloodborns. It's in your blood."

"It's those pills she feeds you." I shook my head and rolled my eyes. "All of you have gone batshit insane. Where's the other one?" I shouted down at Desi, who was currently holding Paulo's head in his lap. He tossed it down and stood. "He went easier than this guy. The captain is taking us back to shore and we can leave. Just take care of this one." He nodded to Landon.

"Why do I have to?" I pouted, stomping my foot.

"Because he's the one that started this all. Fucking do it, Scout," Desi snarled.

"Fine. But then you're explaining what the hell he's talking about." I stepped over Paulo's body and started toward Landon. He put his hands up and started backing away.

"Please, just let me be. I won't tell anyone what happened. You guys can leave without Ginata knowing."

"Why does Ginata care so much about me leaving?" I demanded, continuing to stalk him.

"I told you. You're special. You're related to some high

priestess. That's why people want you so bad. It's why she wanted to keep you safe in her territory."

"Well you did one hell of a job," I replied sarcastically. "You're just as stupid as the others if you think I've got magic powers."

"Ginata wouldn't lie to us. She keeps us safe. She loves us."

"Ginata loves herself. She sees you as another thing to collect. Nothing more." Desi spoke up from behind me. I heard his boots step over the body. I turned just as he came up to me, handing me the knife he had just used on Paulo. I took it and clutched it tight until my pale knuckles went white.

"That's not true. Without her we'd all be lost. She found us, brought us to her sanctuary, and gave us jobs, homes, blood."

"She treats the men here like you're just animals getting a new home. Three or more to every woman. You don't even pick them yourselves." Desi shook his head in disgust.

"It's—" Landon stopped talking and seemed absolutely stumped. Desi did have a point. Polygamy was supposed to be more than having sex slaves. The world Ginata, the Seven Sin of Gluttony, had created was just that—sexual slavery.

We reached Landon. Desi stood behind me, whispering in my ear to kill him quick. I raised the knife and looked Landon directly in the eye. I still couldn't believe what he had planned for me.

Ritual sacrifice?

Then, without time for me to respond, Landon reached into his back pocket, pulled out something quickly and thrust it into my stomach. I let out a quick gasp as I felt the sharp pain of a blade.

Landon's eyes went big as we stared at each other. It took

me a minute to catch my breath, but then I looked down, to were his hand was still on the blade.

"Did you just fucking stab me?" I asked, not entirely sure I was comprehending what actually happened. Landon didn't speak, which was well enough. I dropped my own knife and let it clatter to the wooden deck. I smacked his hand away from my stomach. Then, I wrapped my hand around his knife and bit down while I pulled it from my gut.

I hissed as it hurt almost worse coming out than going in. I forced myself to straighten once it was out. I raised it to my eyes, staring at the blood.

My blood.

"Nah, fuck this."

I let out a loud grunt as I thrust the knife forward and up. It punctured his skin right under his chin and went up through his mouth, and hopefully, his brain.

His mouth fell open and he fell back. I shook my head and held tight to the knife, letting my body heal the gash in my stomach. It didn't feel pleasant, but I knew it'd be over soon.

Landon was helpless. I think I did get his brain, because his eyes were rolling into the back of his head and blood began to trickle from his mouth, nose, and eyes.

When I no longer felt the pain from his stabbing, I stood, smiled, and twisted the knife further into his head. "I am special. Just not the way you think. Sorry about your luck."

I removed it quickly and then sliced it across his neck. He collapsed. I bent down and grabbed Desi's knife to finish him off once and for all.

Desi stood there, silently watching me remove Landon's head from his body. This wasn't new to me, so it went fairly quickly, but it didn't make it any less messy. By the time I stood back up, I was covered head to toe in Landon's blood.

I looked up into Desi's eyes and sighed with exhaustion.

"Why does hanging out with you always lead to murder?"

He laughed and reached for me. I let him pull me into his arms. He reached for my chin and tilted my head up so we could kiss. It had been months since we had touched each other like this, and it was like an explosion of emotions. When our lips pulled away, he laughed again and answered me.

"Because it's fucking fun."

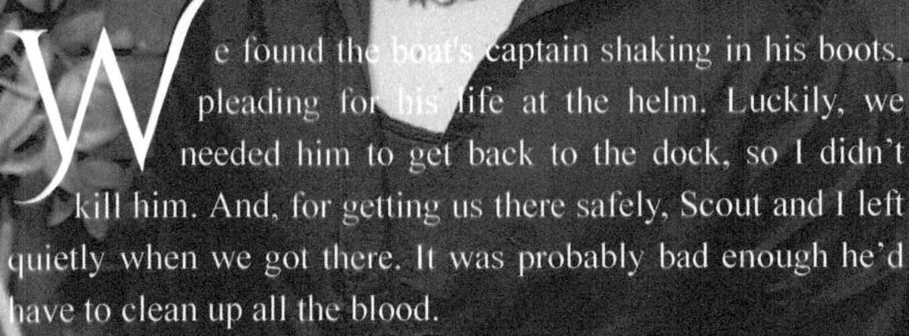

We found the boat's captain shaking in his boots, pleading for his life at the helm. Luckily, we needed him to get back to the dock, so I didn't kill him. And, for getting us there safely, Scout and I left quietly when we got there. It was probably bad enough he'd have to clean up all the blood.

"What do we do now?" Scout asked when we got into my rental car.

"We go home. I cleaned it. I have a few surprises, actually. I think you'll like it."

"Home?" Her voice squeaked. I raised an eyebrow as I shifted into drive and started off toward my hotel.

"Do you have something you want to do before?"

"I mean," she paused. "I don't know. I have some stuff at my apartment. I should probably tell someone I'm leaving."

"Like who?" I demanded. "Fuck Ginata. She hasn't seen me since I got here. She couldn't give me a hello, she doesn't deserve a goodbye."

"She's not horrible." Scout's voice came out in a whisper. "She saved me."

"From what?" I turned a corner a bit sharply and she fell forward. The seatbelt locked and threw her back.

"You."

Silence fell over us then. Would I be able to fix this rift between us? The memory of that night was fuzzy at best. No wonder she hated me. *I hated me.*

"I'm sorry," I said. "I wish I could take that night back."

"Life doesn't work that way," she sighed and turned to look out the window. "If it did, I can think of a hundred different nights I'd like to redo."

"How many of them involve me?"

"What makes you think any of them do?" She turned to me with her own raised eyebrow.

I wasn't sure how to respond, so I didn't. She turned back to the window, and we drove in silence until she asked for me to put on Journey, which I did. *Lights* came on and she reached for my hand. I wasn't entirely sure what to think of that, if anything, but her touch was everything to me.

I passed by my hotel, and drove her to her apartment. When we reached the parking lot she turned with furrowed brows to me.

"I thought we were just gonna leave."

"You wanted to grab whatever you have here. Go for it. You want to go alone, or can I join you?" I asked as I parked the car and undid my seatbelt.

"You can come up. You haven't seen it yet. I mean, it's nothing spectacular, but it was shelter for a few months."

I snickered. "Oh, I've seen it quite a bit, actually."

"What? How?" Her eyes went wide as her thoughts went wild.

I cringed. "Remember that night you saw me in the room when you were with— those two?"

"Yeah, but that wasn't here."

"Well I saw you and the bartender fucking just about everywhere. Cars, apartments, the back room," I grimaced.

She shook her head. "That wasn't real. We only had sex the one time. With Paulo." She looked away from me and I furrowed my brows.

It looked so real.

"I wonder if that's why I could talk to you that time. All the other times I was a ghost."

"I think you may have been seeing... my dreams." Embarrassment flooded her face and I scowled.

"More like nightmares. I guess that makes sense," I laughed. "Even in your dreams he barely satisfied you. I started to feel bad for you, honestly. The threesome." I grinned. "I had better orgasms by myself than you did the entire time you were fucking them."

"I don't doubt that even a bit," she laughed, and leaned forward over the center counsel to kiss me. Again, another simple act of affection that I had spent months starving for. There was no way I'd let her go again.

We got out and went up to her apartment. While I had seen it while I was in that weird corporeal form in her dreams, seeing it in real life was... sad.

"I know, I feel like I'm a teenager again. Broke and just starting out," she chuckled as she began shoving what little clothes she had in a duffel bag. "I'm going to go change." She eyed me up and down. We were both still in our damp clothes. "I don't have anything for you. Sorry."

"All good. I wouldn't wear it if you did. I'll change at the hotel."

She scooped up some clothes and there was a hesitation where she looked at me, then hurried to the bathroom to change. I cocked my head in confusion. Since when was I not allowed to watch her dress?

She returned a moment later with a dry band tee and pleated skirt. Her hair was drying in clumps, her makeup was running, and her lightly tanned skin was still splattered in blood. She was beautiful.

She smiled, and reached for a small stack of sketchbooks. She stuffed them into the bag and then tossed it over her shoulder. "Ready?"

"Are you? This is goodbye." I looked around the studio apartment. "We aren't coming back."

"Consider this place forgotten. Let's go."

We left, and I drove to the hotel I'd been staying at, only to find that I'd been checked out. Elvie too.

"Well can I get a new room then?" I asked the clerk, a little more harshly than I'd intended. He shook his head.

"I'm sorry, sir. Ginata called us herself and told us to. We actually have to ask you to leave."

"Ginata runs your fucking hotel?" I snapped.

"She runs everything here, sir. Now please, I'd appreciate it if you lowered your voice and left the lobby."

"Look here you little shit." I reached over the counter and grabbed the Bloodshed by the shirt collar. I was really racking up a body count here. "I don't think you realize who you're fucking talking to."

"Desi!" Scout's voice caused me to snap out of it. "Let's go. We'll figure something else out."

I let go of the kid and he stumbled backward, shaking with fear. I could smell it on him.

"What about a vampire named Ludovica? Is she still here?" I demanded. He shook his head.

"She was also escorted out. Do I need to call someone?"

Scout stepped forward and pushed me back. "No. Thank you, we're leaving."

Scout grabbed my arm and began pulling me out of the

hotel. I followed begrudgingly and when we were outside I called Elvie immediately. It went straight to her voicemail. I swore.

"Desi, the sun is going to come out soon. We need to find something else."

I nodded and we returned to my car. I gave Scout my phone and she began calling around to hotels, trying to find us shelter from the sun. Every time she did find a place with space, the moment we tried to book a room she was promptly told that our names were not welcome at the establishment.

Ginata worked quick.

"Something isn't right," I mumbled as I processed what was going on. "She's turned on us, but I have no idea why. Ginata has never been like this before."

"She told me you'd never come to her territory because you were afraid of her."

I laughed loudly. I gripped the steering wheel as I glanced at Scout. "Scared? I've never been afraid of the Sin of Gluttony. If anything, it would be reversed, but even then it's a stretch. We've always been close. All of us."

"She's the one who gave me the Sunshine," Scout revealed.

"Elvie gave me the cure. Hmm. Maybe she knows something." I was thinking out loud when my phone rang.

"It's Ludovica." Scout flashed the screen at me.

"Answer it."

There was a click and the vampire's voice I considered closer to family than my actual blood rang through my speakers. "Desiderio?"

"I'm here. With Scout," I added, glancing at her. "Where are you?"

"I had to get a hotel outside of Ginata's territory. I have

one for you too. There's something weird with her. I don't know what, but this is wrong."

"Yeah, I figured that out when I got kicked out of the hotel. Send me the address and I'll head over."

"Drive fast. The sun is coming." She hung up with a click and a moment later, Scout typed the hotel's address into my GPS.

We arrived just as light orange crossed the the sky. I grabbed her bag and hurried us inside. I only realized then that the hotel I had been kicked out of hadn't given me my things.

"I have your bags. I saw them emptying your room as they were escorting me out and I convinced them to let me have them." Ludovica's voice came from the lobby. I blinked and looked around for her. She was sitting in a chair, playing with her phone. She stood and pulled out a key card, handing it to me. "Hello, Scout. Welcome back."

Scout glanced at Elvie with suspicion, understandably. Last time they had spent any real time together the Seven Sin of Sloth had her kidnapped and almost murdered. I reached for Scout's hand, but she flinched away. The movement was so subtle, that only I noticed it.

"Hi," Scout said in a clipped tone. She hadn't been nice to her at the bar either.

Elvie rolled her eyes. "I really wish you'd get over the whole incident at my home. You aren't the first person I've tried to have killed, and you certainly won't be the last. But now, I'm here to save you. Let's go to your room."

Scout blinked rapidly. I smiled at my friend. I couldn't have said that better myself. I brought my hand to Scout's lower back and urged her forward. She started moving then. I looked down at the key card and saw our room number.

As we walked, I raised my arms and cleared my throat.

Elvie turned as we reached the elevator. "Can we get into our room and settle in before we start talking about stuff? I need a shower."

Elvie seemed to just now notice that we were covered in blood and my clothes were extremely damp and basically dragging on me. "Oh, of course. You must have had problems on the boat?" We stepped inside the elevator and it closed. She pushed the button for the third floor and we started to move.

"Something like that. I'll explain in a bit. Are my bags already in my room?"

"They are. I got a room down the hall, so I'll grab some things and be back to yours in an hour."

The doors opened and she hurried out ahead of us. I went for Scout's hand again, but she stepped a hair away, just enough to make it awkward for me to try to grab.

Okay then.

The room was not as nice as the one I had just been in, but we didn't have many options. It had one bed, a TV, table, and dark curtains. Which, was all we needed.

I found my bags on the bed. I tossed hers beside mine and started to open them. I pulled out some clean clothes and then began peeling off my wet ones. I paused when I was down to my boxers. Scout was standing by the door, watching me.

I swallowed the lump in my throat. "Should I have changed in the bathroom?" The lump in my throat turned into a pit in my stomach. The way she looked at me… as if she were scared.

She pressed her lips together for a moment and then shook her head. "No, you're fine." She kicked off the door and came toward the bed. "Sorry, it's been a long night."

I tried to kiss her lips but she moved just in time for my mouth to touch her forehead.

"We'll get some sleep soon. You want to join me in the shower? Getting clean will make you feel better." I was trying to be caring, but she shook her head quickly.

"No, I'm good. You go first, I need to sit down. By the time you get out I'll be ready to shower."

I gave her a tight smile and left her in the room then. I removed my underwear in the bathroom and showered alone. It was becoming abundantly clear that things weren't okay between us. I thought they were good after we kissed on the boat. She seemed like the Scout I knew and loved, but she wasn't. I had done this to her.

The solo shower went fast. I made sure to dry and change in the bathroom. I couldn't stand seeing that look on her face again if I came out with less than pajama pants and a t-shirt. I normally slept in just my boxers, but for her, I'd do whatever she needed me to.

She traded places with me and she too, changed in the bathroom. Her new clothes were long pants and a sweater. In all the time I had known her, in our human life and after, she rarely wore pants.

Elvie came to our door at exactly one hour. We let her in, and if she could feel the tension in the room she ignored it. She went to the table with her tablet and turned to us. "Okay, so what do you know?" she asked Scout.

Scout sat a few feet from me on the bed. "Uh, I know that Ginata is telling people I'm special. The guys on the boat were going to sacrifice me to some fertility demon. I'm not special," she adamantly denied. Elvie and I shared a look, knowing that Scout was very wrong.

"I respectfully disagree," Elvie started with a smile. "You were an orphan, correct?"

"Yes," Scout sighed.

"We found your family. Or, they found us. Desiderio, really. A brother."

Scout stood up quickly. "I have a brother? Who? How do you know that's true?"

"We don't. But based on what he's told your boyfriend, we think it could be true. And, if it is, then your weird powers make sense."

"What weird— oh," Scout's mouth opened and closed. "The ghost thing?"

Ludovica nodded. "I think it has something to do with you two being bonded when you drank each other's blood. Nothing happened when you drank from him thirty years ago. But when he drank yours a few months ago, it sealed whatever this is. The soulmate thing. I'm not entirely sure how it works, but you've got powers that other vampires, Bloodborn or Bloodshed, don't have."

Scout took a moment to process what Elvie was saying to her. She began to pace. "Okay, so what does that have to do with my brother?" She said the word as if it was foreign to her, which I guess... it was.

"The man who claims to be your blood, is the nephew of a high priestess in Mexico. Her people believe that she is the reincarnation of an ancient Aztec Goddess. They didn't give exact details, but it seems that they may have powers too."

"Magdalena?" Scout burst out. Ludovica and I exchanged looks.

"Yes," Elvie said cautiously. "You know about her?"

Scout nodded enthusiastically.

"They know about me? My powers?" Scout asked quickly. Her blood-red eyes went wide. I wasn't sure if there was fear, or the longing for a family that caused them to form a thin line of blood under them.

"No. I didn't give them any information about you because I wanted to let you decide what to do," I said, cautiously. I didn't want to sway her decision about meeting the man who claimed to be her brother. I could take it or leave it, but I understood the desire to know where you came from.

She nodded and sniffled. "Good. But—" she blinked. "Ginata. She knows. How?"

Elvie and I both shook our heads and shrugged. "We don't know. She won't talk to us. I think it's best we just leave and get as far away from here as we can."

Scout nodded again. "Yeah, okay. Tonight?" She glanced at the dark curtains. It was morning now. We would have to wait to leave. I stood and went to her. I tried to embrace her but she turned away, crossing her arms.

Ludovica stood then. "I'll see you both in the evening. We'll formulate a plan to get you away safely then." She left without another word.

Scout finally collapsed, and I was prepared to comfort her as she cried, but she didn't. I stood beside her until she got up.

"I'm tired. I should probably sleep."

"Yeah, let's go." I motioned to the bed. I raised the blankets and let her climb inside. I then shut off all the lights and locked the door. I was nervous about getting into bed with her. She was laying on her side, facing away from me. Cautiously, I lifted the blanket and climbed into bed.

Instantly, she stiffened. Which made me feel like complete shit. It crushed me so completely. I turned on my side as well, and stared at her. She was on the edge of the bed, and I laid as close to the edge on my side.

I stared at her until I could see her breathing. It wasn't relaxing. She was still awake. I decided to try touching her. I needed to feel her. I had missed her body wrapped in mine so much. It nearly killed me having to sleep alone.

I moved closer, and finally, I put my arms around her. She stiffened so hard I started to pull away, but then stopped. I decided I would wait for her to speak. I shifted closer, trying to snuggle my face in her hair. I inhaled deeply and sighed. Finally, she shifted so much she was completely out of my arms.

"I just— I can't. Desi, please. I know it was the candy and not you, but— let's just— not," she finally said, brushing my arms away. I moved away fast, as if she had slapped me, rather than gently moving me off her. It was devastating. She couldn't even bear to let me hold her.

If I couldn't even hug her, kiss her, or soothe her when she cried, how would we manage to spend eternity together?

The answer was simple, but soul-crushing.

We wouldn't.

CHAPTER 30

Desi

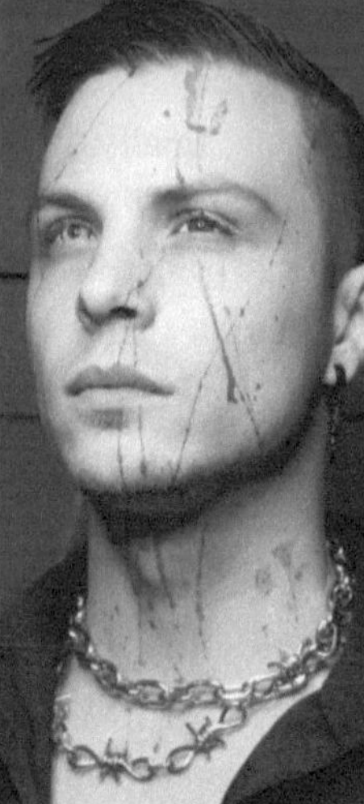

I squinted at my screen. It was still dark in the room. Scout was sleeping lightly on the other side of the bed, but my phone vibrating by my head woke me.

What the hell did that mean?

Without any issue.

Since when was I an issue? Had she turned her back on the Seven Sins? Did Corrine know?

I climbed out of bed carefully. Scout was so relaxed, I didn't want to wake her. The look she gave me when she was awake stung my very core.

I glanced at the time. The sun was down. I could roam freely. I changed as quietly as I could into jeans and my boots. They were still sopping wet from the swim Scout and I took the night before. I grimaced as I forced my feet down into them. My socks instantly soaked through.

I glanced behind me at her before I went to the door.

Ginata and I were going to settle whatever the fuck this was once and for all. Sin to Sin. No sooner had I stepped out the door, was I greeted by two large Bloodsheds waiting for me. I ran into one of them with a hard thud. The door closed behind me, leaving me stuck between him and the door.

"We're here for the Young Blood Priestess."

"The what? Scout?" It took me a minute to process what they were saying. "Don't call her that."

"That's what the High Priestess has decided she shall be called. Where is she?"

"She's sleeping," I said sharply. "You really want to wake up a Goddess in training?" I rolled my eyes and raised my hands up to shove them back. The one directly in front of me took a step away from me. Both seemed to consider what I had said.

"We will wait then." One of them decided.

"Who sent you, Ginata?" I demanded. They didn't answer. "Go tell her I want to see her face. She's a fucking coward if she doesn't come for me herself."

They didn't react to my ranting, so I turned around to go into my room again.

Suddenly, a hand was on my arm, pulling me from the door. I swung, and my fist collided with the brute's jaw. The other one came toward me and I ducked. He stumbled, and soon all three of us were fighting in the hallway.

Eventually, we heard a door open down the hall and we paused just in time to see Ludovica come out. She blinked with surprise, and came toward us slowly.

"What's going on here?"

"I need to get back to Scout. They want to take her." I stood up straight and brushed off my clothes.

"Ginata wants her returned safely to our community," one of her men declared.

Elvie nodded thoughtfully. "Okay. Well, if you won't let Desiderio, why don't I go in and get her?"

"Who are you?"

"I'm Ginata's sister. This is our brother. Why don't you let him go? I'll go get the vampire woman you desire, and then Desiderio and I will leave, peacefully."

"Fuck you!" I laughed. My eyes went wide with incredulity. Did she really think I was just going to surrender Scout to these men? Elvie gave me a stern look and I shut my mouth. She was planning something. I knew that face. I'd seen it many a time in our early Sin days.

"Give me the key card."

I was hesitant, but I handed it to her. She pushed it against the door and the hallway fell silent as she went in.

We waited. All three of us leaned against the opposite wall and stared at the door. Eventually, it opened and the pair came out.

Ludovica was holding on to Scout, and Scout appeared to have been crying. Her eyes were bloodshot and her face, while having slept a full day, looked exhausted.

"Are you ready, Miss?"

Scout nodded but kept her eyes firmly on the ground.

"Yes. Thank you for coming. Will I see Ginata?"

I squinted. *Thank you?*

"Yes, Miss. We're taking you directly to her. Do you have everything you need?"

"Yes. I just want to leave. Let's go." Her chin trembled and I cocked my head. My eyes went wide as Ginata's security team glared at me.

My mouth fell open as Elvie wrapped her small arms around Scout and hugged her tightly. "It's fine. You're safe now. Go."

The men smirked at me triumphantly as Scout went with

them to the elevator. She didn't look back as the doors opened and they stepped inside.

As soon as I heard the elevator's tiny bell descending, I snapped at Ludovica.

"What the fuck was that?"

"Desiderio, stop." She was firm, and motioned for me to return to my room. I glared at her, but did as told. As soon as the door closed I was back on her, demanding answers.

"What did you tell her that got her so upset? Why did she act like she wanted to leave with them?" I was throwing questions at her like knives, but I purposely avoided the one I wanted to ask.

Had Scout changed her mind?

"Desiderio, enough!" Elvie tossed up her hands. "She's acting. We need to get Ginata in the same room as us. She's purposely avoiding us and this might be our only chance to see her."

I paused, trying to understand where she was going with this. "What did you do, put a tracker on her or something?"

She laughed. "Am I some sort of super spy now? I just tossed my cell phone in her bag. We can follow the ping. Let me get my tablet and we can see where they take her."

I was impatient as all hell, but I tried to behave as she made me sit with her at the table while she showed me exactly where Scout was traveling. She was headed back into Ginata's territory.

"Are you sure about this?"

"About what?" Ludovica turned to stare at me. I cringed.

"About Scout." I let the words fall over us. We both knew what I had meant. How much of that was acting?

She could barely look at me, let alone let me touch her. Would she come back?

I couldn't finish the thought, but my friend knew where I

was going with it. She reached a hand out and placed it on my arm in an attempt at comfort.

"She's gonna come back. Trust her."

She *had* trusted me, and look what happened.

"I'm just—confused," I sighed and brushed my hand through my hair. "She kissed me. On the boat." I revealed. I looked to Elvie to see her reaction. Her eyebrows rose with surprise.

"Oh? What exactly happened?" She scrunched up her nose and shook her head. "Let's keep this PG. I don't need bedroom details."

I rolled my eyes. "There aren't any. We were kind of worked up from a thing and then we kissed. She let me hold her until the boat got to the dock, and then it was like a light-switch. It's like— she remembered she hates me."

"What thing got you worked up?" She tilted her head, causing her to look so young, almost child-like.

I shrugged. "We killed the bartender and the other guys she was involved with."

"Desiderio!" Elvie's eyes bulged and her mouth fell open. "Well this is probably why Ginata's angry! You can't go into another Sin's territory and start killing their coven."

I leaned forward. "I don't think Ginata gives a shit about anyone but herself. She was like that before, and now it seems her ego has been inflated even more so. You really think she cares about Scout? No, she wants something she thinks she has."

Elvie put up a finger to stop my rant. "Probably has. I am starting to get on board with this Young Blood Priestess theory. And the soulmates thing, for that matter. I didn't believe in it before, but I think if it was true, you two would be the poster children for it." She crossed her arms and sat back. "You guys are something else."

"What's that supposed to mean?" I shot back. I wasn't sure if I liked her tone.

"The only time she wanted to touch you was after— I'm assuming here—" she put her hands up in innocence. "Slaughtering a group of people. We all know how you got your name, Wrath. But, Scout." She shook her head and smirked. "I think she likes it too."

I ran my tongue over my fangs, considering her words. "I mean, yeah." I shrugged. Then I grinned. "She's a doll, ain't she?"

"A real peach." She shook her head. "You know her aunt's the same way."

"What way?" I asked, standing. I hated sitting here while Scout went somewhere potentially dangerous.

"Gory. That's how she got caught in the first place. She enjoys torturing her blood before drinking it."

"Scout doesn't do that," I defended. "She told me she doesn't drink from people. Familiars." I said that last word with distaste, as if it was sour on my tongue.

"Hey, don't knock it til you try it." Elvie stood with me and grinned. "Some humans get off on it. Although I think it's just them trying to play cool. Warm blood is better than bottled."

She wasn't wrong.

"Any pings on where she is? I can't sit here all night."

She sighed and went to her tablet. She clicked the screen a few times and then nodded.

"Yes and no. They've stopped. But I'm not entirely sure where they are."

I grabbed my keys off the table. "It works. We'll find it in the car. Come on."

"It's a spa." Elvie frowned from the passenger's side. "I think."

"Like, facials and massages?" I glanced at her as I drove back to Ginata's territory.

"Yeah, that's what it looks like." She flashed her tablet, but I couldn't look at the screen. "Take that next exit."

I did as told, and she continued to direct me until we were parked in front of the building she claimed Scout was in.

"My phone is in there, anyway. It is very possible she dropped it or the bag entirely."

"What do we do then?" I shot her a look and she flinched.

"Let's worry about that when it happens."

Only a few cars were in the parking lot, but the lights were on in the building.

"Let's try to find a back door." I mumbled, and we dipped down the alley between the spa and an unmarked building.

We went around the back to find a vampire standing next to the door. I looked at Elvie, who was frowning. She turned around and put her hands over her eyes. "I don't want to watch."

I rolled my eyes and went over to the guy. Bloodshed, I saw, right before I pulled out my switchblade. He turned just as I hurled myself at him. We fell to the concrete and I heard his head hit the pavement with a loud crack! I opened my mouth and sunk my fangs into his throat. His screams were cut off as I brought the knife up and stabbed him in the trachea. I ripped away at his throat and finally, when I pulled away, I moved the blade in and out and around to get his head severed from his body.

I stood and wiped my mouth. "Come on!" I shouted at Elvie. She turned and shook her head sadly at my newest victim.

"Oh, Desiderio. You are so violent. I hate it."

"He would have done the same to us if he had the chance." I kicked his limp body. "Let's go."

Ludovica's sad eyes shifted away and returned to me with a smile. She rose her head high and moved with a grace that came with confidence. The confidence that came from being one of us. A Seven Sin. Despite her often-seemed innocence, Sloth was not a person to be messed with. While I, Wrath, wore my sin in plain sight, her evil was brewing just under the surface. We walked in together as if we owned the place; and in that moment, I was glad to have her here with me to take on our other Seven Sin sister, Gluttony.

The lights were dim and light elevator music played throughout the building. I was alert to every footstep or noise that I heard. I was covered in blood, and there was no way I could explain that away.

We both paused outside an open doorway that had said BATHHOUSE outside of it, when we heard a familiar voice.

Scout.

"Can't I just wear a bra and panties?" she asked.

"No, silly. Everyone gets naked. Come on, get in," a female voice laughed.

"I don't know if this is my thing."

"Why? Are you still nervous? I thought the massage would help. You were naked for that, weren't you?"

"I don't want to be exposed. The water is clear."

"We'll put bubbles in. Get in. And take that tacky necklace off. Even seeing that name gets my blood boiling." There was a pause, and I realized I had inched my way into the doorway. My hand went to the matching necklace I wore. I had stopped breathing entirely as I listened in. Ludovica moved silently beside me.

The woman spoke again. "If you don't drop that towel I'll get one of my men to do it for you. Or is that what you wanted this whole time? They are handsome, aren't they? I suppose I can let you borrow them for a night or two until we get you another set."

I stepped in then, and set my eyes around the room. Scout's back was to me. She was standing at the edge of the large tub. I tilted my head to look at the woman in the water.

Red hair was pulled up in a bun, loose curls dangling on skin so pale it almost hurt to look at. I blinked in confusion as I stared into the face of a rather pretty Bloodborn vampire.

She saw me and Elvie and stood quickly, exposing her naked body to the room unashamedly. Scout turned when she saw her reaction and her mouth fell open. The relief that washed over her expression was only comforting for a moment. My attention returned to the redhead in the water.

"Desi—" Scout started but was cut off. The strange woman was glaring at us. She put her hand up to stop Scout but didn't take her eyes off me.

"Scout," I started. I began inching closer to her, watching the woman closely. "Who is that?"

There was a pause. Scout's face took on a look of confusion before she responded. "That's Ginata."

The woman's eyes went wide and she started to smile, baring her fangs at me. I shook my head and stepped forward, wrapping a hand tightly around Scout's arm. I tugged her back behind me protectively.

"No, it's not."

"Fleck! Jonathon! Get him!" The woman who I thought was Ginata, the the Seven Sin of Gluttony shouted. I spun my head around just in time to see two of her lovers the size of Arsenio come out from doors I hadn't noticed before. They looked to their girlfriend in the pool and followed where she was pointing, right at Desi. They stopped and pivoted, turning on him and Elvie.

"I don't know who you are, but this isn't going to end well for you." Ludovica, the Seven Sin of Sloth put her arm out to stop them. Fleck grabbed her and twisted until she let out a small gasp and bent over. I clutched the towel tightly to my chest and stared in horror. It was then that I saw his eyes.

He was human.

I glanced at Desi. His eye twitched, but he wasn't interfering. That gave me some kind of reassurance.

You don't want to mess with the Seven Sins.

Desi put his arm around me and urged me back. "You might want to go," he muttered through clenched teeth.

"I can't leave you here. If she's not Ginata," I paused, trying to collect all of my thoughts. "Then who is she?"

His focus shifted from Ludovica to the woman in the water. Her red eyes were large and her smile even bigger as she watched her boyfriend hurting the smaller vampire. She ran her manicured hands over the water and cocked her head in amusement.

"Who I am is none of your damn business." She turned to us then, and grinned, straightening to expose her breasts further. Did she think that would entice Desi?

He's mine.

Ludovica let out another small cry. We all turned. "Desiderio, get her out of here," she whimpered.

"I'm staying." I shook my head.

"You're naked." He turned his head. "Go."

"I'm not leaving you," I protested.

"Why now?" he snapped. "You've had no problem with that before." He spun around. "Will you just fucking go?"

I blinked rapidly. Reflexively, my hand went to the necklace he'd given me months ago. I looked toward the ceiling, feeling the blood tears coming. No, this was ridiculous. The sooner I left, the sooner I could return. I turned, and ran from the room.

Thankfully, I was able to remember exactly where the locker rooms where. I hurried in and flew to my bag. I tugged the drawstrings open and my stomach dropped. I pulled out my dress, but that was the only thing left in there. Someone had taken my bra, panties, socks, shoes, and coat. Everything! My wallet with all my money, Ludovica's phone— it was all gone.

I dropped the towel and pulled the dress over my head and down my body. Whatever, I had to get back to Desi. I ran back just in time to see the fake Ginata out of the bath and reaching for Desi.

She was faster than Desi or me. She thrust her hand into

his throat and squeezed. Her pale knuckles went whiter as she tightened her grip. Desi's eyes went wide and blood rushed to his face as she continued to crush his windpipe.

She dug her nails into his skin and tiny red dots began to form under her fingers.

"Stop!" I cried out. She turned her head to me, and then laughed.

"Oh, was that supposed to do something? Please, no one cares about this poor vampire. He's more inconvenience than anything."

Desi's muscles were tight as he struggled. He looked down at her, and then grinned. I watched as he lifted his knee slowly. His eyes flicked from her to me. It hit me then.

Keep her talking.

"They just want me. Right? Magdalena?"

"That's right. You're the important one. He won't be missed."

She was too focused on me to pay attention to anything else. Perfect.

My excitement fell when she turned her head back to Desi. She raised her other hand and reached for his cheek. "What a shame. You are so pretty. I wish we hadn't met this way," she sighed.

Desi's tongue slid out between his lips and only then did her eyes dip down to his raised leg.

He struck then. He launched his boot at her, landing the kick firmly against her bare abdomen. He shoved as hard as he could and she was forced to let go of him as she flew backward into the bath.

Water flew everywhere as she went completely under. Just then, Ludovica let out a loud growl and moved. I watched her sweep her foot under her attacker's ankle. He stumbled, and she took that opportunity to shove him down and hurl herself at his fallen body. She crouched, and reached into her tall boot, pulling out a pink-hilted dagger.

The Ginata impersonator was splashing in the bath, trying to get her balance. The other boyfriend she had called for offered her a hand but before she could grab it, Desi walked over and snatched him back. He shoved him against the wall and quickly pulled out his own knife. It was wet and dripping red. What had he done before coming here?

He flicked it open and brought it up to eye level. Fleck stood still as a stone, eyes wide and body in apparent shock as he stared at the bloody knife.

Desi flicked his tongue across the metal. I cocked my head and leaned against the doorway. A waft of air came through and I smelled the blood coming from the knife. It was from a vampire.

That could not have tasted good.

I was right, because he cringed, then quickly turned it into a laugh instead. "You guys taste so bad. It almost makes killing you not even worth it."

"You're going to kill me?" Fleck asked, his voice shaking. Desi shrugged.

"I think it would be kind of silly to leave you alive. What if you tell the others that I killed your fearless leader?"

"You can't kill Ginata!" Panic flew threw her lover, as if Desi had already hurt her. He shoved my boyfriend and Desi took a few steps back. "She's too important!"

"Well for one, she's not Ginata." Desi glanced at the woman still in the water. "She's pretending to be someone she's not. Not entirely sure why. Being a Seven Sin comes with a lot of baggage."

"You're a Seven Sin?" Fleck asked, looking from Desi to Fake Ginata. "And you?"

"No." Desi reached out and snatched his chin, forcing him

to look at him rather than the woman he was going to sacrifice his life for. "I am Wrath. She is nothing."

"That's not true. She is one. I know she is." Fleck nodded as if saying it enough could make it so. It broke my heart, seeing the devotion so clearly in his blood tears, sliding down his cheeks. Desi squeezed his lips together tightly and shook his own head.

"No, but believe me, before she dies she will tell me who she really is."

Laughter rang out from the other side of the room. "Is that so? You think you can just waltz into my world and take everything I've worked so hard to build, just like that?"

Desi let go of the Bloodshed in his hands and turned to see the redhead. She was stepping over blood puddles being made by Ludovica feasting on the human boyfriend. The noises she was making were ignored by everyone as the phony sauntered over to a rack and pulled a robe down. Slowly, as if she had nowhere to be, she put it on, adjusted it, and then tied it around her waist. Only then, did she look at me. She smiled, then returned to Desi.

"I may not be the person you expected to see today, but that doesn't change the fact that you stormed into my territory, tried to steal my ward, and killed multiple vampires in my coven."

"You really consider hundreds of people your coven?" he smirked. She sighed, her tone and face revealed boredom. She examined her nails and shrugged.

"I don't have to explain anything to you. Why don't you leave before you don't get the option." She flicked a glance at me. Her red eyes were blazing. "You're certainly not leaving with the Young Blood Priestess."

"You're a fucking cult," Desi sneered.

She ignored his words. "You know, I had heard so much

about you all. She would tell me story after story of the things you used to do together. She really liked you." She stepped over the pair on the floor again and came over to me.

I crossed my arms and stood up straight. "Who are you?" I asked.

"That's not important. What is important is who you are."

"I'm no one."

My gaze shifted, as I heard something. Desi's voice. But — not.

He hadn't said anything. I knew he hadn't, because he wasn't looking at me. He was staring down at his feet. But... I had heard his voice.

"You're someone to me."

I blinked, trying to wrap my head around it. Could we—

"Desi!"

He looked up sharply at me, his eyes hardening.

"Did you just—can you—"

It took everything in me not to nod my head. I forced my muscles to behave and thought to him instead.

"Yes. Kill her."

"You got it, boss."

"It's no wonder you were able to pass for Ginata. You look nothing alike, but the way you walk, the way you talk, and the way you attempt seduction," Desi smirked. "That's all Gluttony."

She turned away from me, stepping back to Desi.

"The vampire fallen from grace, she used to say. Desiderio Amato came from a very important family, but he gave it all up for someone he would never remember. He'd been marked, with eyes like no other vampire. Born or Shed." She shook her head and reached for his face. He tensed, but let her touch him. I gulped, watching them with nervousness as she placed her full palm against his cheek. "No wonder you're so angry," she laughed.

"Where is she? The real Ginata?" he asked through gritted teeth and clenched fists.

"For all I know, she could be dead and buried. I left her years ago." She leaned up on her tiptoes, her lips were puckered and she closed her eyes. In an instant I was moving, but Desi had already stepped away.

She stumbled back, surprised, and slipped on the blood from Ludovica. She screamed as she waved her arms wildly, trying to find something to hold.

"Fleck!"

The vampire who Desi had flashed his blade to was cowering in the corner. Desi turned to him and he threw his hands up in innocence. Desi rolled his eyes and let him flee. He leapt up and ran past me without a second look back.

Fake Ginata's mouth fell open as she watched her boyfriend abandon her. She steadied herself and took a step but her bare foot slipped on the blood again. She fell back and bounced her head on the tile. Bone collided with the ceramic with a sickening crack. There was a moment where she lay there, stunned.

"Desi?" I said aloud. "Is—"

"I'm not done here. Can you maybe—" he paused, and looked around. It was a fucking shit show in here. Water and blood flooded the floor. Ludovica was still tearing apart the human, despite him being super dead. Fake Ginata was groaning and rolling in said-blood. "I don't want you to watch me do... *this*."

"Why do you boss her around like that? No wonder she hates you. I would not spend eternity with someone like you," False Ginata moaned.

"No one asked you to," he snapped.

"What am I supposed to do then? Wait outside? Yeah, okay, sure." I crossed my arms and glared at him as I shot the thoughts his way.

"Scout, this is gonna get gory," he warned, responding the same way.

"We're vampires. Our entire lifestyle is gory. We're endgame, remember? I'm staying."

Desi shot me a sarcastic smirk then, and I ignored him. A moan came from where Ludovica was still attacking the guys throat. I grimaced. It sounded like mac and cheese being stirred.

"What is she doing?"

"You don't want to know."

"It sounds disgusting."

"It is. Ignore it."

"I'm— is she moaning?" I squinted to look better. I think tearing apart that human piece by piece was… arousing her. Desi shut his eyes and put a hand on his temple.

"Scout! Shut the fuck up! Focus!"

"Sorry," I said aloud. My hands flew to my mouth then but it was too late. Fake Ginata heard it and saw us shoot looks of panic at each other. She sat up and then stood. She stared at me with bright eyes that made me weary.

"It's true. You are special. Tell me, Young Blood Priestess, what drew you to this vampire?" She shook her head and scrunched up her nose as she looked at Desi. "Out of all the partners you could have had, why this one? He doesn't fit."

"Good question." Desi looked at me.

I crossed my arms and relaxed against the wall. "Because he has loved me when I had nothing. Both as a human, and after I turned. He didn't see red eyes, blue eyes, or my last name. He just wanted me." I reached for my necklace, and he reached for his. I looked at him, and we both smiled.

"You're a fucking loser, but you're my loser."

"Likewise, Nerd."

"He doesn't see me as 'The Young Blood Priestess'." I put my hands up and did air quotes.

"Shame," Fake Ginata sighed. "The High Priestess won't like it. You can't be mated to someone like him."

"Excuse me?" I took a step forward. Instantly, Desi stepped toward me in defense, putting himself between us. "Someone like him? At least he's not a liar. A fake. An imposter. He doesn't need to pretend. What will my aunt think when she finds out you can't be trusted? What did she promise you in exchange for me?"

When Fake Ginata didn't reply I asked again. The redhead stood taller and put her nose to the sky, as if we were truly beneath her.

"She's going to make me more powerful than any of the sins. I won't need to borrow the name anymore."

"Borrow? You've been stealing from our sister." Ludovica stood, finally. Her entire front was covered in thick, dark blood. She wiped her mouth, but it did little to clean her chin, neck, and arms. "You don't get to walk away from that." She clenched her fists and widened her red eyes.

"Oh please. It's too late. The High Priestess is sending her people to come get her, and then I'll be rewarded. I'll be so rich I won't need a single thing from anyone again. Fuck Ginata and all the Seven Sins. Seriously, you two should leave while you still can." She waved them off with a flick of her wrist.

I blinked.

People were coming for me?

The room fell silent for a moment as everyone took in her words. Ludovica came to stand beside me. She reached for my hand and I took it. It was sticky from Jonathon's head. We watched as Desi stuck his hand in his pocket. Ludovica and I shared a look, knowing exactly what was coming.

"Who are you?" He cocked his head to the side.

She grinned. Her eyes were wide with excitement over her future. "My name, before I took over for your friend, was — is, Chelsea. I guess I can just start going by it again. I always liked it more than Ginata."

I couldn't take my eyes off of Desi's back. Every muscle was tense, yet confident. I could feel the excitement radiating off of him.

"It sounds like I have no real choice but to take your word for everything. I will admit, I did not expect any of this tonight. I should probably leave."

Ludovica squeezed my hand and gently tugged it when Desi pulled out his tarot deck. I nodded, and took a small step back with her. I would go, but I wanted to see how it played out.

"Well, Chelsea, one last thing, will you pick a card?" He fanned the deck out and extended my hand. She eyed it with amusement.

"You're a magician now? That explains how you won her over." She laughed and took a card from his hand. She looked at it, then turned it for us to see.

"Justice. Is that good?"

Desi glanced at us, licking his lips and grinning. He then turned back to her and stepped forward.

"That's excellent."

CHAPTER 32

Scout

"Do you really think she deserves whatever he's doing to her in there?" I asked, sitting in the car with Ludovica. I stared at the building. We had left through the front, because apparently in the back, there was another body that I shouldn't see.

"She created a cult centered around convincing men to serve women and the women to treat men like sex slaves." Ludovica didn't look up from her nails, which she attempted to clean. "Definitely Seven Sin material, but no, I think she is going to get everything she deserves. I'm more concerned about where the real Ginata is. I'm sure Desi will try to get the truth out of her before he kills her."

"Polyamory isn't—" I started but Ludovica cut me off.

"No, what she was doing was not Polyamory. I'm cutting off their supply, and hopefully the blood community here can heal and decide for themselves. The people here had no choice."

I considered her words. She wasn't wrong.

I thought about the card Chelsea had drawn. *Justice.* I imagined the card in my head. A woman, wearing a crown, sitting at her throne. A sword in one hand, scales in the other. I shuddered at the images coming to mind about what Desi was doing to her.

"Something new happened in there." I changed the subject. "Desi and I were talking to each other in our heads."

"Oh?" Ludovica raised an eyebrow and rested her blood-stained hands in her lap. She was still covered in Jonathon's blood. "Just you two?"

I shrugged. "I think? I don't know. Try to talk to me. Think something at me."

She scrunched up her nose and stared hard at me. We sat in silence for a solid minute before she slumped and frowned. I shook my head. "Nope. Just us I guess."

"It comes back to you two sharing blood, I think. I find it so odd that your blood tastes good to each other. You guys share a bond that I'll never understand," she laughed. "I wonder if what Chelsea said was true, that Magdalena will be mad about the bond. Oh well."

"I'm not giving him up," I said firmly.

"You did before," she accused.

"Yeah? So?" I shot back. "And he left me for dead thirty years ago, right after I turned. We've both done shitty things to each other. I think we'll be fine."

"Will you? He's worried about you, you know. Why do you act normal in public but won't let him touch you in private?"

I raised an eyebrow. He told her about this morning? I wasn't entirely sure how I felt about that. When I stayed silent, she threw up her hands. "Look, I get it. What he did, I don't know if I could forgive that. Even considering it was the candy that caused it. *My candy*. You have every right to feel how you feel and act like you do. But, talk to him about it."

"Fine. Fuck it," I muttered and reached for the door handle.

"What are you doing?" She sat forward.

"I'm going to talk to him about it." I opened the door and put my foot out onto the ground.

"You think this is an appropriate time?"

"Will there ever be a good time for this?"

The look on her face told me, no, there wouldn't be.

I climbed out then, and shut the door. I glanced back and waved as I headed back into the spa.

Elevator music still played in the dimly lit building. Thankfully, there was no one working tonight. Ginata— or I guess, Chelsea, made sure that we were alone. For what, I wasn't entirely sure now. I wasn't sure who to trust anymore. Was everyone working for this high priestess?

The floor was cold on my bare feet. As vampires, we were cold in general, but still, I shivered slightly with every step on the tile. My breathing became deep and labored as I tried to think of what to say to Desi. What could I say to the man who hurt me deeper than anyone else ever had?

I found the hallway to the bathhouse and started down it, slowly. I listened for screams, crying, or anything, but I heard nothing. Had he left? Inside, I found Desi standing with his hands on his hips, shaking his head and staring at a very dead vampire woman.

I glanced at the body. It was covered in blood, which was not surprising, considering the only way to kill one of us was to remove our heads. Hers, was resting in her hand, reminding me of Shakespeare. I was glad that her eyes were closed. She almost looked peaceful.

I sighed, and that alerted Desi to my presence. He turned quickly and blinked. "I thought I asked you to wait in the car."

I stepped toward him. I couldn't miss the blood. Between Chelsea and Johnathon, it had flooded the floor. I looked at Desi as I moved slow. He was drenched. When he had first come for me, he had red on his chest, but now, he was bathed in it. From his head to his toes, it looked like he'd showered in the blood of his enemies.

"You're dirty," I said.

"You're getting there." He looked down at my naked feet. "Scout, what are you doing here?" he sighed.

"I think we should talk." I reached him, and brought my arms up and rested them on his shoulders. The movements were jerky and almost forced, which he noticed.

"You don't have to do this." Out of habit, his hands went to my hips. "Seriously, I know we have a lot of things to work through. It doesn't have to be tonight."

"But I want to. From the sounds of it, our future might be pretty busy." I stared into his beautiful eyes. The only part of him that wasn't red. My hand went to his cheek, and I took my thumb and rubbed some of the blood away. "Kiss me."

"Why?" His voice came out croaked, as if choking back his own high emotions.

"I need a reason to stay. Show me you want this as much as I do."

He paused, then with a passion I hadn't felt in such an achingly long time, he brushed my hair back behind my ear and bent down, pressing his lips to mine.

The kiss was stiff, but he was determined. As was I. If I wanted to be with Desi, I needed to push past my pain of that night. It wasn't him. It was the candy, that had done that to him. To us.

His hands found mine and we laced them in each other's. Then, something happened. He opened his mouth, and his tongue moved past his fangs and I reacted. I parted my lips and invited him to taste me. My tongue found his and one kiss turned into two, and two, turned into three.

He let go of my hand and he began exploring my body. The familiar feel of his fingers tracing my arms, my hips, and the rest of me was heaven. I pushed against him, and he paused. He pulled his face away from mine and looked down at me. "Should we be doing this here?" His Adam's apple dipped with nervousness.

"I missed this." I smiled.

"Missed what?" His eyebrows went up with pleasant surprise.

"The delightful chaos that is you."

"You like chaos? I can give you chaos." He bent his knees and cupped my ass, lifting me. I let out a small squeal of excitement as I wrapped my arms around his neck. "But let's take this chaos somewhere else." He took a step and our eyes locked in horror as he lost balance, slipping on the blood.

It happened so fast, neither of us could react. I let out a scream as we fell backward, splashing into the bath together!

I went completely under, taking water into my mouth. I let go of him and flung my limbs about in an attempt to reach the surface. It wasn't deep but he had landed on me, and I had to scramble to get from under him.

I came up like an explosion, and Desi joined me a second later, gasping and spitting out water.

I choked trying to get the taste of the water out of my mouth. There was a moment when we gained control of the situation and looked at each other. I was standing, but the bath was deep enough that only my shoulders were visible if I stood on the bottom. For him, standing beside me, it reached his chest.

"You turned the water red!" I giggled.

"Me? Are you sure it wasn't you?" He pulled me into his

arms and kissed me again, as if the passion from moments before hadn't been ruined. I agreed with him, kissing him back.

His hands dipped under the water and resumed exploring my body. My dress flowed up and around me, giving him easier access to the parts he was interested in.

"Are you not wearing a bra?" he whispered. I ignored him, and when his hands went further down my body, he paused at my hips. "Are you not wearing panties? This whole time?"

"Someone stole them." I shrugged.

"I guess I'm glad you didn't tell me. I would have been struggling to kill that vampire if I had a hard on the entire time."

"Do you have one now?" I smirked, my hand going to his wet chest. His Iron Maiden shirt was almost clean now from the sudden bath.

"You're more than welcome to see for yourself."

I gulped. Did I want that? I closed my eyes for a moment, and when I reopened them, I saw Desi staring down at me, watching to see my reaction. I knew then, that he would never force me to do something I didn't want, ever again.

Candy or not.

I nodded, and moved my hands below the water, stopping at his jeans.

"Shower sex is fun and all, but this has potential," I said, finding the buttons.

"That it does. Are you sure?"

I popped a button, and then looked up at him. "Yes."

"What do I do? Do you want to take the reigns? Or…" he trailed off, looking lost. I rolled my eyes and pulled his pants apart. The warm water made the blue jeans hard to maneuver but I was determined.

"Stop overthinking. I want to go back to how we were before." I shoved his pants down, taking his boxers with them. His cock was hard and pointed directly at me.

"And how was that?" He reached for the hem of my dress and tugged upwards. I lifted my arms to let him remove it from me. He tossed the dress onto the tile beside one of the bodies. The splat of it hitting the floor only distracted me a moment.

Both of us looked around the room and then back at each other. Were we really about to give in to our emotions surrounded by blood, gore, and dead bodies?

"Fuck it, they're already dead," I said, pulling his head down to crush his lips against mine. That was all the permission he needed. He cupped my ass again and lifted me up. The water made it easier for him to hold onto my weight. I was raised out of the water slightly, exposing my breasts to the cold air.

My nipples pebbled instantly and Desi grinned at the sight, leaning down to take one into his mouth. I relaxed my head back and savored his tongue running down my nipple and his teeth gently nipping the tip. I bucked, and one of his hands reached down to explore my sex.

My core started to ache then, and I tightened, trying to deal with the pain. I reached down and helped his hand find where I wanted. He let out a low chuckle when he discovered I was already slick with need.

"How long have you been wet like this?" he asked.

"Since you turned around and I saw the glint of your necklace against your chest," I said.

"Okay, now who's being fucking poetic?" he laughed, and then slid a finger into me.

I gasped, and he paused, making sure that I really was okay with this. I nodded and bucked against him again, clueing him in to what I wanted. He began pulling in and out, and soon one finger turned into two.

"You miss this?" he asked. "I knew none of those men were pleasing you like I can," he said into my ear. His tongue flicked against my lobe, and then began trailing down my neck. "How long has it been since you properly came?"

I reached for his cock, still rigid and ready. "I need you," I gasped. I pushed his hand away and he frowned.

"Already? I wasn't done."

"Yes," I growled.

Without another word, he walked me to the edge of the tub and pressed me against the wall. We readjusted and he nudged my head to the side with his nose. I closed my eyes as he entered me, and I really had found heaven.

Nothing felt like Desi did when we were connected in this way. He was the only one who did what he did to me. He knew how to tease, torture, and please me in such a way that as he thrusted deep into me, I was reminded of how much I fucking loved this cursed man.

"God, you're so fucking unbelievable," he gasped as he continued his steady rhythm. "I forgot how this felt. You and I, we're fucking end-game, baby." Our lips met and our tongues tangled as he palmed my breasts with one hand and pulled my hair with the other. I held on to him, my hand on his lower back as he thrust into me with a ferocity that I craved.

Despite the water washing the blood off of him, I could still smell it. His skin smelled like blood, his cologne, and cinnamon. Suddenly, with little warning, my body exploded! I gasped and then screamed as my orgasm overtook me in such powerful waves that I couldn't handle it, and I bit down on his chest.

My fangs sunk into him and he inhaled quickly only once.

He kept moving, helping me to ride my orgasm out and slowly savor it. I drank from him, but only until I stopped coming, at which I pulled out and slumped against him for a moment.

"Are you alright?" he chuckled. "Has it really been that long?"

"You don't even know," I sighed, my entire body was filled with warmth. I felt like I could be glowing with how good I felt.

"Oh, I think I do."

I looked up at him then. I had all but forgotten about our newest connection. His eyes were large and I couldn't quite put my finger on what he was thinking, but all I felt in that moment was his love pouring from everything he could.

"Can we move?" he asked suddenly. I blinked.

"Sure, what do you want to do?"

He removed his cock from inside of me. "Turn around."

I did as told. I felt his hands on my hips, and he spread my legs apart with his feet. I did what he wanted, and his hands found my core again. I enjoyed how he touched me with expert fingers. A moment later, his cock was pressing against me. I arched my back and he slid into me with ease.

He began a steady rhythm, but then, I felt a hand on my ass, and my eyes went wide when I felt his fingers spread my cheeks and press against something we hadn't exactly discussed before.

He felt me stiffen and he paused. "Is this... alright?"

"Um, I don't know," I said, honestly.

"I don't know as in a violation, or in a we've never tried this before situation?" he asked, as his thumb ran over the apparently highly sensitive spot. I was a little taken back by how much I didn't hate it.

"The second one," I gasped as he leaned forward and began kissing my bare neck.

"Good," he purred. "Then try to relax, and let me do something for you."

"What's that?" I asked.

"Make you come again."

He began moving his hips, grinding against me, bringing himself deep into my body. He brought his hand to the front of me and played with my clit, rubbing my slickness all over his fingers. I closed my eyes again and tried to do as he had requested. Relax. As his hand returned to my backside, now slick with arousal, he gently pushed into my most private spot.

I gasped and groaned as my body resisted his prodding, but he continued to kiss and lick my neck while whispering sweet, soothing things into my ear. I tried to steady my breathing as he got one finger inside of me and then began slowly, so achingly slowly, pulling it out and then back in, with the same rhythm his cock was doing to my other hole.

"Do you like it?" he asked eventually, and I answered him honestly.

"I do."

"Good." He pressed deeper into my ass with his finger and moved it in such a way that my mouth fell open. It was a mix of tight pain and unusual pleasure, as he stretched my body in a way I had never experienced. He was right, he was going to make me come again.

My arms went out, gripping the edge of the bath as he continued to take me with his finger and his cock. I was unraveling with each thrust, and finally, I couldn't take it anymore. I let out a scream of utter delight as my second orgasm caused my body to jerk, stiffen, and react in such a way I had never come before. My heart was racing as hot, steaming blood flowed through my body. Desi began pumping harder into me, removing his finger completely. I pressed against him harder, inviting him, encouraging him to find his own release.

He came quickly, barely a minute after I did. His orgasm was just as strong as both of mine had been, and when he pulled away from me, he fell back into the water with a relaxed expression on his face.

I laughed, and hurried to help him up. He blinked, looked around the room and then back at me.

"Alright, I'm just gonna say it. This is kind of a new low, even for me. Let's get out of here."

CHAPTER 33

Desi

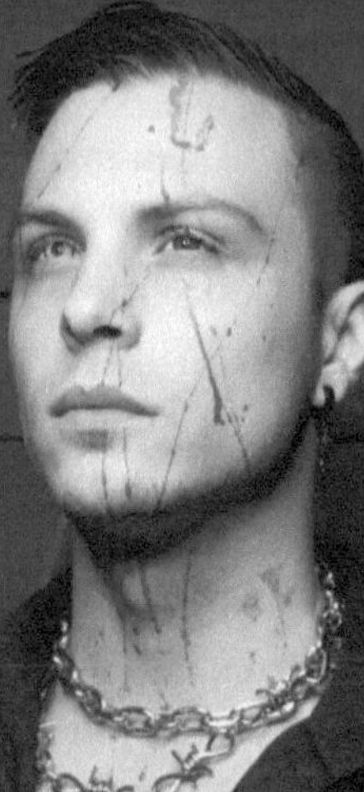

Ludovica insisted we take a flight back to Ohio, rather than drive.

"I am not staying in shitty blood hotels for a week. This way, you'll be back at your apartment in a few hours."

She was right. By morning the three of us were safely in our apartment and exhausted. Ludovica excused herself.

"I need to get all of this off of me." She motioned to the dried blood covering her front. We had gotten on her private plane barely an hour after we had left the imposters territory. I pointed to the bathroom and she went to it, closing the door quietly behind her.

"Wow, you... cleaned." Scout looked around the apartment with unease in her eyes.

"Do you like it?" I asked, cautiously. She didn't look happy. I knew we still had a lot of work to do to repair our relationship, but I had thought she'd like the new look of our home.

"I guess. I mean, I don't hate it. I just... clutter makes me comfortable." She shrugged.

I laughed, and wrapped my arms around her from behind. She stiffened for only a second before relaxing into me. It was amazing.

"Well, you're back and you can clutter it all back up. I have another surprise for you, but we can do all that tomorrow."

My neighbor was probably already asleep. The sun was coming up when we got here. I'd get the bird later.

Scout yawned. "Sure. I'm kind of beat. I need a shower, some blood, and a comfy bed."

"Well good thing, I think I have all those things." I grinned, letting her go. She started toward the kitchen. I followed like a lost puppy. I knew she was probably getting annoyed, but I couldn't help it. I never wanted to be without her again. Even for a second. The pull to be around her was so hard, it felt like if she was out of my sight, she'd disappear.

"What kind of blood do you have?" She opened the fridge and saw a few glass bottles of what she usually got from the banks. She pulled one out and popped the cap off. "Cool. I'm too tired to warm it up." She shrugged and drank the entire bottle quickly.

I leaned against the doorframe and crossed my arms over my chest. God, she always looked so effortlessly gorgeous. She was tough as nails and beautiful every moment of it.

Elvie came out of the bathroom, a towel wrapped around her tiny body. "Scout, may I borrow some pajamas?"

"Sure, yeah. Desi, you want to set her something up on the couch?"

I nodded and went to the closet to grab some extra blankets and pillows. Scout took Elvie to our room and when she came out my Seven Sin sister was wearing one of my shirts and pair of my shorts. I frowned.

She shrugged. "All of your girlfriend's pajamas are a little risqué for a day at my brother's house." She rolled her eyes. "Forgive me for choosing the most modest option."

"Fair enough," I muttered. I finished placing the last blanket on the couch. I stood up and straight and motioned to it. "Here you go."

"Thanks. I don't see myself becoming a permanent guest."

"All good. It's been a long few days. We'll figure out stuff tonight."

We heard the shower turn on, and suddenly I felt tired. While I had managed to get a lot of the blood off in the bathhouse, I still was filthy and exhausted.

"Blood is in the fridge if you need it. I'm gonna go lay down," I told Elvie, and she nodded as she climbed onto the couch and covered herself with the blanket.

I went to the bathroom and knocked.

"Yeah?"

I opened the door. "Is there any room for me to join in? Strictly to clean up?" I put up my hand in innocence.

"Sure."

We were both too tired to even attempt anything sexy. I peeled off my stiff clothes and stepped into the shower. Silently, we shampooed our hair, washed our bodies, and rinsed.

We dried and slipped on comfortable clothes. There was no playful banter, no tangling of our legs to relax. We simply climbed under the covers and both of us were out in an instant.

When we woke up in the evening, we went out into the living room to see Elvie rummaging through her pink suitcase.

She grabbed some clothes and went to the bathroom,

returning in a pink puffy dress. Her normal look relaxed me some. Scout came back from the kitchen holding two glass bottles. She offered Elvie one and together, they drank.

I smiled, looking at the pair of them. After Ludovica's planned kidnapping last year, I didn't think they'd ever be together and smiling.

Scout and Elvie couldn't be more different. While Elvie, the sin of Sloth, lived her life in pastels and puffy dresses, Scout didn't own a single pink item. She was more comfortable in black skirts, fishnet tights, and doc martin boots.

A deep knock on the door caused us all to curiously turn and cock our heads.

My happy mood from Scout's return and her budding friendship with one of my most favorite family members was soured when I realized who was probably at the door.

"Was someone expecting you home?" Scout asked.

"Kind of. Why don't you go get dressed?" I forced a tight smile.

I watched her cock an eyebrow but turn and do as I requested. I waited until I heard the bedroom door before going to the front and opening it. Sure enough, my fears were correct, Jaime was here and ready to take her.

"Hello," I started. "Were you watching my apartment?" I snarled. He had his arms crossed over his chest in an almost impatient manner.

"Your neighbor graciously offered to let me stay with her while I wait."

I glanced behind him at the shut door.

Fucking Amy.

"Where's the bird?" I snapped.

"Is Julieta taking visitors?"

I flinched at the name. Despite her being born with that name, she would always be Scout to me.

"No, but I feel like you're not going to give me a choice." I stared at him. He was easily twice my size. I'd taken down thousands of men like him, but there was no way I'd touch someone that could help Scout learn about herself. He smiled.

"You are correct."

"Come in," I sighed. I opened the door and he walked past me. He saw Elvie and nodded.

"Hello."

"Hi." Elvie stared at him with wide eyes. He eyed the couch, still covered in blankets. I went to it and pulled them off, clearing a spot for him. He sat, rather politely, and offered me a smile that was… friendly. It was a stark difference from the first time we had met each other.

"Ludovica, this is Jaime. Scout's—"

"Brother?" Elvie smiled wide and extended her hand out to him. The vampire looked surprised and shook her hand. I had to look away when he lifted it to his lips and she giggled. They sat on the couch together, and I went to see how Scout was coming along.

She was putting her messy curls into a high pony-tail. She had changed from her pajamas into some black shorts and one of my older band shirts. The words "Accepted Perversion" were emblazoned on her chest with a green cartoon snake eating a zombie underneath it.

"Hey!" She turned when she saw me in the mirror. "Who was here?"

My jaw locked and I had to force myself to relax and answer her. "When you're ready come out, I'll introduce you guys."

She grinned, reaching for her lipstick. "Sure. I'll be out in a second."

I waited for her, rather than go back and listen to Elvie

and Jaime flirt with each other. Scout came over to me finally, and together we left the bedroom. I reached for her hand, and she laced her fingers through mine. I squeezed them as we walked down the hall. I wasn't sure why I was so nervous, but I couldn't shake the feeling of dread from my gut.

"Why are you acting so weird?"

I stopped and turned to face her before we stepped into view of the couch.

"I just don't want you to leave me again."

She frowned, and then nodded. She didn't understand yet, but it'd be pretty clear why I was so nervous in a moment.

Jaime stood when we entered the room. Scout dropped my hand instantly and I felt her stop breathing.

Ludovica and I watched with caution at the two, apparent, siblings. Standing across from each other, I guess I could see the resemblance. Jaime had a darker skin tone than Scout, but living in hot, sunny, Mexico your entire life would do that. But it was their eyes, that I saw it. Were they related? I wasn't sold yet, but perhaps.

"Scout, this is Jaime. He came from Mexico to meet you. He has reason to believe that you two are related."

"Related?" She raised her eyebrows and looked from me to him. "How so?"

"There is no question," Jaime smiled wide. "You are my sister, Julieta."

Scout crossed her arms and popped her hip. She smirked. "Julieta? Sister? Bro, I have no idea who you are."

He shook his head and reached into his pocket, pulling out his phone. "I know. I was raised in Mexico, by my—our Aunt." He didn't look up from his phone as he spoke. He swiped his screen a few times before grinning and bringing the phone up for her to see the screen. "This is her."

I couldn't see the screen, but Scout's reaction was enough

for me to reach for the phone. He let me take it from him, and my mouth fell open when I saw the photo. That woman in the picture had Scout's face. The shape of her nose, her cheek-bones, the eyes, the lips, all of it! It was Scout, but… not. Her eyes were harder, her makeup more intense. Her hair, it was styled and the clothes she wore looked expensive. She could have been Scout's twin, sure, but they were not the same woman.

"Magdalena?" I asked.

He nodded. "Yes." He turned to Scout. "I would like to take you to meet her. And the rest of our coven. We've been looking for you for many years now." He smiled.

Scout took the phone from me again and stared at the photo. There was no denying that the two shared some kind of blood lineage. "She's your aunt?"

"Our aunt," he corrected. "She can do things beyond your imagination, and we would like to see if you can too."

Scout and I exchanged a look, which everyone in the room caught.

"I don't know. Why doesn't she come here?"

"If the High Priestess leaves, her powers go with her. Our coven would struggle without her."

"If I go, it would only be to visit," Scout said, carefully.

"NO." My mind screamed. I stood up.

She shot me a look but said nothing.

"Of course." He nodded. "We just want to meet you, get to know you, and perhaps help nurture the potential hidden inside you."

"It's just another fucking cult."

"Yeah, but it's my cult."

"Your cult?"

"My family's cult. Who cares? It's just a visit." The two of us went back and forth in our minds, arguing.

"When are you going back?" Scout asked aloud to her brother.

Jaime grinned. "As soon as you agree to come with me. I have a plane ready to go."

Scout blinked. Ludovica stood then. "Now hold on, this is all a little fast."

Jaime opened his mouth to protest but was interrupted by another knock on the door. We all turned, and after a second knock, Scout went to the door.

"Can we not just have one normal day?" She pulled the door open and we all leaned forward to see Amy on the other side, holding the bird cage.

"Oh good! You're home. This is yours." She thrust the cage into Scout's hand. "He was good, but I think he misses you guys. He talked a lot." She scrunched up her nose. "Anyway, I've got to head out. See you guys later." She waved uncomfortably and then left quickly.

Scout shut the door and blinked rapidly as she turned. "You got a bird?" She looked at me.

"Well— kind of," I admitted, looking down.

"It was a gift from the High Priestess herself." Jaime declared.

Scout brought the cage over and stared at the cover for a long moment before taking it in her hands and pulling it off. She let out a sharp squeal as the red and black parrot was revealed.

"Oh my God, he looks just like Alfie!" Her head shot up to me, and then Tippi, and then back at me. "Does he have a name?"

"Tippi," I explained. Her eyes took on a far off look before it clicked and she brightened.

"As in Tippi Hedren from *The Birds*?" she asked. I nodded and she laughed. "I love it!"

She looked at me again and I her eyes had a thin red line at the bottom. Her chin trembled with emotion. "How did you know I used to have one?"

"I went to visit Nalida," I revealed.

"Nalida?" She furrowed her brows. "My foster sister?" It took her a minute but then her ruby eyes went wide with realization. "She showed you my stuff!"

I nodded. "She did. Although she wasn't happy about it. She told me all about you guys. When the opportunity came to get one of these, I had to." I shrugged and stuffed my hands in my pockets.

"Oh, Desi," she sighed and bent down to look at the bird some more. "I love it."

"They fly freely in our city. Magdalena loves them. Come with me and see them in flocks," Jaime urged.

I sighed and pulled my hand out of my pocket to run my hands through my hair. He had her with the fucking birds.

She stood then, and I could see in her face that I was right.

"Okay. But only for a few weeks, at most. I can't stay."

"That's fine. Come on." Jaime moved fast, heading to the door.

Scout laughed. "Uh— we have to pack."

Jaime's eyes darkened and he shook his head. "We? No, my plane does not fit all of you. It fits six."

There was a moment where we all took in his words.

"Okay, so how many people do you have?" Ludovica asked.

"The pilot, me, you," he pointed to Scout. "Your bird, and any other belongings will cover the other seats."

"Fuck that. She's not going then," I snarled.

"Now hold on," Scout put her hands out between us. "What if..." she paused as she tried to think. "I bring

Ludovica with me on the plane. Then Desi, you drive down there with the bird and any extra luggage?"

"Why do I have to drive?" I demanded.

"Because I absolutely will not," Ludovica declared. "I like this plan. I could use a vacation."

"Fuck you." I raised my middle finger to her. She was really going to make me drive from Ohio to Mexico? Elvie stuck out her tongue and rolled her eyes. She knew that for Scout I'd do just about anything.

"Desi, can you do that?" Scout reached for my hand, and when I looked into her eyes, I knew I would never, ever tell her no.

I sighed. "I fucking guess. Let's get you packed."

CHAPTER 34

Desi

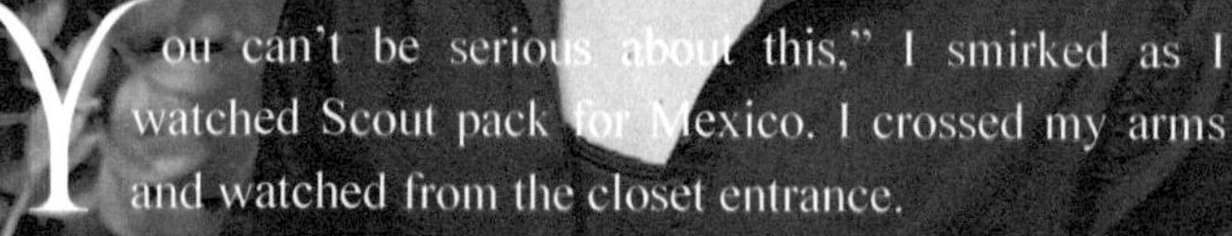

"You can't be serious about this," I smirked as I watched Scout pack for Mexico. I crossed my arms and watched from the closet entrance.

"I am. You don't understand, Desi. I've never known my family. I've spent so long looking for them, this is it. I have to go."

"No, I get that." I shook my head. "I'm talking about just up and leaving with a stranger. Why can't I just take you?"

"Ludovica is coming with me." She shrugged.

I glowered.

"I don't like it," I said.

"I don't care," She shot me right back. The closet went quiet other than the shuffling of clothes into her duffel bag. Finally she stood and picked up, tossing the strap over her shoulder. "I love you, I do. But I need to do this my way."

She came over to me and raised her hand. She started to place her hand on my cheek, but she paused. We both noticed how stiff she was, and she forced a smile and opted to pat my shoulder instead.

I was beyond confused. She was hot and cold. She had

kissed me on the boat, then didn't want me near her in the hotel. Then that night we had some of the hottest sex I'd ever experienced, and now, we were back to being awkward.

"What's going on with us?" I asked softly. I let out a breath. I was lost. "Tell me how to fix this."

Her fake smile fell and was replaced with a natural, more sympathetic one. She nodded and looked away from me.

"I know. I'm still—processing things. I want to be with you, but I just need to work through my feelings. Let me go. Trust me to go without you." She looked back to me and smiled reassuringly. "Give me this, and in time, I'll be able to give you me again."

I stared at her with my brows furrowed, trying to understand.

That's it? She just wanted… time?

"Desi, I love you, you fucking loser," she laughed and stood on her tiptoes to give me the quickest peck on the lips. I took it gratefully, as if I were starving to death and she had just handed me a single roll.

We got everything prepared so she could leave with Ludovica and Jaime. By midnight, we were taking them to the airport, where the private plane was waiting. I gave her a tight hug and let her go, just like she had requested.

After the women vampires boarded, Jaime hung behind. We both shared an awkward look, waiting to hear the other speak. Finally, he dug into his pockets and offered me a tight smile.

"Your brother, Gianni," he struggled with his accent to say the Italian-based name. "Gave me this to hold. He said, if you let her go with me to give this to you."

He then presented me with the familiar velvet box I had requested from my older brother months ago. I took it greedily and my eyes flicked to the plane, where the person I intended to give it to sat, comfortable and unaware.

"Thank you," I said. For the first time, I was genuine. "I appreciate this."

He nodded. "He said it would be very important to you. Good luck." With that, he hurried up the metal stairs and onto the plane. I turned and didn't look back. Now, with the ring in my possession, I had more incentive not to fuck this up again. I'd win Scout's love back, even if it killed me.

Once in my car, I glanced at the backseat. I got a loud squawk from Tippi and I scrunched up my nose. This trip was going to fucking suck if I had to be alone with this... what did Scout call me that first time we met?

Cabrón?

I smiled, remembering that day. For me, for us, actually, it had felt like we'd only just met, but in reality we'd been searching for each other since for each other since nineteen-ninety-four.

The bird squawked again and I pulled out my phone. It connected to the car's Bluetooth. I cleared my throat and grabbed a piece of candy from the cup holder.

"Call Arsenio."

"Greed and Wrath! Back in business!" Arsenio, my giant, overeager friend ripped my car door open, shoved his bag in the back, and hopped into the passenger's seat. He turned to face me, his face lit up with an excitement that made me uncomfortable. He clapped, and started to laugh. "Come on, my friend! I can't tell you how long I've waited for this!"

I blinked and shifted back into drive. "I just didn't want to be alone. Calm down."

"Oh, stop." He was practically bouncing in his seat. He brought his arm over to ruffle my hair. I gritted my teeth and shifted away. "You could have called anyone but you called me. I've missed true Seven Sins fun!"

"Ludovica is on the plane with her," I relented.

"We should invite the others! I mean, the ones we can find. Elvie told me about Ginata." He frowned. "I'll have to do some digging. Corrine might send you to find her next."

"What am I, a fucking bloodhound? I agreed to help find Ludovica because we've always been close. Ginata was always kind of a bitch."

"I never saw her like that."

"She would never take no for an answer," I muttered.

"Well you're not one to talk," Arsenio blurted and then realized where he fucked up and promptly shut his mouth with a loud clack of his fangs on his teeth.

"What did you just fucking say to me?" I pushed on the gas pedal, hitting the highway. As the gauge went higher, so did the red staining my mood.

You think I won't kill us all?

"I'm… I'm sorry friend." Arsenio actually flinched and reached for the shoulder that I had taken a bite out of the last time we fought. "I shouldn't have said that."

"What did you hear?" I raised an eyebrow and relaxed my foot. It calmed him down enough to explain.

"Toulouse called me when it happened. He was worried about you."

"I call bullshit."

"You took too much of his candy. The stuff he got from Elvie. It wasn't your fault."

"Don't pander to me," I snarled.

Silence reigned down in the car, and was only broken

when Tippi ruffled his feathers and made a light cooing. It spooked Arsenio and he jumped.

"What the— is that a bird?"

The tension relaxed and I explained how I came to own such an interesting looking animal.

"You're really working hard to fix things, aren't you?" He said afterward.

"I am. She said she wants to be with me but just needs time to figure things out," I grumbled. I understood, and agreed to give Scout as much time as she needed, but the selfish part of me hated every minute I had to spend in the car with Arsenio and not her.

"I'm sure she will. Scout and I used to fight all the time while we were together. I'd give her a few days to cool down and we'd be fine again." He shrugged.

"Can we not discuss you two again?" I muttered. While I did acknowledge that in some fucked up bizarre twist of events, he was the reason I found her again, I hated knowing that she and he used to screw around.

"Yes, of course. I'm sorry again, my friend. I'm just so excited to be back on the road with you, Desiderio Amato, the Seven Sin of Wrath, with me, Greed. And Mexico! I can't wait to try some of the selection there."

I grimaced as images of Arsenio draining willing victims while taking shots of vodka flew through my head.

"It's a family visit, not a party," I reminded him. He waved off my concerns.

"For you, perhaps. You can go meet her family, I'll stay at the hotel and enjoy myself."

I shook my head, and continued driving. Ohio to Mexico was a twenty-six hour drive, according to my phone. Considering our limitations, it'd take us almost a week to get there.

At this rate, I wasn't sure Arsenio would make it to Mexico alive.

"What city exactly is it?" He reached for my phone with the map on the screen. I slapped his hand away.

"Tamaulipas."

"Never heard of it," he said, pulling his phone out and looking it up.

"I'll get us a good hotel," he assured me. "So Scout has a brother?"

"That's what he claims. He showed us a picture of the aunt. She's the spitting image of Scout. I'm inclined to believe there is some truth to it." I was still slightly bitter and nervous about it all.

"Interesting. I've heard about her, the High Priestess of Blood. She's violent, even by your standards."

"That's what I keep hearing."

The bird started muttering in its cage. I could tell that Arsenio really did not like him.

"Gianni brought him, you said? Did he ever give you the ring you asked for?"

I nodded. "Yes and no. Jaime, Scout's brother, gave it to me. Gianni gave it to him. I think it was some stupid power move for him. Apparently he had instructions to only let me have it if I let Scout go." I rolled my eyes.

"Of course. Sounds just like your brother. What are you going to do with the ring?"

I scoffed. "I'm going to propose. I told you that, didn't I?"

"Yes, but that was before all of this. I wasn't sure if your plans had changed."

"Why would they? I love Scout more than I love myself." I grinned, knowing it'd get a chuckle from my good friend. It did.

"That is one thing about you I can agree with! So, a proposal. When will that be? What are you planning? I want to help you make this moment spectacular!" He waved his hands across the car, as if envisioning it now. I blinked.

"I don't know." I squinted my eyes. "What would you do?"

"For Scout? I never considered marriage. Our relationship barely made it out of the bedroom."

I growled and he got back on track.

"Sorry. For a woman I truly loved? Something momentous. Grand! Larger than life. A whole event, with her in the spotlight. Tell me, are you going to do it in Mexico or back home?"

I shrugged. "I really hadn't planned anything. I was just going to do it."

He swore. "No. That won't work. You need to do something she'll remember."

"Okay, well you figure it out then!" I snapped. "This shit isn't my thing. It's a fucking ring. I'll give it to her. She'll say yes. Boom, done."

"No, no no no. Look," he put his hand up and then lifted his phone to his ear. "I'll take care of it. All you need to do is show up." I turned slightly to see him giving me an up and down look and then a grimace. "And a suit."

"Who are you calling?" I asked.

"The family. If we meet Scout's family, they will meet ours."

I blinked.

What?

"And how do you think that's going to work? We can't just strut into a vampire den and say, "hi, we're a fucking organized crime family, can we hang?"

"We won't." He rolled his eyes. "We'll be your real family."

"But Jaime has met my brother."

There was a pause in his plans. "Well who cares, we'll be fine." He put a finger up and spoke into the phone. "Dante! My friend! I need you to come to Mexico with me and Desiderio."

I drove through the night as Arsenio spent our first leg of the trip making phone calls to Corrine, Toulouse, and Dante.

The conversations went about the same as ours had been. They were skeptical, and had lots of questions, but finally, all three agreed to come.

As we pulled into our first hotel, Arsenio discussed Ginata and what to do about her situation as a whole. None of us had known about her imposter. Discovering the truth had caused some major issues. Organized crime was only as good as it's weakest member, and currently ours was MIA.

I checked us in and handed Arsenio his room card as he continued his phone call. Finally, as I was taking Tippi into my room, Arsenio hung up and smiled wide.

"This is great. The seven of us, under one roof again. I can't wait!"

I shook my head. "What about Ginata?"

He waved off my concerns. "Corrine is on the case, she'll figure it out. She always does. There's a reason for her sin."

Pride.

"Thanks for doing this, man," I said, putting my hand on the door. He came over to me. His room was directly across from mine. He put his hand on my back and patted it hard, causing me to jerk forward.

"No problem, friend. It's going to be perfect. I can see it now. The six of us, all standing beside you on your wedding day. I couldn't think of anything better. Well, other than being your best man, naturally," he laughed.

"You want to be my best man?" I blinked with surprise.

"Of course!" he boomed. "Who else better to give her away than the man who did originally!"

"That's not how—" I started, then shook my head. His laughter, energy, and overall good mood was growing on me. I grinned. "Yeah, okay. I'd like that."

CHAPTER 35

Scout

The flight didn't take long. In fact, it was a little too short for my liking. I had hoped for more time to process everything. I had a brother, and an aunt. They lived in Mexico, as I had thought, and they were special.

I was special.

I was hesitant to tell Jaime about what I had only recently learned I could do. So far, my new abilities were only activated with Desi. None of it really mattered if he wasn't with me.

And he wasn't. I specifically asked him to back off. I needed time to process this entire week.

I told myself that I would never go back to Desiderio Amato, but the moment he came for me, I was putty in his hands. I couldn't resist the pull I had to him. Despite his violent actions, he still had my heart.

"Are you okay?" Ludovica reached for my hand. I blinked and turned to her on the plane.

"Yeah, just nervous. I've spent half a century looking for these people, only to have it thrust on me in a few hours." I glanced over at Jaime. I supposed if I were to have a sibling he'd be it. It was hard for me to see similar features in us, but the aunt was undeniable. We could almost be twins.

Jaime heard us and nodded. He said something in Spanish and I shook my head.

"No sé Español," I told him, shrugging apologetically.

He cocked his head and an eyebrow. "I thought you spent time in Mexico?"

"I did. But my friends translated, mostly. I can only catch a few words here and there."

He nodded thoughtfully. "Well we can help you learn."

I almost replied with, —*"I won't be there long enough to learn a new language."* But I decided to keep it inside, not wanting to upset him.

I leaned forward, and opted for a slightly different topic. "Tell me about my parents. Or my aunt. Anything. Actually." I smiled politely.

Jaime relaxed again. "You were born Julieta, not Scout, after our mother. Juanito was our father. We are from Tamaulipas, which is where we are going now." He glanced out the dark window.

"Did you know her? Our mother? Or our dad? How big of an age gap is there between me and you?" I shot question after question at him; he was patient and answered as many of them as he could.

"Sixteen years between you and I. It's not unheard of in the undead society to have children years apart."

"What about our parents? What were they like?"

He was hesitant, his face contorted as if struggling with what to say. "They were nice, but selfish," he finally said.

It was then that he explained our aunt's imprisonment, and the trade that was supposed to happen.

"If she hadn't gotten pregnant with me, our mom would have kept with the plan to die for her sister?"

Jaime nodded. "It was save you or save the entire vampire village. She chose you."

Awkwardness filled the plane. To which, Ludovica perked up.

"Yeah, but it seems to have worked out in the end, right? Scout's alive and well, your village survived, that's good."

"Yes, it is," he agreed. "But our parents paid with their lives for the risk they had put us under to protect you."

"So why am I being asked back then?" I shot at him. It sounded like he was still bitter about something that happened fifty years ago. He didn't seem fazed by my quick anger.

"Because the High Priestess wants to leave her grudges behind. She wants to get to know the child our parents felt so strongly about to risk everything. She wants you to join our court."

"Are you part of it?" I asked.

"Yes." He didn't elaborate, and we were landing before I could ask him more.

For being a smaller, private plane, the ride was relatively smooth. We arrived just as the sun was coming up, and had to stay in a hotel until nightfall.

The heat in Mexico was high and dry. I recalled it with bittersweet memories. Even as a human I wasn't a fan of the hot climate. I much preferred places where autumn was the prevailing season.

Ludovica and I shared a room. I didn't have a cell phone, so I had to use hers to call Desi and see how his trip was going. His words were reassuring, but I knew he wasn't happy with the situation.

That next night, Jaime knocked on our door and told us a car was here to take us to meet my aunt.

"What should I call her?" I asked.

"High Priestess, unless she tells you otherwise. She may try to call you Julieta," He warned.

"I kind of like the name. It's pretty," Ludovica said. She was helping the tension almost constantly with her comments. "Weren't people calling you a priestess too, back in the fake Ginata's territory?"

I furrowed my brows. While it had only been a few days, it felt like ages ago. "Yeah, the Young Blood Priestess."

Jaime nodded. "Yes, the High Priestess of Blood has high hopes for you," he told me cryptically.

I watched out the window, but I was completely unfamiliar with where we were so it was pointless. We drove for almost an hour before reaching a large white brick wall. It was at least twenty feet high and I couldn't see the ends on either side in the dark. Two large wooden doors reminded me of a castle's gates.

The driver got out and spoke to someone standing by the doors.

They were guarding it.

A moment later they were slowly pulled open and the driver returned to the car, and drove us in.

Torches were everywhere, lighting up the small village. Music played loudly in the streets as vampires danced, their shadows dancing with them.

It felt almost as if we had gone back in time. Many of the cities I had visited in Mexico decades ago were somewhat modern. This town was clearly not.

We drove slowly until we reached a large mansion on top of a small hill.

Jaime got out and opened the door wide. "This is it. Let's go."

Ludovica and I joined him. The car took off instantly, leaving us with our carry-on bags to climb up the hill.

The concrete stairs were white, the same as the walls. Everything about this village gave me ancient aztec vibes. The art around us, from the buildings to the paintings on the walls, were old in style but freshly done. It was… beautiful here.

I heard the noises of the birds before I saw them. As we walked, I heard a caw and stopped to see a gorgeous Dracula parrot fly over us. And then, as we continued our trek, another one was perched in a tree, and another. I pointed and Jaime chuckled.

"They are all over the village. The High Priestess loves them too."

For a moment, I wondered how Desi and Tippi were getting along. But before I could make a mental note to call him, we reached the house and stopped. There were a few more stairs on the flat part of the hill, taking us up, and the three of us practically flew up and to the door. Jaime knocked, and was greeted by a handsome Bloodborn vampire.

He recognized Jaime and led us in. Again, I stared in awe of the beautiful home, all decorated in Aztec art. I hadn't stepped into the nineteen sixties as I had previously thought. I was in the fourteen hundreds!

We stopped short when the butler did. He took a step back at a large, open entrance. I could hear the crackle of a fire and I smelled warm, fresh blood. My mouth began to water, as I realized how thirsty I was.

I stood on my tiptoes to see over Jaime's shoulders. A figure stood, but it was dark in the room, lit only by the fire.

A voice came from the room. It was feminine, but spoke in Spanish.

Jaime, considerate of my needs, spoke in English. "I brought the Young Blood Priestess home. She only speaks English."

She hissed.

"Come in," she said a moment later, in my native tongue.

Jaime moved to the side and allowed me to enter first. My heart was racing and suddenly I felt the coldness in my vampire body. I was frozen to the spot but Ludovica's hand pushed on my back, moving me forward.

I entered the room slowly, as if I could step on a wrong tile and a booby-trap could crush me. I looked onwards toward the shadowy figure until my eyes adjusted. When I could see her face clearly, I gasped.

Her eyes lit up as she saw me as well. We truly did look so much alike.

"You are Magdalena?" I whispered. She giggled, and nodded.

"Yes. Welcome home, Young Blood Priestess."

I cleared my throat as I stared at her, trying to catch the differences. Her skin was unblemished, while mine was covered in tattoos. Her hair, while long, dark, and curly, like mine, was more taken care of. It was shiny and framed her face perfectly. Mine was what I called 'permanent just-fucked hair.'

I had more makeup on than her. My eyes were dark with eyeliner while hers were not. But we both had the same shade of red lipstick, which I found interesting.

"It's Scout, actually," I clarified.

She nodded and sauntered over to me. She was wearing a crimson wrap dress with gold trimming. It was clasped over one shoulder with a gold brooch of the sun. She extended her arms out and pulled me in for a hug. I realized as I cautiously hugged her back that the dress was the only thing she was wearing.

I inhaled deeply and she smelled of jasmine. It was relaxing. When she pulled away, I felt as if I truly had come home.

"Jaime, why don't you take her and get a drink." She looked to my brother and Ludovica. Ludovica raised an eyebrow in my direction and I nodded for her to go.

I'd be fine.

As soon as the pair were gone, Magdalena took my hands and urged me to join her in front of the fire, on the floor, surrounded by fluffy pillows.

I was offered a large goblet of warm blood as soon as I crossed my legs. I took it greedily and drank it. The blood was delicious, and I told her so. She smiled, and said nothing as she too drank.

"Tell me about yourself," she demanded.

"What do you want to know?" I asked in reply.

"Do you enjoy life? Do you have powers that other Bloodborns do not? Do you have a mate?" she asked me in rapid-fire succession.

I swayed my head side to side, considering them. "My life is okay. Could be better, could be worse. I like to draw. I want to go to art school."

"Art? Interesting." She smiled, but I could tell she did not find it interesting.

"What kind of powers are you talking about?" I asked instead of answering her second question. Her grin grew so large her fangs became exposed and her eyes widened. She turned to the fire and put her hand out. She quickly closed her hand into a fist and the fire went out, darkness swarming over us. Then, a moment later it roared back to life and I blinked to see her hand open.

"I can do wondrous things."

I shook my head. "I can't do that."

Something in the back of my head was telling me not to tell her about my powers linked directly to Desi. She frowned, but nodded.

"What about a mate? Have you taken a lover?"

I laughed. "I've been on this earth for fifty years."

She laughed with me. "Yes, of course. You have multiple then?"

"No, just the one. We're soulmates."

She cocked her head at the unfamiliar word.

I licked my lips and looked down at my goblet, half-full. "Desi and I fell in love when we were humans. There was an accident, and we both thought the other was going to die, so we made deals with a demon to save each other."

She swore and her red eyes went wide. "Which demon?"

"Samson," I gulped. "Do you know him?"

"I am familiar." Her eyes darkened. "Go on."

"For me, he saved Desi's life, but took my memory of him. I had to give him a thousand evil souls if I wanted it back."

"And him? Desi?" she said his name with almost a confusion in her tone.

"Desiderio," I clarified. I did not like her using my nickname for him. "He had to do ten-thousand."

"How long did it take?"

"Thirty years."

"And you were still in love?"

"Kind of. We had actually met again, before we remembered each other and fell in love without knowing the truth."

"Are you married?"

I shook my head.

"So just in love?"

"Well no, we're bonded."

She shook her head. "I do not understand."

"We drank each other's blood, and now we…" I hesitated, trying to convey things without revealing everything. "Can't live without each other."

Her eyebrows shot straight up. "The demon did this to you?" she demanded, standing up quickly.

I joined her. "No, not at all. We did, on our own."

She didn't seem to be listening. Her fists were clenched at her sides, and her jaw was tight. Suddenly, the almost girlish vampire who sat with me just moments before had switched to the leader everyone claimed she was. She stiffened and started out. I opened my mouth to speak but she clearly didn't care what I had to say.

"We'll see about all of this."

I didn't see Magdalena the rest of the night. I sat by the fire, enjoying the delicious tasting blood and when I had drained the cup I heard someone clear their throat from behind me. I turned to see two beautiful vampire women, dressed similarly to my aunt, smiling at me.

"Do you want a bath?" one of them asked. Her English wasn't great, but it was absurd to go to a different country and expect them to know your native tongue. I nodded.

"We will take care of you," the other woman said, and offered me her hand. I took it and stood up. She squeezed my hand in an almost comforting way and led me out of the room. We went down the hall, and I tried to remember the way back but they were walking so fast, I could barely keep up let alone memorize turns and rooms.

We reached a door, and they let go of me to open it. I blinked when I saw it was the back door. I peered out, and was pleasantly surprised to see tons of candles around a large wooden bath.

"The water is warm and ready for you." They both smiled reassuringly, and I walked outside.

The bath was scented with jasmine and flower petals were floating above the surface. I turned nervously back to them. I watched them close the door and turn their faces to give me privacy.

I was slightly hesitant but I put a finger in the bath and the heat enticed me enough to strip down and climb in.

I sighed as the warm water heated my perma-cold body, slowly thawing it. I spread my arms out and stretched my legs, letting them float up. While I had spent more time than not an undead creature of the night, I still missed being naturally warm. The moment I left this water, I'd begin to cool again.

I was handed a bar of yellow soap. I sniffed it and thought I recognized papaya as a main ingredient. I washed my body and thanked her.

"What is your name?" I asked them both. They smiled, but it didn't quite reach their eyes. It was as if they were on the clock, more than doing a favor for a friend.

"Alicia," said the one who offered me the soap.

"Anita," said the other.

"Were did Magdalena go?" I asked when I finally got out. I didn't want to, but my fingers were pruning.

"She went to see the demon that cursed you." Anita handed me a warm towel. I blinked as I dried myself off.

"What? How?"

The pair exchanged smirks. "The High Priestess does not explain her ways, but we always see the results."

I frowned, unsure of how to take that.

"I broke my curse already, there's no need to stir up old things."

"We do not ask why the High Priestess does things," Alicia said very matter of factly.

"We are to take you to your room." Anita changed the

subject. She had my clothes folded in her arms. I tried to take them back but she shook her head.

"They are dirty. We have a dress for you."

I wasn't entirely enthused, but I was getting tired, and when I looked up I saw that it was getting lighter in the sky. I hurried inside with them and they led me through the large home again, twisting and turning until they stopped to open a door and usher me inside.

The room was decorated in reds and yellows. There was a giant bed with red silk sheets that looked divine. There was a yellow rug on the wooden floor, and I had an armoire and vanity table. Simple, but lovely.

I walked in slowly, taking in my surroundings. I hadn't expected this level of hospitality. When I heard cult, blood sacrifices, and orgies, I had imagined a cave, hidden deep in the mountains. This was nothing of what I had prepared myself for. This was… nice.

Anita and Alicia moved fast. Anita went to the armoire and Alicia ushered me to the vanity. I sat down and looked at the table. There were lotions and oils, brushes for makeup and hair. Ribbons, and jeweled pins. All of this was… beautiful.

Alicia picked up a white cream and dumped it into her hands. She then began running her fingers through my unruly curls. I flinched as she hit snarl after snarl, but whatever was in that cream seemed to work with the curls. She reached for a comb and continued working until slowly but surely, my curls became less 'just-fucked tangles' and more… 'Aztec priestess'. I looked so much more like Magdalena now with my hair detangled it took my breath away.

Alicia put something on my face that smelled heavenly. She rubbed it in and murmured something about it keeping my face youthful. I smirked, considering that. I saw her lips curve upward just slightly as well.

After my hair was under control I stood and Anita was ready with a dress just like the one Magdalena had been wearing.

"Do I get underwear?" I asked. They exchanged looks and shook their heads.

I guess… when in Rome.

They helped me put the dress on. While letting them see me nude was mildly uncomfortable, I pushed past it. It was obvious that this was their job. This was nothing new to them.

"Go to sleep. The High Priestess will come for you tomorrow," Anita promised. They waited until I climbed into bed to leave. I was so refreshed and the bed was so luxurious that sleep came easy that morning.

The next evening I was greeted by the same two servants and warm, fresh blood. I greedily downed it and took in another full goblet. This blood was different. It was delicious.

"Where is Ludovica? The woman I came with?" I asked. They gave me polite nods.

"She is being entertained by Jaime. Magdalena would like to see you first."

I opened my mouth to protest, but it seemed trivial. Jaime and Ludovica seemed to get along well. I should just let them relax.

I was given a fresh dress. Alicia brushed my hair again and insisted on doing my makeup. When I turned back to the mirror, Magdalena and I could be twins.

I stood and together, the three of us returned to that room I had first met my aunt in. There she was again, relaxing on pillows in front of the fire.

I came to sit with her. She looked me over and nodded approvingly.

"The vampire you took that curse for is here," she said, her voice rather deadpan. She didn't look at me when she said it.

I perked up. "Desi! Where is he?" I looked around, almost as if he were going to pop out of the shadows.

"He brought a friend. He is very handsome."

"Who? Desi?"

"No. The friend. Arsenio." She struggled with his name. I blinked. He brought Arsenio? Why?

"Can I go see them? Are they staying here?"

"You can." She turned to me then and shrugged. "I will send for them." She snapped her fingers and the two servant vampires I had been given disappeared.

"You are an artist," she said, not asking.

I grinned. "I am. You have beautiful art all around your community. I'd love to study it."

She beamed, flashing her fangs. "Take all the time you'd like. This is your home, and I want you to love it as much as I do."

We sat in comfortable silence for a moment before I turned to ask a question.

"You went to see the demon who cursed me. Why?"

Her eyebrows went up, but she seemed otherwise unfazed. She seemed to enjoy staring into the fire.

"A demon does not make deals with uninteresting vampires. He thought you were special, and I wanted to know why."

I swallowed. "How did you get a meeting with a demon like that?"

"I have many powers."

"Were you satisfied with the conversation?" I asked, not knowing what else to say.

She lifted her hand and wavered it. "Demons are tricky folk. I wanted to know who he thought he was, cursing my niece!" She laughed, waving a finger in the air. "He scurried away before I could ask any more questions."

A knock came then, and we turned to see Anita and Alicia.

"Your guests," Anita announced and stepped away to let Desi, Arsenio, and Ludovica enter the room.

Three of the Seven Sins in one room. They weren't in one of the other's territory, this was out in the wild. Was this safe?

Magdalena stood and held out her hand. Arsenio moved quickly to kiss it.

"You are very beautiful," Arsenio said to her. I heard a low growl come from behind him, and Arsenio snapped back, with a tight, awkward smile to me. "Hello again, Scout."

"Are you comfortable in your rooms?" Magdalena asked. All three gave various positive answers and she motioned for everyone to sit. I stepped over a pillow to go to Desi. He grinned, and reached for my hand. I took it, lacing my fingers through his. I pulled him forward, to sit beside me by the fire.

Ludovica and Arsenio sat in the middle, between Magdalena and I.

"Tell me about yourself, Desi."

"Desiderio," Desi corrected. I grinned.

Only I got to call him that.

Magdalena raised her eyebrows but adjusted quickly.

"Desiderio, the vampire who has stolen my niece's heart. Tell me, what makes you interesting?"

My thoughts went back to our conversation right before

they got here. How demons only make deals with special vampires.

"The only thing interesting about me is my namesake." Desi shrugged. "I have nothing impressive to list."

"Your eyes are interesting."

"That was a product of my curse. Since I was shot before turning, I was offered a sort of deal. A half-in, half-out situation."

She smirked, almost as if she had assumed he was not special and now it was confirmed. "Scout made a deal to kill one thousand men to get you back. What was your agreement with the demon they call Samson?"

Desi looked taken back by her bluntness. He cleared his throat and glanced around the room. "Ten thousand."

"Why was your number so high, I wonder?" she mused.

"I couldn't tell you. Maybe he was doing Scout a favor, considering the blood running through her."

"And what blood runs through you?" Magdalena's tone turned icy and she turned from the fire.

"I come from a long line of Bloodborns. My family, the Amato's, are well known in the United States."

"Fame is relative," Magdalena sighed. "I was rather famous many years ago."

"You aren't anymore?" I tilted my head in confusion.

She shook hers sadly. "No. Me and my people had to go into hiding. The Mexican people did not like us. There is a protection spell, keeping everyone inside the village safe and secret from the humans. But, not anymore. I want us to take back everything we lost."

I gulped. The determination in her blood-red eyes unnerved me. What did she mean by that?

"For too long my people have been trapped here, afraid to leave for fear of capture, torture, and death. With our power," she leaned forward and snatched my hand up. "We can fight back."

I pulled my hand back. "I don't want to fight anyone. Can't you just co-exist? We do in the United States."

She nodded, but rolled her eyes. "We can, but we want *more*. We've earned more."

"Is that why you went looking for me? To ambush humans?" I grimaced.

"No." She grinned. "That is just a bonus." There was a long pause before she snapped her fingers again and a moment later we were being served large goblets of tasty blood. "Do not worry about any of that. I've been planning this for years. It is not happening tomorrow. Desiderio, tell me about your life before the curse."

As Desi regaled her with stories of his life as a human, I sat and muddled over her seemingly flippant plans. She clearly wanted to see if I could help her overtake the humans. I could never do that. I wasn't a monster.

Or was I?

Flashes of all the brutal murders I'd committed over the years ran through my mind. Was I just in denial about how much I enjoyed ripping a heart out?

"That entire night was a rough one," Desi said. I popped back into the conversation just as he told the room about the night we both turned, died, and were cursed.

"Our birthdays are a day apart. And I had no idea she was a vampire. I thought I was going to turn and we could never be together."

"You abandoned her," she accused. I raised an eyebrow. How did she know about the bridge?

Desi gulped, glanced at me, then nodded. "I did. I was a coward. I let her drink my blood to give her enough sustenance to complete the change and survive, but then I ran. I didn't know how to process everything."

Magdalena shook her head. "You created the bond then. Giving her your blood."

"And then I gave him mine, when we met a second time thirty years later," I told her, feeling the need to defend him.

"Soulmates. Such an interesting concept." Magdalena looked to the two silent members of our group. They both sat up straight and blinked at her, remaining silent. "Could it be real? What happens if one person betrays the other?"

Desi and I glanced at each other. We both were thinking about his odd ghost form.

"Don't tell her anything!"

Desi raised an eyebrow and nodded ever so slightly to tell me he heard it in his mind.

"I don't think we could," Desi told her. "Fate has other plans for us. Regardless of what happens, our lives are tied together, and we can't move forward without the other."

"I was in love before. More than once." She smiled softly. "Deep down, the need for survival is too strong. You make sacrifices for the ones you love, and time and time again I have had to make those sacrifices," she paused, her eyes changing from the wistful, almost childlike expression to bone-chillingly cold. She leaned forward, only inches from Desi's face as she spoke the chilling words.

"Tell me, Desiderio, could you?"

CHAPTER 37

Desi

This place gave me the creeps. Which, was laughable, considering who and what I was.

It was like we were transported through time. The architecture, the art, the clothing. All of it gave me chills before I had even been taken to seeing Scout.

They had turned her into a doppelgänger of her aunt. At a quick glance, I couldn't tell them apart, which I felt was the whole point.

We stayed in that room, with Arsenio, Ludovica, and Magdalena. Our host interrogated me most of the night, wanting to know more details about the curse. I was not enthused, but every time I glanced at Scout, I saw her expression and relented. She looked so worried, so desperate to have her newfound family member like her, how could I destroy that?

When morning finally came, we all stood. Our bodies were full of warm blood and our brains, well, mine anyway, were exhausted.

"My servants will take you back to your rooms to rest," Magdalena nodded.

Arsenio and Ludovica went first, and I clung to Scout's side. We started out and Magdalena reached for Scout's empty hand.

"You two are not married?"

I blinked. Seriously? This was the route she was taking?

"No." Scout shook her head. "Why? Can we not share a room?"

Magdalena glanced at me, and I glared down at her. Fuck her if she was going to try to say that shit.

"Are you really going to try to judge us for sleeping together?" I asked sharply. She glared at me, and irritation swelled in me. "I heard about your past. You used to be a sex worker. And you still do blood orgies, do you not? Me sleeping with my long-term partner was nothing compared to that."

She seemed to reconsider and sniffled.

"No. I'll see you tonight." She let us go then, but I could see she was not pleased.

"What the hell was all that?" Scout hissed, once the bedroom door was closed and Scout's assigned servants had left. They insisted on brushing her hair again and putting her in a nightdress.

"Sorry. I don't know about her. She rubs me the wrong way," I admitted.

"What do you mean?" Scout asked. She slipped under the covers and invited me in as well. I had been allowed to keep my clothes. So I peeled off my Iron Maiden shirt and jeans and slid in beside her. I pulled her cold body into my own and let out a deep sigh as she stiffened but relaxed an instant later.

Baby steps.

"She hates me, obviously. Like I'm not good enough for you or something."

Scout laughed. "How does it feel to be on the other side of that?"

"What do you mean?" I lifted my head. She turned hers to look at me.

"When we visited your family they seemed absolutely repulsed by the idea that you wanted to be with me and not Aleida. It sucked. This is the same thing."

"So, I'm right. She doesn't like me."

Scout turned her head back and snuggled closer to my body. "Maybe. But it doesn't matter. I like you and I'm keeping you."

I watched her close her eyes and I tried to relax with her to do the same, but I couldn't shake the feeling that coming here was a bad idea.

That next evening, we were greeted by her two women in waiting.

"Jaime would like to take you to meet the people of the city," one of them told her.

The other turned to me. "The High Priestess would like to speak to you this evening."

"Again? We talked all last night," I protested, but the looks on all three vampire women told me I had no other option. "Fine. Let me get dressed."

One of them handed me my bag and I thanked them. They turned as I got dressed. They were more focused on Scout. I watched with mild interest as they washed her arms and face. They then reapplied makeup and styled her hair to resemble her aunt's. They wrapped her in another white dress, this time with red trim the color of their eyes. Then, they brought out a gold crown to place on her head. It was small and delicate, but truly made her look like royalty.

Why were they doing this? All of this was so— off.

They finished by rubbing her down with perfumed oils

and then let her go. They split then, one coming toward me, the other staying with her.

"I will take you to the High Priestess now."

I looked at Scout, lingering for a moment. She was beautiful; but she was not Scout. The only difference between the two women was the ink on Scout's body, where Magdalena had none.

"How do I look?" Scout asked, her voice perky. I smiled.

"Gorgeous. I'll see you in a bit, okay?" I went to her and she let me kiss her. I wanted to press deeper, stay longer, but she pulled away, gently pushing her hands on my chest.

"Yes. Later tonight. I love you," she said.

I pressed my lips together, fangs sinking into my lower lip, but I relished the pain. "I love you too," I told her before I left.

I expected to return to the fire room but was lead through the house, past that room and all the others. Finally, the woman opened a door and I heard the bugs chirping outside. I blinked, looking out. There were candles lit, but it was dark.

"Are you kicking me out?" I blinked in surprise, although, I felt stupid for being surprised. The servant shook her head and motioned for me to go through the door. Hesitantly, I forced my feet forward and out of the house.

I relaxed only slightly when I saw it must be the backyard, for there was a large wooden hot tub. Steam rolled off the surface and large flowers floated around inside.

"Join me, Desiderio."

I whipped my head around to see Magdalena dropping her dress to the ground and stepping out of it, completely naked.

"Uh, no?" I raised an eyebrow and looked away. Was this a weird test to see if I'd cheat on her niece? Even if that were possible, it wouldn't be with her.

"I insist. I promise I won't touch you," she laughed

deeply and I didn't believe her for a second. We stood there for a long moment. I stared at her feet, my hands in my pockets, fingering my cards. Finally she stepped toward the hot tub and used the stairs attached to get in. She lowered herself slowly, and once again asked me to join her. "We have another guest coming soon."

That relaxed me some. A third person could be safe. Or would it be even worse? Still, I stayed put. I watched her sigh and then raise her hand. She flicked her wrist and suddenly, I felt a presence beside me.

"Hello again, Desiderio Amato." The voice caused me to jump so hard I fell face first to the ground. I spun around and quickly scurried back, hitting my head on the hot tub. There, in the flesh, was the demon I dealt with once upon a time. With his suit and all.

"What the fuck." I swallowed hard. "What are you doing here?"

"I told you we'd have a guest. Why don't you join us, Desiderio." Magdalena reached down and ruffled my hair. I jerked away.

Samson, the demon in his human form, reached out his hand for me. His smile was polite, but I knew better. I ignored his help and stood up on my own.

I watched him roll his eyes, and then a moment later he was gone. He reappeared an instant later, in the hot tub, seemingly bare. "Join us for a talk, would you?"

Reluctantly, I took off my shirt, jeans, and shoes. I kept my boxers on, and climbed into the bath. I made a point to splash Magdalena. I sat directly between them. I was stiff and ready to fight for my life if needed. How I would in just my boxers and no weapons other than my teeth, I didn't know, but I'd try.

"What do you want?" I snapped.

"Why do you want my niece?" Magdalena asked quickly.

"What do you mean? Because I'm in fucking love with her. That's why," I snarled.

"You are different. She is a queen in the making," she argued.

I cocked my head. "And what am I? A monster?" I laughed. "She's no angel either. She had her own curse she took for me all too gladly, if you don't remember." I pointed to Samson. "And she broke it. She's just like me."

"She didn't know any better."

"Know any better? What did you expect her to do? Come home to a place that never wanted her, and marry some.... Cabrón you pick for her?" I shot the word Scout had called me that first time at the theater back at her aunt. The vampire blinked rapidly. I turned to my other side.

"And what the fuck are you here for? To take me to hell with you? Sorry pal, but I'm done making deals with the devil. I learned my lesson."

Samson held his hands up in innocence and laughed. "I'm not here for your soul. I'll take anyone's. I'm not picky."

I furrowed my brow in confusion but didn't have time to focus on him. I turned back to Magdalena. "What are you planning?"

She stood, baring her slick, oiled body to the chilled air. "My niece, the Young Blood Priestess, has returned to her rightful place beside me. She will reign over our village, and together we will slowly take over Mexico."

"And you think she's up for this? Scout isn't like you," I scoffed. She took a step and slipped halfway back under the water. She came toward me. I pressed my back against the hot tub as she moved closer, pressing her naked body against me.

"You lie. Scout has powers that she's hiding."

"What are you talking about?" I snapped, my hands

reaching out for her wrists under the water. I squeezed and shoved her away. She didn't budge, instead, she tilted her head to whisper into my ear.

"Samson keeps no secrets." She licked my ear lobe, and traced her tongue down my neck. Slowly, my head turned to look at the demon. I ignored Magdalena completely.

"What did you tell her?"

Samson shrugged. A small smile slipped onto his face. He chose to reply to me through his mind as well.

"She's not the only one I make deals with. You want favors, make me an offer."

Magdalena's hand reached for my boxers and I snapped out of it. I shoved her away with all of my strength and I stood.

"I don't know what you think you know, but you're wrong. Scout would never stay here just to kill thousands of innocent people for you. She doesn't want world fucking domination. She wants to paint!" I screamed at her.

"Paint?" Magdalena scoffed. "You want her to stay beside you as a pet. It is you who should bow down to her," She growled. Her fangs flashed as she stood again. "It is you that will leave this place tonight and never return. It is you she will forget. You!" She kept screaming.

I blinked. What? She was looking from me to Samson, as if they had already planned my demise and I was moments from it.

Samson shook his head. I stood and jumped out of the tub. My wet feet hit the stone ground and I looked for my clothes. The servant was scooping them up quickly to hide them from me.

I turned to keep my eyes on the tub and the servant vampire. Suddenly, Samson disappeared and reappeared, dry and in his suit, beside me. "End his bond!" Magdalena shrieked.

"I told you. I don't do anything for free. Make me an offer."

"You want a soul? Fine." Magdalena stood and pointed to the servant girl. She made a swishing movement with her finger and the girl let out a quick, sharp scream before her body stiffened, a thin line of blood started from one side of her throat to her other, and then, she crumpled as her head separated from her body. Both pieces of the vampire woman fell to the stone, bleeding profusely. "Now do it."

Samson seemed to consider her offering. "Fine." He turned to me then, and I looked at him, my eyes wide with horror. I put my hands up to defend myself. "You've got my card if you want to make me a stronger offer."

"But—"

I didn't get to finish my sentence. Samson snapped his fingers and everything went black.

CHAPTER 38

Desi

I woke up in an unfamiliar dark place. I sat up and groaned. "Where am I?"

"Desiderio? My friend, you are awake!" Arsenio's voice was hushed but elated. "Ludovica! He's awake!"

I blinked. My eyes burned and my entire body felt heavy. My arms collapsed under me, making me drop back onto the bed.

"Steady now. You've been sick."

"What do you mean?" I asked. I closed my eyes and steadied myself. I felt dizzy.

"The fucker woke up?" Tully's voice came from the other side of the room.

"It looks like it," Dante replied.

"Who's all here?" I tried to sit up again and a feminine hand was placed on my back to help me.

"Everyone, dear," Corrine answered.

"Minus Ginata," Tully snickered.

"Yes. Of course. We're working on that one," Corrine replied. I opened my eyes cautiously. The room was dimly lit by candles, but I quickly realized that it was not Scout's room or the one I had been originally given in Magdalena's home.

"How long was I out?" I was offered a large pitcher of blood. I gulped it down with a ferocity that wasn't like me. I usually had better control than this, but I was…thirsty.

"A week," Ludovica said.

"A week?" I choked on the last of the blood. It spurted out of my mouth and dribbled down my chin like a child. "What the fuck happened?" Already, I could feel my strength returning.

"We're not entirely sure." Arsenio scratched his head. "Ludovica and I were seized and told that we had to leave. We tried to fight, but that woman, the high priestess, she's stronger than the two of us." He hung his head.

"We were taken to the edge of her protective spells. She keeps her coven under magic. Once you're out, you can't come back unless you're invited," Ludovica added.

"Then how did you guys find me?"

Corrine offered me a cloth to wipe my face. I took it and quickly attempted to clean myself.

"They brought you to us, shortly after. We took you to the nearest town and got a hotel room. We've been here, watching over you."

"I've just been unconscious? For a week?" I was so confused. I couldn't remember how any of this happened.

"Yes. Your shallow breaths were the only indicator that you weren't dead. I think the Bloodborn blood in you has been fighting whatever is trying to kill you." Corrine nodded to the room, as if they'd been discussing this.

"I feel fine now. Confused, but I'm ready. Where's Scout?" I demanded. Everyone's eyes turned down to the floor. I repeated myself, and once again, I received no answer.

I clenched my fists and I narrowed my gaze. "I need answers now before I go fucking feral."

"She seems to have forgotten you."

My mouth fell open, and I wasn't entirely sure how to respond. What?

"Again?" I blurted, finally.

All the heads in the room fell with the defeat I felt. Ludovica came to sit beside me on the bed. She put her arm over my shoulder and leaned her head on my side.

"Again."

I ran my tongue across my fangs trying to process things.

"But I still remember her. All of it. I know who she is to me."

No one spoke. I stood and my legs wavered. I stretched and slowly began to pace.

"What happened then? Did she get cursed, again? I don't understand." I pressed my palms to my temples. "None of this makes sense."

"What is the last thing you remember?" Corrine asked. I scrunched up my nose, trying to think.

"Scout. I was there with her. She was going with her brother, and I had to go see Magdalena. Magdalena!" I blinked. "It was her! She did this."

"Did what?" Arsenio stood quickly. I shrugged and waved an arm over my body.

"Whatever this last week was. She put me under some weird sleep and made Scout forget me. She doesn't want us to be together. She wants Scout to stay here."

I flinched. My brain felt fuzzy. Every time I tried to push past the gray shadows hiding what happened that night, something was pushing back, causing my brain to scream for me to stop. What had that priestess done to us?

"I'm going to go find her." I looked around for a door.

"Who? The High Priestess? Desiderio, don't you realize we've been trying to do that all week?" Arsenio reached for my forearm but I pulled away.

"Dude, you're not getting in there. We've basically circled the perimeter. She's got solid magic," Tully told me.

"It's true. I don't know how to get in," Dante added.

"I'll find a fucking way," I gritted my teeth. My vision was turning red. I don't know what that woman was doing, but I wasn't going to let her take Scout from me. I'd die fighting for her if I had to.

I saw the door and stalked over to it. Suddenly chairs squealed and everyone clamored up and toward me. I reached the knob but was tackled by Dante. We fell to the ground with a hard thump.

"What the hell was that for?" I demanded.

"Dude," he sat halfway up and thrust his hand toward a window. "It's still daylight."

"How do you know she's forgotten about me?" I sat, frustrated and impatient, waiting for the sun to go down. It had been a week since I had woken up, and still I was stuck in this hotel with all but one of my Seven Sins clan, with no real update on what Scout was doing.

"Last week, she and a group of Bloodborns came down into the human village. I caught her alone and said hello, and she didn't recognize me." Ludovica frowned. "When I told her I was your sister, she told me she didn't know anyone by that name. She was genuinely confused."

"Desi. She calls me Desi. That's why," I insisted, but I knew it was a frail attempt at bargaining with myself. She would have known.

"She's coming again tonight, and we're ready to distract her new group and give you a chance to speak to her. Don't worry." Corrine patted my thigh, but it wasn't as comforting as she had meant.

"Come on, friend. This will work!" Arsenio, ever the optimist, grinned at me. "Seeing your face will break the spell she's under and she'll run back to you. Then, we can work on your proposal."

"Proposal?" Tully grimaced. "You want to get married?" He stuck out his tongue in distaste.

"Well not right now, obviously," I shot back. Then, I turned to Arsenio and shook my head. "One thing at a time, man. I can't even think about that shit right now. I can't get married if she doesn't know what name to say at the altar."

Silence filled the room for a moment, but Dante broke it by announcing it was officially nighttime. We could leave the room.

The room was the only one available to us close by. It was a large family room, but with six adult vampires, it was… cozy. I needed to stretch my legs and fill my lungs with fresh air.

The only one that had left the room so far had been Tully, who, surprisingly, was fluent in Spanish.

"Immortality gets boring," he explained in his jersey accent and a casual shrug. He left every night, returning with blood to share.

"This tastes like shit," Dante grimaced as he downed his cup.

"It's from a fucking donkey, what do you expect?" Tully smirked. "This is laying low."

Dante rolled his eyes and looked down toward me. "Please, for the love of God, get your girl so we can fucking go."

"Fine by me," I said, and stormed out into the night.

The village we were staying at was small, but lively. It was loud day and night, despite a large vampire coven living only miles away.

I stepped out and was actually a little taken back by how lit up the town was. Lanterns lit up the town square, a band was playing music and humans were laughing and dancing. Was it a holiday?

For such a small village, it was odd they had a motel, I realized as I walked. There couldn't be more than a thousand people in this town, and half of them were in the middle of it right now.

Tully sidled up next to me, wearing tinted glasses. Corrine had supplied everyone with them so as to not spook the humans. I however, the only one without red eyes, could walk amongst them unseen. Tully caught the eye of an older man and he smiled, mouth closed, at him. He said something I didn't understand and the man nodded eagerly. He replied and I stood there awkwardly as the two conversed.

Finally, he shook his hand and turned away.

"They are having a party because tonight the vampires are coming down. It's the High Priestess' birthday."

"They know about the vampires?"

He nodded.

"They make the best of it. If they show fear they die. So instead, they party until dawn, celebrating the monster on top of the hill, so to speak. There's going to be a blood parade, he says." He pointed his thumb back at the guy.

"A blood parade?" I blinked, trying to imagine how messy that could be.

"That's just what they call it. The vampires come down wearing red, walk through the city, then leave. That's your window. It's small, so don't miss it."

I flipped him off.

I waited, smiling and bobbing my head with the crowd, as we all watched the clock. They'd come at midnight, Tully told me.

Sure enough, a large bell gonged at the top of twelve and the city grew quiet. The music stopped playing, the people stopped dancing, and the air stopped moving.

My head turned, and I stood taller to get a good view of the parade. It wasn't a large one. In fact, I'd say only about twenty vampires came down to visit. One of them being Scout.

She was dressed magnificently. Her makeup reminded me of a Greek goddess. Her dress was the rich ruby color of her eyes, and my heart longed for her. It pulled me through the crowd. As I got closer, I noticed that she was wearing a shawl to cover her tattoos. Were they intentionally trying to mislead the humans? Sure, if they only saw the high priestess sparingly it would be hard to tell the difference, but I could see it instantly. That was Scout, my scout.

I reached the front of the crowd and just as Scout was going to reach us, they turned. My mouth fell open.

No!

I scurried around the humans, trying to keep up with the fast-moving parade. However, by the time I got in front of them again, the parade was done. They were heading out of town.

I slumped, but then decided to follow them as far as I could.

Fuck it.

As soon as they were out of the lantern light, the clump of vampires relaxed and spread out. Most had started a sprint toward the safety of their spell-protected village, but others walked at a slower pace, one of them being Scout.

I was surprised to see that no one was hovering over her. She was still at the edge of the village, her back turned toward the forest. Within minutes, she was the only one left. Did they trust her to return back to them?

I gulped and stepped out of the shadows, only a few feet away from her. She jumped and let out a sharp inhale.

"Hey Nerd," I said with a light chuckle. My eyes flicked to her neck, and disappointment flooded me as I saw that the necklace was gone. Scout shook her head and furrowed her brows.

"No se inglés."

I blinked.

"You fucking liar."

The face she made told me that despite her not recognizing my face, she did still know English.

"What?"

"I said, you're a fucking liar."

"How dare you. Do you know who I am?" She glared at me, dropping the façade. Her eyes grew large.

I laughed. "Do you?"

"Do I what?" Her upper lip twitched in a snarl. Her fangs peeked out with her anger, sitting just under the surface.

"Know who you are? Do you know who I am?" I pressed my lips together, trying to suppress my grin. I couldn't. My smile spread over my lips, seeing her small frame so pissed off. I slid my hand in my pocket. Her eyes dipped down, watching me with caution.

I pulled out a deck of cards that I'd banded with a red rubber band. I slid it off and onto my wrist, and spread the cards out in my hand. I extended my arms out to show them to her.

She looked down at them and furrowed her brows.

"What am I supposed to be looking at? Are you some kind of street magician?"

I gulped. My mouth opened and closed for a moment. "These were— are—" I corrected myself. "Your cards."

She shook her head. "I'm sorry." She took a step back and put her hands up. "I think you're mistaking me for someone else."

My eyes began to well up against my will. In her eyes, I had realized true hell. Knowing our history when she had no clue, was a sucker punch to my heart. I could barely breathe as she stared down at the weather-worn cards.

"I found every single one of them," I choked up as she stared at me in shock and confusion. "We had a fight, and you left them in the woods." Suddenly, my hurt was replaced by anger. How could she not remember? "By the time I found them they'd been rained on, stepped on, wrinkled, and torn. But you know what?" I gathered them tightly in my hand and pulled back. "It was worth it. I dug through that God damn woods for two nights to make sure I got each and every card back, and you still have no clue who I am!" A single tear finally got through, sliding down my cheek.

I wiped the blood away with the back of my hand and sniffled. I closed my eyes and steadied my breathing.

"I'm sorry." Her voice was gentle, and she reached for the cards. I looked up from the ground in surprise as she took them from my hands. "I'm sorry you're hurt."

I laughed then. I dropped my now empty hand and then put both behind my head. I stepped back, and another laugh came out. This was literal hell.

"Thanks. I gave up everything for you. Fucking every-thing!" I shouted. She blanched and took another step toward the dark trees. "You see this?" I stormed over to her and bent down, shoving my face into hers. I pointed at my eyes.

"That's my permanent reminder of what I gave up to have you. I shed literal blood for you. Over and over. I went to the ends of the world for you, and you don't even fucking remember that you're my fucking soulmate, Scout."

She shook her head furiously, her red eyes large and horrified. Clutching the cards in her hands, she stepped back until she was just at the edge of the trees.

"I don't know who hurt you, but it wasn't me. My name is Julieta."

I stared at her as she stepped into the shadows, her eyes the only thing I was able to see anymore.

My tongue slipped between my lips as I shook my head, trying to figure out a way to fix this, but my mind was blank.

"You're really fucking leaving, aren't you?" I scoffed.

"I have to. My people need me." Her voice came out tiny, but I could hear it clearly.

"Your people? Scout— those aren't your people."

"How do you know my name?" She demanded.

"I thought you were Julieta," I shot back.

She repeated her question.

I blinked. "I've already told you," I snarled.

"I— I don't believe you," she stammered. "What is your name?"

I stiffened. She took a step back and I knew this was my last chance to speak. I made perfect eye contact as I answered her silently, connecting our minds with the bond only she and I still shared.

"Desiderio. You call me Desi."

CHAPTER 39

Scout

I stared down at the cards. They were faded and wrinkled from moisture, some ripped, some folded, but there were four cards that were completely unharmed.

I picked them up and held them to my face one by one. The Fool. I scrunched up my nose, trying to feel something. A memory, a thought, an idea of what this card could mean. But once again, I felt nothing.

I tossed the Five of Cups, Three of Swords, and the Ten of Swords on my bed and sighed. This was pointless.

A knock on my door had me scrambling to pick up the entire deck and shove them under my pillow.

"Entras!" I called, letting the person know they could come in. My Spanish education was slow going, but I was trying to do better every day. Magdalena had told everyone they were not to speak English to me anymore, so I had no choice but to learn the language.

I exhaled some relief as Jaime came through the door, and no one else.

"Hi!" I exclaimed. I hopped off the bed and went to

embrace him. He had been the only one willing to defy her rules since I'd returned back to Mexico, months ago.

"How are you, Blood Priestess?" he asked me. I rolled my eyes. That was the one thing he didn't budge on. Everyone called me that, or sometimes, the Young Blood Priestess. I just wanted to be the name my aunt had told me I was given at birth, Julieta.

Since I couldn't be Scout.

"I'm okay. Bored." My eyes flicked to the window. Warm air was coming through at a leisurely pace. It brought music and the scent of fresh blood from the Bloodborns down below. Here, every night was a celebration. One that I very much wanted to be a part of. "Can I go down today?"

He frowned and my heart sank. I hated the nights I was forced to remain in the house on top of the hill. I wanted to dance, laugh, and sing, with all the other vampires of the village.

"I'm sorry. The High Priestess wants to see you tonight."

"Oh?" I glanced down at myself. I was still in my night-dress. I rarely changed these days unless I was leaving. "What about?"

"She wants to see if your memories have returned."

I blinked. "Oh."

It had been almost two months since the accident. I didn't even remember that, let alone anything else. I was almost a stranger in my own skin. I couldn't remember my childhood or my life after I turned. I had tattoos all over my body I didn't recall getting, a gnarly scar on my thigh that confused me, and a deck of cards under my pillow I desperately hoped would give me answers.

I shook my head. "I still don't."

He reached out and hugged me again. "It's okay. She only

worries. Go visit, have some fresh blood, and maybe I can suggest I take you down to visit with the others."

"Thank you Jaime, thank you."

He grinned. "Get dressed. I'll wait outside for you." He exited and shut the door behind him, letting me prepare for a visit with the high priestess.

All of my clothing was similar. Long, swooping dresses that reminded me of Ancient Greece. I picked one the color of rust and draped it around me. I then went to my vanity, quickly put my hair up in a ribbon of matching color and applied some makeup. I looked like death without it.

Finally, I left the room and saw Jaime leaning against the wall, waiting for me. We started down the hall, toward the high priestess' blood den.

"Jaime, I did have one thing that might be something." I clasped my hands in front of me and squeezed my fingers nervously.

He stopped short and turned to me. "A memory?"

"Maybe. It was a dream." I swallowed hard and my eyes drifted to my feet. "Does the name Desiderio mean anything to me?" I glanced up and saw his face turn from surprise to a scowl in an instant. His jaw tightened and his eyes narrowed.

"We don't use that name in this village. Do not speak of him again." He started forward but I reached for his arm. I grabbed his wrist and pulled to stop him.

"Hold on. Why? What is he?"

"He's a monster," Jaime snarled. He turned to me and pointed to his eyes with his other hand. "He has the mark of the beast."

"What do you mean?" I let go of him. Jaime didn't relax his furious stance. I had gone rounds with him and everyone else serving in this house for two months. I was sick of it. I glared right back at him. I refused to back down on this one. I crossed my arms.

"Desiderio is a monster. He is neither welcome here nor in the village where he currently resides. He roams the streets, preying on the innocent. He hides in plain sight. If you ever see him, in dreams or in front of you…" he leaned down and got face to face with me. "Run."

He turned then and stormed down the hall. I hurried after him. "He didn't look evil. He seemed to know me. Surely someone who I was close with couldn't be evil."

"No more! Where did you see him?" Jaime demanded without looking back at me.

"In my dream," I lied and then steeled myself. "No. Tell me exactly what he did to warrant such— such—" I stumbled, looking for the words to describe my normally calm brother's current state. "Wrath!"

He stopped then, and seemed to take a few long, deep breaths. His next words came through gritted teeth and a clenched jaw. "That man has admitted to slaughtering ten thousand people. He is the worst kind of monster."

I hesitated in responding. My mouth went dry and I opened and closed my mouth a few times before asking. "What kind?" The words came out so softly I wasn't sure he heard me.

"The ones hidden amongst us."

The conversation ended then. Jaime was done talking about Desiderio and his odd eyes. I walked behind him silently, as if walking toward my death. I paused at the entrance to Magdalena's private relaxing room. The tension in the air between my brother and I was thick.

"I'm sorry. For arguing."

He blinked rapidly, but turned away and headed back to his own part of the house without speaking.

"Julieta?"

I sighed, and stepped in. The room was dimly lit and she sat by the fire, as she did almost every night. The room smelled of flowers freshly picked and blood freshly shed. The fire crackled but other than that, it was quiet.

"I forbid English and still, you insist on speaking it," she said in English. I raised my eyebrows and my heart sped up with nerves. Had she heard Jaime and I? I opened my mouth to reply, but she put her hand up. She still hadn't turned to even glance at me. "Come sit."

I did as told, spreading my dress out over my legs. She had chastised me on my tattoos numerous times, despite my memories of getting them were gone.

"You wanted to see me?" I replied, also in English. While I had been working hard at learning, I was still much faster at English. It was as if the accident had completely washed away my knowledge of any Spanish words I knew.

"Yes. I want to talk about your gifts."

"Gifts?" I cocked my head. The beautifully scary vampire woman finally turned her head. The look on her face shook me to the core. Her eyes were blank, as if looking through me, talking to a different dimension.

"Yes. You share my blood, you must have gifts like me."

I shook my head. "I don't think so."

She put her hand up again and suddenly my tongue felt heavy. I couldn't speak. I clamped my mouth shut and widened my eyes. What did she do?

"You have them. You don't know how to use them." She put her hand down and instantly I could use my mouth again.

"Is that why I have to stay here? I won't use my powers, if that's what you're worried about. Is that what caused my accident?" My brain was lighting up with the possibilities. That would make so much sense.

Magdalena nodded. "I have to protect you. I have to protect the others from your gifts."

Guilt flooded through me. Had I hurt someone along with myself that night? It was no wonder no one would tell me what had happened to cause the memory loss.

"I promise, I won't ever use them again." I put my hands up in innocence. "If they hurt someone, I don't want them."

"The full moon is soon."

I furrowed my brow in confusion. Her eyes were still blank. If I didn't know her well, I'd think she was blind. Still looking through me, she reached to the side and grabbed a large goblet of blood. She handed it to me. I took it and drank the sweet blood slowly.

"Does that mean something?" I asked.

"The accident in which you speak. It is time I tell you what happened."

Eagerly, I sat up straighter. She nodded, and her eyes went even wider.

"Your gifts are great. We have spent many decades trying to calm the storm within you, but your mind resists. The evil takes over and you can not control yourself. I was given the same gifts and struggled many years. I was able to beat the evil. You were not."

I raised my eyebrows in surprise. "The evil? I'm evil?" I pointed to myself. She shook her head.

"No. You are good. You are pure. The devil does not like that. He wants to corrupt but can not corrupt if you fight back."

"I don't understand. What happened? What did I do?" I fired questions at her, one after the other. I was horrified with what she was telling me. Was I a monster and I didn't even know it?

"We found a way to save you. I would take your gifts, but a mistake was made."

My heart was beating out of my chest. I could hear every single thump in my ears. The blood rushing through my veins sounded like a rushing river. My mouth fell open and I could feel my face taking on a look of pure horror. What did I do?

"A sacrifice has to be made to complete the spell. A soul of pure evil."

I blinked.

"The soul you took was not."

Oh my God. I murdered someone in cold blood?

"Who was it?" I exclaimed.

She shook her head. "It does not matter. What matters is that this time, we do it exactly." She stressed that last bit, and I nodded. Yes, of course. No more. I couldn't live, knowing what a monster I was— I am. Whatever powers my mind holds, I don't want them.

"Fine. Let's do this. We have to wait until the full moon?" I asked quickly.

"Yes. I will gather all the items we need to complete the ritual, but it is you who will need to collect the soul to sacrifice."

"What makes you so sure I won't get it wrong again? I don't want to kill another innocent person."

"We will keep trying until you are rid of the monster inside you," she said and then collapsed back into the pillows behind her. "Tomorrow, you will leave this house, and you are not to return until you have a soul to break your curse."

"Curse?" I said, my voice nearly a whisper. Were the powers inside of me that bad?

She waved me off and I stood then, completely unsure of myself. As I walked back to my room, I looked at all the art on the walls, studying the decor. All of it felt so foreign to me, but I had supposedly grown up here. I had lost everything I held precious to me while trying to break my curse. It had to have been horrible.

And for Magdalena to offer to take them for me. She was always the stronger one. I knew in my heart of hearts that she could handle more than I could. If she was willing to take on my burdens to let me live a normal eternity, I could find her that soul to sacrifice.

I went to my room and spent the rest of the night pacing, trying to piece things together. None of it made sense, and yet, it all did. This was why the villagers feared me. Why I was only allowed out with supervision.

I cried. I cried for the life I took, thinking I was doing good. Whoever that person was, I prayed to a God I didn't believe in to save him. To take pity on his soul and help him. Please, this evil in me needed to be stopped, before it hurt more people.

The next day I was greeted by the same group of people that had escorted me the first few times I had gone to the human village. We dressed in all red, and silently, we trudged through the forest.

The humans were all out, like they had been each time before. There was music, laughter, and the smell of warm food to greet us. I was permitted to walk around the village at my leisure tonight.

My heart was racing, my stomach completely soured and swishing around nervously. My palms, always cold, felt hot and sweaty as I hid them in my cloak.

I walked through the stalls of people showing off their wares. The humans smiled kindly at me, but I could see the fear in their eyes. I could feel their hands shaking under tables, and I could smell the terror as I passed them. Every person I made eye contact with only made my decision to rid myself and the world of the monster inside me stronger.

I walked alone at times, and other times Jaime or another court member would walk with me. I'd ask questions in English about the villagers. I wanted their backstories.

After hours of looking for someone that could break my curse, I was beginning to panic. These villagers were innocent. I couldn't kill one of them to save myself. I couldn't!

I needed to get away from the party. I found a dark alley and hurried down it. I could see the forest, only a few hundred feet away. What if I just ran away? That home didn't mean much to me anymore, now that I couldn't remember it. I could try to start fresh somewhere else. I could control the beast inside me if I didn't try to bring it out. I'd gone two months without it, hadn't I?

I made it to the trees. I stared at them for a long time. The realization of what I was doing hit me then. It was fight or flight, and I was running. That wasn't fair. To the people who loved me, the innocents I could potentially harm, or… myself.

I heard a twig break and I spun around. My eyes went wide and my heart stopped.

I gulped as my stomach twisted so hard I thought I would vomit all the blood I had drunk tonight.

There it was, my solution.

He stared at me cautiously, the devilishly handsome man with the mismatched eyes and the dangerous smile.

He said I used to call him Desi.

Slowly, I stepped forward. His eyes darkened for a moment, and he took a step toward me. We reached each other in moments, and then, I pulled my hand from beneath my cloak and lunged.

There was a slicing sound followed by a squish. I gritted

my teeth and buckled down, but he had tons of muscle on me. I was shoved back, and when we locked gazes, he was staring at me with a mix of confusion, hurt, and anger in his face. He shook his head as he removed the knife from his belly and glared at me with almost disbelief in his eyes.

"Did you just fucking stab me?"

CHAPTER 40

Scout

I stared at him in horror at what I'd done. He ripped his shirt over his head and was using it to wipe the blood off his abdomen, already healing.

He was a vampire too.

"I—I—" I stumbled, trying to process everything. He glared at me, his eyes, one green, one blue, looking more annoyed than anything. "I didn't know you were immortal."

"Oh, well thinking that the knife would kill me makes it all better." He tossed the black shirt, now damp, on the ground in front of my feet. "Not fucking cool."

"What are you?" I demanded. "Your eyes…" I swallowed hard, trying to wrap my brain around what I just saw. His wound sealed up as if it had never happened.

He grinned, and that's when I saw them. Fangs. "Why, I'm just like you, dear *Scout*."

"Why do you keep calling me that? That's not my name." My voice trembled. He laughed. He was gripping the knife in his hand tightly. He put his hands behind his head, and laughed again.

"I can't believe this. I come to help you, and you fucking

stab me. Why?" He swung his arms out and I flinched. He rolled his eyes and then turned to examine the knife. It was nothing of note. Just a pocket knife that Jaime had given me to protect myself.

"Stay away, Desiderio," I warned. I put my hands out. "I've got gifts that I will use on you."

His eyebrows went up. "Gifts? What, like super powers? That's news to me." He took one solitary step forward and I spread my fingers as if I was going to cast a spell. He froze and then laughed.

"Unless you're talking about this power."

His voice sang inside my head and I nearly screamed. He did this the last time I saw him too. The gleam in his eyes as he looked at me, knowing I had heard him, was terrifying. He put his hands up.

"Alright, you've got me. I won't move. But I gotta know, what was your plan here? Why are you going around stabbing people?" His voice was kinder then, and I relaxed some.

"I need an evil person to give her," I said, my voice shaking as I revealed my intentions.

"To give? You mean… sacrifice?" He shook his head. "And you thought… me."

I nodded.

"Wow, okay. Why don't you look a little closer at yourself. You don't even know me. How do you know I'm evil at all?" He stepped forward, and I let him come close. My heart was beating out of my chest as my eyes flicked from his stunningly beautiful eyes to the dangerous knife, still covered in his blood. He saw me, and he lifted the knife up to his lips.

His tongue came out and slid along the sharp blade, lapping at the red liquid. He kept eye contact with me the entire time, and I didn't breath as I watched. Arousal suddenly hit me, low in my belly. My core pulsed as I watched his tongue dart out of his mouth.

"Your own blood is never as good as someone else's. I'd like to taste yours." He leaned down to whisper in my ear. "Will you let me?"

I shook my head and suddenly I remembered to breathe and move. I pushed him away. "No!"

He smirked and flicked the knife around, offering me the hilt. He stepped back when I took it.

"I'm not the evil soul you're looking for. Good luck." He turned, and disappeared back into the village.

I picked up his shirt and closed the knife. I stuffed it back into my pocket and turned, running into the forest.

I couldn't believe myself. I had just tried to kill someone. An innocent! How could I do that? That wasn't me.

I dropped to the cold ground and clutched my knees as I sobbed. What kind of monster was I? I couldn't live knowing I'd sacrificed someone to have my freedom. Someone who didn't try to hurt me after I stabbed him.

He let me go.

He was right. I pulled my head up and wiped the blood tears off my face. I was looking for the wrong person. I knew exactly what I had to do to eliminate whatever evil was clinging to me and my village.

I stood then, and wiped the earth from my dress. I braced myself and started back to my home.

"Are you sure?" The High Priestess asked. Her face was covered in worry for me. I was fiddling with my hands, but I nodded.

"It's the only way. No more innocent blood shall be shed in the pursuit of happiness. This is the only way to break the curse."

She nodded, and leaned forward to pour me another cup of warmed blood.

"I was afraid of that. I think you are right. I think this has to happen if we want to save our coven."

"Once you have my powers, you can turn it to good energy and use it to help the ones I leave behind."

Magdalena, my precious aunt, smiled, and reached for my hands. She was always so kind. "Yes, child. The Young Blood priestess will live on through my blood. Our coven will do great things with your gift."

"How many days do I have left?" I gulped.

"Two moons." She stood and reached to take my hand, helping me up. "We must prepare."

"What do we need to do?" I cocked my head. I couldn't remember what we'd done in past full moons.

"We are going to have a celebration. Everyone must be told. The more people come, the stronger the spell will be."

"The servants will take care of you." She snapped her fingers, and suddenly two Bloodborn women appeared, bobbing their heads.

"The Young Blood Priestess must be prepared for the ritual."

They nodded, and when she disappeared, I was taken to a milk bath. The water smelled of flowers and honey. Normally, I would wash myself, but tonight they scrubbed my skin and washed my hair.

When I was brought back to my room I was given a brand new nightgown and the brushed my hair until it shown like the high priestess'.

I was tucked into bed and visited by Magdalena in my room before sunrise. She smiled as she came to my bed.

"You are a true goddess," she told me, kissing my forehead.

The next night I was told that I'd be staying in my room. They were planning a celebration of my sacrifice, and the High Blood Priestess was worried that someone would come to stop us.

"There are many men who want to use your gifts to destroy us. Never again." Her eyes took on a far off look, as if remembering something I didn't.

While I had no idea what she was talking about, I understood, and spent my last night being pampered. The women assigned to me made me a special dress for the full moon. I had asked for black, and they had delivered. The fabric they had brought was as dark as the dogs that howled in the night. When you looked closely, there were thin, shiny red swirls weaved throughout the fabric, creating a hint of a sparkle when I walked into the light.

I went to bed that morning at peace with my decision. But, as I tried to fall asleep, my mind went to the last person outside of these walls I talked to.

Desiderio.

Desi.

He was incredibly handsome. Which was how he got away with all of his wicked deeds, I was sure. He was close to seducing me completely in that forest, with only a few words and his eyes.

Those eyes.

The mark of the beast, Jaime said.

My mind drifted to that first conversation I'd had with him, and I suddenly could feel the thick bump underneath my pillow. I lifted my head and pulled out the cards. I stared at the ones that had somehow remained un damaged.

What did they mean?

The three of swords.

"It's the card for broken hearts."

I heard his voice clearly in my head. He had told me that once. When?

Had he been telling the truth? That these were in fact my cards?

I closed my eyes and ran my hands over the cards, trying to feel their power.

Please, I pleaded. Help me remember.

Flashes of Desiderio smiling at me, laughing with me, and… kissing me, flew threw my mind so fast I wasn't sure if I had really been given the memories or if I'd imagined them. I'd be lying if I said I hadn't thought of what it'd feel like to have my lips pressed against his. To have his tongue between my thighs, doing what he did to that knife. How could I love someone so evil?

How could he love me back?

Considering this only solidified my decision. Whatever connection I had with Desiderio, it was not worth staying around to figure it out. This evil needed to die with me.

I had a five women team waiting for me when I woke up. I was bathed again and they did my hair and makeup. I looked beautiful as I was escorted out and down the hill.

"Where are we going?" I asked.

"To the caves," someone said. Everyone had abolished the facade of speaking Spanish with me after I had offered to sacrifice myself.

"The caves?" I had never heard of the caves. Where were they?

"We will take you," another said.

As soon as we reached the bottom of the hill, I was ushered into a carriage. The bed had large purple pillows thrown about it, creating a rather comfortable bed for my ride. I looked around for horses or donkeys, but large Blood-born men took the handles and began pulling me along.

I was nervous, but I was given a warm goblet of blood that made me sleepy. I relaxed into the pillows and closed my eyes.

I was woken up later by Jaime. I smiled softly.

"Are we at the caves?" I asked, yawning.

"Yes, Young Blood Priestess. We are celebrating until midnight. Would you like to join us?"

I sat up and nodded eagerly. A party?

Jaime offered to escort me to where I could hear drums and loud chatter. I saw the cave opening a distance away. There was dim lights inside, but the party was at the mouth of the cave.

Magdalena was holding court in the center of the party. She was dressed in full Aztec royalty garb. She looked beautiful with her large necklaces and flowing dress. She held a large scepter in one hand, and a goblet of blood in the other as she watched with approval at the people dancing around her.

She saw me and smiled. I smiled back as she motioned to the empty chair on her left. I hurried to take my seat.

"You see all of this?" She swooped her arm over the crowd. "This is all for you. Everyone here loves you, and wants to see our coven grow and succeed."

"Succeed with what?" I tilted my head. "Existing without fear?"

"Exactly, yes," she said.

I looked around. Blood was aplenty, being served from large barrels. The music was loud and the dancing was vigorous. The fire crackled as people threw in colored powder to create rainbow flames.

I watched alongside my aunt, trying to remain in a good mood. The realization that I would never get to experience this or any other fun moments again began to sink in. This was my final night on earth.

What happened to eternity?

The High Priestess climbed off her throne, and went to dance. I perked up and forced another smile as I tried my hardest to be happy for her. She was gaining my powers tonight, and would be stronger than ever.

"Hey!" A voice I heard only twice before jolted me in my seat. I whipped my head around and looked for the sound. "Behind you. Don't freak out."

"Desi?" I asked. My hands flew to my mouth in surprise. He was standing off to the side, dressed in all black. He put a finger to his lips and shook his head.

I listened, only nodding my head.

"You can't do this. We're here to save you. Come on."

"We're?" I whispered back.

"My family. Stand up, we're going."

"I can't. I need to do this." I stood then and looked to see if anyone was looking at me. I didn't catch any eyes, so I raised my dress off the ground and slipped behind the chairs.

"You can't possibly think this is a good idea," he argued.

"I have no other choice. The evil inside me is hurting people."

"Says who?" He crossed his arms and cocked his hip. He was clearly unamused.

"The High Blood Priestess. I can't remember, but she can, and she knows the evil that has plagued me and our coven for years."

"She's lying to you."

The words hung in the air for a moment, but I shook my head. My lips trembled and I backed away from him. "No she's not."

He stepped forward and glared down at me, his eyes boring into mine. "Yes she is, and I'm taking you with me."

Just then, someone cleared their throat and we both turned. It was one of the male guards.

"Who is this?" he asked me.

I opened and shut my mouth. I couldn't explain it.

"We are about to begin the ritual. Come." He snatched my wrist up and tugged. I reached with my other hand for Desi in a panic. His hand shot out and grabbed me, but the other man was much stronger. Instead of Desi saving me from his grasp, he was dragged forward with us.

The music stopped as we were pulled back into the party. All eyes were on us. The guard dropped my arm and I fell to the ground. Desi helped me stand and then took a large, deep breathe. He shook his head at me, and we shared a deep look for a moment.

"I love you so much, you have no clue."

I blinked, hearing his voice in my head again. How was he doing that? He stepped forward, and spread his arms out, dropping his head back to the sky.

"What are you doing?" I thought, looking at him, and he replied, again, in my head.

"Saving your fucking life."

Then, I watched him open his mouth and shout to the High Blood Priestess herself.

"You want an evil soul, Magdalena? You can have mine!"

"What are you doing?" She reached for me. "You can't!"

I smirked. "I'm not going to spend my immortality without you. If you think you're the evil soul that has to die, then I'll gladly take your place. I've done many a deed worse than you can ever even consider."

I swallowed, and dug my hand into my pocket. I pulled out the blank white rectangle card I'd been studying for the last few days. I never thought I'd need to use this, but it was time.

"Alright, let's make a deal."

Just then, a figure caught my eye, stepping directly out of the fire. He turned his head to me and waved.

Samson.

"You called?" he asked, coming toward me. My eyes looked around to see if anyone else was seeing him. I didn't think so. In fact, I realized then that everyone had stopped moving completely. It was as if time had been stopped for me to call him.

Everyone that is, but Scout. Her chest was heaving and

her eyes and mouth were wide. I didn't see recognition in her face, but it was shock.

"Desiderio. I knew I wasn't done with you." Samson gave me a sly grin that made me want to fight a demon.

"I don't think you've given me any other choice. You took the one thing I cared about."

His eyes flicked to Scout beside me. "You want me to give her memories back to her?"

I locked my jaw and said through gritted teeth. "Yes."

"Done." He snapped his fingers and Scout collapsed. I flew to the side to catch her before she hit the hard ground. "She'll be fine. Just give it a second." He assured me as I slid to the dirt with her in my arms. "But, you know that everything I do for someone comes with a price."

"What do you want?" I snapped.

"You run with a group. You call yourself The Seven Sins."

I nodded solemnly. I didn't like where this was going. "Why does that matter?"

"I know of another group. The Heavenly Virtues. I'd like to add them to my collection."

I hesitated, looking for the angle in which I'd truly get fucked. "To clarify. Scout will return to how she was before coming to Mexico this very last time; and in exchange, I have to hunt down these seven virtues?"

He shook his head from side to side as if weighing the offer himself. "Yes," he finally said.

"And what if I don't?"

"How about we put a timer on things? You've got a year to do it. If you can't manage it, your soulmate," he paused and crouched down. He brushed the back of his hand against Scout's soft cheek. I swatted it away and he looked surprised at the offense I took. "Will return to never knowing of the love you feel for her."

I stared down at her unmoving form. Her eyes were closed and her mouth partially open. She looked almost peaceful. I sighed, trying to make sure I do this fucking right this time.

"Do I have to be the one to kill them? What if I find them already dead or they die by accident before I can physically touch them?"

"Do you mean, what if she tries to do it for you?" he smirked. I rolled my eyes, but nodded. He knew both of us too well. "I'll allow it. Just make sure they are all dead before the next year, and you can pretend your dealings with me are done forever."

"Fuck you, man."

"Indeed. Deal?" He offered me his hand. I stared at it for a long moment before steeling myself and shaking his hand.

"Deal."

The world around us exploded. The drums boomed, the loud laughter hurt my ears, and I could almost feel the ground vibrating with the dancing. Scout opened her eyes and I stared down at her, praying that I hadn't fucked up.

"Do you remember me?"

The first thing she saw was my face. She scrunched up her nose. "What is going on? Desi?" She blinked and began wiggling. I helped her sit up and watched as she looked all around. "Oh fuck."

"Yeah, we need to get out of here. Come on," I muttered low. The guard was standing near us, but he seemed to be talking to someone a distance away.

"How? Desi, I'm like— a priestess or some shit. They aren't going to let me just run."

"I told you, I'll lay my body down before I let them put

you on that table. Come on." I urged her up. We stood and I reached for her hand. She took it and squeezed. I turned and immediately ran into a hard chest.

"You are to take the Young Blood Priestess's place?" he asked.

I pressed my lips together tightly, but nodded.

"The High Blood Priestess wants to talk to you."

Scout and I exchanged looks but we both knew we had little choice.

"Where is she?" Scout asked beside me. The brute motioned with his chin behind us. We glanced back and saw that he was motioning to the cave.

I licked my lips and tried to quickly work out an escape. Where the fuck was everyone? We were pushed and told to turn and walk with the guard, and we did as told. As I walked, I looked for my friends.

I had planned on going alone, but Elvie wanted to come, which made Tully get protective. If he went then Dante had to come. Arsenio, the biggest one of all of us couldn't be shown up by the others so he agreed to come, and Corrine, well, she felt the need to be backup.

"Just in case. I'll stay hidden," she assured me. We spent all last night trying to formulate a plan based on absolutely no knowledge of what we'd be walking into.

Everyone was supposed to be spaced out and trying to blend in. While I hadn't given a fuck what I'd be wearing since I'd be risking everything anyway, the rest of them had made sure to wear clothes they had seen humans wear. I had chosen my jeans and one of my faded band shirts. I stuck out, but I had wanted to. Scout and I both didn't belong here. Magdalena needed to know that when I took Scout away. If I was able to.

"You saw Samson. Did you make another deal with him?" Scout's voice filled my brain.

I looked down at her. She didn't look at me; her gaze focused on the walk.

"I did. I had no choice." I replied silently.

"How is he going to save us from being sacrificed?"

Crickets.

"Desi?"

"I didn't."

"What?" Her eyes darted to me quickly.

I shrugged and offered her an awkward smile. "I was more focused on getting your memories back. It's fine. I'll figure it out," I said aloud.

"How?"

I didn't reply, as we walked into the cave. Torches were on both sides, lighting the way. It was rather bright, actually. I paused in my steps and was shoved roughly forward. I snarled, but kept moving.

It felt like a quarter of a mile, but finally the cave opened up into a large cavern. The room was gigantic, actually. It could easily fit everyone outside still partying. On the far end sat a large throne, and in the very center of the room was a table, standing atop a pedestal. There were leather straps bolted to it, and beside that, was a smaller table. It held a large bowl, several goblets, and an array of knives. It reminded me of my roll of knives I used back home.

"I hear you'd like to trade her life for yours," a voice called from behind us. We both turned quickly to see Magdalena. "That won't work. It's too late."

"What do you mean?" I demanded. "An evil soul is an evil soul. What does it matter?"

She shook her head. Her red eyes were cold and unfeeling. "We didn't need any soul. We need her. This was all to convince her to do it herself." She motioned with her hand and the brute who brought us here pushed us forward. "However, I think we shall sacrifice both of you tonight."

She said something in Spanish, and suddenly more people appeared. They came from a different cave entrance, carrying a second table. They brought it to the pedestal and placed it beside the first one. It too, had the straps attached.

"How many people do you sacrifice?" I smirked. Magdalena didn't smile.

"Many," she said firmly. My stomach soured. She was really doing this. I had heard stories of all the horrific things she had done to people. Humans and vampires alike.

Would she take my still-beating heart out and eat it?

"Desi!" A small cry came from Scout's lips. I embraced her, putting her head against my chest.

"Shh, it's okay. I'll get us out of this." I licked my lips, trying to think. Suddenly, I could hear the drums again, and they were actually getting louder. Where people coming inside?

"It's too late. It is time." Magdalena snapped her fingers and suddenly both of us were seized and by two men each. Both of us went kicking and screaming to the altars.

"You touch her I'll fucking slaughter you!" I snarled as they tossed us onto the tables. Two people turned into five, and I was held tight at the wrists and ankles as they took the straps and bolted us to the tables.

One of them reached for a knife on the table and came toward me. Her eyes were blank as she reached for me.

"Don't you fucking dare."

I glared but she didn't seem to register my words. She grabbed my shirt and sliced the knife right through it, pulling it off me. Another person took my shoes and socks, and the woman with my shirt cut off my jeans and boxers.

What the fuck?

I turned my head to see that they had done the same to Scout, although undressing her had been easier.

The rhythmic drumming was so loud now I could barely think. I lifted my head and saw that the party outside had indeed come in to watch the show.

I fought and struggled against my bindings, but to no avail. Scout was wiggling, and thin streams of blood fell from her eyes as she looked over at me.

"I love you. After everything we've been through, just know I loved you in the end."

I bit down hard and glared at her.

"Don't say that."

If she heard my thoughts, she didn't register them. A horn sounded and silence fell over the room like a thick blanket. Magdalena walked over to us then, with a large book in her hand.

She spoke in Spanish loudly to the crowd. I closed my eyes and began violently thrashing my head against the wood, trying to break it. She only spoke louder, drowning out my sounds.

The crowd began to holler and whistle when she finished her introduction. I opened my eyes then and watched her saunter to the equipment table. Was this karma for all of the deaths I had directly caused? Was this the right way for a Bloodborn like me to die?

She went to me first, and rested her hand on my thigh. I jerked, the leather cut into my ankles. It healed immediately but the sting remained.

She reached for my cock and it was almost as if watching in slow motion. My eyes went wide and I started to shake my head as she grabbed me and wrapped her fingers around it.

"Take your hands off my brother." A feminine voice

called from the entrance. Magdalena dropped my cock and I relaxed only slightly. I searched for the source of the sound, but only heard a sharp clicking. "I heard people were looking for me."

I realized then that the clicking was that of heels, and the voice was that of the one, the only, Ginata De Santis, the Seven Sin of Gluttony. She looked exactly as I remembered, stunningly beautiful and an eternal badass. Her brunette hair was in soft waves, her makeup was dark and only enhanced her natural beauty. She walked toward the table, tall and confident as the room stared at her. She was dressed in a women's suit, and a fedora. She looked entirely out of place with her six inch heels and leather gloves.

"We're done here," she spoke to Magdalena. The High Blood Priestess snatched a knife up but Ginata waved her off. She looked almost bored as she came up the small stairs and to the tables. "Did you not hear me?" she asked her.

"Who are you?" Magdalena demanded.

"I'm one of the most feared Bloodborns in the States. I'm hear to bring my brother and his partner home. We can do this with or without blood. Your choice."

She stepped up to Magdalena. Ginata had almost a full foot over the Scout look-alike.

"The ritual must be completed tonight." Magdalena doubled down but Ginata didn't even raise an eyebrow.

"Ronald," Ginata said, and suddenly we heard a man scream and a loud slice, followed by a squishing sound. Heads turned to see a dark skinned vampire holding a native vampire's head in the air. "That's one. How many more will you let die to keep these two?"

Magdalena growled and launched for Ginata. Ginata sidestepped her casually, as if dodging a soccer ball. "Bruno."

Another scream rang out, followed by a head being

thrown toward us. Ginata crossed her arms. "I'm fully prepared to wipe your coven out tonight if I have to."

People began to call to Magdalena frantically. They were chanting the same thing in Spanish, but my lack of understanding made me panicky. What were they saying?

"See, even they are telling you to let them go. Will your vanity win tonight, Magdalena, High Priestess of Blood?"

Magdalena seemed to be thinking, but then she threw her head back and let out a high pitched howl. It lasted almost thirty seconds, sending a shiver of fear through me. It was as if she was calling to someone.

I heard a rustling, and I turned my head to see Scout being released from her leather banding by a third darker skinned man, dressed like Ginata. He had a gray suit and fedora. Scout sat up quickly and was handed her black dress.

Magdalena spun around to grab Scout but Ginata raised her leg and kicked her hard! She stumbled forward and hit her head on the side of the table I was still tied to. She didn't move, but we all knew that wouldn't last.

"Alright, now you two. This is a sex cult, is it not?" Ginata pointed her gloved finger at Scout. "Be a doll, climb onto the table and show us how to finish the ritual properly." She pointed to me. My eyebrows shot way up and I shook my head furiously. Scout's face was that of pure horror.

"What? Why does everyone want to watch us have sex? No!" I tugged on my restraints as hard as I could as I looked from her to Ginata.

Ginata's harsh look failed instantly when we locked eyes and she burst into laughter, relaxing me. "Yeah, I'm just fucking with you. Thomas, let's get him out too and get going." She nodded at the man who was walking from Scout's table to mine. "The others are waiting outside."

"What about her?" I asked as I was stripped of my bonds.

Magdalena's servants had cut off my clothes, so I had to stand there with a hand over my crotch. Thomas looked around and snatched the tablecloth off the equipment table, sending everything spilling all over. He handed it to me, and I stood, tying it around me. Beggars couldn't be choosers.

Ginata crouched down and removed her glove. Her nails were ruby red and sharp. I watched with curiosity as she reached forward and ran her finger along the side of Magdalena's cheek. The touch seemed gentle, but blood spurted from her face almost as if she'd been fatally wounded. A sizzling sound came as Magdalena's eyes burst open and she began to scream as she clutched her face.

Ginata stood and wiggled her fingers at me. "Sunrise is not as rare as people think it is. You just gotta know who to ask." She slid her glove back on and pointed to Scout and I. Suddenly, the three men she had brought with stepped up behind her. "Let's blow this joint."

CHAPTER 42

Desi

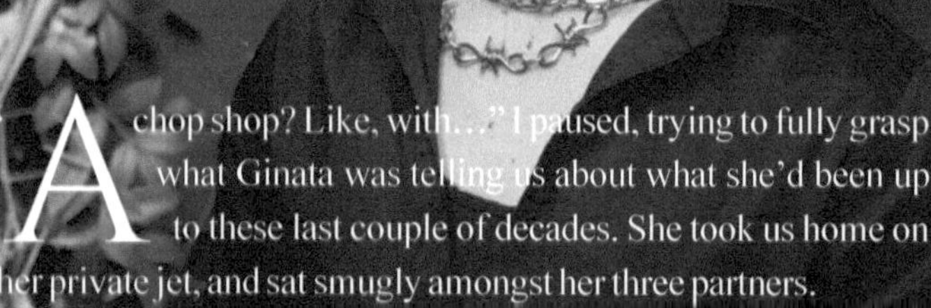

"A chop shop? Like, with…" I paused, trying to fully grasp what Ginata was telling us about what she'd been up to these last couple of decades. She took us home on her private jet, and sat smugly amongst her three partners.

"I'll explain later. But yes." She grinned. "You all look like hell."

"Just got back," Dante muttered. He had struggled the worst with drinking animal blood for months. He'd grown too accustomed to humans giving it willingly for a little more gambling time. Ginata laughed again. The sound seemed to relax everyone.

Scout slumped against me, struggling to stay awake. I wrapped my arm around her and pulled her closer. I kissed the top of her head. "It's okay. We're heading home."

"They took Tippi from me," she frowned. "I mean, he wasn't really nice, but I loved his coloring."

"I'll get you another Dracula parrot. This one we'll pick together," I assured her.

"Before we all split again, why don't you stay a few days

at my place?" Ginata interrupted our moment. "A plane ride is not enough time to catch up."

"Agreed. I am curious about your nails. I want some!" Elvie giggled.

"Yes, and I'd like to know your supplier," Corrine added in a more subdued tone.

"Or the whole stolen identity thing, can we talk about that?" Tully added loudly, throwing up his hands. "That was insane!"

Ginata laughed. "Oh yes. I've been quite busy these last few years. I'll call ahead and get rooms prepared for you all."

Out of all the homes the Seven Sins had, Ginata's was the most lavish. I didn't think that was possible after seeing Arsenio's white marble palace. The Seven Sin of Greed walked into Gluttony's home, and I could see him sizing up everything.

We reached her place by morning, and we all agreed to go rest. It had been an insane night.

The room Scout and I had been given was a mini-suite. There was a large bathroom attached, and we took a shower together. It was silent but in a way, comforting. When we fell into bed, we laid there, bare, skin to skin, and fell asleep in each other's arms.

The next evening, we had clothes waiting for us. Scout was given a simple black dress, and I was given a black business suit. I frowned, but having no other options, I slipped it on.

We joined the rest of the party downstairs. Ginata was entertaining everyone with wild stories of what she'd been doing. Everyone chimed in with their own crazy moments.

"So, it wasn't just the phony that was obsessed with

harems?" Elvie asked when the three rather attractive darker skinned Bloodborns came in and sat with Ginata.

"Mm, I don't like that sentence." Ginata scrunched up her nose. "Thomas, Ronald, Bruno, and I have been in a loving relationship for over twenty years. It's more than just physical. What she had over there," she waved the air as if wanting it gone. "Was not what healthy polyamory is. None of my men are bound to stay, nor are they sex slaves." The foursome shared knowing smiles, and the topic was dropped.

We spent the evening telling tales and drinking blood. Ginata had gotten fireball whiskey for me and made sure to get something Arsenio enjoyed drinking.

"You look odd, in that suit, baby brother," Ginata smirked. "Thomas was the closest to your frame, and it does fit, but that's not you."

"Agreed. Any way you can get me a band shirt and some jeans?"

She winked. "Consider it done."

As we were going to bed that morning, Arsenio stopped me. Scout went up without me, and I assured her I'd only be a moment.

"It's the perfect time to pop the question with all of us here. Just say the word, and I can plan a grand affair. Ginata has a wonderful garden that would be perfect."

I shook my head sadly. "The ring was left in Mexico. It was in my pants."

He grinned wide. "Actually, I had a feeling that I would need to move my best man duties forward." He dug his hand into his pocket and pulled out the velvet box. I snatched it with surprise.

"Holy shit. You really got it." I opened the box to check, and sure enough, my family ring sat in its rightful place, safe and sound.

"I did, as well as a few other items. Your deck. And hers." He dug into his other pocket and handed me the two tarot decks. "We found them under her pillow. Oh, and this. This was in a bowl in her room." He dug into his pocket one last time and pulled out the necklace I had given her with the nickname she had for me.

"I recalled the matching one you wore and thought it was hers."

I stared at everything in wonder. "Thanks, man. You risked so much to get these. I appreciate it." I shoved the items in my jacket and pulled him into a giant hug. He patted my back hard, and I jerked forward. He laughed.

"Yes. I know. So, the garden then?" He let me go and put up his hands. His eyes lit up with his ideas. "Lights everywhere. Soft violins playing. We'll have the finest champagne ready, and we can all hide in the flowers, waiting for the right moment. And then you'll bend down, wearing the finest suit I can find, and ask her to be your wife for eternity."

I grimaced. "Is this what you sit around all night and think about? This romantic shit is too much for me. What happened to the plan of you doing it all and I just show up? Surprise me. I'm too tired for this shit." We shared a laugh, and I went upstairs to Scout.

I found her already sound asleep and realized I was just as tired. I stripped down and slid in beside her. When I woke up, I found two outfits waiting for me. One from Arsenio, the other from Ginata.

"Aw, who got me this?" Scout beamed as she pulled on her thigh-high socks. She took, had been supplied with two outfits. I looked at the expensive suit and the Iron Maiden shirt, opting for my comfort over style. I could always come back up for the suit.

"You're fucking gorgeous, you know that?" I told her as

she slipped on hi-top sneakers. She had been given a black tulle skirt, a black shirt, and a leopard print jacket. "That High Priestess look wasn't you."

"I kind of miss the hair," she laughed. She stood and sauntered over to me, putting her arms around me. Despite her naturally cold vampire skin, she felt warm to me. She felt… like home. I reached up and gently fisted her hair.

"I don't know. I think I'll always love the 'freshly-fucked' look." I laughed. She looked at me, and I planted a quick peck on her lips. "You're a wild one, and I never want that to go away."

"I don't ever plan on it," she grinned.

We went downstairs together, and I saw Arsenio first. He scowled when he saw me. I shrugged and flicked my eyes to Scout.

"We were just about to do a tour of the garden," Ginata announced when she saw us. "Are you interested?"

"Sure," Scout answered for us. Together, our large group went to the back of her enormous home. Scout gasped when she saw the fairy lights.

Ginata beamed. "It's lovely. Come. I want to show you all of it. It's my favorite part of my home."

Ginata became our tour guide through the rows of flowers. The trees were aplenty, and it felt like we had been transported to a botanical museum. Ginata would point out this flower or that, explaining how hard it was to either get it here or take care of it. Especially considering our condition. "Being a vampire who loves to garden has its difficulties," she laughed.

Scout and I stayed in the back, taking our time exploring the flowers. The group took a hard left, and Scout tugged on my arm, causing me to stop. I cocked my head, and she wiggled her eyebrows.

"Care to explore on our own?"

"You want to get lost?" I grinned.

"Yes, please."

I took her hand, and we went the opposite way. Casual strolling quickly turned into a light jog, which then turned into laughter as we began to sprint. The garden was never-ending!

Scout stopped suddenly, and I fell into her. I straightened and looked over her shoulder, seeing a bench. "There. We're finally alone," she said.

"Do you not like everyone?" I frowned. She walked over to a bush with red flowers. She reached for the leaves and shook her head.

"It's weird, seeing Tully and Dante," she admitted. Guilt flooded through me instantly.

"Scout I—"

She put her hand up. "It's fine. I'll get over it, eventually. I just really wanted to spend time with you. Alone."

"Oh?" Instantly, my body roused. I glanced around and saw no one.

"Yes. I missed you. And, I wanted to talk. You found my tarot deck. All of them. You didn't have to do that." She went and sat down on the bench. I opted to sit on the ground by her feet. I crossed my legs and looked down at the grass.

"I know. But I wanted to. I messed up big time that night. I'm so sorry for everything. I wish I could go back and change things."

"I know." She reached for my hair, running her fingers through it. I closed my eyes and groaned. I loved it when she tugged on my hair. I turned and put my head in her lap.

"I think we've both made some mistakes and done damage to each other. Scout, I never want to hurt you like that ever again. If you let me, I'll spend the rest of eternity together trying to make it right."

She stopped moving her hands. "Together?" Her voice came off almost confused.

I looked up and nodded. "Yes. I want together, forever. What do you think?"

"I'd like that."

We sat in quiet for a moment. She began running her hands through my hair again, and a moan slipped from my lips. I closed my eyes. I placed my hand on her leg and began sliding it up her socks. She parted her legs ever so slightly as my fingers reached the line where the socks stopped, and her thighs were fully exposed. I moved under her skirt and discovered with utter delight that she was completely bare underneath.

"When did this happen?" I chuckled.

"I didn't even bother tonight."

"You had this planned all along," I accused.

"Maybe…" she giggled.

"Well, if you don't mind." I positioned myself between her legs, parting them further to expose her bare pussy. I slid my hand under her skirt and parted her lips. "How long have you been this ready for me?" I asked as I discovered her to be already wet.

She groaned as I slid a finger in with ease and began to fuck her slowly. "Ages." She tilted her head back and arched her body. I slipped another finger inside, and she began bucking her hips, matching my thrusts. I kissed her thighs.

"Bite me."

I paused. "Are you sure?" I asked. I always wanted to ask multiple times before we did this. It felt like such an invasion, drinking another vampire's blood, that I had to make sure before I did.

"Yes. Desi, please. I need to feel— close, again." Her eyes pleaded with me to take her in the way that only I could. I nodded and sunk my teeth directly into the original bite marks I had made on her thigh.

She gasped and groaned as I fucked her with my fingers and drank from her open wound. Her blood was divine on my tongue. It warmed my belly, and my brain, and my cock. When she finally ripped my head and hands away, I couldn't take it anymore. I picked her up with ease and found the nearest tree. She wrapped her legs around me, and I quickly unbuttoned my jeans, ripping them down. I shoved my throbbing cock into her, and she let out a sharp cry. In the past, I had waited for the pain to subside and her body to adjust, but tonight I couldn't. I needed that release.

Her nails dug into my shoulders as I thrust against her. "Oh, Desi, oh God," she moaned into my ear. I ran my tongue down her ear. "I love it when you say my fucking name. Do it again."

"Desi," she obliged. "I'm— I'm there, I'm so close."

"Bite me," I growled. She didn't need to hear me ask twice. She jerked her head forward, and her fangs pierced my skin ferociously. She lapped at the blood as I fucked her. I started to go harder. With each thrust, I went deeper, and our movements were those with the same goal. Suddenly she ripped her head away from my shoulder and let out a high cry. Her body tensed, and I could feel her orgasm rippling through her as if it were my own. Blood pounded in my ears, and I knew I had to finish quickly. The rush of her venom warming my veins would only last so long.

She collapsed against me, and with one last gentle lap with her tongue against the wound, I came. I groaned loudly and pumped into her as hot waves of pleasure flew through me. My eyes rolled in the back of my head as I reveled in the feel of her tight pussy against my cock. This was paradise for me.

Both of us drained. In more than one sense, I let her down, and we straightened our clothes.

Suddenly, from behind us, someone cleared their throat. We spun around quickly to see all of my Seven Sins family peeking out of the bushes with varying levels of embarrassment.

"Holy hell, that was hot," Ginata exclaimed.

"I—uh, thought it was the thing." Arsenio couldn't look me in the eye.

"What thing?" Scout asked. I shot a glare at Arsenio but then realized that this was kind of perfect. I took a long, deep breath and turned to face Scout. I smiled wide and reached for her hands. She was deeply confused.

I pressed my lips together tightly and then got down on one knee, as Arsenio had directed.

Scout's eyes went wide with realization. I cringed and glanced back at my crew. "I'm not in a suit."

Scout giggled, but her eyes were shiny. She was trying not to cry.

I let go of one hand to reach into my pocket and pull out the box. I opened it quickly and offered it to her.

"You said before that you want forever— together. What do you think about making it real?" I wished I had rehearsed a speech. This wasn't the grand event Scout deserved. I shook my head and laughed. "I should have done something better, made it more mind-blowing, but that's not us."

She pressed her lips together. "Oh?"

I nodded, deciding on what to say then. "Yeah, this is us. Me in a fucking shirt and you in your ripped tights. We've never been extravagant or cheesy-romantic." I glanced at Arsenio, who was smiling tightly, holding back tears. My eyes went back to Scout. I squeezed her hand and then let go. I needed both hands to remove the ring from its box and offer it to her again. "I'm laying it all on the table now. You aren't getting a fancy future filled with amazing, wondrous things. It's gonna be a wile time. You're just getting—me."

I looked her directly in the eyes then and waited. Each second felt like a decade. I could hear each beat my heart took as it waited for her to react.

"Promise?" she asked. I blinked.

"Promise what?"

"That it's going to be a wild time."

I laughed and stood. "Baby, Nerd, it's going to be such a fucking ride."

My mind flashed back to the deal I had made with Samson. Yeah, what a trip that was going to be.

She grinned wide then and offered me her hand. I slid the ring on and brought my lips to hers. The kiss was so gentle, but it was a promise. When we pulled away, my forehead paused to rest against hers. She giggled, and my heart soared as she put her arms around my waist.

"Yes, let's do forever, together."

THE END.

Afterword

Thank you for reaching the end of Lay Your Body Down. If you enjoyed the book, please consider leaving a review wherever you leave reviews, and if you do so on instagram, tag me in it!

Acknowledgments

I'm not entirely sure who to thank first, as it's a lot of the same people from book one. Victoria from Eve's Graphic Designs. Your artwork is amazing, and I'm grateful to have found you. You do great work and I look forward to seeing what you come up for my next books!

Cult Podcast, or specifically, to name the hosts, Paige Wesley, Armando Torres, and Andrea Guzzetta (although I know you're not there anymore, you do play a part in this.)

I was listening to an episode. I can't remember what one, but in the back of my head, I was thinking about the work I needed to do when I got home. Writing. Then suddenly, it was either Paige or Armando that said the phrase, "Lay your body down." And it clicked.

That was the title for my next book. Specifically this book. It was set in stone, no doubts about it. I don't know why, but it hit just right, and now here we are, getting published.

You also talked about a cult that I added to this book. Without you, I would have not known about Magdalena and her vampire cult in the 1960's.

Thank you for the inadvertent inspiration for both the title, and a major plot point in the book. I wish I could remember the episode for the title to sight it. Maybe upon a second listen I'll catch it. Anyways, thanks.

My street team, my Whorror Babies. Oh, how you've grown! Thank you for the support each and every day. And all the members of my Bitchcraft Coven. No, I'm not just talking about my Facebook group. I'm talking about every single one of my readers. You all make this worthwhile. Every single kind thing you say or type, I remember it. When things get really low, I try to think about you guys.

Oh! Speaking of a fan base, I want to talk about all the people who came and supported me from Justhauntr's shout out's.

It's been super cool hearing from you guys! Seriously, I absolutely love it. It's always a nice surprise to see one of you pop up with a message somewhere to mention my book or just say something nice. Please do it more, I encourage it. I love hearing from people, and it's even better when it's people with stuff in common. Let's watch some horror movies together sometime!

And finally, Wes and Marie.

Wes, this journey has been great from the start. I'll never stop saying thank you for answering that email. You helped launch my dark romance career, and everyone involved, I'll be forever grateful for.

Marie, you are wild boo and I love your energy. You make a great Scout.

Thank you all so much for taking a chance on me and my books.

I am so glad to have reached the end of book two in this series.

Firstly, before I start anything else, let's talk about real life versus fiction. This is reminder that any person that is on a book cover or is part of mine or anyone else's marketing and/or inspiration is only playing a character. Desi was completely fabricated from my brain and is a work of fiction. Considering how much darker book two is to book one, I really want to make that clear.

Be cool guys. Thanks.

It was a struggle, I'll admit, to get this book done. While book one only took about fifteen days to write (once I sat down to do it), this book took much longer. This book was my first true leap into dark, dark romance, but also, my life completely changed while writing this.

My dad died August 20th, 2022. It was unexpected, and horrible. I have spoken before about my parents, and their drug addictions. My parents have been addicts for almost twenty years, and still, I did not see his death coming.

It was incredibly hard for me to deal with. None of his

children had good relationships with him by the end, and we all struggled to come to terms with the fact that now, there would never be a chance to change that. Before his death, I hadn't seen my father in six years.

However, as I grieve for Justin Standish, I think about him the way he was before his addiction turned him into something else. When he was still my dad.

Justin, was not my biological father. We met when I was two, and he formally adopted me when I was sixteen. However, since day one, he was my dad.

I was raised in an environment where sharing your feelings or expressing any sort of love to someone was not normal. (Mexican Catholic, if that helps explain a bit) But somehow, my dad showed me how to love. I never once felt like I was different from his biological children, and for that, I'll feel forever grateful. While I was being bounced home to home most of my childhood, he stood up for me, and made sure that I knew I was loved and always welcome to come home when I needed to.

He would do anything for me. And, I only wish that everyone could have seen those good parts of him.

Why am I going on about this? Because without his encouragement when I was a teen, I would have never started writing.

When I told people I wanted to be a writer when I grew up, every single member of my family (traditional, Chicano, catholic roots) had something negative to say. I was actually sat down and lectured about how being a writer was bad and that I could never consider something that would pay nothing. I needed to tell the schools I was going to be a lawyer. But you know what my dad did?

He bought me a typewriter.

After watching Heathers and listening to My Chemical Romance one too many times in her teens, Chicana author, Tylor Paige, was drawn to the darkness where the villains were still villains, but deserved love stories too.

Shifting her focus to Horror Romance, Tylor writes snarky, psycho vampires, troubled but beautiful Goblin Kings, and slashers so sexy you'll be begging your partner to buy a mask.

When she's not writing about women railing the villains, she enjoys watching horror films, sewing, comic books, and overall trolling her readers, one DM at a time. At the time of this update Tylor has now written and published thirteen full length novels.

Oh, and feel free to call her Ty. She prefers it.

Also by Tylor Paige

Final Girl Series:

Slash or Pass

Slay Less

Book 3

Book 4

Little Deaths: a Vampire Mafia series

Seven Little Deaths

Lay Your Body Down

Bury Me In Blood- Prequel

Little Taste of Death (FREE VALENTINES SHORT!)

Standalones:

Surrender to Forever- a Goblin King reimagining

Final Girl Featurettes:

Like Father Like Slaughter- a dystopian horror romance novella

Get in touch with me

Get in touch with me:

- Www.Tylorpaige.com
- https://linktr.ee/Tylorpaige
- Facebook.com/Tylorpaigeauthor
- Instagram: @Tylorpaige
- TikTok: @authortylorpaige
- Join the Coven of Bitchcraft group on Facebook!
- https://www.facebook.com/groups/376190999768893/?ref=share